Clemency Burton-Hill is an actress, journalist and broadcaster. She is a contributing editor for the *Spectator*, has written for many UK publications including the *Observer*, *Guardian*, *Telegraph*, *Daily Mail* and *New Statesman*, and appears regularly on arts and current affairs programmes including *Question Time*, *Andrew Marr*, and BBC Radios 3, 4 and 5. She was a presenter at the *BBC Proms* and on the series *Visionaries*, and her recent acting credits include leading roles in *Poirot*, *The Palace*, and *Party Animals*. *The Other Side of the Stars* is her first novel.

The
Other Side
of the
Stars

clemency burton-hill

THE HEADLINE PUBLISHING GROUP
An Hachette Live UK Company
338 Euston Road
London NW1 3BH

headline
review

For my mother

This being human is a guest house.
Every morning a new arrival.

A joy, a depression, a meanness,
some momentary awareness comes
as an unexpected visitor.

Welcome and entertain them all!
Even if they are a crowd of sorrows,
who violently sweep your house
empty of its furniture . . .

Rumi

. . . Why then
Have to be human — and, avoiding destiny,
Yearn for destiny?

Rilke

PROLOGUE

As she steps out of the airport terminal she can see that the world has turned white, and this makes her gasp. It is beautiful, and beauty is not what she is expecting. Giant snowclouds are beginning their weighty drift earthwards, icing like cakes the cars and taxis that hum along the kerb, surprising with their damp flakes the arriving travellers, who scurry even more urgently into the building, and delighting the little ones who now strain eagerly to break free of their mothers' hands and play. At the sight of the children, she wraps her coat tighter around her body and holds her face to the sky. The brightness is dazzling. She closes her eyes and feels icy snowflakes settle on her nose, and wonders if she might be dreaming. Where is she? Why has she come here? Noises are echoing oddly in her head: words are floating, the disjointed sounds of surrounding conversation merging with the shrieks from the kids in the snow and the distant Tannoy announcements inside and the screeches of brakes as a bus pulls up in front of the terminal to offload more bustling people. She hears what she supposes is the sound of someone laughing. A baby crying. Another car horn. She opens her eyes and watches the great expanse of white nothing above her dissolve into further blankness as the snow begins to fall more heavily.

'Excuse me,' somebody is saying – how many moments later? The words sound close, but she does not move. She remains staring at the sky, the stray flakes that nestle at the edges of her eyes glinting like frozen tears. And again: 'Excuse me!' This time it is more intrusive, somehow, urgent. 'Aren't you . . . ?'

She drops her head down from the sky and shuffles away from her unwelcome interrogator towards a blue taxi that has just pulled up to the rank. The shouts she can hear as she opens the door seem to blur into all the other peculiar, underwatery sounds around her. She does not even realise they are directed at her.

'Madam, there's a queue,' the driver begins to say. But as he glances at his rear-view mirror, and sees the face of the passenger who is now seated on the cracked navy leather, he falls silent. Immediately he cranks the machine into gear and pulls away from the airport, before any of the angry people in the snow-sodden line can tug her out again.

'Where can I take you, madam?' he asks, his voice a little tremulous as he swings the car into the lane that will direct them towards the city. The woman is silent, staring out of the window. The driver watches her face in the mirror. He should keep his eyes on the road in this weather, he knows, but it is only for a moment, and he can't help it. He asks his question again. This time, he calls the woman by her name. She turns her head, slowly, and stares at him, her green eyes muddy with confusion. And then, suddenly, her eyes begin to focus. Now she knows where she is, and she knows what she has to say.

'Just drive, please,' she asks politely, her voice sounding distant to her ears, as if it might not be her own. Is it her own? Is she really here, in this taxi, in this city? Why is she here? But she knows.

'Of course, madam. Where would you like me to go?'

'Where?'

'Where?'

She hesitates for a moment. And then, in a half-whisper, she says the word: 'Anywhere.'

As soon as she sees the street, she knows she is in the right place. 'I would like to walk from here,' she tells the driver quickly. 'Stop, please.'

He glances at her reflection in surprise, but obediently pulls the car over and dashes round to open his passenger's door. The street is so empty. He sees she has no luggage with her. She seems to have nothing at all. The snow is whipping up more ferociously now, and he feels a faint ripple of concern as the woman eases herself gracefully out of his cab into the blizzard. He smiles nervously at her, though; he cannot help it. And the smile she gives him in response suddenly dissolves his worries. He feels like the luckiest man in the world, just to be standing on this street with her. He watches as the woman pulls off one of her grey leather gloves, and then, with a little cry of shock, drops it in the snow. Her hand flies to her mouth and he automatically bends down to retrieve the glove.

'Please,' she is saying, her lovely voice a croak. 'It's just, I don't seem to have any money. I don't seem to have any things . . .'

The taxi driver smiles again and hands her back the glove.

The leather, he will remember afterwards, is unthinkably soft, just as he imagines her hands must be. 'Then it is my pleasure, madam.' He gives a gallant little bow, believing this to be the right gesture in such unlikely circumstances. 'My honour and pleasure. But are you sure you will be all right here? You haven't far to go?'

The air is freezing and the snow now blankets the street around them. He feels another twinge of worry about leaving this woman alone in the storm. Surely she does not belong out here. Can he not, perhaps, put her back in his cab and take her somewhere else?

But she is shaking her head.

'I haven't far to go,' she assures him.

She watches the driver get back into his cab and listens to the splutter of the engine as it starts up in the cold. Her heart starts to beat faster, and she feels her throat constrict, and now she almost calls out to him to wait, *wait!*, she has made a mistake, such a terrible mistake! She is not supposed to be here at all, here, in this blank, empty theatre! But as the car chugs slowly down the street, her mouth remains closed. She does not move. Standing perfectly still, on her white, white stage, with the snowflakes now whirling ever more frantically around her, the woman is suffused with calm. She knows why she is here. She knows what she has to do. I haven't far to go. Not far.

Just to the other side of the stars.

Her eyes trail the taxi until it has turned the corner of the street and she is alone on her white stage once more. She closes her eyes. She takes a deep breath.

And then she begins to walk.

Part One

Part One

ONE

Through the slats of the shutters in their bedroom, Lara could hear Alex outside, whistling as he prepared food and drinks for the party. She smiled to herself and walked over to the window, leaning her elbows on the wide ledge. The late afternoon sun was hovering lazily over the rooftops of West London, and the wooden deck on their new flat, which they had been redecorating for the past month, was pink in its glow. Even the housing estate on the other side of the square looked rather lovely in this light, and Lara was momentarily dazzled by the flare from one of its windows as the sun hit the glass. Beyond the faint bass emanating from the council flats and the music coming from the speakers in her own living room, she could hear the comforting hum of traffic from the surrounding streets and the drifting laughter of Portobello Market stragglers somewhere down the road. It was the first of July. Lara breathed in the balmy air and felt relieved that, after a June of seemingly relentless slate-grey skies, summer had finally arrived. She called down to Alex, who looked up from the ingredients he was chopping for Pimm's and waved his beer bottle at her.

'You coming to help me, Lady Latner?' He grinned. 'It's nearly six. What are you doing up there?'

She laughed. 'Sorry. Getting dressed. I'll be right down.'

'There's a very cold beer and a kiss waiting for you when you get here.' He brandished a half-chopped cucumber. 'And this. So hurry up.'

After pulling on a pair of jeans and a suitably summery top, Lara paused at her dressing-table and glanced at her reflection in the mirror. The antique piece of furniture, a relic from a dressing room in a famous old Parisian theatre, had once belonged to her mother, Eve. Gilt-edged and lined with bulbs that no longer worked, its rose-glass mirror was spotted with age but still contained, for Lara, the magic of a million once-reflected images. Looking into it, she could sometimes see herself as a small child, watching her actress mother make herself up – for a performance, a dinner, a party. Eve would sweep Lara onto her knee and dab powder on her nose, or a drop of Chanel No. 5 on her tiny wrists. She'd brush Lara's hair and kiss her ears, singing made-up songs to her in French as a filterless cigarette smouldered in the ashtray and cast them both in the romantic, smoky light of one of her films. At other times, Eve would sit with a script in her lap, reciting lines to herself, as her daughter crouched in the corner of the bedroom, apparently transfixed by the reflection of her mother in the mirror. Sometimes, Lara remembered, her father Oliver, a British diplomat, would appear in another corner of the bedroom. He too would watch Eve for a moment, before clearing his throat and saying, 'Darling, you shouldn't smoke in front of the children.'

Now, all these years later, Lara saw only her twenty-six-year-old self. But somewhere, she knew, the ghost of Eve was still there, held for ever in the mirror's flecked old surface. Leaning forward and narrowing her eyes at her own reflection, Lara drew a coat of mascara over her lashes and pressed a touch of that same Chanel scent into her neck. She pulled her dark hair into a messy knot, then selected a pair of earrings, grabbed her cigarettes and headed outside to join Alex at the cocktail table.

As promised, Cassie and Liz, Lara's former flatmates, were the first to turn up. Having deposited a bottle of wine, with a quick hello, into Alex's hands, Cassie threw her arms around Lara. 'I don't know why we're celebrating the fact that you've left us!' she exclaimed. 'We miss you!'

'It's true,' Liz said warmly, next in line for a hug. 'It's not the same without you.'

'Well, I miss you too.' Lara laughed, motioning them into the flat. 'But I'm not exactly far away.' The trio, who had happily found themselves sharing a corridor as nervous freshers at university, had been renting a flat in Shepherd's Bush for the past two years. Lara and Alex's new place, just north of Ladbroke Grove, was no more than a fifteen-minute bus ride away.

'I know, but it's still not the same as having you right there,' Cassie protested. 'I have to keep reminding myself that you've gone. I keep expecting you to appear in the kitchen in your pyjamas . . .' She stopped as they reached the living room. 'Bloody hell, La, this is amazing.'

'Wow,' Liz agreed. 'It's *gorgeous*. And it was such a dump before.'

Lara beamed. 'Good. I'm glad you like it.'

'Are you kidding? I *love* it.' Cassie walked over to the french windows that led out onto the deck. 'Especially what you've done with this outside bit.'

'I know – isn't it great? That's what we're most proud of.' Lara pulled a face. 'God. Listen to me. I've turned into a middle-aged housewife already. "We're so proud of this", "You must look at what we did with the bathroom", blah, blah. I never saw myself as DIY-girl. It's been quite a revelation.' She chuckled, relishing the irony. 'But, you know, you really *should* see the bathroom.'

The doorbell rang and Alex walked back into the living room, barbecue tongs in hand. 'Drinks, ladies? How d'you like the new gaff, then? Not too shabby?'

'Yeah, I'll say,' Liz laughed. 'Your middle-aged housewife of a girlfriend has just been showing us around. The bathroom next, was it, La?'

'You'll see that later,' Alex remonstrated. 'Drinks. Much more important. Outside.' He kissed the back of Lara's head. 'I'll get the door.'

The guests were soon flowing as readily as the drinks, and by eight the place was packed. As more and more people arrived the hip-hop from the estate opposite got steadily louder and Lara, loving the carnival atmosphere on the square, wondered if this might be some territorial attempt to battle it out with the tunes being spun on the deck by her younger brother Lucas and his two mates. She allowed herself the vaguest flicker of concern about the noise, then promptly dismissed it. It was the first proper day of summer! And the rest of the building was empty tonight anyway. Since moving in six weeks ago, Alex and Lara had discovered that the inhabitants of the ground-floor flat, a publisher and his wife, went off to the country every weekend and never seemed to return until Monday morning. The hedge-fund manager who occupied the first floor was on holiday for two weeks. And the good will of their neighbours on the second floor, an investment banker from Sydney called Sam and his girlfriend Heidi, had been secured last weekend when Lara and Alex had popped downstairs to introduce themselves properly. Offering a bottle of Australian red they'd picked up in Oddbins down the road, Lara had mentioned they were hoping to throw a housewarming party the following Sunday night – it had to be Sunday, she explained, because she was acting in a play called *Night Games* in the West End and Sunday was her only night off – to which they were, of course, warmly invited. Sam and Heidi had seemed very keen, and Alex had joked later that they were probably a bit starstruck by their upstairs neighbour: Lara was currently gracing the nation's TV screens again as the star of *The Chronicles of Mary*, a popular twenty-something series now in its third season on Channel 4. Lara, who was still amazed (and embarrassed) when anyone even recognised her from the TV, had rubbished that idea and decided instead that they were just being friendly.

Nevertheless, she noticed now that Heidi did seem a little flustered, as a group of the *Mary* cast suddenly arrived on the deck bearing champagne and drawing inevitable attention to themselves. Out of the corner of her eye, as she poured drinks and handed round paper plates, Lara spotted Heidi frantically trying to take pictures on her phone of Charlie Fox – Lara's co-star and the show's resident heart-throb – and gushing about how much she loved the programme. Amused, but mildly concerned about how this might affect neighbourly relations, Lara was relieved when Alex, still holding court at the barbecue, told her that it turned out Sam worked at the same investment bank as their friend Joe and was clearly quite happy talking credit crunch and derivatives over beers with him.

'They work at the same bank?' Lara asked, nicking a sausage off the grill and dipping it into the bowl of ketchup that was balanced on the edge of the table. 'Small world.'

'More to the point, someone who actually knows what Joe *does* all day.' Alex chuckled, deftly flipping a beefburger. 'That must be a nice change for him.' He put his free arm around Lara's waist and leant over to kiss her. 'Good party, monkey,' he said.

'Good party,' she agreed, grinning at him through her sausage before dancing off to welcome the latest arrivals.

It *was* a good party. Evening dissolved into night and a few brave London stars came out and still nobody showed signs of slowing down. At one point Lara, feeling a bit drunk and not a little overwhelmed by all the snatched half-conversations and exclaimed hellos and quickly downed cocktails demanded by her role as hostess, escaped upstairs for a quiet cigarette. Returning to her favourite spot by the window, she surveyed the scene on the deck below. The sky, emptied of its sun, had faded to a dusky pinkish-blue but the air remained warm. Still holding the late afternoon's balmy perfume, it was infused now with other scents – her cigarette, forgotten bits of food that were still grilling slowly on the dying embers of the barbecue, the marijuana smoke which curled upwards from two distinct centres: her brother's crowd in one corner and the *Mary* actors in another. Lara leant her head against the window and marvelled for a moment at the music Lucas was mixing. A trademark Lucas sound, some kind of deep-funk, soul-infused hip-hop concoction, overlaid with the evocative strains of Nina Simone, it suited the almost melancholy beauty of this first summer evening perfectly.

Focusing on her little brother, busy at the turntables with his DJ face on, Lara felt a pang. They'd had a brief chat when he arrived – he had admired the flat, lingering over a framed monochrome photograph of their mother playing Cleopatra at the National Theatre, which Lara had hung over the fireplace. She'd mentioned that their father had emailed to say he was coming back to London for a memorial service soon, and said she hoped they could all get together when he was in town. Lucas had said something like 'Yeah, cool, whatever,' but had been characteristically laconic when she'd asked how he was doing. He'd been working in a record shop in Soho for most of the summer – they'd bumped into each other on Shaftesbury Avenue a couple of weeks ago on her way into the theatre. That was when she'd had the idea of asking him to DJ at the party. He had told her then that he was staying in Oliver's pied-à-terre in Pimlico, coaching cricket at the weekends and trying to save up for a trip to a Moroccan music festival.

That much she had learnt. But when was the last time she had had a proper conversation with him? she wondered. Lucas had just finished his second year at university, coasting through his social-anthropology degree like he'd coasted through his school days; no care for anything much except making music and playing football. Lara did try to visit him in Bristol as much as possible, taking him out for Sunday lunch at one of the nicer local pubs and transferring him money every now and again: he knew she would never tell their father. They made small-talk easily enough, could drink a few pints together or go and see a film without awkwardness, but Lara always found herself stepping onto the train home with a leaden realisation that the great chasm of the unsaid between them had just widened. After their mother's fatal accident in Paris ten years ago, Lara's relationship with her brother had necessarily been wrenched from the sisterly to the maternal. But she had been only sixteen herself, equally paralysed by grief and disbelief, and it had faltered, perhaps inevitably. Although some had questioned the wisdom of Oliver Latner dispatching his newly motherless children back to their respective boarding schools in England while he returned to the embassy in Beirut to pick up the pieces, Lara had been inwardly grateful for his approach. Father and brother were a walking, breathing, inescapable reminder of her loss; and she'd found it easier, or rather, less difficult to get through the shock of her mother's death by shutting down, focusing on her A levels and distancing herself from the two people who might have any real understanding of what she was going through.

Still, tonight Lara felt something sharp, regretful, bite into her when she looked down at her brother. She knew so little about Lucas these days. She wasn't even sure if he had a girlfriend, although there always seemed to be a clutch of impossibly beautiful girls buzzing around him and his entourage – like the creature here tonight, a long-legged blonde who never seemed to take her eyes off him. Over the years, Lara knew, Lucas had cultivated two versions of himself. There was the one on the outside that most people saw – a tall, good-looking boy with distant sea-blue eyes and mean skills on the decks – and then there was the real, inner one; the one who sat very still and watched the world going on around him in bemused, peaceful silence. Lara had always prided herself on having access to the real Luc, the inner Luc, but somewhere along the way, she now saw with a shock, she had lost that sisterly privilege. And, knowing what her brother was like, it would not be easily won back either.

Lara watched as Lucas removed his headphones and accepted a bottle of Becks and a spliff from one of his friends, a black guy with dreadlocks who took over as DJ. Taking a drag from the joint between his teeth, Lucas hoisted himself up onto the wall and positioned his battered *djembe* drum between his knees. And then something remarkable happened. Despite people's absorption in their own conversations, despite all the general party chatter and the surrounding urban drone, it seemed to Lara that there was a collective gasp as her brother began drumming over the track his friend was playing. For a moment, everyone fell silent in appreciation. Lucas had started drumming as a kid when they lived in Lebanon, then taken it more seriously when the family had been posted to Kinshasa, then Dakar. He'd learnt properly on the streets of Mali and Senegal in his gap year and had clearly honed his talent at clubs and parties in Bristol over the past couple of years. He was amazing. Lara felt a swell of pride and would almost have joined in the whoops of delight from her guests, had she had not wanted to remain up here, invisible to the party, for just a little longer.

As Lucas played, Lara cast her eye over the collection of her and Alex's friends below and felt any latent regret about her brother melt away in a surge of happiness and drumbeats. I love these people, she thought, the loosening effect of all those cocktails gilding everyone in a warm glow. Lots were mutual friends of theirs from university – so many of them now lawyers and bankers and management consultants that it was good to see them dressed down and letting rip on a Sunday night. But there were others she and Alex had picked up here and there too – at her drama school, his law school, on random holidays. It was good to have so many of them in one place; and especially this place, she reflected, feeling again a sense of incredulity that these bricks, this mortar, were really theirs to call 'home'.

The flat had cost a fortune, even despite the credit crunch, but after four years of renting post-university, Lara had decided it was worth it. Following a stretch of almost constant employment, and a few fat residuals cheques for *Mary*, the series that had given her a big break following her post-grad year at drama school, this was certainly the moment she could afford it. She and Alex had never officially cohabited during their six years together, but this spring, with the leases up for renewal on both their rental places, had also seemed the right time for that. They had been joking about being together for ever since about a month into their relationship, so taking the plunge and getting a place together hadn't seemed like that big a deal.

What had become a big deal, however, was *where* they were going to buy, with Alex, native northerner and latterly dedicated resident of Camden Town, declaring that 'no fucking way' was he going to live 'in a half-million-quid cupboard among the posh twats in Notting Hill'; and Lara, with her secret predilection for organic groceries and nice cocktail bars, beginning to despair. For three months they'd slogged around London, failing to find a flat they both loved but eventually agreeing on a place in Angel, mostly out of frustration. Lawyers were instructed, surveys were carried out, the whole excruciating process had shunted along until, at the very point of exchanging contracts, they were gazumped.

'The bastard!' Alex had exclaimed, lightly, on hearing the news. They were sitting in the pub down the road from his flat, drowning their sorrows.

'You know, Al,' Lara had said tentatively, 'we *can* afford to match the other offer . . .'

He'd looked up at her and touched her cheek affectionately.

'Let's forget about it, princess. As you might say, it clearly wasn't *meant to be*.'

'Are you sure?'

'Sure, baby. Forget about it. We'll go back to the estate fuckers tomorrow and we'll find somewhere better. You'll see, it'll all work out for the best.' He held up his pint glass. 'Cheers, you.'

And then, just the following Saturday, Lara had been woken up by the plummy tones of Barnaby-from-Foxtons, whom she had in desperation called upon to help her look for somewhere 'at least in North Kensington'. Something had *just* come on the market, the very obliging Barnaby had explained urgently to her through her sleep fug; it needed 'a bit of attention', he conceded, but was in the right area and an 'absolute bargain', having belonged to an old lady who had recently died and whose bickering sons, aware of the current pitch of the London market, were keen to get rid of it as soon as possible.

Within minutes, Lara had pushed a mildly grumbling Alex out of bed. 'It's a two-bed split top-floor flat, with a terrace, on St Charles Square,' she'd told him on the way, anticipation catching in her throat. 'Number twenty-nine, I think he said. You know where I mean? Just up from Ladbroke Grove tube.'

'Yeah, yeah,' Alex had joked. 'But it's still in W10, my posh little love.'

Once inside the property, though, Lara – heart beating frantically for she adored it even in its dilapidation and despite the hideous fifties furnishings – had raised her eyes to meet Alex's and found him smiling at her. She had laughed out loud. With its lofty position above the square, near enough to the chic dim sum restaurants and the French candle emporia but closer in spirit to the grotty pubs and vegetal grunge of Portobello

Market, it had retained enough of the area's historic character and charm to seduce even the wary northerner. Not long afterwards, back in Barnaby's bottle-green office, Lara was pledging away her considerable chunk of the capital required, Alex was adding his own, more modest, contribution, surveys were being arranged, and bingo: two weeks later they had themselves a mortgage. Much as Alex teased Lara about her funny little superstitions, her faith in the random interventions of fate in everyday life, she would never be able to shake the feeling that this flat was somehow destined to be theirs. Of all the many houses she had lived in across the world, she had never felt so happy anywhere.

Lara watched her boyfriend on the terrace now as he darted between clusters of people, refilling drinks, laughing, making everyone feel at ease, as was his way. She saw him shake hands with arriving boys, kiss departing girls goodbye, segue effortlessly into the ends or beginnings of conversations. Spreading joy, that was what Alex did. It was what he had always done.

She'd had a sense of it the very first time she'd met him, at a party in her second year at university. Alex had been standing by a makeshift drinks table chatting to a girl, holding a bottle of Tesco value cola in one hand while he sloshed vodka into the girl's glass with the other. Lara had waited patiently by the table – ostensibly for the vodka, but actually quite content just to watch, unobserved, the tall boy with the floppy dark hair and animated brown eyes. He'd suddenly turned and caught her eye; she'd motioned at the vodka. 'Oh, sorry, didn't mean to be hogging it all night,' he'd chuckled, in his broad northern accent, cracking her the most enormous grin. 'I'm Alex, by the way.' The other girl seemed to have disappeared – although in reality she was probably still standing there, daggers in her eyes, clutching her vodka and coke – and for the rest of the party, Alex and Lara had never left each other's side.

He was a history finalist, he told her, a politics-obsessed footballer from a small town just outside Manchester, heading to law school in London next year. She was reading French and Italian, she explained, 'basically cheating' her way through her degree because she was half French and could already, thanks to being the daughter of a diplomat, speak lots of languages. 'I've seen you somewhere before, haven't I?' he'd said, at which point she'd blushed and, being a few vodkas down, admitted that she'd probably remember if that had been the case. But he'd insisted, and finally remembered: of course! The theatre! He'd seen her in that 'legendary' production of *Romeo and Juliet* last year; the one that had acquired a sort of mythical status across the university because it had been so good, critics from London had come up to review it. As if reflecting the connection he had just made, a shadow crossed Alex's lovely, open face and he seemed to be looking into Lara's eyes with a new understanding. Wasn't she the girl with the famous mother, the dead mother, the French actress? But he hadn't said anything about that. He'd simply gone, 'Yeah, well, I suppose you were okay in that play, weren't you?' with a twinkle in his eye. She'd laughed.

They'd talked all night, and continued to talk as the party gradually dwindled to a close. Emerging from the noisy, smoke-filled rooms to discover a university town tranquil and peaceful under the stars, they'd kept walking, talking and walking, vodka-happy, love-drunk, until pausing at the river. The sun had nudged its way out of the darkness, then, and dawn light had flooded the bank of grass where they were sat, huddled together for warmth. Alex had taken Lara's face in his hands and kissed her. 'Well I never,' his eyes had said, laughing. 'Who'd have thought?'

And that had been that, really. Alex had become Lara's rock: her best friend, her protector, the first person she had dared to trust after four post-Eve years of wondering if everybody she loved would one day desert her. 'Thank you for the sunshine in my head,' she used to say to him, wishing there were somehow words that could convey just how much she loved him; just how grateful she was for the peace he'd restored to her soul.

As if sensing Lara's green eyes on him again, Alex looked up at their window, spotted her sitting on her favourite seat, and winked. Lara felt a rush of affection, a familiar surge of warmth and security – and then caught her breath as a spasm of dread suddenly gripped her insides. The happy scene below her was starting to blur and buckle, and her head spun with the sensation that she might be watching it all – her boyfriend, her friends, brother, her flat, her life – from a great distance; as if she were no longer part of it. Lara shut her eyes and, to her astonishment, felt tears sear the backs of her eyelids. Turning away from the window she took a deep breath and pulled the shutters tightly closed. *What the hell was that?* she wondered at her reflection, furiously stubbing her cigarette in the ashtray on the dressing-table. Her face in the mirror wondered back, impassive. Lara closed the bedroom door and went slowly downstairs to rejoin the party, trying to banish Nina Simone and her heart-wrenching melody from her head.

TWO

'Remind me never to listen to you again when you decide you want to throw a party on a Sunday night.' Alex was groaning into his pillow when the alarm went off the next morning. Last night's diehards had still been lounging in their living room drinking the dregs of a bottle of whisky at four a.m., and the hosts had only fallen into bed a couple of hours ago.

'Excuse me,' Lara groaned back. 'Whose idea was it to start a full-scale political debate at three in the fucking morning?'

He rolled over and flung his arm around her, continuing to talk into his pillow. 'It wasn't my fault,' he yawned. 'It was that awful girl Harriet, the one Ben brought, who started it with all that crap about the Tories being ready to win the next election . . . Baby, can you call work and tell them I'm not coming in because I'm sick? *Please?*'

Despite her throbbing temples, her furry throat, Lara let out a hoot of laughter. 'Yeah, right,' she said, prodding his shoulder.

21

'Half your bloody chambers were here last night.' Alex was a junior barrister in one of London's top criminal sets, and the colleagues he had invited had done little to dispel the notion that lawyers could drink everyone else under the table.

Alex emitted a moan of resignation and sat up, rubbing his eyes. Kissing Lara's forehead and looking blearily into her eyes, he said, 'Ah, my little slacker, you're so lucky you don't have to go to work today.'

'Excuse me!' Lara cried. 'I have to work tonight! And at least you don't have to clear up this place. Now, stop being so pathetic and get in that shower.'

'Fine, fine.' He slumped back down and didn't move.

'Listen, if you can't handle a few drinks, Mr Craig . . .'

And he was up. Lara smiled and rolled over to take a sip from the glass of water by the bed. She switched on the radio, which Alex had left tuned to Radio 4, as usual. Willing her head to stop hammering, she lay there, half listening to the familiar voice of the *Today* presenter interviewing some minister about NHS reform, half thinking about the night before. Random images floated in and out of her chemically imbalanced consciousness: the loveliness of the candle-lit deck as the sun went down; her brother clutching the drum between his knees with that dreamy look in his eyes; marshmallows and burgers grilling under the stars; Alex in full party-host mode; her girlfriends, looking fabulous in their summer dresses, drinking cocktails and gossiping; that poor girl Heidi getting trashed with the boys from the show; that incredible music . . .

With a jolt, Lara recalled the feeling she'd had at the window, completely out of the blue, as if the night, as if everything, was just too perfect and could not hold. As if something in her life was about to spin, shift, change. Shuddering, she hauled herself out of bed and dug out a packet of Nurofen Plus from the cabinet in the bathroom where Alex, towel around his waist and still a little bleary-eyed, was shaving with the utmost concentration.

'You okay?' he asked, swilling the razor in the basin.

'Yep,' she answered, chucking two pills down her throat and turning on the shower. 'Just feel like shit.'

'Poor monkey,' he soothed. 'Listen, I was only joking. You don't have to do all the tidying up. Leave it and I'll finish it when I get back from work.'

'Don't be stupid,' she heard herself snap. 'Of course I'll do it.'

He raised an eyebrow and went back to his shaky shave. She sighed, and moved over to him. Kissing his shoulder blade where a few water drops still quivered, she rested her head against his warm skin. 'Sorry,' she murmured. 'Just feel monstrous. I love you. Have a good day.'

By the time Lara had taken a long hot shower she was feeling altogether more human. Downstairs, she finished the remains of Alex's pot of coffee and made some toast, which she ate while skimming the newspaper he'd left half read on the table. Then, after turning the iPod in the living room to full volume, she set to work, clearing up the glasses and ashtrays, filling the dishwasher, recycling the wine and beer bottles, the paper plates. Marvelling at the amount of alcohol that had been consumed, the number of cigarettes and joints smoked and, even more miraculously, the apparent lack of red-wine stains on the new carpet, she swept and wiped and dusted and hoovered until the flat was sparkling again. Every now and again she would glance up at the photo of Eve/Cleopatra on the mantelpiece and a familiar, piercing regret would momentarily undo her. *I wish, I wish, I wish you were here to see all this . . .*

23

But she was used to that.

At midday, Lara finally collapsed on the sofa and called Cassie.

'What a great party,' Cassie said, a little groggily. 'Haven't been that pissed in *ages*. I've only just got out of bed.'

'Lucky you. I've been clearing up all bloody morning.'

'Oh, honey! You should have called earlier. I'll come round and help if you want.'

'Don't worry, I'm nearly done now.'

'Shall we go for a BMC then?' A Bloody Mary and Chips was Lara, Cassie and Liz's tried and trusted hangover cure, born one rainy morning in a university greasy spoon and refined along the way in various London cafés.

'As a matter of urgency,' Lara said, cheered immediately by the prospect. 'See you at the Electric in half an hour? Oh, and bring your camera. I want to see your pictures from last night.'

Portobello was buzzing sleepily, Monday's atmosphere one of renewal and relief as the streets recovered from the weekend and geared up for next Saturday's inevitable onslaught of teenagers and tourists. Lara pulled her sunglasses onto her nose and wiggled her bare toes in their flip-flops, happy to discover that yesterday's glorious weather had lasted the night. She waved to Phil and Lou, a couple of the vegetable traders stationed opposite the Electric Cinema, and went upstairs to the members' floor.

'Hmm. A little hungover, are we?' Simon, the barman, enquired, when Lara had given him her double Bloody Mary order with a wry grimace.

'Er, well spotted. Alex and I had our flatwarming last night. Let's just say it went on pretty late.'

'Wouldn't have been much of a party if it hadn't,' he pointed out, reasonably.

'Well, that,' she laughed, 'is very true.'

At that moment Lara's phone rang – she had forgotten to turn it off up here where, in a bid to create a relative haven of peace and quiet, mobiles were not allowed. She glanced at the number, saw it was her agent, Milton Hewison, and pressed cancel as Cassie walked in. The girls embraced, and Cassie leant over the bar to kiss Simon.

'Looks like you need this as much as she does,' he said cheerfully, handing her a glass.

'Hell, you can say that again,' Cassie deadpanned. 'It was some party. Her boyfriend mixes a mean cocktail.' She took a sip. 'Not as good as yours, though.'

'The chips are on their way, ladies.'

Smiling, Lara and Cassie moved towards their usual table by the window and, as they had done on so many occasions over the years, promptly started deconstructing the events of the night before. They were at that stage of their mid-twenties when couples who had been together for years were splitting up, causing divorce-settlement ructions among joint-friendship groups, while other university sweethearts who had broken up long ago were getting back together.

'Can you believe Emma and Tom?' Cassie mused, looking at a photo on her camera. 'How many years was it you couldn't have them in the same *room* as each other? Now they look as if they should be on the cover of *Hello!* welcoming us into their marital home.'

'Weird, isn't it?' Lara agreed. 'How people just drift apart and back towards each other as if controlled by some magnetic tide.'

'Except for the likes of you two, of course, constant as the morning star. God, Al was on good form last night.'

Lara snorted. 'You should have seen him this morning. Anyway, missy, what was going on with you and that guy? The one Charlie brought along. He was cute.'

Cassie giggled. 'Who, *Ed Fletcher*, you mean?' she asked innocently. 'It was just a kiss.'

Lara raised an eyebrow.

'Honestly,' Cassie laughed again. 'Just a kiss. But he is fit.' She grinned. 'Anyway, talking about *fit*, how amazing is your little brother?' She handed her camera to Lara to point out a photo of Lucas perched on the wall. 'I don't know how long it's been since I've even seen him, but not only is he seriously *gorgeous* that drumming was incredible.'

'I know.' Lara looked at the photo and felt her throat prickle. 'Hey, Cass, will you print this one for me?'

'Course. How often do you see him, these days?'

'Not often. He keeps himself to himself, you know.'

'Has he been to see the play?'

Lara removed the stick of celery from her glass and crunched down on it. She shook her head.

Cassie frowned. 'That's a shame.'

'He's working in some record shop on Poland Street. I bumped into him the other day on my way into the theatre and told him he should come. I said I'd get him tickets and everything, said Al and I would take him out for supper afterwards, told him to bring whoever he wanted. He said he'd call me about it, but he never did. It's no big deal. Theatre was never really his thing.' Lara drained her glass and shivered as the vodka hit kicked in. 'Even when Mum was alive.'

After a pause, Cassie said, 'Will your dad come and see it, do you think?'

Staring at a column of dust motes that were caught in a shaft of sunlight, Lara felt her headache inch back through the Bloody Mary barrier. 'Funnily enough, he emailed me the other day,' she murmured. 'He's coming to London soon, the week before it ends. So I don't know. Maybe.'

She felt knackered and disgustingly hungover now. Her phone was still vibrating insistently in her bag so she pulled it out, happy to change the subject. 'I'm sorry, babe,' she said. 'This thing's going crazy. It's Milton. I'd better answer it.'

'Of course you must.' Cassie smiled widely. 'Maybe you've got a job!'

'I doubt it. But it's not like him to do this. I'll be two minutes. Can you ask Simon for a Coke for me?'

Going all the way down to the sunny street so she could sneak a cigarette at the same time, Lara rang her agent's number and got through to Christian, his assistant.

'*Great* party,' Christian said. 'Sunday night, though – tsk. I hope you're not suffering as much as I am.'

'Put it this way, Chris, I've felt better.'

He feigned shock. 'Miss Latner, you have to be on *stage* tonight.'

'I know,' she replied guiltily. 'But I'm getting there. I think I'll pull through. Now, do you have any idea why Milton's been calling me a thousand times today?'

'He's been in the weirdest mood since he read his emails this morning. Really quite agitated. I can't get out of him why, though, and frankly, with this hangover, I'm loath to try. But I know he's desperate to speak to you. I'll put you through now. Have a good show tonight, doll.'

Seconds later, Milton was on the phone. 'What are you doing at the moment?' he asked.

'Nothing much, I'm just with Cassie, trying to mend my headache,' Lara replied, taking a drag of her cigarette. 'Remember I told you we were having our flatwarming party last night?'

'What?' he said vaguely. 'Oh, yes. Well. Listen, can you come and see me in the office as soon as possible?'

'In the office? Why? What's going on?'

Milton cleared his throat.

'I think we should talk about it face to face.'

Lara was amazed. In all the years he had been her agent, Milton had never once demanded that she come into his office. She was suddenly worried. 'Is everything okay, Mil? Are you okay?'

'Me? Yes, yes, of course. I'm fine. Believe me, you'll understand.'

'O-kay.' She looked at her watch. 'How's four?' The agency was in Covent Garden, conveniently just around the corner from the Donmar Warehouse where she was performing. 'Then I can stay with you for an hour or so and still get to the theatre for my call.'

'Four is fine,' he said. 'Lara—'

'Yes?'

'Oh, nothing. Listen, darling, I'm sorry to sound a bit cryptic. You'll understand when you get here.'

'Well, that was weird.'

'Why?' Cassie asked, taking a deep breath. 'Have you got a new film?'

'No, course I haven't. It's nothing like that.'

'What is it, then?'

'I don't know. He just sounded really odd on the phone and

asked me to go in to see him at the office. He's never done that before, ever.'

'He's not ill or anything, is he?'

'That's what I'm worried about. It's so unlike him.' Lara waved at Simon for the bill. 'Sorry, lovely, I'm gonna have to make a move if I'm going to sort myself out and get into town in time. What are your plans for the afternoon?'

Cassie stuffed a final chip into her mouth and sighed dramatically. 'Not much. I wish I could say *my* agent had rung and urgently requested that I go into his office and see him.' Her pretty face clouded. 'Although, actually, I don't really, because then he might be telling me he wanted to let me go and that would be awful.'

Lara inclined her head. 'Oh, Cass, don't say that.'

'I know, I'm being gloomy. It's probably my hangover. It's just sometimes I feel *soooooo* fed up. I haven't worked for more than six months now. I don't know how long I can keep going and keep smiling and pretending everything's going to be fine.'

Lara handed her credit card to Simon. 'You don't have to *pretend* that everything's going to be fine. Everything *is* going to be fine.'

'Easy for you to say, Latner,' Cassie said lightly. 'You wouldn't know what unemployment was if it hit you in the face.'

'Yeah, well, I've just been very, very lucky,' Lara said levelly, tapping her pin number into the machine. 'You know that that's the only thing that really matters in this business.' She looked up. 'I've been bloody lucky, C, but my luck could run out any time.'

'Yeah, right. Like *that*'s going to happen!'

'You never know,' Lara countered, although she had to concede that Cassie probably had a point. She'd definitely had a break getting the lead in *The Chronicles of Mary*, when breaks counted for almost everything in this most arbitrary of industries, but

Lara recognised she'd also had a genetic head-start when it came to the acting profession. To be Eve's daughter – the revered Eve Lacloche, Oscar-nominated French icon, star of some of France's most celebrated films and dead at forty-five – often felt like a curse, but there was no question that this biological fact, which asserted itself so visibly in Lara's green eyes and high cheekbones, had cleared an initial path, invited curiosity, opened doors. How could Cassandra Kearney, daughter of a Welsh schoolteacher and a sales manager from Luton, ever compete with that? Lara almost envied her best friend for it.

'Anyway, forget about it, my duck.' Cassie was smiling again. 'It's cool. I shall sit in Kensington Gardens and read my *Grazia* and have an ice-cream and I'll be fine. Make sure you call me as soon as you've seen Milton, though, okay? I want to know what it was all about.'

'Will do,' said Lara, standing up. 'Now, I really should run. I'll see you soon.'

'Have a good show!' Cassie called, but Lara had already disappeared down the stairs.

THREE

Settling into his seat towards the front of the plane, Oliver Latner declined the glass of champagne being proffered by the stewardess and sent a final few emails from his BlackBerry before switching the device into flight mode. Then he opened his briefcase and removed the sheaf of papers that his personal assistant Julia had handed him as he jumped into the car waiting outside the embassy in Tel Aviv.

After just a few minutes' reading, though, he found himself unable to concentrate. Frustrated by this uncharacteristic lack of focus, Oliver told himself it must be the bumpy take-off that was bothering him, perhaps combined with the grim fact that what awaited him at the other end was the memorial service of a dear colleague, Andrew Muirhead, who had surrendered to liver cancer eight weeks ago. He and Andrew had known each other for thirty-odd years, ever since their days on the NATO desk back in 1975. Fresh out of a two-year commission in Northern Ireland, it had been Oliver's first job at the Foreign Office, and the lively twenty-six-year-old Scot had rather shown him the ropes. Andrew had gone on to specialise in Eastern Europe and the Baltics, and had been partway through a term as Her Majesty's Ambassador in Moscow when the terminal diagnosis had come in. Thinking back to those early days with Andrew in King Charles Street – the days before he even left for Paris – Oliver felt the lurching judder of time passed, and an unexpected wave of deep regret. For what, he was not quite sure, but he would certainly miss Andrew: a good man, a great squash player, and a diplomat of the very finest degree.

As the plane levelled off and he found his mind unwittingly replaying the conversation he had had with his daughter last week, Oliver was dismayed to have to admit that it probably wasn't just Andrew's death that was proving such a distraction tonight. Placing the papers on the table in front of him, he removed his glasses, rubbed his eyes and requested a whisky and soda from the hovering stewardess. Lara had rung him at the residence last Monday evening, and Oliver had listened in stunned silence as she explained that a Hollywood production company was planning to do a remake of *La Belle Hélène*. Predictably enough, he supposed, they had approached her to play the lead. Hélène. Eve's Hélène. Except it wasn't really Eve's Hélène, Lara was saying: they were updating the story, setting it in modern-day New York. Her part would be 'Helen'. What had she said they were calling it? *This Being Human*. Still, the strangeness of assuming what was, to all intents and purposes, her mother's most famous role had clearly not eluded her. 'Can we talk about it when you're back next week?' she had asked awkwardly. 'I've just got so many questions.'

Oliver had heard how the words clotted Lara's throat, and had felt his own tighten just to hear them. He liked to believe he had buried his feelings about that film, along with his wife, ten years ago, but evidently not: listening to his daughter, he found himself gripping the telephone so hard that his knuckles turned white. Silently, he wondered who was directing the film, whether it had any connection to the original beyond its storyline, who might be behind the decision to remake it. But he dared not ask, of course. At some subconscious level he had worried, perhaps from the moment his daughter had announced, the year after Eve's death, that she was going to be an actress too, that something like this might one day happen. And now, apparently, it had. Confronted with the prospect of dredging up the past and having to talk to Lara about *La Belle Hélène* – perhaps having to tell her the truth – Oliver could not staunch the sense of foreboding that was gathering apace at the pit of his stomach.

He hadn't mentioned any of this on the phone, of course, he had merely said, 'Right. Well, I'll see what I can help you with next week, then,' and had gone on to suggest a game of tennis or lunch at his club. Now, taking a grateful sip of whisky, he took up his papers again and stared at the words in front of him, trying to stay focused on the latest negotiations between the Israeli government and Fatah leaders in the West Bank. But it was too late. Suddenly, unwittingly, he was back in Paris; back on the night when he had first encountered Eve . . .

He had gone along to the gala performance of *Phèdre* at the Théâtre du Chatelet as part of a British Embassy delegation; he couldn't even remember now what the occasion had been. A fuss had been made before the curtain went up, though, because due to the indisposition of the famous star, a relatively unknown and unfeasibly young actress was stepping in at the last minute to play the title role. People had felt cheated, but in the event the girl had been remarkable. At that point in his life, Oliver had known almost nothing about the theatre – being more used to observing politicians at the dispatch box. But even he had grasped as much. There had been a dinner in the Elysée Palace afterwards, and this Eve Lacloche had been invited with some of her fellow cast. Although her physical loveliness was the most obvious thing about her, it had become increasingly apparent, as the evening wore on and she had held her own in a room full of male statesmen and diplomats, that she was not just a pretty face. But while Oliver's colleagues had fallen over themselves to try to catch her attention with garrulous witticisms and verbal one-upmanship, the twenty-seven-year-old Oliver had found himself tongue-tied whenever he tried to open his mouth.

And yet, over the course of the dinner, he had gradually become aware that a pair of beautiful green eyes were turning towards him with increasing regularity. And the feeling of being looked at, even just looked at by this creature had sent a peculiar thrill through him. Although he had had a number of girlfriends at Oxford and Sandhurst, and was, to the ribbing of his mates in the embassy, apparently quite popular with the prettiest girls in Paris, it was something inexplicable and almost unsettling that Oliver felt stir within him as the girl threw back her dark head and laughed, then cast her dizzying green gaze on him before asking him a question across the table.

'What about you, Monsieur?' she was saying, her English husky and almost comically sexy. 'Where do you stand on the issue? I hear you are quite the rising star of the British Embassy here.'

There were good-natured jeers from down the table and Oliver blushed hotly. Taking a great slug of Dutch courage in the form of the vintage Bordeaux on offer, he told himself to pull himself to-bloody-gether and nodded at the *sommelier* for a refill.

'*Pas du tout*, Mademoiselle Lacloche,' he declared – he'd checked her place card instinctively to make sure she was indeed still 'mademoiselle', and had been absurdly (he recognised) relieved to discover she was. 'I believe you are the only star in this room.' He smiled, she smiled, and at that moment a bolt of electricity had passed across the table between them. 'As for where I stand on the issue of Anglo-French trade relations . . .'

Was that the moment? Oliver, on the plane, decades later, wondered again. Was it really then, just an hour or two after they had first set eyes on each other, that the 'fate' in which his late wife had always placed such child-like trust had swooped down to intervene? Redirecting their formerly independent lives on a collision course towards each other, eternally intertwining their futures? He couldn't imagine how he'd answered Eve's question now, but he recalled being wildly grateful to the Bordeaux for helping to invest, he hoped, his response with a dash of flair: certainly she had looked suitably impressed, eyes glittering, mouth twitching into its perfect smile. Eve Lacloche had stared across the table at him under those sooty lashes as everyone else continued to chatter around them; and Oliver Latner, buoyed up with all the wine and the candlelight and the sumptuous surroundings and the whatever-the-hell-it-was that was happening inside him, had stared back at her for longer than was perhaps polite in such company.

When the meal had drawn to a close in the early hours and the guests were making their way down the grandiose staircase towards the exit, Oliver heard Eve, a few steps in front of him, graciously telling one of the other men that, no, she lived on the other side of town, and that she would be 'completely fine' to get a taxi on her own. Despite this, when he managed to bump into her at the cloakroom a few moments later and was helping her on with a little black jacket over a very pretty dress, he found himself asking, impetuously: 'Mademoiselle Lacloche, might I get you a taxi?'

Eve had turned to him then, a strand of hair that had escaped from her chignon glancing across her forehead, and Oliver had felt his insides tumble at the knowledge that something momentous had occurred to him this evening; that he would, perhaps, never be the same again.

'Où allez-vous, Monsieur Olivier?'

'Oh, no – I mean, I'll put you in your own cab . . .' He trailed off. 'Where am *I* going?'

'Oui, Monsieur Olivier. Où allez-vous?'

'I'm, er, going back to my apartment. On Avenue de Friedland,' he managed.

'C'est parfait!' she had laughed. 'I live nearby. I will come with you.'

Draining his whisky in a bid to stop his brain continuing this futile little exercise, Oliver clutched his papers and attempted once more to make sense of the briefing document in his hand. It was going to be a busy few days in London: a number of meetings had been scheduled, including one with the foreign secretary tomorrow afternoon, and a breakfast at Downing Street the following morning. He had visits to make to DFID and the MOD and was due to give a lecture about the latest security situation in Israel and Palestine to Chatham House. There were lunches pencilled with various people, including William Davenport, now political director of the Foreign Office and one of his staunchest allies. (Davenport had been particularly supportive after Eve's death, standing by Oliver when he refused to take gardening leave; Oliver was convinced that had people like Davenport not been so vociferously on his side he would have lost traction within the Office completely.) On Thursday night there was Andrew's memorial service, at which he was giving a speech; on Friday, dinner with some old friends; at the weekend the annual Foreign Office versus Commonwealth Secretariat cricket match at Blenheim Palace, to which he was hoping to take Lucas. And, of course, there was the promise he'd made to Lara to try to get along to her play before it closed. It was by one of the UK's brightest young playwrights, apparently. She'd said the reviews had 'generally been pretty okay', but when Julia helpfully printed a selection off the Internet, he'd discovered that the notoriously savage London theatre critics had in fact been rather rapturous. Oliver had felt a curious flicker of both pride and detachment when he saw the name 'Lara Latner' in print and read complete strangers talking about her in such breathless terms –

radiant, vulnerable, magnetic . . . This is the kind of performance that makes careers . . . Beg, borrow or steal your way into the Donmar Warehouse to catch Rufus Elliot's breathtaking production of Sam Kerrigan's bold new play Night Games, *with a star-making central performance by Lara Latner, daughter of the late, great Eve Lacloche . . .*

And so on. Was that really Lara, his Lara, they were talking about, that gawky little girl with her skinny legs and scabbed knees? His – and, of course, the 'late, great' Eve's – Lara?

It was hard to imagine. In all the years he'd been married to an actress, Oliver had never quite got used to how disturbing, even alienating, it could be to watch the person he felt closest to become daily transformed into somebody else; how like a betrayal, an infidelity it could seem. He would always catch his heart beating a little faster when he made his way round to the stage door after watching Eve perform. Would she really be *his* Eve again when he walked into her dressing room and kissed her, her greasepaint smudged, her hair in pins? Or would some residue of whoever's soul she had been inhabiting for the past three hours under the spotlights remain, somewhere inside her, invisible to his eyes? Where did they go, all these souls, after that? Eve would invariably be frayed but elated after a performance, human again, high on adrenalin, demanding kisses and a dry martini and to be fed; it would take everything in Oliver's power for him to act normally around his wife in the immediate aftermath of having seen her turn calmly into another woman. The prospect of watching his daughter on stage again next week did not, therefore, overjoy Oliver, who had discovered in the past few years that it was no less perplexing to witness that transforming process in his own flesh and blood. Nevertheless, he told himself: no matter how busy he was, no matter how much he secretly dreaded it, he must find a way to get there.

By the time dinner arrived, Oliver's head felt much clearer. Having selected a decent-looking sauvignon to drink with his fish, he whizzed through the rest of the briefing document as he ate, pausing now and again, fork aloft, to underline something. Some of his fellow business-class passengers were also still hard at work, tapping away on laptops, but many had given up and succumbed to the guilty pleasures of a film.

Not so Oliver. As soon as the stewardess had removed his

meal paraphernalia he opened his briefcase again and swapped the embassy papers for a book about Iraq, which he was reviewing for *Foreign Affairs*. Its author, Edward T. Lowenstein, was a former official in the American State Department whom Oliver had worked alongside whilst the UK's Permanent Representative at the United Nations a few years ago. Reclining in his seat and taking a sip of his wine – really not bad, considering he was on an aeroplane – he found his place, about a quarter of the way through, and attempted to start reading again.

But it was no good. Images of Eve kept flashing into Oliver's head and mocking his determination to stay with the words in front of him. This was deeply disturbing: it was almost a decade since his wife had died, and over the years he had evolved mechanisms by which he could keep thoughts of her, of their life together, under control. What had unleashed this mutiny of his memories, usually so well-behaved? Was it simply Lara's revelation about *La Belle Hélène*? Andy's death? The impending tenth anniversary in December of Eve's? Yet that was still months away. Sighing, Oliver took a glug of water and turned resolutely back to the book. But it was a pitiful 'Coalition security preparations in the southern province of—' that he could manage, before she was there again, dancing between the dense lines of text. He closed his eyes.

It had turned out that Eve lived nowhere near him in Paris. In fact, she admitted with a shy giggle the next morning, she lived much closer to the other man who had offered her a ride home in his taxi.

'So why . . . ?' Oliver had asked, dazed, wondering if he had perhaps imagined this whole glorious episode. Rubbing his eyes, he had inclined his head and tried to make sense of the fact that there was, indeed, an exceptionally attractive female stretched out on his bed. He was not imagining it. There she was: coltish limbs twisted around his white linen sheets, the slender curve of her hip gilded in a wash of dawn light, a faint scent of rose petals in the air. The girl laughed her smoky, wicked laugh again. It was going to be dangerous, this laugh, he could tell.

'Pourquoi, Monsieur Olivier? *Pourquoi?*' Eve drew herself up to his face, like a cat, and kissed him fully on the lips. 'But isn't it obvious?' she teased in English, in that intoxicating voice.

Oliver leant back on his elbows and gently manoeuvred her lithe body onto his own once more. 'I'm not sure it's obvious to me,' he had admitted, through a moan of pleasure. 'But I'm very, very glad it's obvious to you.'

A couple of hours later, after Oliver and Eve had made love again and fallen asleep in each other's arms – a first for him, for until now he had preferred to sleep on his front making no contact with anything else (a constant source of grievance with former girlfriends) – they awoke to a Paris bathed in slanting September sunlight. It was after eight, time for work, but somehow Eve had convinced him to call the embassy and say he was sick. In all his years, throughout boarding-school, Oxford, Sandhurst, the army, the Foreign Office, Oliver Latner had never once pulled a 'sickie' – and nor would he ever again. But he was smitten, for the first time in his life. He knew he'd have to endure endless barracking from his colleagues for this – he'd be buying the beers on Friday night, that was for sure – but he didn't care. He felt quite enchanted.

Ignoring his entreaties to stay right where she was, as he came back to bed after making the phone call to the embassy switchboard, Eve had leapt up, giggling that they had 'things to do'. Coyly, but somewhat theatrically, she had wound the sheet around her body (even more miraculous to him in the light of day) and crossed to the bathroom, leaving Oliver lying naked, charmed, and astonished on his bed. His unlikely guest had sung as she showered, and he had lasted only a few minutes before jumping up to join her.

Back in the bedroom, clean and rosy-cheeked, Eve had thrown one of his blue work shirts over the black dress she'd been wearing last night, rolled up the sleeves, flung her damp dark hair into a ponytail, wound a scarf around her neck – his old Balliol scarf, no less – and pulled on her boots. '*Vas y!*' she had cried, and bustled him out of his front door. Taking his hand and flying down the stairs (quite ignoring the rickety lift he usually stepped into without thinking), she seemed to dance onto the street. And for the rest of the day, so it seemed to Oliver, Eve never stopped dancing, even when she was perfectly still.

They had walked for hours, that luminous chilly day, as she introduced him to her city – its parks, its cafés, its museums, churches, river, islands, hidden treasures. (Oliver had been in Paris for the best part of six months and had barely scratched the city's surface, he discovered with a touch of shame.) Eve never let go of his hand, and to Oliver's amazement, for he had never been one for physical displays of affection, he was happy to let her hold it. At one point he even found himself taking hers and was surprised by how natural it felt to have this girl's delicate fingers interlaced with his own. Alighting on café table after café table like a pair of giddy sparrows, they drank black coffee with their breakfast, red wine with their lunchtime steak at Café de Flore, where Eve seemed to know the entire room, and finally champagne as dusk began to sink over the streets of Paris and she pulled him down some Montmartre alley into a hidden jazz bar; the sort of place Oliver would never have dreamt of venturing into before tonight. His eyes had widened in disbelief as he listened to Eve, perched on a stool by the bar, tell him that her father Bernard was a jazz pianist and had played there often – as if that were somehow the most normal thing in the world! He had thought of his own father, Thomas, a quiet, mild-mannered Jewish accountant back in Berkshire, and wondered how it was possible that his life could have intersected with this – sprite. '*Who are you?*' he wanted to say, as Eve, laughing, reached over in the middle of their conversation and kissed him on the lips. '*Who are you?*' And '*Why me?*'

But Oliver had kept his wonderment to himself and, cool as a cucumber, had called for another bottle of champagne. He had asked Eve, still dressed ridiculously in his blue work shirt, how it was that she spoke such good English, and she had broken into peals of laughter. 'It's not perfect, not at all,' she had insisted. 'I just finished this film, playing in English, *Blue Gardenia*, you know, and I was *terrible!*' Explaining that a visiting professor at the Paris Conservatoire, an American, had made her promise to learn English properly so that she could go to Hollywood, Eve had scoffed wickedly.

'Have you ever heard of a more crazy reason to learn English than to *go to Hollywood*?' She cackled. 'I mean, learn English to read Shakespeare, *bien sûr*, learn English to read Donne, okay, but learn English to go to Hollywood? *Bof!*' She had taken a sip of her champagne and gazed dreamily around the faded, crumbling décor of the famous old bar, which was plastered with images of the great musicians who had once played there. 'Who wants to go to stupid Hollywood anyway when you can be here, in Paris? It's the centre of life, Oliver. *N'est-ce pas?*'

And it had been, for a while. The centre of life. Within three months, Oliver had been persuaded to sublet his rather sterile Foreign Office apartment in the Eighth Arrondissement, and move into his new girlfriend's light-filled, ramshackle studio flat on rue Jacob. Within three years, their lives had changed for ever. Eve had rocketed from unknown stage actress to major French film star and been thrust into the public eye accordingly. Oliver had moved impressively through the ranks of the British Embassy in Paris and was being tipped for great things by his managers back in King Charles Street. They were young, gifted and beautiful: bright stars in the veritable firmament of writers, artists, actors, politicians, philosophers, musicians, directors and fashion designers who flocked around Eve and made up their circle of friends. They had talked hopes and dreams, passions and ideals, politics and poetry, love and life. They had talked post-1968 artistic freedom and intellectual adventure. The only thing they had tried *not* to talk about was what would happen when Oliver's current posting finished and he had to go back to London to take up his next position. Those halcyon days in Paris had not been without difficulties, of course – Oliver found Eve's whimsical, flirtatious nature testing, especially after she became a star and was deemed 'public property' in France; Eve in turn found Oliver's 'English repressiveness' when it came to expressing his emotions infuriating. But, mostly, they were in love, and they were happy. And just when they were wondering how life could get any happier, a film script called *La Belle Hélène*, to be directed by Eve's favourite *auteur*, Dominique St Clair, had dropped through their letterbox on rue Jacob . . .

Unclipping his seat-belt now, so many moons later, Oliver stood up and paced to the end of the cabin, trying to stem the swell of sadness that was rising within him. Returning to his seat, he dug into his briefcase for his emergency sleeping pills, and, swilling them down with another whisky, was finally, for a few hours at least, able to shut his dead wife, his daughter, that film – everything – from his mind.

FOUR

Lara was late, as usual. Oliver was standing on the steps of the Travellers' Club, casting his eyes distractedly over the front section of the *Financial Times* and inwardly frowning at his daughter's timekeeping. It was another few minutes before he caught sight of her dashing down Pall Mall from the direction of the park, but as he took in the sight of her, his irritation melted away. This green-eyed creature in a white sundress, her dark hair flying, could almost have been his wife; and that, as ever, had the capacity to floor him.

'Sorry, sorry, sorry!' Lara cried, as she reached him and stood on tiptoe to kiss his cheek. 'Sorry.' She was wearing huge sunglasses and a chunky wooden necklace that Oliver thought he recognised as one of Eve's, picked up in the Congo or somewhere. 'I thought I'd walk because it's such a lovely day, but I managed to completely misjudge the time.'

'No problem,' Oliver said, giving her a peck in return. 'Although I'm afraid I don't have long.'

She stood back to inspect her father. 'I imagined you wouldn't. But, hey, it's good to see you, Dad. You look great.'

'Good to see you too, Lals,' he said, tucking his paper under his arm as they walked up the stairs into the club. 'Are you hungry?'

'*Starving*,' she told him, following him in.

This place always seemed to Lara as if it were stuck in some Edwardian time warp: ancient men in jackets and ties sipping gin and tonic over their *Telegraph*s; powdered old ladies in twinsets and pearls enjoying a little midday sherry with their *Daily Mail*. Even with its modern membership of worldly politicians, foreign correspondents and diplomats, to Lara the establishment still felt like an antiquated cocoon, all soft furnishings and hushed voices, but nevertheless she sort of loved it. Feeling as though she was stepping into a theatre set and rising to the occasion accordingly, she straightened her shoulders, removed her sunglasses, and took a deep breath.

'So, how are things?' Oliver asked, once they were tucking into their starters in the chandeliered dining room upstairs. 'How's the play been going? And the new flat?'

'Everything's great,' Lara told him, dipping a hunk of bread into her soup. 'The play's been a joy, the flat's amazing. You should definitely come and see it while you're here. Did Luc tell you we had a party there the other night? He came to DJ and ended up drumming too. It was brilliant.' She paused to study her father's face, which looked tanned and healthy; all that Middle Eastern sunshine, she supposed. 'How about you? How's it going?'

'Everything's fine', Oliver replied. 'Very busy, as you can imagine.'

'Of course.' Lara nodded. 'I hate the idea of you being out there, stuck in the middle of everything. Is everything really okay? It sounds like such a nightmare, what I read of it in the papers.'

'I'm not actually stuck in the middle, thankfully. There are many worse places I could be.'

'Well, I suppose that's true,' she conceded, with a sly grin. 'I suppose I should be grateful you didn't take the Baghdad job, right?' Oliver's inclination towards the world's war zones had been a defining feature of their lives; the Latner family had learnt that to joke about it was perhaps the only way to stomach it.

'Quite.' Oliver grinned back.

'Dad, I haven't made up my mind whether to do this film or not.'

Ambushed by the switch in topic, Oliver cleared his throat and suddenly found himself giving undue concentration to the task of spreading some potted shrimps on a thin triangle of brown toast as he heard his daughter saying, 'Alex and I watched *La Belle Hélène* again last night.'

'Ah,' he said, looking up and taking a bite. 'How is Alex? Enjoying the new chambers?'

Lara put down her spoon. 'He's fine,' she said. 'He sends you his best. But, Dad, I really want to ask you about Mum.' She looked him bang in the eye – but not without trepidation, it appeared to Oliver. 'I can't explain it, exactly, but I really feel I need to *know* more before I can say yes or no to the film.'

Oliver nodded slowly. It was a long time, especially in his line of work, since he had felt truly lost for words. He wished that his renowned ability to hit smoothly upon diplomatic solutions in sticky political situations could somehow be applied to his daughter.

'Okay,' he said, feeling quite the opposite. 'What is it, exactly, that you want to know about?'

Lara hesitated. It was also difficult for her to have to admit that, much as she wanted to believe she remembered everything there was to remember about her mother, so many details of their sixteen years together had dissolved into oblivion. What continued to be preserved of Eve in glossy celluloid was not, she knew, *Eve*: what was still real to her, on the other hand, was a collection of grainy memories that were becoming terrifyingly less substantial with every year that passed.

'Everything,' she told him, 'I suppose. Everything. I have all these memories, these moments I can recall, this fragmented picture that I can put together, of smells and looks and words . . . and her voice, of course. I can remember her voice. But it's not enough, Dad. I need more. I want to know what was going on in her life, her head, when she made that film. I mean, she was so young. You were both so young. You weren't even married yet. It just must have been such a different *time* . . . And she must have been such a different person. Or maybe not. I don't know. That's the problem.' Lara broke off, frustrated by her inability to express herself more articulately. She watched her father's handsome jaw twitch, his brow furrow, almost imperceptibly, and wondered how it was possible that the great tragedy he had endured in his life had not etched itself into his face. The lines around his blue eyes only added to their twinkle, somehow; the grey at his temples to the general air of distinction about him. Why did he not look ravaged, she wondered, by all the things he'd lived through?

Nevertheless, he seemed faintly uncomfortable now, his diplomatic equilibrium thrown off-kilter by the thrust of her conversation. Lara gulped another spoonful of soup and plunged back into the weighty silence hovering between them. 'The thing is, Dad, it's such an extraordinary performance. And it's not that her other performances weren't great, because of course they were. But there's something about the way she is *in that film*. You must know what I'm talking about. Maybe I feel completely, sort of, spiritually connected to it or something because I know that she became pregnant with me halfway through filming it, but who knows?' She offered her father a shy smile. 'I suppose I just want to know where that performance *came* from. Because at the moment, I have to admit, I'm a long way from believing I can replicate it.'

Oliver did indeed know what Lara was talking about, and it was too painful to contemplate. As a waiter swooped over to remove their starter plates, he took full advantage of the distraction. 'I think I might have another glass of wine,' he said affably to Lara. 'Would you like one? Perhaps we should have got a bottle after all.'

He smiled pleasantly at the waiter and Lara caught a flash of her father's legendary charm in recovery. Suddenly, the discomfort vanished, and here was Oliver the Diplomat again. 'Another glass of claret, please, Ian, if you wouldn't mind,' he was saying. 'And for my daughter?'

'I'm fine, thanks. I have to work tonight.'

'Ah, of course. *Night Games*! The toast of the West End! So, have you got me a ticket? I hear it's completely sold out and people are queuing from dawn to pick up returns, or shelling out thousands on eBay.' He winked at her.

'Of course you've got a ticket, if you want one,' Lara replied, surprised. When she'd talked about the play on the phone last week, he'd said he would try his hardest to make it, but it had sounded highly improbable. 'Just let me know when you want to come,' she said. 'Do you realise I'm almost exactly the same age as Mum was when she was making *La Belle Hélène*?'

And there it was. Oliver, defeated, carefully cut off a corner of his lamb chop. 'It had crossed my mind,' he murmured. Gazing across the room for the first time that afternoon, he spotted Derek Langton, former editor of the *Telegraph*, lunching at the Members' Table with Steven Tompkins MP, both old acquaintances. There was Rory Edwards from the BBC, talking to someone he vaguely recognised. And in the corner by the window, Belinda Strong, a parliamentary private secretary, was deep in discussion with a fellow he knew even from the back to be Lord Norman, the former home secretary. At that moment, Oliver conceded, he would rather have been seated among any of them than opposite his daughter, whose haunting eyes seemed to accuse him of something even as they begged at him so imploringly.

'If I'm going to be honest, Lara, the prospect of you taking your mother's role in anything, let alone that particular film, is perplexing.'

Lara swallowed. 'Okay. I understand that in principle. But why?'

'Well, I suppose I think you have to be careful, that's all. People will inevitably make comparisons . . . I know many think it was her greatest film.' He looked down. 'And it might be a little raw, for all of us, especially this year.'

For a moment, with the echo of 'this year' reverberating in the space between them, father and daughter collapsed into silence again, each struggling with their own decade-long, private grief.

'Yes,' Lara said quietly. 'Of course.' She bit her lip, trying furiously to hold back the tears that had sprung up like hot little daggers behind her eyelids. 'I know it's pathetic,' she continued in a half-whisper, 'but I just also thought, maybe, that doing the film might bring me ... I don't know ... closer to her.'

The sight of Lara trying so obviously but unconsciously to bite back tears in the same manner that her mother had often done made Oliver feel even more wretched. Evidently this had not been an easy conversation for his daughter to initiate, and he was suddenly filled with love for her. Love, and pity, and remorse. A devastating combination. He should tell her the truth, he knew, but how?

'Well,' he said, 'perhaps it would. Perhaps it wouldn't.'

'Oh!' Lara let her cutlery clatter to her plate. '*Dad!* How can you just sit there like that, all unruffled, and issue the standard bloody diplomatic response to everything? All I want is for you to tell me a bit more about my mother, a bit more about what she was like, a bit more about what was going on when she was making that film! It can't be hard!'

Can't be hard? Oliver wondered. Can't be hard to have to revisit those times, those gilded years in Paris when Eve had been at her most captivating, at her most free, at her most happy, because she was young and beautiful and in demand, in her own city, her own life? *Can't be hard?* For him to have to remember what Eve had been like in her twenties, before they had left Paris and moved to London in 1982? Before he had made the fateful decision to bid for first secretary in Beirut, a post he took up in January 1985? Before any of the things that happened later: his snap decision to go to the Middle East Peace Process desk rather than the Europe desk when he returned to London, despite having made a promise to the contrary; or the impending chaos in Lebanon, years later, which had meant he was asked to cut short his job on the UN desk and, years after he'd first been posted there, return to Beirut? Of course, he could not have *foreseen* what would happen later, he could hardly have known, but for him to have to revisit the days when Eve had been Lara's age, and most truly herself, was somehow for him to have to concede that what happened later had been, at least in part, his fault. But no! Not his fault! He had never deceived her, never said it would be anything other than what it was: a life of constant upheaval and disruption, where certain codes of behaviour were not just expected but demanded in a diplomat's wife; a life of excitement and new experiences, yes, a life of travel and exposure to other ways of being, a life even of a certain glamour, but a life, nonetheless, that would not be conducive to furthering her own career. She'd been told what it would be like during those tumultuous days in Paris when they had tried to wrest back a semblance of their life together after *La Belle Hélène*. But she had said she didn't care, said she loved him and would go anywhere just to be with him, said she'd known they were *meant to be together* from the first 'fateful' moment she had laid eyes on him in those State Rooms after the play. Eve had said, nay, promised, that a life with him was all she needed in the world. So it wasn't his fault that this had turned out not to be the case, was it? Couldn't be his fault . . .

But Eve had sacrificed so much, Oliver knew, with a terrible, metallic certainty in his mouth. And could he say the same of himself? What about that moment in Beirut, after Eve had returned from Paris following Lucas's birth – it must have been around February 1987, he recalled, because Syria had just occupied the west of the city – when his wife had begged him to consider taking a job on a European desk when they returned to London the following year? Oliver's heart had sunk because, for whatever reason, the Middle East was calling him, and he was less than cheered by the prospect of spending the rest of his career in and out of Brussels.

'Because at least that would mean we could spend some time in Europe,' Eve had pointed out, the prospect of cities where the sound of mortar shells did not serenade her babies to sleep a sort of wildly unthinkable fantasy. She had taken a deep breath. 'Maybe, even, we can go back to Paris . . .'

Oh, God, he remembered it so clearly. She had been sitting under the shade of a parasol on the sun-soaked stone terrace of the residence in Lebanon, holding her tiny sleeping son to her breast while five-year-old Lara played on the stone flags nearby. Even so soon after giving birth for the second time, Eve looked sensational, and Oliver had been struck anew, as he was every so often, by the unlikely perfection of the way his wife had been put together. With her hair wrapped in a bright turquoise scarf to beat the heat and large sunglasses perched on her nose, she was seated in shadow but a sliver of sunlight had escaped across her face, illuminating its fine bone structure. Eight, nearly nine years on and her uncommon beauty was still transfixing.

'I could even, maybe, start working again,' she had ventured. It had been a while since she had acted in anything, but people still called her agents all the time; people still wanted her. Hardly a week went by when some Parisian couture house or magazine editor was not on the phone, requesting interviews, photo-shoots, fashion shows, while the quantity of dresses and other expensive gifts that arrived weekly at the residence via airmail for 'La Lacloche' continued to make the staff wide-eyed with wonder. 'Although I'm so fat and old, these days, probably nobody would *think* of employing me.'

Oliver had walked slowly over and sat by his wife. 'Darling,' he had said, resting a hand on her flat belly, 'don't be ridiculous.'

53

She'd pulled off the sunglasses, he remembered, and the intensity of her gaze had liquefied his resolve. 'Will you please at least think about it, Oliver?' she had asked. 'For me – for us? Will you?'

'Of course I'll think about it,' he had heard himself say. 'In fact, I'll do better than that. I'll ring my line manager tomorrow and tell him I'm withdrawing from the Middle East bid.'

Eve had giggled joyfully then, the bewitching laugh he had not heard for so long. She had stretched out her right hand and stroked his cheek, her face the image of sincerity and gratitude. Occasionally, and just for a moment, all the years of life and children and stardom and experience would vanish from Eve's face and she would become, in that instant, simply the most beautiful, innocent girl, with such a light in her eyes it made the heart catch.

'Thank you,' she had whispered. 'I love you. You are my life.'

The memory of that light now made Oliver reel. Because he had never made that phone call, had he? Was he responsible for extinguishing it for ever?

'Dad?' he heard his daughter ask. Lara was reaching out to touch his shaking hand. Crashing back into the present, Oliver cleared his throat. His face must have been giving something away, for Lara was open-mouthed, apparently astonished.

'Yes, yes,' he assured her. 'Fine. I was just – remembering.'

'Listen,' Lara said gently, 'I'm really sorry if I was being horrible back then. I don't know what's going on with me at the moment. I'm just finding it increasingly hard to deal with what happened.' She stared out of the window. The London sky was so playfully bright today, especially in contrast to the muted propriety of this room, that it almost hurt to look at it. 'I don't know why. Her death should get easier really, shouldn't it, with time? But, somehow, it's always harder. And this film offer – I don't know. It came so out of the blue and it was after I'd had this really *devastating* feeling the night before about how my life might be about to change in some scary way. I know it sounds stupid but I just can't help feeling they're somehow connected.' She sighed. 'Listen to me, I sound like a nutcase. But that's the thing – this is all making me feel a little crazy. The prospect of doing the film, playing Mum's most . . . *defining* role, a role that I was *inside* her when she created, fills me at one level with dread. But at the same time I feel like I'll regret it for ever if I turn it down . . .' She squeezed his hand again. 'But I am sorry for saying what I said.'

He demurred. 'No need.'

'Anyway, you know just now you said you were *remembering*?' Lara speared a lone green bean with her fork and looked up hopefully. 'Do you think, maybe, you could try to share some of those memories with me?'

Oliver, to his relief, had fully recovered his composure. He leant back in his chair and raised a hand in greeting to Rory Edwards, who had spotted him now from across the room. 'Well, let's see,' he started, turning back to Lara and cradling his glass of wine in his hands. It would not, Oliver knew, be possible to conjure up for his daughter a true picture of the woman they had lost without conjuring up the loss itself; and he was loath to be derailed again by more memories like that Beirut one. So he would play it safe, he decided. Stick to the platitudes and hope they would suffice, for now at least. 'When I met your mother, Lara, she was very passionate, very full of energy. She had a way of walking into a room and commanding the absolute attention of everybody in it. She wasn't unaware of this effect.

55

You might say she was alive to her own power, I suppose, but she was modest, and she used it wisely. People used to say Eve was like sunlight: she'd arrive somewhere, and everyone would light up. And, of course,' he smiled, 'your mother was always the best-dressed girl in Paris.'

'Of course.' Lara smiled back.

'You know, she was quite political when we first met, campaigning for women's rights, marching with the MLF, the feminist liberation movement, on abortion law and so on. She became friends with Simone Veil and Monique Pelletier through my contacts at the embassy, and she used her fame to bring attention to the things she cared about. Freedom, inequality, poverty, women's rights – those were the things she got exercised about at that stage in her life. Later, when we were overseas, she was constantly frustrated that I couldn't make the British government "do something", especially when we were in Africa. She didn't believe in being somewhere, knowing what was "going on", and apparently not doing anything about it. I could never, unfortunately, get her to understand that we were trying to make things better, most of the time. We were simply operating on a different level, a governmental level. Progress was slow, and not always visible. But that wasn't enough for her. In many ways I think she grew to mistrust the power of governments and, quite often, me. It was as if she blamed us for all the horrors she was witnessing out there in the Middle East, in Africa. As if to see suffering and apparently do nothing about it was as bad as inflicting it in the first place. And then, of course, she started to blame herself for doing nothing, which wasn't very helpful at all . . .'

Oliver frowned slightly and took a sip of wine, swiftly changing direction. 'Of course, as you would expect, Eve had a voracious love of the arts – she used to read endlessly: poetry, plays, novels, everything she could get her hands on, really. When we first went out to Beirut she taught herself a bit of Arabic and discovered all these unknown poets and writers and became a great champion of Levantine literature. I seem to remember she even bewitched some poor publisher into setting up an imprint for their work and then translated some of it herself from the French or Arabic into English.' He paused. 'She loved theatre practically more than life itself, and she adored opera, dance – and jazz, of course, because of her father, but really all sorts of music, couldn't get enough of it. She wasn't so into the cinema, strangely, no matter how many films she made. She always felt it lacked the "vibration", she said, the perfume, the oxygen of being on stage.' He smiled brightly. 'What else? Well, she loathed cooking, of course, but you know that.'

Oliver allowed himself a little chuckle here, and Lara laughed with him, remembering the paroxysms of despair her mother would work herself into whenever she had to throw a diplomatic dinner party in London without the backroom support of an embassy or high-commission cook, plus teams of obliging staff. While Lara was still laughing, Oliver said, 'She was very like you, actually, Lara.'

That stopped Lara short. 'What do you mean?' she breathed.

'Well, the physical resemblance at least is uncanny.' He gave a little shrug. 'I can't help it. I look at my daughter and I see my dead wife. It's a very strange thing.'

A chill unease whispered through Lara at her father's words. When she was younger, she had taken a great, secret solace in the fact she looked like her mother – as if the genetic and aesthetic echo of Eve in her raven-haired, emerald-eyed daughter was a way of assuring the world, and the daughter, of Eve's continued presence in it. Increasingly, however, Lara was finding the similitude unsettling; and she sometimes found herself wondering how it could be that she should have so little of her father in her face – especially when her brother, with his sandier hair and his grey-blue eyes, had so much. Until recently, moreover, Lara had never questioned her decision to follow in her mother's professional footsteps. Acting hadn't really felt like a decision: just the thing she 'had' to do. And yet the older Lara got, and the more defined she became in the public eye as 'Eve Lacloche's daughter', thanks to her own blossoming career, the more the question plagued her of *why* she was doing what she was doing. Why had she voluntarily chosen a path that would constantly invite comparison between mother and daughter, constantly remind Lara of her loss, constantly make her feel trapped in some sort of inescapable fate? Her inability to answer those questions was partly why this latest film offer had thrown her into such a tumult, and she was desperate now to ask her father: 'Do you think I'm crazy to do what I do?'

But Oliver was looking at his watch and scraping his cutlery together over the remains of his meal. 'Darling, I'm sorry,' he said, beckoning the waiter. 'I'm going to have to get a move on. I have a meeting with the foreign sec in twenty minutes and I need to make some calls on the way.'

'You're going?' Lara asked incredulously. 'Right now?' She wanted to cry, 'How can you leave me now, Dad, in the middle of this conversation?' but managed, instead, 'Oh . . . I hoped we might be able to take a walk through the park at least.' She trailed off. 'It was looking so pretty.'

'I'm sorry,' he said kindly, choosing not to point out that if she'd turned up on time they'd have had an extra fifteen minutes. 'Look, I'll try to come to your play this week, I really will. And

I'd love us to fit in some tennis one morning, perhaps with Alex and Luc if they're around. But I must go now.'

Lara watched her father as he began matter-of-factly to gather up his briefcase and newspaper, nodding a cheerful 'Hello, Derek. Steven, hi, how are you?' to the men in suits walking past them.

'Dad,' she said, not moving, their freighted history as father and daughter burning in her eyes.

Oliver turned back to the table and, for the first time, he noticed the dark half-moons that shadowed the skin under Lara's eyes; how the earlier glow had faded from her cheeks; how, despite the dazzling impression she gave at first glance, his daughter seemed exhausted.

'Dad,' Lara repeated, her voice trembling, 'I need to know if you think Mum would have wanted me to do this.' She took a deep breath. 'I need to know if *you* want me to do it.'

Oliver sighed and extended a hand to help her up. He swallowed. 'Lara,' he said, 'I promise I'll think about it.'

FIVE

For the rest of the week in London Oliver, to his shame, avoided his daughter. He didn't get to *Night Games* in the end, deciding that he couldn't face it and using his workload as an excuse. He did email to remind her about the Blenheim day out on Saturday, but in the knowledge that it was her final matinée and evening performance on the same day. In a sort of asymmetric compensation for what he knew was pretty feeble behaviour towards his daughter, he lavished attention on Lucas, who was staying at the flat for the summer. They played tennis together in Vincent Square; on Friday afternoon Oliver met him on Tottenham Court Road to buy him some new contraption for his turntables; and on Saturday they proved to be a perfect father-son partnership on the victorious Foreign Office cricket team. It was pathetic, Oliver knew, to try to salvage the idea that he was being a good father to his children by acting like this, but after the difficulties of the lunch he'd endured with Lara, he found his son's uncomplicated company and his absence of questions about the past a blessed relief. It was only on the Sunday, in fact, when Oliver went alone to evensong at Westminster Abbey that, thinking about his son, he felt a jolt of grief. Sitting in the choir stalls, he was unexpectedly overcome by a memory of Lucas as he had once been there, so many years ago, when they lived down the road in Tachbrook Street and the little boy had attended the Abbey Choir School. Remembering a rambunctious, angelic-looking choirboy with scraped football knees under his red gown, who never stopped beaming at his mother and father as they watched him proudly from the stall opposite, Oliver contemplated the great rift of time which separated that Luc – who had once been full of mischief and noise and affection – from this Luc, this towering, silent dreamer – and for a brief, painful moment, he wondered how it was possible to bear it.

But bear it he did. Because from the moment Oliver touched down in Ben Gurion airport the next day and hopped into the armoured car that was waiting to convey him straight to the embassy, via a stop at the residence for a quick shower and change of suit, London and its familial complications felt a world away. The situation here was rapidly deteriorating. In the early hours of that morning, as the ambassador was reclining on his British Airways flatbed somewhere high over the Mediterranean, three more Israeli soldiers had been captured on the border with Lebanon. Hezbollah militants, Oliver now learnt from the emails pouring into his BlackBerry as he sat in the back of the car speeding past the modern high-rises and ancient date trees which shared this blighted landscape, were threatening to execute if Israel did not release certain political prisoners. (Oliver allowed himself a little snort at that likelihood.)

Meanwhile, as his political secretary Paul Conway was now informing him on his mobile phone, various NGOs, including two major British outfits, had announced they were making plans to evacuate their aid workers from the area; worth bearing in mind, given he was due to have meetings with the country head of Oxfam and the regional director of Save the Children in the next few hours.

The situation on the ground was grim, by anybody's standards, but during his years as a diplomatic veteran of wars of this region, Oliver had seen worse. In any case, the truth was that he rather thrived on the politics that such conflict threw up – something his late wife, for whom each sighting of a starving child or a maimed political refugee had been an intensely distressing ordeal, had never been able to grasp. As Oliver reverted to work mode – holding meetings, moving processes forward, hosting a dinner for the US secretary of state, who was in town with the EU envoy from the international 'quartet' tasked with forging a viable peace in the Middle East – he was certainly provided with plenty of distractions to take his mind off the now-distant concerns of his daughter. Without really meaning to, Oliver managed to forget about the messages Lara was leaving in his office and on his mobile; and he replied only cursorily, on his BlackBerry during a journey up to the consulate in East Jerusalem, to the earnest email she had sent him, which outlined the pros and cons, as she apparently saw them, of making this film. '*Not sure I'm the best person to advise you on this one, I'm afraid,*' he tapped speedily in the back of the car, as Paul read him the contents of a briefing note from the post security officer on the Gaza border. '*But I'm sure whatever decision you make will be the right one, Dad x.*'

And then, out of the blue a few days later, an email from

Lara popped into his inbox that knocked the breath right out of his body.

Date: 24 July
To: oliver.latner@fco.gov.uk
From: llama@gmail.com
Re: A thought??

Hey Dad, Just tried to call you again but you're understandably impossible to reach at the moment: hope everything's okay.

The film company are really pressing me for an answer about *This Being Human*, the *La Belle* project, and I am still all over the place. I got your email saying you didn't know how to advise me – that's okay (Alex is being equally unhelpful, telling me to 'follow my heart' in v. un-Alex fashion!) and everyone else seems to think I'd be bonkers not to do it. But I had what I think might be a good idea this morning & wondered what you thought of that at least . . . Shall I contact Dominique St Clair about the original film, see if he can help me in my decision? I'm sure he'd be happy to see me and talk me through my questions and issues, wouldn't he? I've got time on my hands now the play's over – in fact I'm going a bit nuts with work withdrawal and I can't even say yes to any of the other offers on the table until I decide what to do about this one – so I could easily pop down to Paris for a few days. I really owe Mamie Colette a visit anyway, haven't seen her for so long . . .

What d'you think? Ideally I'd go over asap, so long as I can track Dominique down, but don't think that'll be a problem; I'll just call his agent (unless you by any chance have contact details for him, although I suspect they'd be rather out of date now). I know he's still around because I saw a film he directed last year.

Anyway, really hope you're safe and well. I read such a terrible story in the paper this week about what was happening in Gaza – world's worst humanitarian crisis, etc. You'll no doubt tell me there is more than one side of the story and not to be swayed by my emotions when I read stuff like that, but even so, made me v depressed indeed.

Was so nice to see you in London, wish you'd been able to see the play – but come and visit again soon, please, and next time you MUST come to the flat. The sun's streaming through the windows as I write this – really quite pretty, even for London. Alex sends his love too, and lots from me.

Take care of yourself,

Lals xx

That night, a man unaccustomed to dreaming much awoke from a nightmare with sweat pouring from his brow and his heart thumping madly in his chest.

Oliver had been dreaming he was in the little flat off Kennington Lane that he, Eve and the baby Lara had moved into when they first came back from Paris to London in the early eighties. There was some awful pop song playing at deafening volume on the radio, and Eve, dressed and made up like Hélène from the film *La Belle Hélène*, for which she had recently been nominated for an Oscar, was screaming at him, thrusting the baby towards him. But he, for some reason, was refusing to take her. He couldn't hear what his wife was screaming about, couldn't make sense of the words, and still there was this awful din coming from the radio. Tears were pouring out of his wife's eyes, just like a scene from the film; but then suddenly the tears were blood, and now the green eyes were Lara's, and now it *was* Lara, dressed as Eve had been, as Hélène, in that same little kitchen, screaming at him, pointing at him, until he looked down and saw blood dripping and dripping off his hands and all over the floor and still that music. 'Where's my mother?' Lara was screaming. 'What have you done to my mother?' He kept trying to open his mouth, to speak, to explain, but no words would come out. And then Lara was suddenly weeping, repeating over and over again, *Why didn't you believe her? Why didn't you believe her? Why didn't you believe her?*

Gasping as he sat bolt upright in bed, his throat as dry as ash, Oliver wiped his forehead and swung his feet shakily to the floor. He staggered downstairs to the reception room, and poured a large whisky to steady himself. The nightmare had felt so gut-wrenchingly real because it was redolent of a real scene: the night they'd had the fight about whether Oliver should accompany Eve to the Oscars ceremony in Los Angeles.

'You don't value what I do,' Eve had announced darkly, that February evening. They were in the Kennington kitchen, which was cold and still only half finished, filled with builders' clutter. Something was cooking in the oven and the radio was playing some god-awful pop song at an infuriating volume. Oliver remembered that his new wife – looking exhausted, what with the baby and having just started rehearsals for a play at the National – was wearing huge oven gloves which gave her the appearance of having giant Mickey Mouse hands. 'It's true, isn't it?' Eve was goading him. 'You have never valued what I do. It's all just stupid and frivolous to you, isn't it?'

Oliver had just arrived home after a long day in King Charles Street and was also tired. He'd only had a few weeks in the job as head of the FCO Security Policy Department and was finding the new work, which focused on the nuclear threat, an unexpected challenge – especially with a young baby who, unsettled by her new circumstances, was still only sleeping a few hours a night.

'That is utter nonsense,' he'd countered, taking a beer out of the fridge and trying to ignore the defiant manner in which Eve was standing, with her faintly comedic hands planted firmly on her hips. 'Of course I value what you do.'

'*Vraiment?* How so, exactly?' she had questioned. 'You think it's *every* year your wife will be nominated for an Oscar? Your *wife*, Oliver!' She had shaken her head. 'If you had even the slightest interest in what I do you would surely be coming with me!'

'We've been through this,' Oliver protested sharply, trying hard to contain his irritation as he cracked open his beer and spun the bottle top deftly into the rubbish. 'I'm not coming with you, Eve, because I have to chair a joint-intelligence conference on counter-proliferation policy on the Tuesday morning and I'm afraid I cannot take the risk that I won't be back in London in time. It's as simple as that.' He collapsed into a chair and waved to Lara, who was seated in her high chair at the table. The baby made a goo-goo noise at him.

'Yes, it is very simple, isn't it?' Eve agreed, coming to stand in front of Oliver and fixing him with her eyes. 'Oh, yes, very, very simple. You have to do a *conference*, a stupid conference that probably anyone could chair, but that will always come before me, won't it?' She turned away from him, slightly, and the lone tear that shivered on her cheek was briefly illuminated in the last embers of the winter light that cut through the kitchen window. She nodded towards Lara, who was gurgling merrily to the music coming out of the radio. 'It will always come before us, won't it? *You cannot take a risk . . .*' Eve had laughed, bitterly, and gone to the oven, where she whipped out a casserole dish. 'Well, you take a risk with me every day.'

Something in Oliver snapped. 'What was that?' he said, his chair scraping on the unfinished floor tiles as he leapt up.

Eve was silent and still, her back turned to him.

'What did you say?' he repeated.

Eve spun around. 'I said, you take a risk with me every day!'

'Well, quite!' Oliver exclaimed. 'I think we both know I took a pretty bloody great risk, didn't I, marrying you?'

She had banged the oven door shut, her eyes blazing, and wrenched off the gloves, flinging them to the ground. 'How . . . fucking . . . *dare* you?' she breathed. 'After everything.' Her voice seemed to boil in her chest and now she was screaming. '*HOW?*'

'Eve – I'm so sorry.' Oliver had dropped his beer bottle and moved quickly towards his wife, but she was holding her arms out in front of her in self-defence. 'I didn't mean that, I swear – I'm sorry. I'm just tired, and—'

'Don't you come near me,' she hissed. 'Don't you come anywhere fucking near me.'

'I'm sorry,' he pleaded, trying to reach an arm around her again. As she ducked away and held up her left hand in warning, he could see the platinum band of her wedding ring glinting in the light.

'I mean it, Oliver,' she said. 'Don't touch me. You're a coward. We both know why you're not coming with me, and I think you're pathetic. You're fucking pathetic.'

'Eve, stop swearing, please.'

'Don't you *fucking* tell me what to do!'

'Okay – listen, I'm sorry. Eve!'

But it was too late: Eve had grabbed Lara, who was now wailing, and fled from the room. Oliver had punched off the maddening radio and, in the deafening silence that descended, could hear his wife sobbing wildly upstairs. He let his head drop into his hands.

Eve, Oliver whispered to himself now, his head in his hands once again. *Oh, Eve.* Half a world away, in another lifetime, sitting in a dressing-gown with a tumbler of whisky in his shaking hands as the cold blue light of a Middle Eastern dawn began to filter through the thin curtains, the terrible reality that his wife had been right – that there had been another, pathetic reason that he wouldn't accompany her to the Oscars – taunted him again. And what a tragic risk he had taken with her indeed! All because of his jealousy and his insecurity and his suspicions about the world she inhabited and his stupid, unforgivable, misguided pride. And, of course, the most painful irony of it all: that he should have accused *Eve* of a lack of faith when all along it had been he who had exhibited the most reprehensible sort of faithlessness.

Having drained his glass, Oliver walked back upstairs to his bedroom and resolved to call Lara in the morning, to tell her the decision he had made about her film – to tell her the truth.

But an hour or so later, having just dropped back to sleep, he was woken by an emergency call from his duty officer. It was looking like all-out civil war in Gaza, the voice was telling him, and two female British nationals working for an NGO had apparently been kidnapped. Could HMA please make his way to the office immediately?

SIX

'You'll never guess who they've cast opposite you!'

Lara had arrived deliberately early for the meeting, to steady her nerves and look over the script of *This Being Human* yet again, and was therefore surprised to hear Milton's voice behind her already. More than three weeks had passed since that hot and hungover afternoon when she had sat in her agent's office and learnt that a Hollywood production company was planning to remake the classic French film *La Belle Hélène* as a modern-day New York story and wanted her to play the lead role. The role that a twenty-seven-year-old Eve Lacloche had created all those years ago to the acclaim of the world. Trying to focus on what Milton was telling her, as her head hammered from the flatwarming party and the lunchtime Bloody Mary – shooting in New York, so-and-so directing, such-and-such producing, budget of this-or-that – Lara had felt herself be slowly undone by the memory of another lovely summer's afternoon . . .

Clemency Burton-Hill

It was six months after Eve's death; Lara was seventeen. She'd just finished her end-of-year exams, but rather than go straight to the pub with the rest of her year, she'd split from her friends and headed to the railway station. She'd be in trouble with her housemaster, she knew, but she didn't care. She'd had a bit of an epiphany that morning, during her history exam (of all things) and knew she had to go to London. At Victoria station she had walked, zombie-like, towards the music and video outlet. She had to get her hands on a video of *La Belle Hélène*. It was possibly the best-known film her mother had made, but Lara had never watched it – initially because her mum had told her she was too young for its emotionally sophisticated story, a take on the original Helen myth; and later because Eve said it made her too sad even to have a copy in the house.

Two minutes and twelve-pounds-ninety-nine later, though, and Lara had the precious video cassette in her possession. As commuters whirled all around her, Lara's hand had closed defiantly over the keyring in her pocket. She should go back to school and watch the film there before anyone noticed she was missing, she knew, but even as she told herself that, she was touching what she recognised by its shape to be the key to the family house on Tachbrook Street. As she crossed Wilton Road and started to walk in the direction of Pimlico, Lara wondered if she was mad. She could still abandon the whole thing, she told herself, as she dodged the traffic on Warwick Way: go back to Victoria, jump on a train and join her celebrating friends, who would, no doubt, still be buying underage pints galore in the Old Red Lion in the neighbouring village. She could hide the video in her room and forget she'd ever made this impulsive journey at all. But no. The feeling she'd had earlier, midway through her not-very-good essay on Hitler's rise to power, had been luminously clear. There was something she knew she had to do, and this, without question, was where she had to do it.

Lara had not been back to their old house since Eve had died in December; the prospect had always seemed pointlessly unbearable. She'd had the few things from the house that she needed sent down to school by the Foreign Office counselling people who were looking after them – there wasn't much anyway: she'd left most of her stuff in her room at the end of the Christmas term, before the catastrophe. Then she'd spent the Easter holidays in Paris with Colette, Lucas, and Oliver. There had been no reason to go anywhere near Tachbrook Street until now.

In the six months since Eve had been killed her daughter had already learnt the hardest thing about tragedy: that nothing around you changes in its wake. Beauty does not leave the world, nor ugliness. The sun still rises, rain still pours. The clocks still tick, the tube still runs; life as you knew it grinds relentlessly on, though you have changed for ever. Despite knowing all this, however, and trying mentally to prepare herself for it, Lara still gasped in shock when she turned right onto Tachbrook Street to discover that their road, with its elegant stucco houses, its cherry and magnolia trees and its red-brick council housing, looked exactly the same as it always had done. The same as it had looked when they'd first moved there, fresh off a plane from the Middle East, when she was eight. The same as it had looked whenever she and Lucas came back during the holidays from postings overseas and ran upstairs to their old bedrooms, whooping with delight to be 'home'.

Lara let herself gingerly into number forty-two, and was suddenly winded by grief. She had not been prepared for the *smell* – the smell of home, so familiar, and yet a home that would never be home again. She had steadied herself and forced back the tears that threatened to engulf her, knowing that if she let herself cry now she might never stop. In the kitchen she took long, deep breaths and drank a glass of water from the tap. All the time she had been putting off coming here, she had been putting off facing that truth. But now here she was, and the stillness of the empty house wrapped her in the most piercing loneliness she had ever known. Sipping her water, Lara glanced around the kitchen. A framed photograph of the four of them, taken so recently, less than a year ago on holiday in Damascus, sat mockingly on the dresser. She resisted the urge to pick it up and instead wandered, with the plastic HMV bag now sticky in her palm, into the living room. The blinds were drawn, casting the room in a dusky half-light. Lara sat cross-legged on the floor and took out the video box. And there it was, the iconic shot: Eve leaning over a balcony. *La Belle Hélène.*

Lara had placed the cassette in the machine and forced herself to press play, and then she had watched, entranced, as her mother came back into the living room to join her. She had sat for more than two hours without moving, barely breathing, feeling teeteringly alone, yet somehow connected by *blood* to this performance. The history-exam epiphany had been true. She was going to be an actress. *One day*, she had vowed, instinctively reaching out to touch Hélène's face on the screen in a tender and futile attempt to touch her mother again, *I will honour your memory by giving a performance like this. One day. I promise you.*

'Opposite me?' Lara asked now, standing up to greet Milton. 'Er, I might remind you that I haven't actually said yes yet. Isn't that the whole point of this meeting?'

Having had no answer from Lara Latner's 'people' after what was approaching a month, the producers and director of *This*

Being Human were apparently getting so edgy they'd decided to fly over to convince her in person. Pre-production had already started at the Steiner Studios in Brooklyn; they needed their chosen lead to say yes. Milton had called Lara sternly at the end of last week to inform her of their intentions. 'Tuesday,' he'd announced, in his don't-even-try-to-mess-with-me voice, the one he usually reserved for errant producers who hadn't put funds in an escrow account. 'Midday. Covent Garden Hotel. You're meeting the director, Kevin Goldberg, and two of the producers, Alison Kennedy and Eric somebody. I'll be there too. All right?'

'Fine,' Lara had muttered, knowing she could not put off this decision for ever. But her head was still in turmoil. Deep down she loved this script, which had, she was forced to admit, been beautifully adapted by Martin O'Connor, the Academy Award-Winning Screenwriter (as it helpfully reminded everyone on the title page). But whenever her heart skipped with excitement at the prospect of playing Helen, it would also constrict with fear as she contemplated the terrifying significance of what she had been asked to do.

Oliver's recent visit had not illuminated anything, except the gaping hole inside her where her mother should have been. For the first time in her life Lara had become aware of a latent jealousy towards her father. Jealousy that he should have had all those years with Eve, all those happy times. Jealousy that he should have all those extra *memories*. She'd detected something in his face at lunch, as if behind the mask of diplomatic decorum he assumed so completely there might be hidden a roiling history of emotion and pain. It was an amazing thing, Lara realised, to witness somebody who had always tended to do his remembering in private being flooded with memory and grief right in front of her eyes – and she couldn't help but wish he had shared more of those memories with her. Oliver had gone on to deliver some spiel about how Eve had lit up every room she'd walked into and had loved the theatre – thanks, Dad, would never have been able to work *that* one out – and had subsequently disappeared into the hell that was the current situation in Palestine.

Alex had also been completely unhelpful, appreciating Lara's dilemma but insisting she should do whatever her instinct told her to do. 'Follow your heart,' he'd said, ironically channelling a romantic-movie parlance of which he would usually be so scathing. When she'd admitted that one of the reasons she was dithering about the decision was because she was reluctant to leave him and their lovely new flat for so long, he'd taken her shoulders in his hands and told her, 'Lara, our flat's not going anywhere, and neither am I. Not a good enough reason.'

Nearly everybody else she had spoken to, including her friends, and obviously Milton, had been convinced it was a god-given opportunity to play a very special part. 'It'll send you into a different league!' she had heard more than once, a prospect that left her strangely cold. Only her dear grandmother, Colette, had reacted somewhat differently when Lara had rung her in Paris to tell her what was going on. 'Oh, non, *chérie*, non,' Lara had heard Colette whisper, her voice quiet as dust after a moment of desiccating silence. '*Non.*' Lara had put down the phone, promising to call her grandmother back soon, but perplexed in the extreme that Colette's definitive answer had not stopped the nagging question in her head.

Because still she did not know what to do.

'Now, darling,' Milton was saying, as he settled his portly frame onto the maroon leather banquette next to her. 'You're not really still deliberating over this, are you? It's such an opportunity for you. That part's got Oscar written all over it. It will send you stratospheric.' He waved the waiter over. '*And* . . . do you *know* who they've cast opposite you?'

'No, Milton, I don't,' Lara sighed. 'Who is it?'

Milton paused dramatically. 'Jacob Moss. *Jacob Moss*, darling.'

Lara raised an eyebrow in surprise. She had been deeply moved by the American actor Jacob Moss's performance in his latest film, which was about a soldier who murders his brother in Afghanistan. It was the kind of film that could have dissolved into the most abject Hollywood cliché, but had been salvaged by a remarkable central performance.

'Wow,' she said. 'Jacob Moss. He's good, isn't he?'

'Pot of Earl Grey tea, please,' Milton said to the waiter. He looked at Lara. 'Cappuccino?' She nodded thoughtfully. 'And a cappuccino for Miss Latner. Oh, and bring us some of those nice little macaroony things you do, will you?' The guy disappeared and Milton turned back to his client. '*Good?* Darling, he's probably the best screen actor of his generation. You know that. Everybody knows that.'

'Mmm,' Lara murmured. 'Jacob Moss . . . Well, that's interesting casting. That's definitely interesting.'

'*Interesting?*' Milton cried. 'Oh, Lara, for God's sake.'

She bit her lip, opened her mouth, then closed it again. Then she said, very quietly, 'I'm sorry, Mil. I know you really want me to do this, and believe me, a lot of me wants to do it too. But I'm just not sure I'm up to it.'

'Up to it?' Milton echoed.

'Can you *imagine* what people will say if I'm bad in this film? And I might be, you know. There is every chance I might not be able to pull this one off. I've never felt so scared by the prospect of anything in my entire life.'

'Darling,' Milton soothed, 'stop being melodramatic. You're going to blow everybody away, like you always do.'

Melodramatic? Lara thought, but swallowed her irritation.

'And what if I don't?' she pointed out. 'It's not like this is just some normal film. This is a remake of the film that made my mother a star, the film she was nominated for a bloody Oscar for!' Lara was tempted to add, *'This is the film Eve was making when she got pregnant with me! I was there, inside her, while she was doing it! It's part of me! It's in my blood, my molecules!',* but conceded that that really *would* be a touch melodramatic and managed to restrain herself. She took a gulp of hot coffee, burning her tongue, and was grateful for the physical distraction.

Milton put a hand on her arm. 'I'm sorry, darling,' he said kindly. 'Of course I understand this is a sensitive issue for you. I was lost for words when I first read the offer email. That was why I wanted to tell you about it face to face. But, honestly, I think you're being far too hard on yourself.' He looked up and lowered his voice. 'Oh, bugger, they're here. Bloody Yanks, always early. Listen, we'll talk about it later, all right, but not a word of this "I'm going to be rubbish" nonsense in front of them now? Please?'

Kevin Goldberg, a lean thirty-one-year-old from Williamsburg, had started his career making music videos and documentaries, and had won an Academy award earlier in the year for Best Short Film. *This Being Human* would be his second feature; the first, *Retributive Justice*, starring two of Hollywood's megastars, was yet to be released, but the industry seemed to be completely overexcited about it. The last time Lara had been in LA, doing a smallish part in a film called *Out of the Darkness* earlier in the year, everyone had been talking about it in quite rhapsodic terms. Tall, pale and unshaven, wearing skinny black jeans, Converse trainers, a tatty *keffiyeh* around his neck and a black leather jacket despite the heat, Goldberg looked every inch the *über*-East Coast film director, and Lara smiled knowingly to herself. But then again, she could hear Alex pointing out in the mocking tone he reserved for exactly these moments, didn't she look every inch the up-and-coming starlet right now? She was in equally skinny jeans, Marc Jacobs flats and a vintage Balenciaga top she'd worn on a *Vogue* shoot recently and loved so much the stylist had let her keep it at the end of the afternoon. Much as Lara occasionally fantasised about giving up acting and running off to have a normal life, here she was. She wasn't an aid worker sweating it out in Darfur; she wasn't even a journalist, or a banker, or a lawyer, like so many of her friends. She was just an actress. Like her mother had been – just an actress.

But she wasn't her mother.

Having ordered drinks and supplied the requisite comments about London's weather, the Americans wasted no time. 'There's obviously nobody else who can play this part,' Kevin Goldberg was soon drawling earnestly over his latte. 'Seriously, ever since I saw you in *High Tide* I've wanted to work with you.'

'Um, thanks,' Lara said.

'Look, the truth is I've been obsessed with your mother's work since I was a kid. I always wanted to make *Hélène* in English. I even tracked down some of the guys who worked on the original film. Sabine de Sévigné, the costumier, now lives in New York and she's agreed to be a consultant on our film.' He smiled a slightly goofy smile. 'It's pretty exciting. But the thing you have to know, Lara, is that I *totally* developed this project with you in mind. I know you will be amazing in this film.'

There was a pause, as Lara wondered how to react to this, when a loud 'Oh, *ab*solutely' broke the moment. Producer Alison Kennedy could have come straight out of Central Casting for 'neurotically slim, super-driven, female Hollywood executive'. She was probably fortyish, although it was hard to tell: impeccably groomed, she had a neatly Botoxed forehead that precluded any extreme facial expression and gave her a seemingly permanent look of insincerity. The first thing she had done, after shaking Lara's hand vigorously, was to remove two mobiles and a BlackBerry from her briefcase and place them on the table in front of her. One or another had since rung or beeped every few minutes. 'You are *ab*solutely our first choice for this role.'

'And we want to know what we can do to make you say Yes!' cut in Eric Liebermann, the other one. He was also super-groomed, with unfeasibly neat fingernails, a deep suntan and an intense look in his eyes. Oh, Hollywood, Lara mused. Could she really work with these crazy people? More importantly, could they really be trusted with that precious story?

'That's – very kind,' she replied. 'Really, so very kind. It means a lot to me, and the first thing I want to say is how grateful I am that you've even considered me. Obviously. It's amazing. Thank you.' She gave them a nervous smile. 'But I hope you can also understand that it's all a bit daunting for me, the prospect of actually doing this . . . And I just can't help wondering—'

'What Lara's wondering about,' Milton interrupted, 'is, you know, the basics. She's got a lot of other projects trying to attach her, so we'd have to try to make it work around them.'

Lara glared at him. 'Actually,' she said, 'I'm not worried about that at all. I couldn't care less about that. I'm just—'

'Are you saying that there *are* issues you're worried about?'

Kevin asked. 'You know we've attached Jacob Moss to play Peter? I *really* think you guys will work amazingly together. And the rest of the cast are shaping up really well.' He started to count on his fingers. 'We've got, let's see, Robert Dickinson to play your father, Chris Emmett playing Michael, Amelia Epstein as—'

'Kevin,' she stopped him, 'please. It's not that. I'm sure you'll get the most wonderful cast. It's a wonderful film. I mean, who wouldn't want to do it – right?' She gave a wry grin, then fell serious. 'Look. I'm sure you understand that it's a big deal for me that this film is going to be remade. It has huge emotional significance for us as a family, and me . . . as, I suppose, my mother's daughter, and I just want to make sure that . . .'

Lara trailed off. How could she *articulate* this? How could she explain to these manicured strangers that even though nobody had ever told her as much, she knew, intuitively, that some secret about her mother and father swirled around the original movie? How could she tell them how *sacred* the fact that she'd been conceived during the filming of *La Belle Hélène* was to her? Or how violently jealous she felt at the prospect of some other girl playing the part, despite being utterly terrified of doing it herself? How could she admit that, for some reason, every time she contemplated their offer, she was reminded of the sensation of pure dread that had crept through her the night before she'd learnt about it – the night of her and Alex's flatwarming party? How could she stop herself screaming that, oh, she wished they'd never had the idea to do the remake in the first place, and that they must be crazy, not to mention arrogant beyond belief, to meddle with a film that was already as perfect as any film could be?

As the group around the table watched her tensely, Lara cleared her throat and opened her mouth again to try and say something, anything. But suddenly Kevin was talking, and with a determination she had not previously detected in his languorous Brooklynite intonation.

'Okay, Lara,' he was saying. 'I'm gonna just come out and be straight with you here. That okay with you?'

She nodded weakly.

'You have this quality on camera which translates into a vulnerability that I absolutely *need* for this character. Believe me, I have searched, but I have not found this ability in any other actress of your generation. I haven't seen it in anyone on screen, I guess, since maybe Eve. I saw it in your performance in *High Tide* and in everything I've watched of yours since. Hell, I even watched the entire DVD box set of your little British TV show, *The Chronicles of Mary*. Larry Finkelstein let me view a rough cut of *Out of the Darkness* recently and I was totally blown away. More so than ever. So, please believe me when I say that I know you have to do this. I don't mean to blow myself right now, but I've had literally every young actress in Los Angeles begging to work with me. And this is, like, every girl's *dream*, right, to play this part? Seriously, I could take my pick: *who*ever. But I do not wanna make this movie unless I make it with you.'

'What Kevin's trying to say, Lara, is that all of us at the studio are *very* eager to attach you as Helen.' Alison Kennedy was nodding sincerely but her artificially structured face looked so insincere that Lara was reminded of the wagging toy dogs that people put in the backs of cars. She bit her lip to repress a dangerous chuckle.

'*To*tally,' Eric added. 'Like, as soon as possible.'

'Well, like, today,' Alison declared. 'You know, Lara, we are due to start principal photography in less than six weeks, so if you're not going to accept our offer, which we of course sincerely hope you *will*, we will need to start actioning our other options.'

Lara gulped. Six weeks? Other options? What did 'actioning' even mean?

'As Kevin mentioned,' Alison continued pleasantly, 'there are many other actresses out there who would kill for the chance to play such a part.' She smiled. 'And, Lara, I'm sorry to have to say it, but I'm sure you're very aware that we are *kind of* going out on a limb for you here. Lots of producers wouldn't be prepared to take such a risk. Think about it. You've never played a lead in Hollywood and the other actresses we're thinking of for the part are already *very* well established.'

Milton let out a fruity scoff. Lara knew, with a kind of bleak resignation, that they were right. There must be a million actresses out there who could play her part – interesting that she had already started to think of it as 'her' part – and her stomach lurched at the prospect of any single one of them doing it instead of her. Was that her answer, then?

'Can you let us know what you're thinking?' Kevin asked.

Lara looked at them all, at the expectant American faces, at Milton, who had put his head in his hands in apparent despair. She took a deep breath, and smiled. 'I'm thinking, it's lovely to meet you all, and although this opportunity is a huge honour, it's also a huge responsibility. And I'm sorry, but I just need a bit more time.' She scrambled to her feet. 'Will you excuse me for a few minutes? I'll be straight back. I just – I really need to call my father.'

Out on Monmouth Street, in the baking sunlight, amid the tourists with their cameras and shopping bags, the lunchtime Londoners scurrying to pick up a sandwich, the builders and the taxis and the tramps, Lara felt as if her legs might buckle beneath her. She hurried towards Seven Dials and pulled a cigarette from her bag. *One more chance*, she thought, lighting the cigarette. *I'm going to give you one more chance to tell me what I want to hear.* Sitting on the sundial, she took a deep drag, and dialled the embassy switchboard in Tel Aviv.

'I'm sorry, Lara,' she heard Oliver's secretary Julia apologising, once she'd been put through to his outer office. 'I know you've been trying to reach him recently, but he's in the West Bank. I'll try to patch you through to his mobile now but they're having problems. Lots of the power lines have been cut.'

'Oh – of course they have,' Lara said, guilt at the relative luxury of her own predicament temporarily flooding her with shame. 'I'm sorry . . .'

'If you hold on, I'll try and get him to call through to you now.'

'Thanks so much.'

Clutching her phone, Lara waited in the middle of the roundabout, watching the cars and the people circling like vultures, her head spinning, her mind reeling. It rang again a minute later and she snatched it up to her ear. 'Dad?'

'Sorry, it's me again. The switchboard can't get through to any of them over there at the moment. I'll get him to ring you as soon as he can. Can I give him a message?'

'Tell him . . .' Lara exhaled. 'Actually, no. No message.'

That night, when Lara and Alex got home from having dinner with David, one of Alex's colleagues from chambers, and his fiancée Ashley, Lara went into the kitchen to make tea while Alex kicked off his shoes and sorted through the post in the hall.

'Baby, your dad left a message on the home phone,' she heard him call a few minutes later, as she dropped the teabags into the rubbish bin.

She'd been humming to herself, feeling the lightest she'd felt for weeks, having finally made the decision. Now she froze. 'Why would he call on the home phone?' she cried. 'Nobody calls on the home phone.'

Alex appeared in the kitchen. 'Dunno. Maybe he couldn't get through on your mobile. Everything's fine though, princess, don't sweat. Didn't hear the whole thing but he said he'd call you tomorrow.' She frowned, and he stroked her arm. 'Hey, it's fine, nothing's happened or anything. Terrible line, though. Go and have a listen.'

She pushed past him into the hall, her head pounding. 'Lara, it's your dad.' She could just make out Oliver's words – the line was truly appalling. 'I'm sorry you haven't been able to get through to me. I've actually been meaning to give you a ring for a few days . . . Things are a bit sticky here, as I'm sure you can imagine.' Crackle. 'I tried to call you on your mobile but I can't get through on that at all, so I thought this was best. Listen. I'll phone again tomorrow, but I've been thinking about it.' Crackle, crackle. 'I don't think you should do the film.'

Lara stared at the phone in stunned disbelief. 'Too late,' she breathed. 'Too fucking late.'

SEVEN

By August, the rains of June felt like a distant dream: for the past few weeks London had been basking in almost permanent sunshine. While her fellow city-dwellers substituted moaning about the cold for groaning about the lack of air-conditioning on the tube, Lara, who had grown up with Middle Eastern and African suns soaking into her bones, lapped up the hot weather like a cat, lazing on the roof terrace with a cold glass of juice and her much-highlighted script in her hands after Alex had gone to work each morning, or wandering down to Hyde Park to swim in the Serpentine, reciting Helen's lines over and over again in her head.

Not long before she was due to leave for New York to start filming *This Being Human*, she and Alex drove up north for the weekend, where his grandmother Maggie was celebrating her eightieth birthday at his parents' house. They had hired a car so that he could bring back all the stuff he'd left in storage while they did up the flat. Lara watched the skies broaden as they slowly inched out of the capital – late, after a morning mucking around in bed – and felt her soul soar at the sight of field after field of rolling green. How strange it was, she thought, that by the time she came back from New York it would be winter in England; and she was struck again by how unnatural the existence of a film actor was. Out of nowhere a job offer; and then a total transplanting of circumstances for a brief, intense period; after which, a thankless parachute back into 'real' life once again and the expected resumption of immediate normality, as if the original seam of time had never been interrupted in the first place.

Lara had had an unwitting sort of training, as a child, for becoming a grown-up nomad: uprooted from one diplomatic posting to another, she and Lucas had shuttled obligingly between continents, making friends of every colour and creed, filling their ears with a symphony of languages. This had given her some mechanisms to cope with the zooming between different time zones and modes of existence she'd had to get used to as an actress; but nevertheless, as she was rudely reminded every time she came back from shooting on location, a residue of what Eve used to describe as being '*dépaysée*', literally decountrified, always threatened to knock her off-balance.

It helped to have someone like Alex to come back to, of course. Lara inclined her head to study her boyfriend surreptitiously as he hummed along to the radio, his right arm leaning out of the open window and his brown hair, sun-lightened from all the cricket and tennis he'd been playing outdoors this summer, ruffling gently in the breeze. She grinned and leant over the gearstick to murmur into his ear, 'You look very sexy when you drive, Mr Craig. I'll miss you when I go.'

Alex grinned back and kept his eyes steadily on the road,

reaching his left hand across to play with the lace edging of Lara's skirt. He squeezed her thigh. 'I'll miss you too, monkey,' he said, indicating left and swinging into the exit lane for the Manchester turn-off. 'But it's fine. You'll be home soon.'

The semi-detached house that Michael and Stella Craig lived in was already packed with well-wishers by the time Alex and Lara rang the doorbell.

'Sorry we're late, Mum,' Alex cried, throwing his arms around his mother when she opened the door, an apron around her waist and an open bottle of white wine in her hand. 'Lara took for ever to leave the house.'

'Hah! It's all lies!' exclaimed Lara, sheepishly kissing Stella hello.

'Of course it is!' Stella joked warmly. 'Remember, I had that many years of trying to drag this one out of bed in the mornings.' She took a step back and beamed. 'Oh, but it's so good to *see* you! You look so well. Now, come through to the garden and say hello to everyone.' She nodded towards the wine bottle. 'I was just mid-pour. What can I get you both?'

'We'll sort it out, Mum, don't worry.'

'You must go and find Nick. I know he and Kate are dying to see you.'

Lara and Alex followed Stella through the hall and the kitchen, where all sorts of delicious smells were congregating, and out into the little garden, which was crammed with various members of the Craig family and friends. Alex headed straight towards his brother Nick and gave him a massive hug.

'Good to see you, bro,' Nick said to Alex, turning to greet Lara with a kiss on her cheek. 'And how are you, gorgeous? Haven't seen you in ages, not since your play.'

'I know!' Lara exclaimed. 'Why weren't you at our flatwarming?'

'We were still on holiday,' Nick told her, motioning for his girlfriend, Kate, to join them. 'Sorry to miss it. I hear it was a blast.'

'Party of the year, mate,' quipped Alex.

'You should come over and have dinner with us, though,' Lara said, 'before I go away. Are you around this week? The flat's looking a *bit* better than the last time you saw it.'

'It was covered with paint and tarpaulin then, from what I remember!' Kate chuckled in her Glaswegian lilt. 'Nice to see you two.'

'And you,' said Lara. 'You look lovely.' Kate seemed to be positively glowing. 'How was your holiday? You were in Italy, right?'

'Incredible.' Kate smiled, glancing at Nick. 'Really incredible. We went to meet some of his friends at Lake Como – one of them has a house there, can you believe it? Then we travelled around for another week. It was so beautiful.'

'You and your posh mates.' Alex punched his brother's arm. 'Houses in Lake Como. Fucking hell. Who wants a drink. La?'

'Yeah. I'll come and help you.'

Heading off in the direction of the drinks table, Lara and Alex were soon apprehended by other guests, all with their hellos and how-are-yous and what-are-you-up-tos. Lara dealt happily with the barrage of questions from distant aunts and next-door neighbours alike, all of whom seemed interested in just one thing: what was going to happen next in *The Chronicles of Mary*? She accepted a glass of white wine gratefully from Stella and thought how glorious it was just to be here in this sunny, familial haven, as she spotted Michael Craig, out of the corner of her eye, wrapping his younger son in a bear-hug. After a while, having tried not to give away all the season's storylines, she sidled over to join them, and was duly given her own hug by Michael, before he went straight back into the conversation he and Alex were having about politics.

Michael was a professor of Marxist history at Manchester University, and whenever he went home Alex always spent hours and hours just talking to his dad, if not about the latest woes of the government or the specious policies being proffered by the opposition, then about football, cricket, poetry, climbing, his latest criminal case – anything. Lara would sometimes watch them chatting so easily with a dull thud of envy in her heart. She did love being here in the Craig household, with its mess and its family photos everywhere, its almost palpable sense of love, support and – Lara had to admit – 'ordinariness'. She soaked it up, poring over albums and listening in wry amusement at the dinner table as ancient arguments popped raucously between family members. The Craigs had always been incredibly warm and welcoming to her: she knew they looked upon her as a member of the family and certainly treated her as 'one of them' – she was as likely to be berated for not doing the washing-up as either Alex or Nick. But no matter how comfortable, how 'at home' Lara felt there in some ways, in others she could never quite shake the feeling that she would always be an outsider in this kind of life. Her own family years had never been like this, even before they were ruptured by Eve's death, and that simple truth could generate a storm of conflicting emotions inside her: a longing to create something similar to what she saw here with Alex for her own future, and fierce, almost primal resistance to the idea. Sometimes she looked at Stella and Michael and marvelled in wonder at the blissful nest of security and love they'd created for their two sons; at others she felt a flash of disdain for their apparent parochialism, and was newly grateful for her own international, cosmopolitan upbringing – complicated though it had been.

None of the Craigs would ever have guessed at Lara's internal emotional struggle when she came to stay, however. In the six years she'd been visiting as Alex's girlfriend, she had reverted to what was her default position for any emotionally perplexing situation: she played a role. The role of a girl for whom all this ordinariness was *normal* – getting stuck in with the washing-up, lazing on the sofa with the Sunday papers, helping Stella with the grocery shopping.

It was only when Lara lay awake, entwined in a sleeping Alex's arms on the single bed in his boyhood room, with its team photos and preserved adolescent clutter everywhere, that she would let her role slip, her costume fall to the floor. And she would remember her own family homes: the silences, the unspoken tensions, the immaculate but sterile interiors of the embassy or high commission residences, the requisite portraits of Queen Elizabeth II, which used to enrage her mother so much, the suppers placed reverently on grand dinner tables by white-uniformed staff ... While Alex slept on soundly beside her, Lara would feel tears run hotly down her cheeks as she scrambled back over the dunes of time in her mind to try to remember the happy periods in her own family's history. Because there had been happiness, she was certain. It had never been 'normal', exactly, never been like *this*, but it hadn't always been sad either. The more time that slipped past, however, the harder the happy memories were to retrieve ...

Lara shook herself out of her reverie. Stella was standing on the garden step, clinking her glass with a fork to try to get people to shut up. 'As you all know,' she smiled, 'it's my wonderful mum Mag's eightieth birthday today and we're delighted to see so many of you here. Thank you all so much for coming.' Maggie, who was beady-eyed and still bright as a button, beamed as everyone clapped and cheered. 'I've put out a buffet in the sitting room, but I think we should bring our plates out into the garden as it's such a nice day.'

There were murmurs of agreement as people started to drift inside to get their lunch. Stella came over and rested her head against her husband's shoulder. 'Darlings,' she said to Alex and Lara, 'would you mind going into the other room and fetching all the extra chairs we put in there?' She lowered her voice. 'I think some of Mum's friends might appreciate being able to sit down, don't you?'

'Sure.' Alex took Lara's hand. 'See you in a bit, Dad.'

Alex led Lara into the house, but where he should have turned left into the sitting room, he ducked right instead, pulling her up the stairs.

'Oi, what are you doing?' Lara hissed. 'We need to get the chairs for your mum!'

'Ssh, one minute, that's all.'

Up on the landing outside his old bedroom, Alex cupped Lara's face in his hands. 'I just wanted to tell you that you're still the most beautiful girl I've ever seen in my life.' He tucked a stray lock of hair behind her ear. 'I love you a lot, La, and I'm going to miss you so much when you're gone.'

He grinned, but Lara frowned as she felt a brimming pressure behind her eyelids. It seemed the waves of foreboding that had overwhelmed her on the night of the flatwarming party, then plagued her until she'd made the decision to accept *This Being Human*, were returning to dash her out of her complacency –

and Lara was dumbstruck. *Why*, when Alex was standing in front of her, solid flesh and breath and bone in her arms, why was she again paralysed with apprehension that one day he might not be? Why was she filled with a presentiment that going away to do this film would wreak some sort of havoc in her life? Why could she not just smile back at him and say, 'I love you too'?

Alex was carrying on, his brown eyes twinkling at her. 'I know you know all this anyway,' he was joking, 'but you're about to disappear again for three months, so I may as well say it all over again.' He put a finger to her lips before she could protest. 'Lara, you're my favourite person in the world, and don't ever think I don't realise how lucky I am to be with you.'

Lara caught her breath and tried to hold back the tears that now hovered precariously in the corners of her eyes.

'Hey, pretty girl,' he murmured, 'don't cry. It's a happy thing.' He kissed her forehead. 'That's all I wanted to say to you. Happy days, okay? Now we can go and get Mum's chairs.'

Later that evening, after Maggie's guests had gone, the family collapsed in the sitting room with another bottle of wine, balancing plates of leftover lunch on their knees as they chatted. Alex kept his arm loosely around Lara's shoulders and she, thankful to have pulled herself together during the blessedly distracting afternoon of party games and general birthday celebrations, leant back on the sofa, helping herself to the occasional cocktail sausage or handful of crisps. Then, out of the jumble of conversation, Nick was leaping up to stand in the centre of the room.

'Right, everyone, I have something to say,' he announced. 'I didn't do it earlier cos I didn't want to take any attention away from Gran's big day.' He raised his wine glass in the direction of his grandmother and cracked a great smile. 'Happy birthday again, Gran. But . . . we've got news.' He paused, enjoying the suspense. 'While we were in Italy, I asked Kate to marry me. And, amazingly enough, she said yes!'

There were gasps from the women, then, and splutters of congratulations from the men. Stella and Maggie both shot up to hug Kate, who was shedding a little tear as she clutched Nick's hand. Alex slapped his brother on the back and went to give Kate a hug. 'Welcome to the family, you crazy girl.' He laughed. 'Do you know what you're letting yourself in for?'

'I think this calls for more champagne,' Michael declared at the doorway, brandishing a bottle in each hand.

'*Dad*, you sly dog,' joked Nick, 'where were you hiding that?'

'Couple of bottles left over from lunch.'

'I'll go and get glasses,' Alex said.

'There'll be clean ones in the machine,' Stella called, also weeping delightedly.

Lara put a hand on Alex's arm. 'I'll go,' she said, jumping up. 'You stay here.'

In the kitchen, Lara leant against the fridge and tried to stop her heart pounding. It was definitely back. The feeling. It was back. The news of Nick and Kate's engagement in the midst of all the usual Craig familial bliss seemed only to have intensified it. Remembering that she'd been drinking like a trooper all afternoon, Lara snatched at the possibility that her feeling of wretchedness might simply be *l'alcool tristesse*, as Eve had called it; the plunging sadness that would sometimes come over her of an evening if she'd had a few too many. She walked over to the dishwasher.

But that wasn't it, she knew very deep down. That wasn't it

at all. There was something else. It was the way Alex had taken her hand after Nick had said the words 'marry me'; the calm, reasonable expectation she had detected in his eyes. But why should that unsettle her? She and Alex had always joked about being together for ever – of course there would be expectation in his eyes . . . Taking a deep breath, Lara willed herself to get back into character. Then she pulled six steaming champagne flutes from the dishwasher, reassumed her happiest-looking smile, and marched determinedly back into the Craigs' living room.

EIGHT

'So I walk into the waiting room at Spotlight and the world and his bloody wife are sitting there reading your script and I'm in for this *dismal* play, which is going on a number-one tour and, frankly, I felt like screaming.'

It was Thursday night. Cassie was perched on a stool in one of the girls' favourite Soho dives; sipping something lurid and pink in a martini glass as they waited for Liz to arrive.

'I'm *serious*,' she insisted, as Lara, studying Cassie's face, tried to gauge exactly how serious her friend was being. 'I walked in there and saw all these girls, all the usual suspects, all the nemeses, you know, Annabel Lewis, Jessica Cole, Gemma Baxter, all of them sitting there looking like fucking skeletons and I thought, *Oh, wow*, how fantastic, actually – it's not just me who has to go up for this life-sapping shite, these days. Everyone else is up for this stinking play too. But, oh, no . . .' Cassie paused theatrically, mid-flow, for a sip, before continuing. '*Oh*, no. Those girls are all up to play your best friend in *This Being Human*, and I, your *actual* best friend, can't even get seen for the part.' With a flourish – for Lara reckoned there might be an element to this performance that was, indeed, a performance – Cassie downed the contents of her glass and gestured flamboyantly to the barman for another.

Lara hesitated. 'I did mention it again to Kevin the other day', she ventured, shredding a corner of the napkin upon which her own drink sat, 'and he promised he'd do his best to get you in for Julianne. The trouble is the bloody studio people. Although everyone's like, this is some great little indie movie, you start to realise there is actually no such thing as an indie movie in Hollywood these days. Even the independents are owned by huge fuck-off studios, and if you're not a "name", forget it.' She picked up her glass. 'You know what the producer actually said to me in our meeting? That they were really *going out on a limb* offering it to me, basically because of the Eve connection, when there were queues of superstar actresses who would chop off their right arm for the part.'

'So, no pressure, then?' Cassie laughed, then gave a little sigh. 'Honestly, though, sometimes I just despair.' She put a hand on Lara's knee. 'Listen, babe, I'm not trying to get you to pull favours on my behalf, I promise I'm not. I know I'm not a big enough "name" for them. I just feel particularly frustrated about this one because I can't think of anything better in the world than going out there with you to do this film, and also because when I see all those anti-life, size-zero bores auditioning for it, it does actually make me want to murder that fucking casting director.' She sipped her Cosmopolitan and grinned. '*Damn*. I wish we could still smoke in these places.'

'I know,' Lara agreed. 'I'm desperate for one. Look, I'll call

Kevin again tomorrow and see what's going on, okay? It'd be outrageous if you can't even get in for it when they're seeing all those other girls. Gemma Baxter? Jessica Cole?' She raised her glass in Cassie's direction. 'They ain't got *nothing* on you, shweedie.'

Clink.

'Except for the fact they're all anorexic, obviously.'

Lara rolled her eyes.

'No, seriously,' Cassie continued. 'What I want to know is, since when did we all have to be *athletes*? I went into acting because I was rubbish at sport, not because I wanted to starve myself and look like a fourteen-year-old Russian gymnast with no boobs and hip bones like icebergs!'

Lara couldn't help but chuckle, although inside she felt terrible. Since she'd said yes to the film she had been bugging Kevin to consider Cassie for the part of Julianne, Helen's friend and ally, but had met with an infuriating response that she was not about to divulge.

'Look, we totally *love* her,' Kevin had said on the phone the other day. 'We know she's your best friend and all, and we would love to cast her. I thought she was *fabulous* that night we all went to the Groucho when I was in town. But we just can't put her in that role, honey. The truth is, she's not acceptable to the sales company because they haven't seen any of her work, and also . . . they think . . . well, she's a little . . . *big*.'

Lara, confused, had started to say, 'Um, Kevin, I really don't think it matters what *size* Julianne is, or anyone else, for that matter . . .' but had tailed off when Kevin had sighed, 'Honey, it's LA.' End of conversation, apparently. This was a world where actresses got sacked all the time for not being thin enough, and Lara knew it, but still, the conversation made all her old doubts about whether she should even be making this film with these people flood back. *Too big?* Did she really want to make a film with studio executives who thought her gorgeous and completely normal-sized best friend was *too big?* What did *too big* even mean? Lara, tall and slender as a bluebell thanks to her six-two father and her gamine little mother, would have killed for Cassie's curves. Biting into the olive in her martini, Lara was grateful to spot Liz, looking a tad dishevelled, bounding down the stairs.

'Greetings, sisters.' She sighed. 'Sorry I'm so late. Bloody client decided it'd be a *great* time to hold an international conference call at seven p.m. Have we still got time for a drink or are we going to be late?' They were going to Sketch as a girls'-night treat before Lara left town next week.

'We're fine,' Lara said, checking her watch. 'We've got about fifteen minutes.'

'Great. In that case, what are we having? Bottle of wine? Or more cocktails?' Liz shook out her hair and hung her suit jacket on the hook under the bar. 'God, what's the matter with you two? You both look so gloomy! I'm the one who's been stuck in an office all day.'

'We're not gloomy,' Cassie protested. 'I just had a horrible audition this afternoon, which made me feel like strangling someone, and poor old La's feeling guilty because she can't help me get a part in her film. Fuck it, let's have a bottle.'

Lara shrugged. 'I'm also in denial about the fact that I'm about to up sticks and disappear again for three months. I leave in less than a *week* and I've got so much to sort out before I go.'

'You'll be in New York, though, you lucky cow!' Liz cried, handing her card to the barman.

'With Jacob Moss!' Cassie reasoned helpfully.

'Exactly. With Jacob Moss.' Liz whistled. 'That guy is so dreamy.'

'You reckon?' Lara asked, amazed. 'I always think he looks a bit . . . I don't know . . . grubby. I mean, he's a great actor and everything, but I've never got the sex-appeal thing. Not my type at all.'

'Er, hello? You are clinically insane, in that case,' Cassie diagnosed. 'Did you not see him in *Long Road Home*?'

'Don't *talk* about it, man!' Liz cackled. 'That scene where he's stripped naked by the guards? Mmm-mmm.' She turned to Lara. 'Anyway, I'm trying to convince work that they urgently need to send me over to our Manhattan office. I haven't got any more goddamn holiday this year but I'd love to come and visit. So long as you get me an introduction to Mr Moss, that is! Here you go, girls.'

'Of course you have to come and visit!' Lara exclaimed. 'They're putting me up in this ridiculous apartment. That was one of the advantages of keeping them waiting for so long: they kept chucking more and more things into the deal. Milton emailed me pictures the other day and it looks amazing. It's open house. Plus Dan Peters is out there, you know, and Lucy Drew, Jack Taylor, so many people.'

Cassie snorted. 'Of course, I'd forgotten about that lot, no doubt taking over the world via their management consultancies and investment banks. Woo-hoo.'

'Shut up, Cass.' Liz grinned. 'You're just jealous because they can actually pay their rent.'

'*Touché.*' Cassie nodded, with a gracious wink at her munificent flatmate. 'Next month I'll be on time, I promise.'

'Will Al come out for a bit?'

'I hope so,' Lara said. 'Things are pretty busy at work at the moment, but I hope he'll be able to take off a week or two.' She smiled. 'Poor Al, I think he was hoping for a nice hiking trip to the Highlands or the Lakes or something for his holiday and instead I'm dragging him to Manhattan.'

'I'm sure he'll live,' Cassie said drily.

'So, are you excited?' Liz asked.

Lara hesitated. 'Yeah . . . I am. But you know what? I'm also shitting myself. I was thinking about it the other day: this is the first time in my life I've ever just been offered a job. Without having to audition, I mean. And I keep thinking, What if I'm *rubbish*? I just feel like the stakes are so high on this one, because of Mum and everything . . .'

'You're not going to be rubbish, you idiot,' Liz admonished. 'You'll be fantastic.'

'Yeah, well. I'm not so sure. I feel as if I'm about to be found out. And the other thing is, I wish I wasn't going away for so long. I *love* London in the autumn, and it'll practically be Christmas by the time I'm back.'

Liz groaned. 'Oh, my God, don't say it. Seems about five minutes since last Christmas and I'm sure I've spent the whole time since stuck behind my bloody computer screen.' She took a generous swig of her wine. 'You know, I'm actually so jealous of you two, living the life you really want to live. I'm terrified that one day I'm gonna wake up and the years will have just passed me by. I'll be middle-aged and single and still in PR, and I'll be bitter as all hell.' She grimaced. 'Bit like my boss, come to think of it.'

Lara and Cassie looked at each other and smirked. '*Are* we living the lives we really want?' Cassie giggled. 'News to me!'

'You *know* what I mean.'

'Not really, babe. At least you're actually getting on with

things. While you lot all go off and do grown-up stuff, like get mortgages and take out life-insurance policies, I am technically regressing.'

Lara laughed. 'What are you talking about, C?'

'Think about it: I'm unemployed, still kissing random boys and, as Liz has already helpfully pointed out tonight, my poor dad has to pay my rent. I'm basically a teenager.'

'Ooo, kissing random boys.' Liz elbowed her in the ribs. 'How's it going with that guy Ed?'

Cassie smiled mysteriously. 'Let's just say it's going.'

'Oh, come on, Cass. You have to tell us! You know we like to relive our lascivious youth through you.'

'You'll have to get me drunk first.'

'Like that's going to be a problem,' Liz quipped.

Cassie squealed with indignation, but then raised her glass. 'Actually, I'm going to drink to regression. You know, I was talking to my sister the other day, and she was like, very sternly, "Cassandra, you are the Wrong Side of Twenty-five to be behaving like this any more." Said with her nose wrinkled in disdain, of course. "When are you going to think about getting a proper boyfriend and *settling down*?" And I was horrified! Wrong side of twenty-five, *my arse*! Last thing I want to be doing is settling down and marrying a boring *lawyer* like she is. Oops . . .' Cassie grinned at Lara. 'You know I don't think *all* lawyers are boring, babe. It's just Louisa does my *head* in, especially now she's engaged, and what's more annoying is she's winding up Mum and Dad about me all the time. So: regression!'

'To regression!' The others clinked, laughing.

'Actually, talking about getting engaged,' Lara remembered, 'did I tell you about Nick?'

'Alex's brother Nick?' said Liz. 'What? Is he?'

'Yeah, to Kate. We were up there last weekend and he announced it in front of us all. It was quite sweet.'

'Damn!' Cassie giggled. 'I always had a bit of a crush on Nick Craig. Can't believe *he*'s been snapped up too, what with Alex long gone and everything . . .'

'I suppose you two will be next, then?' Liz joked pointedly at Lara.

Downing the rest of her glass of wine, Lara snorted and stood up a little too quickly. 'Yeah, right,' she said, grabbing her bag and throwing a tip onto the bar. 'Come on, you minxes. Now we really are going to be late.'

Cassie and Liz turned to each other and smiled knowingly as they followed their friend up the stairs.

Lara's remaining few days in London were a frantic maelstrom of admin, line-learning, rushing around to say goodbye to friends, and shopping for last-minute 'essentials' – much to Alex's amusement. 'They do apparently have shops in New York, you know,' he reminded her, as she outlined her plans to him one morning. 'Meet me for lunch instead?' But for all her rushing around, there was something Lara knew she must just *do*. Ever since Oliver's crackly phone message that he didn't want her to accept the film, she had given her father a taste of his own medicine and largely ignored his emails and phone messages: as long as he was physically safe in that war zone, she told herself, she didn't want to hear anything else. He might think she had defied his wishes by saying yes to the film, but Lara was not prepared to be guilt-tripped about the anguished decision she had made: as far as she was concerned, she'd given him every opportunity to tell her what he thought, and he had left it too late. There was someone else, however, to whom she badly felt she needed to explain herself, so she spent the best part of one hot afternoon writing a letter.

Sitting in the shade on the deck, with a glass of lemonade and a ten-pack of Marlboro Lights, Lara slid out a crisp sheet of the blue Smythson's paper she'd bought for this very purpose and did battle with her soul, her conscience, her French, and her leaky old fountain pen to attempt to explain to Colette Lacloche the reasons why, despite both their reservations, she had opted to re-create Eve's most legendary part. As she wrote, and smoked, and wrote, and smoked, black ink flying over blue pages, it became clear to Lara that the letter to her Mamie was as much a justification to herself as anybody else. The words 'exploration' and 'reconciliation' emerged a number of times and, with a new tremor of bewilderment and fear as she sealed the envelope and carefully wrote out Colette's familiar avenue Bosquet address, Lara wondered again what the ramifications of her decision would be.

With the missive winging its way irrevocably across the Channel by the late afternoon, Lara jumped on her bike to go and break her next bit of bad news.

'Cass, I'm so, so sorry,' she said. 'I've just found out they've definitely cast Jessica Cole in that part. Kevin sent me an email.' They were drinking muddy, cardamom-scented coffee and sharing a plate of sticky baklava at an Iranian café on Shepherd's Bush Road. Lara pushed the rest of her sweets in her friend's direction as a kind of peace-offering.

With a noble smile, though, Cassie tossed her blond hair over her shoulders. 'Oh, well, sod it then. I shall miss you something chronic, though. Wouldn't it have been fun to work together?'

'Amazing,' Lara agreed. 'Next time.'

'Next time', Cassie echoed, and Lara felt a twinge of real regret.

'I'll miss you, Cass.'

'I hope she's nice, that Jessica Cole.'

'You'll come and visit, though, won't you?'

'I'll try.'

'*Try?* You have to!'

Cassie shrugged.

'I'll get your ticket, if that's the issue?' Lara said tentatively.

Cassie shook her head. 'You're sweet, babe, thanks. But no – it's actually that I've just signed up to a temping agency. I'm starting next week.'

Lara nearly choked on her coffee. 'Are you serious?'

'Yeah. I thought it would be good for me, you know, to actually *do* something with my days, rather than just sitting around waiting for the phone to ring. Plus my dad, understandably, is getting a bit pissed off about having to subsidise me all the time. So we'll see. Obviously I'd love to come and visit if I can. I haven't been to New York for years.'

'Fair enough,' Lara said. 'But hang in there, lovely. I know you'll get another acting job soon, and those stupid perma-tanned producers will be kicking themselves.'

Quick as a flash, Cassie reached out to pop Lara's baklava into her mouth. She winked.

'Hey, what are you doing tonight?' Lara asked. 'Will you come and see Lucas DJ with me? It's at some club in Hoxton.'

Cassie blushed. '*Well*,' I was supposed to be having a drink with Ed . . .'

'Oh, were you now?' Lara grinned. 'Well, bring him along too. I'd love to meet him properly.'

Later that night, Lara left Cassie and her evidently very smitten Ed on the dance-floor while she went to buy a drink for her brother and catch him at the end of his set. As Lucas emerged, flushed with adrenalin, from the DJ booth, Lara handed him his beer and they embraced, briefly.

'Cheers for coming,' he called, over the boisterous house music that was booming out of the speakers.

'Pleasure,' she yelled back. 'It's great. I'm not going to stay long, though – got so much to do tomorrow before I go. But I wanted to give you this.' Lara pulled an envelope out of her bag and pressed it into her brother's hands. 'Just a little something for next term,' she explained.

Lucas looked grateful. 'Thanks, Lals,' he said. 'Thanks a lot.' He led his sister out into a corridor of the club where, although the beat still reached them, they could hear each other speak without shouting. 'So you're really off to play Mum's part in that film?'

'I am.' Lara bit her lip. 'Hey – are you okay with that?' For all the people she'd consulted, all the different feelings she'd tried to take into consideration as she made her decision about *This Being Human*, she had never once thought – or was it dared? – to ask her little brother how it would affect him. Perhaps she hadn't wanted to know the answer.

But Lucas, after a moment, nodded thoughtfully. 'Yeah,' he said. 'I'm cool with it.' He turned to Lara and smiled. 'You know what? I actually think it's the right thing to do. She loved that film so much. So it's got a sort of harmony, you doing it now – you know what I mean?'

Understanding suddenly sweetened the air between them, the sort of intuitive comprehension that only siblings who have grown up in the same house, breathed the same air, known the same touch of a parent's hand can share. Lara was flooded with relief. She wanted to throw her arms around her little brother and tell him she loved him so, so much. But she restrained herself, and said, simply, 'Yeah. I think I do.' Just then a drug-eyed reveller crashed through the door into the corridor and the music bombarded them again. After the clubber had staggered past them towards the toilets, Lucas turned back to his sister. 'Good luck, yeah?'

'Thanks, Luc,' she replied. 'That really means a lot. Keep in touch, okay? And come and visit for a weekend or whatever . . . Remember how much fun we had in New York when Dad was at the UN?'

He grinned. 'Yeah. We had a laugh.' He glanced back towards the door. 'Okay, well I'd better get back in there. I'll Facebook you.'

'Take care of yourself.'

'Yeah, you too.'

'And I'll see you at Christmas.'

'Yep. See you at Christmas.'

Lara smiled at her brother, then watched him head back through the door. After a few moments she followed him in, scanning the dance-floor. Spotting Cassie and Ed looking completely absorbed in each other, Lara decided to leave them to it and make her exit. Cassie would understand. Another Christmas meant another year since Eve died; this year it would be ten. And how – how? – could it be a whole decade, Lara wondered in the cab on the way home, watching her city spin and blur behind her tears, and yet still the grief could ravage, bite, tear, as fresh and raw as if the accident had happened yesterday?

Lara had developed a sort of ritual when she was preparing for going away on location: she liked to select the elements of her normal life that would be accompanying her on her next adventure in peace and quiet, on her own, to music, with no chance of being disturbed. Her last afternoon in London, after she returned from her film insurance medical in the morning, would therefore be ideal: she'd finished the rest of her pre-departure admin, Alex was at work, her phone could be switched off.

Having wolfed down a quick bowl of pasta, she dragged a couple of suitcases out of the cupboard and onto the living-room floor, then began scrolling through her iPod. Looking for the perfect packing playlist, she glanced up at her mother as Cleopatra for inspiration, then paused. Cleopatra's scornful expression was right: today was not a day for iPods and electric speakers: it was a day for live, electrifying, silky, scratchy jazz. Reverently, Lara slid out some of her grandfather Bernard's original 78s from the protective case she had kept them in since inheriting them twelve years ago. Then she opened the lid of the cherrywood gramophone Eve had bought her in an antiques shop in Paris the spring after Bernard had died, and allowed herself to linger briefly on the sofa as the cool melancholy of Miles Davis's trumpet sliced through the air.

Some hours later, surrounded by the selection of her belongings that had made the suitcase cut, Lara was shocked to hear the noise of the landline phone ringing on the table in the hall. She looked at her watch and cursed out loud, realising she was already twenty minutes late to meet Alex for dinner at their favourite local Italian. She grabbed the phone.

'Hello?' she said breathlessly.

'Babe, where are you? I've been calling you on your mobile for the past half an hour!'

'God, I'm sorry!' she cried. 'I was packing and daydreaming! I'm literally walking out of the house now. I'll see you soon.'

Rushing upstairs to the bedroom and swearing at herself for

being such a ditz, Lara yanked off her tracksuit bottoms and Alex's old university football T-shirt, and wriggled her way into a dress and heels, brushing her hair and grabbing a squirt of perfume along the way. Out on Ladbroke Grove she hailed a cab, guiltily, for the eight-minute journey to the other side of Notting Hill, flung the driver a tenner, and dropped down the stairs of the restaurant.

Expecting to find her boyfriend sitting there with an open bottle of Chianti, a half-eaten basket of bread and the sports pages of the paper, Lara instead discovered the whole of the downstairs section taken up by a single long table, around which were seated about twenty of her friends. 'Surprise!' they chorused, as she appeared.

'Oh, my goodness!' she exclaimed, blood rushing to her cheeks. 'What are you all doing here? This is so embarrassing! And I'm so *late*! I didn't . . . I mean, I didn't want to make a fuss or anything and now I'm . . .'

'You're rambling, babe, is what you're doing,' said Cassie, standing up to give her a hug. 'Although we *were* starting to get a little worried that you were never going to turn up.'

'I'm such an idiot, I'd switched off my phone, and I thought—'

'Ssh,' Liz cut in. 'This is for you.' She deposited a large glass of red wine in Lara's hands.

'And so is this.' Cassie leant underneath the table and pulled out a long, rectangular package, upon which was stuck a big card. 'It's from all of us. You didn't really think we were going to let you disappear for another million years without giving you a proper send-off, did you?'

Lara laughed, seeking out Alex's eyes. 'Did you know about this?' she asked him, mock-accusingly.

'Of course he did,' Cassie said. 'It was his idea, duh.'

'But Cass found the present,' Alex said. 'Are you going to open it?'

'Yes!' Lara cried. 'I just don't know what to say. I feel a bit overwhelmed. Thank you all so much.'

'You haven't seen it yet,' Liz pointed out. 'Open the damn thing.'

'Jesus, it's heavy!' Lara laughed. 'What the hell is it?' Ripping off the wrapping paper and unwinding a length of bubble wrap from around a long frame, her skin quickened with goosebumps as she saw what it was. She let out a little gasp as a familiar image worked its old power on her soul. It was Eve, as Hélène, leaning on the balcony and gazing out across the stars.

'It's the original poster!' she cried. And there it was. *La Belle Hélène*. Starring Gabriel Dufy and Eve Lacloche. Directed by Dominique St Clair. Released the year she was born. 'I – I— Now I *really* don't know what to say,' she said, looking around at her friends, the enormity of what she was about to embark upon fully sinking in. 'This is the most special present ever, and I can't tell you how much it means to me. Thank you all. So much. Thank you for being here, thank you for understanding what a massive deal this is. Thank you all for being amazing and for being my friends. I love you all so much.'

'If you win a bloody Oscar for this film,' Cassie said, throwing her arm around Lara's shoulders, 'please promise me you'll work on your speech. Now, let's eat!'

The next morning, after weeks of unbroken blue, the sky over West London was smudged with grey. With a leaden heart, Lara kissed Alex goodbye at the front door. As usual, she had refused to let him take the morning off work to accompany her to

Heathrow because the last time she had seen her mother alive had been at an airport, and she had nurtured a phobia about departures-gate farewells ever since. Leaning against the doorframe as he sauntered across the square to unlock his bike, she watched her boyfriend turn one last time to blow her another kiss. 'I'll see you in a few weeks, princess!' he called. 'I love you!'

Once Alex was completely out of view, swallowed up into the everyday blur of morning commuters on Ladbroke Grove, Lara turned back into the hall and walked steadily up the stairs to their flat. Then, trying to staunch the tide of panic that was threatening to break banks inside her, she wandered around their home, touching surfaces, opening cupboards, peering inside the fridge, feeling a little deranged. She unlocked the door to the deck and stood outside for a moment, listening to the buzz of traffic emanating from Notting Hill Gate and gulping in the air, which seemed, on this greyer morning, to contain the first cooler particles of autumn, the onset of which was surely no more than a few days away now. She felt her heart twist as she remembered that the next time she would be home it would be the middle of winter; and suffered a pang of irrational nostalgia for the season she would miss. And then, suddenly, the nostalgia was for something else altogether: it was for this, just this. A moment in her life when everything was just as it was.

But how, she wondered, locking the french windows and heading up to her bedroom, was it possible to miss something you did not yet know you had lost?

Upstairs, Lara paused at the old dressing-table and gazed at her reflection. 'I hope I'm doing the right thing,' she breathed, instinctively searching (as she always did) for Eve's face in the glass, and feeling bereft (as she always did) to find only her own. She closed her eyes. 'I am so scared that nothing is ever going

109

to be the same from this moment on, but I'm being stupid, aren't I?' She paused, and opened her eyes. 'I'm doing this for you. I know you know that. Wherever you are.' In a moment of gut instinct, she placed a kiss on the history-worn wood of the frame around the mirror and whispered an ancient promise to her mother. *I'll see you on the other side of the stars.*

Just then, the doorbell buzzed. Lara took a deep breath. A few minutes later she was sitting, with her suitcases and the original poster of *La Belle Hélène*, in the back of a black Mercedes as it wove its way westwards through the streets of London; past the water towers and the housing estates; past the football stadiums and the green spaces, the Victorian terraces and the sparkling new factories; past all the familiar landscape of her known life, until now they were flying, flying along the motorway towards Heathrow airport.

A few hours later, she boarded a plane.

Part Two

Part Two

ONE

Emerging into the noisy, neon-bright arrivals hall, she was surprised to discover that this airport looked like any other. She didn't know why such a banal thing should cross her mind; she had just expected this place to be different, somehow. It was a country so far away. It was a country at war. And yet everywhere there was French being spoken. That was a sort of dim comfort to her reeling mind, even if it didn't sound quite like the French she was used to. There was Arabic, too, a melodious racket to which she was drawn almost instantly. But police and soldiers, everywhere. And people, so many people. Picking up her daughter, who was staring with her eyes on stalks at the thronging crowds and the military Arabs with their guns, Eve put her lips to Lara's forehead. 'Here we are, *ma chérie*,' she murmured, into the place where the downy roots of her little girl's dark hair began. 'Here we are. The adventure begins. *Alors*. Where on earth is Daddy?'

'Madame Latner?'

She heard a voice in her ear, and spun around, peering over the top of her sunglasses to see a blue-eyed, coffee-skinned young Lebanese man holding a placard with the royal British Embassy crest and her name on it. 'Oui, c'est moi.'

'Je m'appelle Walid. Bienvenue à Beirut.'

'Merci, Walid. Êtes-vous venu nous chercher?' She couldn't believe he'd be there to pick them up – where was Oliver? 'Où est Monsieur Latner?'

'Il est au bureau, Madame. Il m'a demandé de nous dire qu'il est désolé.'

'Ah. D'accord.' So he was sorry, at least. She found a way to smile, brightly. 'Allons-y?'

The man motioned to take her small valise, and Eve nodded a gracious '*merci*'. All of their other belongings had arrived from London last week, via the international courier service. She was still trying to come to terms with the idea that they had essentially transplanted their home in London across an entire continent to resurrect it here in Lebanon; that this process, moreover, was something they would now have to do every few years for as long as her husband remained dedicated to serving his monarch in such fashion. Swallowing the lump of disappointment in her throat that Oliver had not come to meet them as promised, Eve let Lara jump down from her arms as they walked out into the blinding sunlight of the car park, where more armed guards were clustered, smoking, chatting loudly, and where an armoured embassy vehicle was waiting to speed them through the crazy traffic to their new house, their new city, their new life.

'Hello, darling,' Oliver said, as he welcomed his wife and daughter up the driveway and into the residence. 'So sorry I couldn't be there to meet you off the plane. I thought it made more sense for me to come straight here and be back by the time you arrived. Hello, there, little one!' He ruffled the top of Lara's head and she beamed at him.

Eve said nothing, but flung her arms around her husband. Burying her face in his neck, she breathed in the familiar smell of his skin and felt her insides uncoil as she did so. They had only been apart for a week – he had flown out early to get a handle on the office and ensure everything was in place at this end – but, oh, how she had missed him; and what a relief it was to be back in his arms. Eve clung to Oliver now, deliberately ignoring the stiffening of his arms as he tried to nudge her out of view of the row of servants who were waiting patiently to meet the new mistress of the house. She didn't care about the servants: she just wanted to hold him, this man she loved, and let his firm flesh and his clean smell and his broad shoulders and his clear blue eyes remind her just why it was that she had uprooted her life yet again, and why it was that she now found herself in a war-torn country in the Middle East, with no friends, no family and no career. (Later, of course, Eve would come to learn that the staff in any given residence would become her saviours, her friends; they would make the difference between a posting being bearable or unbearable. But for now, Eve had no idea about any of the realities of diplomatic life, and was still finding the prospect of living in a house with a team of people at her disposal very strange.)

'My God, I missed you so much,' she murmured into his neck.

'I missed you too, darling,' Oliver replied, gently trying to ease himself out of her tight embrace. Now was definitely not the time for over-emotional reunions. 'It's wonderful to have you both here. Now, you must come and meet everyone.'

'That can wait. Oliver, I *missed* you.'

'And it's very good to see you too. Come here, Lara.'

Lara, who was hovering shyly by the corner of a low wooden reception table, dropped her tiny blue rucksack and her teddy bear and skipped into her father's arms as he bent down to pick her up.

'Hello, there,' he said again, in the voice that still sounded to Eve as if he did not quite believe this living, breathing creature was really his. 'This is our new home, Lara. Welcome to our new home. Do you like it?'

Lara cast her eyes around the light-filled, white room, with its Oriental carpets and great ceramic pots, its bright colours and big cushions, and nodded. 'Are we going back to our real home soon?' she asked.

Oliver chuckled uncomfortably, and glanced at Eve. She met his gaze levelly. 'This is our real home for the time being, my dear,' Oliver said. 'You can start thinking of this place as home now. You've got your own new room waiting for you upstairs. Mummy will show you in a minute, after we meet all the people who work here.'

Lara nodded again, but she looked puzzled. 'Why do the people work in our real home?'

Eve bit her lip. She came over and kissed her daughter's cheek, then placed her hand on Oliver's back, so that father, mother and child were connected once more in an intimate triangle. 'Come on, my lovely girl. Papa wants us to meet the nice people who are going to look after us while we live here.'

Are we going back to our real home soon?

Eve would later look back and remember those early days in Lebanon; the beginning, she later told herself, of the end. It wasn't that she hadn't felt the occasional skip of excitement to be in Beirut with Oliver then; even in 1985, in the midst of civil war, the city exuded a certain cosmopolitan glamour, a chic and a glitz that could sometimes even remind her of her own beloved Paris. Perhaps it was the luxury of having her native language all around her, but initially Eve almost felt more at home here than she had in the great grey metropolis of London. The Lebanese skies were never anything but the bluest of blues, and the breezes that blew into the city off the sea or rolled down over the mountains had a clarity and freshness that filled her soul with real joy. They went to cocktail parties and the opera; she saw wonderful visiting pianists and chamber ensembles, and even a few passable theatre productions in French. Although her entire being still ached to be on a stage every day – and it was certainly galling to keep having to turn down film offers from Paris, London, Los Angeles – for a while Eve embraced her new role, that of wife and mother, and tried to live with the withdrawal. She would scribble for hours in her diaries and send long letters to her friends overseas and go to her Arabic lessons and teach drama at the refugee camps and try, desperately and with only moderate success, to learn how to cook. She would read endless local histories, she would attempt to make friends with her staff, in their starchy white outfits with gold EⅡR crests stitched on the pockets, she would ignore the beady eyes of Oliver's queen bearing down on her in the breakfast room every morning, and she would act. She would act harder, better than she had ever acted in her life. Play the role, she would tell herself, every time she felt her delicate façade crumbling. Play the role.

And for a time, Eve managed to do just that. But in May, two days after Lara's third birthday, the trouble started at the camps, and from that day onwards, the fear – that had clenched at Eve's guts since Oliver had come home from King Charles Street with the news he'd got the Lebanon job – was transmuted

117

into a more primal instinct. Now, it wasn't just fear about the lifestyle and career and friendships she had abandoned to marry Oliver that gave her pause: it was fear for her life and, moreover, for that of her child. Although Oliver reassured her countless times that the carnage being wreaked down in Shatila and Sabra and Bourj al-Barajneh, those names she heard intoned again and again on French breakfast news or by her own husband on the telephone, was far away and being contained, she was not stupid. Eve saw the skies darken over Beirut and watched footage on television of mauled, skeletal children screaming in the refugee camps, and felt her arms immediately fly out to find Lara's chubby pink limbs and draw them into her body. She listened, with the thump of anxiety in her heart and a dry, metallic taste in her mouth, to the news that Israel had done this or Syria had done that and wondered what would happen next.

People talked in low voices about occupation, she *heard* them, and she lived in dread of the morning when she would wake to discover rows of new troops lining the city streets, planes droning overhead. The very word 'occupation' made her recall her father Bernard's terrible stories of Paris during the war, and it made her stomach tumble. It made her head hurt too, because, try as she might, she did not understand this war. As much as Oliver patiently explained the complex situation to her over dinner, as much as she pored over daily articles in *L'Orient-Le Jour* or *La Revue du Liban* after he left each morning, her brain simply refused to latch onto the details. She forgot who the PSP were, and the PNSF, and the PLO; she forgot whether Amal was a bad guy and Aoun a good guy or the other way around; she was confused by the proliferating factions and by the fact that although Lebanon's civil war was supposedly being waged between Christians and Muslims, these terrible outbreaks of fighting in the refugee camps were between different Muslim sects. Shi'ite and Sunni, Maronite and Druze, Arab and Jew, Christian and Muslim. The labels spun around her head, unlatched from whatever meaning they might once have had, and with every day that passed she began to feel herself further untethered from the information on the page or the names on the news, conscious only of the vast human tragedy and sickening waste of it all.

As the months of civil war drew on and Oliver, determined to add value to the British Embassy presence, spent longer and longer hours at the office, Eve discovered, to her panic, that feelings and impulses she had always been aware of, very deep inside, were intensifying here as never before, mutating in the seemingly endless hours of vacancy into something altogether darker. Despite the unbroken sunshine around her, she was finding it harder and harder to see light in anything.

On many mornings; she struggled to get up, and, knowing that Oliver would have left for work hours ago and that Lara would have been fed and taken to nursery school by the housekeepers, Eve would often languish in bed until midday, one o'clock, writing in her diary if she could face it, or occasionally picking up one of the volumes of Flaubert or Zola that sat on her dressing-table as a source of quiet comfort. In this foreign land, now, with the days yawning emptily ahead of her and the starry nights filled with terrible dreams, Eve had lost her early interest in the local literature and had reverted to burying herself in that of her homeland and childhood. When the morning had ticked by and it was verging on indecent to remain upstairs any longer, Eve would at last shower and dress and trudge downstairs, forcing herself to smile gratefully at the staff as they busied themselves around her, pouring her grapefruit juice, preparing her a lunch she could hardly bear to eat.

It had never been like this before. There had been times, in Paris, and occasionally in London, when a dark cloud would descend upon Eve's soul and for a few days she would privately battle a toxic sense of futility and misery, but she had usually been able to wrench herself out of it with a good book, a thought-provoking matinée, a particular song, a long walk around the city. And Oliver, of course. But never this. Now, she could no longer bring herself to browse an afternoon away at the French bookshop, she stopped going down to the Gemmayzeh to devour the international newspapers over Arabic coffee in the cafés, she ceased writing to her friends and parents, or begging for news from the arts world, and she refused, with increasing frequency, the endless round of diplomatic engagements she was obliged, as the spouse of a senior British diplomat, to take part in. To her fear, Eve even found herself withdrawing from her beloved husband and her beautiful daughter: when things were really bad, she was occasionally taunted by the possibility that she did not deserve them at all.

And although there were moments of lucidity, when Eve understood that what was happening to her was not normal, could not be normal, mostly she was filled with self-loathing by her helpless inability to 'snap out of it', as Oliver had recently been hinting he wished she would. No doubt he thought she was being melodramatic – sulking because she wasn't working and was no longer surrounded by endless opportunities for further stardom and her adulatory public, her adulatory male suitors. But that wasn't it, not it at all. When Eve looked back over the past five years and wondered how her life had turned into this, she didn't worry about the absence now of the awards ceremonies and the adoring fans, the pretty dresses and the champagne-soaked cocktail parties (there were enough of the latter out here, in any case: the expats, as far as she could see, were all drunks). She didn't even, really, mind that she was not acting any more, despite her passion for her trade. In Eve's heart, she was certain that the only thing that mattered in this world was love; and she was confident that any sacrifices she had made had been for the sake of love. Not a great sacrifice at all, then. So why, why did she feel like this?

As the months went by, and ceasefire after ceasefire was broken, and the death tolls rose on a daily basis, Eve increasingly took refuge within the cool white walls of the residence. She would try to hide her despair from Oliver, whose emotional radar was hardly highly tuned, forcing herself to brush her hair and put on some lipstick and sit down with him at dinner as he recounted his tales of horror from the day. But when, exactly one year after the troubles had first started at the camps, heavy fighting resumed and the news became gloomier, Eve stopped leaving the house altogether.

'But, darling, it's quite safe here in the city,' Oliver would say, when he returned home from the embassy. 'Syria's about to deploy, which should calm things down. Can I get you a drink?'

Just to see him. Just to see him, this man. She would be curled up on a sofa, smoking, perhaps staring out of a window or into space, but at the sight of her husband, looking shattered by what he had witnessed that day but with a glow in his eyes nevertheless, something within her would vivify. He would pull off his tie, pour them both a whisky and collapse into an armchair, repeating, 'Eve, darling, it's quite safe. I promise you. Now, what have you done today? How's the little one?'

But she knew he was lying. He must be. How could it really be *quite safe*? Sometimes, in the middle of the inky blue night, when Eve awoke breathless from a particularly vivid nightmare, her throat dry as bone and her heart in pieces, she would stare

121

at Oliver as he slept, amazed but strangely vindicated – ha! – to see a muscle twitching fretfully inside his beautiful jaw, his teeth grinding together in what must have been worry, surely. And yet every morning he would wake bright-eyed and refreshed, not a hint of anxiety anywhere about him. Her own eyes hollowed with fatigue, she would wrap the sheets around her increasingly thin frame while he went about his morning business, showering, shaving, dressing. (Oh, how she loved to watch her husband in the simple quotidian act of getting dressed – his charmingly unconscious routine, the little tugs at his shirtsleeves as he fitted his cufflinks and knotted his tie, the graceful bend of his knee as he pulled on a shoe. She wondered if Oliver knew he did exactly the same thing every day. And that she loved him all the more for it, every day.)

Sometimes he would turn around hopefully. 'Fancy going for a walk this evening?' he'd suggest cheerfully. Or, from the bathroom, brushing his teeth: 'Darling, how about we go out for dinner later?' Rinse, and spit. 'Hugo Armistead and his wife said they'd love to see us. She, Jane I think her name is, she's particularly keen to get to know you better. She's a great admirer of your work, apparently. How about that French restaurant you liked so much when we first arrived?' Hearing silence, his shoulders would drop, but then, having finished in the bathroom, he'd come back to the bedroom to kiss her goodbye. He wouldn't push the matter.

For all Oliver was exhilarated by his work out here, he sometimes recalled, with a stab of regret, the wondrously free spirit his wife had been in Paris and London. He remembered how she would soar through those cities, enchanting all she touched, and he wondered how it was possible that one year in Lebanon could have sucked the life out of the woman who, for the six he had known her previously, had seemed the very essence of vivacity. 'What are you two up to today, then?' he'd ask, knowing already that, unless there was something vital to attend to, Eve would very likely not be leaving the house.

One evening that springtime, Oliver returned home a little drunk from a formal dinner to which Eve had refused to accompany him. When she, sitting rigidly up in bed waiting for him, heard him enter the room, she relaxed. But Oliver's face, as he yanked off his bowtie, swaying a little, was flushed with anger.

'I've had enough of this,' he announced, leaning heavily against the bedpost. 'I've just about had enough.'

Her heart pounding, she wondered, Enough of what? Of Lebanon? Of the war? Surely not. Of her?

'The way you're behaving is nothing short of selfish, Eve,' he continued, slurring slightly so that 'selfish' almost sounded like 'shellfish'. She stared at him. 'I tell you, if I have to make up another bloody excuse as to why my *wife* is "indisposed" and can't make it . . .' He wrenched off his dress shirt and cummerbund, and moved into the bathroom, where she heard him crashing around and turning on the shower. She waited, silently begging the tears that scorched and scratched at her eyelids not to fall.

What did he mean, he had had enough? Had something happened? Had Dominique written to him? Did he suspect her, again? Was he going to threaten to leave her, again? For a fleeting moment Eve realised that if they divorced she could take Lara away from here, back to Paris, back to her real life – to the theatre, to the movie set, to peace. It was almost liberating to contemplate that; until the truth that she did not want to – and would not – live a life without Oliver insisted itself within her again. The thought of going back to working non-stop, as she had done for the past ten years in Paris and London, was in any case exhausting. At least here that temptation had been removed, and she did not have to navigate her way through those ups and downs too.

There was no sound from the bathroom for what felt to Eve like an eternity, before her husband appeared, a towel around his waist, his face scrubbed and pink. His expression had changed: the blurry post-dinner fuzz had been sharpened by his shower and a couple of headache tablets and a long hard think on the edge of the bath, and now he was gentler with her. He came and sat on their bed and touched Eve's hand. 'Eve,' he began, 'I'm sorry, I just . . . I can't bear this any more. I don't understand . . .'

Eve was silent.

'I don't understand what the problem is,' Oliver continued, meeting her eye. 'I know you're far from home and I know you feel uneasy about the situation out there, but you must understand that you'll be fine. You'll both be fine. We'll all be fine.' He looked at her earnestly. 'I will never let anything happen to you. You have to believe me.'

There was a long, heavy silence in that room then, until Eve whispered, 'I'm just so afraid.'

'Tell me,' Oliver said, 'Please. What are you afraid of, exactly?'

Eve bit her lip. Only to her diary had she attempted to explain the misery and emptiness she was experiencing here – and how she partly blamed herself for having accepted this life, having wilfully entered into it. 'I just feel so lost,' she said simply. 'I am lost. I don't know what I'm doing here, I don't know what the point of me being here is.'

Oliver frowned. 'The "point", Eve, is that you're my wife,' he said. 'You're here because I'm here, and I need to be here because the work we're doing is important. You know that.'

She shook her head sadly. 'No, my darling. You misunderstand. I don't know what the point of me *being here* is. Being here, in the world. I feel so utterly empty and lost. I don't know what purpose I have or what I can do or why I should be here at all.'

Oliver gazed at her, his frustration crumbling in the face of her loveliness. 'Eve,' he said, 'I wish you wouldn't say such things.' What he wanted to tell her was that the world would be an altogether less beautiful place without her in it, and that he could not bear to listen to her talk like this. But the sentiments caught in his throat and he could only manage another quiet 'I wish you wouldn't say such things.' And then, suddenly, he felt angry again; angry that he was even in the position of having to respond to this nonsense at all. Surely it was perfectly obvious: why did she insist on trying to draw these words out of him?

'Why?' he heard her ask quietly.

'Why?'

'Why do you wish I wouldn't say such things?'

'Eve, don't do this, please. Don't be ridiculous. It should be perfectly obvious why I wish you wouldn't say such things. You're my wife, you're the mother of my child, I . . . How can I sit here and listen to you say you have no purpose in life? Honestly.' Oliver rose and, with his back turned to her, removed the towel from his waist and rubbed it over his damp head.

Honestly. How she hated that loaded little word, the way he said it, like his awful mother, with such an underlying sense of aggression and disappointed you-should-know-better. Eve watched her husband's naked back for a moment, then swung herself out of bed and ignored his entreaties to come back as she pulled a silk gown around herself and went down to Lara's room.

The little girl was sleeping in her bed, her cheeks flushed peacefully and one arm flung out over the thin white quilt, clutching her teddy. A moon-shaped night-light brought from London cast the room in a soft golden glow. Eve watched her daughter's chest rise and fall rhythmically and forced herself, with each movement of Lara's breathing, to calm down. Lara was alive. Oliver was right. How could she wonder why she was here when there was this child, this miracle, this beautiful fusion of her and him, with her gurgling laugh and her tireless curiosity and her sparkling eyes and the beguiling sense of *peace* she exuded, despite the war raging around her?

Lara stirred as the tears began to drop from her mother's eyes on to her face. She made a small snuffling sound. Eve knew she shouldn't, that this was terrible parenting, but still she could not stop herself reaching out and scooping her child's warm body in its pink pyjamas into her arms. Lara woke then, a look of confusion and then fright fogging her sleep-filled little face. 'Maman?'

'Ssh, *ma chérie*. Ssh. Everything's okay.' Eve kissed Lara's forehead and held her tightly. 'Mummy couldn't sleep, that's all. I'm sorry for waking you. I love you so much. So much.' She felt Lara's limbs flop sleepily in her arms and placed her back gently on the bed. 'I love you. I'm sorry. Go back to sleep, *chérie*.'

'Mm,' Lara murmured.

'Goodnight, my precious girl,' Eve whispered, pausing for a few more moments to watch her daughter succumb to sleep, before going back upstairs to the bedroom, where she found her husband passed out on the bed, snoring lightly.

TWO

By the end of June that year, the fighting had eased, and for the rest of the summer Eve really tried to make an effort. She had devised ways. Whenever she had to accompany Oliver to one of his dreaded diplomatic or political functions, she would take a long bath at five, with rose petals, a stiff gin and tonic and a cigarette, and spend an hour or so psyching herself up. She would remove, from layers of scented French tissue paper, one of the dresses that had recently been sent to her from Yves, or Karl at Chanel, or Azzedine Alaïa, in Paris, and take a graceful turn in front of the mirror, just as if she were back in a couture house at home. She would sit at the beloved dressing-table that had been presented to her after she completed the triumphant *Phèdre* gala at the Théâtre du Chatelet all those years ago, and which had subsequently been shipped from Paris to London and from London to Beirut, and slowly, calmly, make herself up into the role. A little touch of rouge here, a smile's worth of red lipstick, some face powder – she almost enjoyed it. Who would she become tonight?

Sometimes, Lara would sit on her knee and they would sing together as Eve smoked and dabbed perfume playfully on her daughter's nose. Then Eve would rise, as if she really were about to go on stage, and Oliver would appear in the doorway, her leading man, so dashing in his dinner jacket with his hair slicked darkly back, and she would feel like a bird in flight, just to see him standing there, smiling at her.

'Ready to go?' he'd ask. 'You look lovely, darling.'

She'd bend down to pick up Lara, and they would each kiss their daughter's cheek as they assured her they would be home soon. Then Oliver would offer his wife his arm and they would glide out of the residence into the waiting car, and Eve would turn back to give a final wave to Lara, watching from the arms of Berthe, the housekeeper, and at that moment, just for a moment, all would be perfect. Just for a moment.

'I suppose all this is a far cry from treading the boards? Must have been a bit of a shock to the system, coming out here, eh?'

They were at one of those diplomatic functions tonight. Eve was standing on one leg in a corner of the grand room, bored, while the man with his rosy cheeks and broken veins leant so close into her face she could smell the reek of alcohol on his breath. He made her feel physically sick. She turned her head slightly away and took another sip of champagne, wishing she had not already smoked her last cigarette.

'Yes, it has been a bit of a shock to the system,' she said, the English phrase rolling charmingly off her tongue. 'I don't suppose I could trouble you for a cigarette, Mr . . .' *Merde*, she had forgotten his name. What had Oliver said when he introduced them in the group? He wasn't the ambassador, she knew that, but she'd got the sense from Oliver's reverent tone that he was somebody frightfully important, not that she cared. Somehow, Oliver had then been swept into another conversation, or this man had manoeuvred Eve into a corner, or something had happened that now meant she was stuck here alone with him and having to cast her eyes desperately around the room for her husband.

The man looked surprised. 'A cigarette? Um, yah, shouldn't be a problem.' He dug his pudgy fingers into the pocket of his trousers, fished around and pulled out a silver case. Removing two cigarettes, he handed one to Eve, who placed it delicately in the corner of her mouth.

'Here, allow me,' he said, putting his face uncomfortably close to hers once more as he brandished a silver lighter. She nodded gracefully towards the flame, drawing so deeply on the cigarette that she felt light-headed.

The man, one Rupert Longstaff CMG, sighed heavily, desire stirring inside him. Christ, she was exquisite. How the hell had that bastard Latner ended up with this girl? Yes, all right, so he himself had matinée-idol looks, and was a rising star in the FCO, *and* a bloody good sport to boot – but, oh, God, why Latner?

And now his own wife was waddling towards them.

'Ah! Darling. Mrs Latner, have you met my wife, Mary?'

'I don't think we've had the pleasure,' Eve said politely. 'I'm Eve.'

'I've seen you, of course, on the silver screen,' brayed Mary Longstaff. 'Not sure we've ever met, though.' She stuck out a hand. 'Delighted. How are you finding things? Bit of a shock to the old system, I should say.'

129

Eve took another drag on her cigarette and blew the smoke neatly away from Mary's horsy face, with its shiny eyeshadow and its lacquered Mrs Thatcher hair. 'Everything's perfect,' she recited. 'Thank you.'

'And your daughter? How's she settling in?'

Eve smiled instinctively at the thought of Lara, the way she had taken so effortlessly to life in Lebanon; the way she had so charmed the staff at the residence that they were eating out of her hand; the way she skipped to the international school each morning, with a beam on her little face, and came back chattering in a chorus of languages. She nodded. 'Lara is very wonderful, thank you. She's settled in here so well. Even with all the troubles.'

'Well, indeed. I hope you haven't been too affected by all that palaver. Bloody Muslims, always fighting each other like dogs. Anyway. Well, that's great. Good stuff. How old is she now?'

'Um, she turned four in April.'

'Any more on the way?'

Eve stared at the woman, stunned at the impertinence of the question, and alarmed that perhaps the longing she was nurturing deep inside for another child was visible on her face. Rupert Longstaff, meanwhile, felt his stomach turn to liquid at the prospect of this woman naked, making love, making babies with that young upstart Latner.

'I . . . er . . .' Eve started, then laughed nervously. Play the role, play the fucking role, she reminded herself. She shrugged graciously. 'I don't know. Who knows? I hope so.' She swallowed the rest of her champagne and stubbed out her cigarette in a nearby ashtray. 'If you will excuse me? I must find my husband.' She composed her mouth into a smile. 'It was very nice to meet you both.'

And then she disappeared into the crowd, the sliver of her back shimmering in its cream silk sheath, and it seemed to Rupert Longstaff, and indeed to all the men in the room who watched her, that the lamps in the drawing room somehow glowed brighter as she passed, as if her very presence illuminated them with her grace. The only man who didn't notice, in fact, was Oliver, whose back was turned, deep in conversation with a military attaché from Moscow.

'Seems a perfectly nice woman,' Longstaff managed, his voice weak with desire. 'Don't know why they all have such a problem with her.'

His wife shook her meaty head and tutted. 'Well, you know what they say. You can never trust an actress.'

Eve was quiet in the car on the way home, but it was a tranquil quiet as she rested her head against the window and watched the city of Beirut, charred and broken in some parts, still modern and gleaming in others, roll past in the deep blue haze that signified night in this country. Oliver had his hand resting lightly on her thigh and she loved how its warmth spread deep into her skin through the silk. She'd done it, she'd got through it, and he was pleased with her, she could tell.

Eve knew that her husband, so excruciatingly decorous and sensitive to social protocol, had found it extremely trying last year when she had refused to accompany him anywhere, while his colleagues and their awful wives gossiped about her. At the time, when she was going through it, she had felt justified: after everything she had sacrificed to leave Paris, to discover that the life she had locked herself into was *this*, simply *this*, how could he expect her not to be downhearted? But now she felt guilty for having put him through that.

Oliver had looked so beautiful and relaxed tonight, holding the attention of the room and talking so intelligently that she had quite wanted to climb into his brain, to understand what it would be like to have that level of brilliance in one's head! For all the ghastly conversations she had had to endure with the likes of the Longstaffs, Eve felt proud to have been there with her husband. The thought that Oliver was her husband, *her husband*, *hers*, could not help but bring a smile to the corners of her lips and she sighed contentedly. Oliver. At that moment Eve knew, again, that it was only about him, only about love. Everything was about love. The other stuff, all the films and the plays and the fashion shows and the newspapers and the awards ceremonies, it was just froth and fizz, the bubbles in a glass of champagne, the smoke from a cigarette – impermanent, untrue. This, though, this feeling: this was love. This was truth. She sighed again.

Hearing her sigh, Oliver turned his head better to glance at his wife. Eve was ravishing tonight in a silk dress that had recently arrived in a sleek black box from Saint-Laurent or someone in Paris, diamonds in her hair, a heady scent of Chanel and smoke and roses radiating from her skin. But as he watched her gazing out of the window, Oliver caught himself wondering for a split second what she was thinking – and was taunted again by the old worry that he would never know what was really going on inside his wife's head; that as great an actress as she undoubtedly was, she might always be playing a part with him, always have the capacity to deceive him.

As she turned softly to him and smiled, though, his most deep-seated fears dissolved, and he reproached himself for not keeping those dangerous thoughts in check. Eve had married him, after all. *Him!* And it was already five years since all that . . . Of course, the men here stared at Eve, lust clouding their eyes, but men would look at her like that wherever they were, Oliver knew now; and surely nowhere again would be as bad as Paris.

It was the way those French men had shown no respect for him, as they continued to try to woo Eve throughout their relationship – that was what Oliver had found so utterly contemptible. She, of course, had always laughed it off, dismissed the endless propositions with an expressive flick of her hand and a girlish '*Bof*!' And, all right, so he understood that his Eve had become quite the darling of late 1970s Paris; and why the media were therefore so up in arms when her relationship with '*le rosbif diplomatique*' (as they had insisted on dubbing him in *Paris Match* and the like) had got serious. But why, he wanted to know, did outrage that their favourite homegrown star had fallen in love with an Englishman automatically grant every bloody man in the city (and some women too) licence to try to get into bed with her? Oliver thought bitterly of Edouard Valence, that weak-chinned actor, how he had sent Eve white roses every single day for a year, the cheek! Or François Marchand, chief aide to the *French foreign minister* of all people, how he had solicited Eve quite openly at an official function!

And then, of course, there was St Clair . . . Oliver shivered involuntarily at the memory of the dark-haired director, with his ridiculous black polo-necked sweaters and his roll-up cigarettes and the way he professed such devotion to Eve, his so-called 'muse', that he'd sworn publicly after the furore over *La Belle Hélène* that he'd never make another film if she left France and married *le rosbif*. Oliver tasted blood in his mouth as he remembered the morning he'd spent on rue de Fleurus, waiting . . . And then, a week later, when he'd left the embassy and found Dominique St Clair lurking in the rain at the end of the rue du Faubourg Saint-Honoré. 'Good evening, Oliver,' St Clair had sneered in his nasal French. 'Eve asked me to come. I have a little something to tell you . . .'

In London, things had been a bit better, because at least the English had some respect. The males still gawped at her, at the fine bones of her cheeks and shoulders, at the glitter of her cat-like eyes, the gracefulness of her long arms and legs. But Eve was a film star, of course they stared. Oliver accepted they were unlikely to try to seduce her; and, good as his word in Paris, he now made every effort to trust his wife when she swore to him she could not *be* seduced. It wasn't, even, that he still doubted Eve's fidelity – truly it wasn't, not after everything she had 'given up', as she so often reminded him. It was rather that, deep down, Oliver, who was by his nature a controlling sort of man, was terrified that he could not control his feelings for Eve – and, moreover, could not control Eve's feelings for him. She was, by her nature, so *whimsical*. Think of the way they themselves had met! How could he, really, honestly, how *could he* possibly rule out the risk that at some time in the future she might simply turn around to some other stranger at some other dinner party and say, 'It's you! It's *meant to be* you,' as she had once done with him?

'What are you thinking, my darling?' Oliver heard Eve ask quietly as she turned back towards him. Her face was almost unbearably lovely tonight, so young and fresh in the moonlight, and he swallowed, a touch guiltily. It was precisely that sort of reasoning – *you once did this so how can I be certain you won't once do that?* – which had so enraged and hurt her five years ago in Paris; and he now felt muddy with betrayal for even entertaining such thoughts again as he saw her trusting green eyes and knew that she loved him. She loved him! What a fool he was. Oliver wished he could tell Eve how much he worshipped her, how terrified he was by the strength of his love for her and by the thought that she might one day slip away from him. But, to what would be his eternal regret, he couldn't. He didn't have the words. He didn't know how to say any of that.

'Nothing,' he managed, eventually. Eve looked at him for a moment, looked deep into his eyes, and Oliver moved to take her hand in his. 'Nothing,' he repeated, squeezing her fingers. 'Thanks for tonight, Eve. I thought you did very well.'

Eve kept looking at him, and bit her lip, inclining her head ever so slightly. Then, with her free hand, she stroked his cheek. 'You and your nothings,' she said, with a little sigh. But she was smiling. 'You and your nothings.'

She rested her head on his shoulder then, and remained there until the car slid up the drive to the residence and they stepped out into the moonlight, both aware that this sense of unity between them might not last, but that its transience would be part of its grace. Holding hands, they went to check on Lara, watching their little creation sleeping, and then Oliver placed a hand on the small of Eve's back and they moved silently upstairs to the bedroom, where they made love slowly, tenderly, as if it were the last night in the world.

THREE

The meeting was wrapping up, to Oliver's immense relief. September had arrived but it was still sweltering in the office; he could feel a trickle of sweat sliding down the long groove of his back. He took another swig of water and squeezed his temples, conscious of his hangover. He and Eve had thrown a dinner party last night, their first in ages (Oliver, thankful to have redeemed himself in the eyes of his colleagues, had laughed off their jovial 'about bloody time's in good humour). Eve had certainly bloomed in the last few weeks – a light had come back to her eyes – but Oliver had still been amazed when she had agreed to host a collection of other foreign diplomats and their wives for supper.

The meal itself had proved a drama, of course, but after a tearful hour-long conversation to her mother in Paris about how to do a *coq au vin*, and assistance from an army of embassy servants, the food had been fine. Excellent, actually. And she'd played the hostess with her typical aplomb, dressed in a killer black cocktail dress and red lipstick, her hair swept back off her face; Oliver had had to stop himself tearing off her clothes for a second time before the guests started to arrive. Even now, in fact, he felt a twinge of desire at the very thought of his wife, and coughed, trying to focus on the closing words of the Defence Attaché.

Things were apparently looking problematic again down on the southern coast, thanks to the presence of so many Sunni Palestinians in what was a predominantly Shia area, and Oliver found himself hoping vaguely that if more fighting broke out, Eve would not collapse back into the frozen stupor she had existed in for so many months previously. He wanted this fragile sense of normality, of being a functioning husband-and-wife team, to hold. Essentially he wanted more dinner parties like last night's if at all possible, with Eve rising perfectly to the occasion and behaving so brilliantly he could have burst with pride (although perhaps, he conceded, as he stood up at the end of the meeting and felt his head throb again, with a little less to drink).

The meeting concluded, Oliver gathered up his papers and walked towards the door. Before he could reach it, though, he heard a voice bellow, 'Latner', and felt a hand on his shoulder. 'Bloody good show last night.' It was Rupert Longstaff.

'Thanks, Rupert,' Oliver replied.

'Wondered if we might return the favour next week.'

'Next week?'

Eve would have a heart attack. One of the conditions of doing last night's dinner was that she wouldn't have to suffer another in the near future; and of all the 'deathly bores' in the room last night, she'd declared the pompous Longstaff and his awful shoulder-padded wife the absolute worst. In secret, Oliver agreed. But Longstaff was important. If Oliver was to be promoted early next year, as people had hinted and he was hoping, Longstaff's support would be key to his appraisal.

'Next week, yup, I'm sure that would be great. I'll check with Eve.'

'Oh, yes.' Longstaff agreed. 'Check with Eve.' He said her name as if with a mouth full of clotted cream, looked self-conscious for a flash, then recovered. 'Mary was hoping maybe Tuesday.'

Tuesday. That was less than a week away. She'd go crazy.

'Great. That sounds great. I'll, er, telephone you to confirm.'

'Good stuff.'

'Are you fucking out of your *mind*?' Eve wondered when Oliver broached the subject with her that night. 'I have to sit through another dinner with those terrible people *next week*?' But she was in a good mood today, aware that she had pulled off a masterstroke last night and that her husband was thrilled with her; thrilled by her. So she laughed, beating her fists against his chest in mock fury.

He swooped her up into his arms and kissed her fully on the lips. 'I'll make it up to you, I promise,' he said, but, kissing him passionately, she seemed not to care any more. 'I've been wanting you all day,' he said into her ear, bounding up the stairs and, for once in his life, not giving a toss if the staff saw them. 'I can't get the thought of you in that sexy black dress out of my mind.'

'*Vraiment?*' She giggled. 'I shall wear it more often.'

'Right now,' he said, throwing her on the bed, 'I want you wearing nothing at all.' He moved down her body, kissing each part of her as he stripped off her clothes, then sat up suddenly. 'Where's Lara?'

Eve stretched her body back on the bed like a cat. 'She's asleep, *mon cher*. She's having a little nap before supper.'

'We'd better be quick, then, hadn't we?' Oliver reasoned, removing the last of his wife's underwear with a well-practised tug. 'Now. Where was I?'

Somebody else was also having trouble getting Eve in her black dress out of his mind. Rupert Longstaff felt like a lovesick teenager as he counted down the seemingly endless hours before Tuesday night. He'd got around Mary's surprise at the Latners' new-found social enthusiasm and her husband's eagerness to indulge it by telling her some ridiculous story about Eve promising to help Mary's niece Camilla in her bid to get into RADA. If the story caught up with him later, he had already planned his excuse: to blame Eve's English and suggest that the conversation had evidently been at linguistic cross-purposes.

'How wonderful to see you again!' he roared at the couple, as the moment finally arrived for the doorman to usher them in. 'What'll you have?'

'Hello there,' Mary yelled from the kitchen. 'Be with you in a tick.'

'Go on, old boy. Whisky? Gin?'

'I'll have a gin and tonic please,' interrupted Eve, and Oliver could detect the boredom already lacing her husky voice. 'Do you mind if I smoke? Thanks.' She'd had two strong martinis already this evening, to ease her nerves, she'd said, but he'd seen a wicked glint in her eye and was hoping she wasn't planning on doing anything rash. She'd been so much better of late but, over the past two days, had seemed to sink back into one of her dark moods. He'd tried to get out of her why, but she'd apparently been incapable of explaining it; he was beginning to find her unpredictability somewhat trying.

Oliver cleared his throat. 'Whisky sour would be lovely, thanks, Rupert. Thanks.'

Mary bustled in then and planted damp kisses on their faces. Eve could see beads of sweat glistening through the oily pink patches of her makeup and felt slightly queasy. She took a long swig of her drink and looked around the room. It was an impressive house, of course (they all were), with grand staircases, pristine white walls and generic Middle Eastern furnishings, but to her it felt as life-sapping and sterile as the rest. How she longed sometimes to be back in her apartment on rue Jacob, or even in the sweet Kennington garden flat that she and Oliver had made home together in London. Her heart shuddering with a vicious stab of homesickness, she sat down quickly on one of the sofas as the question *What is this life you are living?* dangled itself again in front of her eyes like a cancerous black spot.

'Darling?' Oliver enquired.

'Sorry. I just felt a little dizzy.'

'Perhaps a glass of water would be more sensible, then.'

Eve glared at him and took a deliberately long sip of her gin, smoothing her palms on her green dress before turning pointedly to their host. 'May I use your bathroom, please, Rupert?'

Longstaff, giddy at the music she had created out of his name, clanged the whisky bottle onto the silver tray and said, 'Ah, yes, of course. Ramzi, see to Mr Latner's drink, will you? I'll escort Mrs Latner to the bathroom.'

'I really don't need escorting, thank you,' said Eve. 'Just point me in the right direction.'

'No, no,' he insisted. 'We'll take you upstairs. You don't want to use the one down here.' Longstaff was adamant, allowing his hand to rest against Eve's back as he showed her up the curving staircase. Just as she seemed to move away from his touch, he found a spot slightly lower down her back, at the top of her buttock, and planted his hand there, more firmly this time.

'Here it is,' he said, stopping outside a door on a corridor that looked identical to all the others. He stared at her, as if mesmerised.

She met his gaze quizzically. 'Thank you.'

'My pleasure.' He didn't move, but let his eyes drop to her breasts, those perfect little breasts with their pert nipples standing up against the green fabric of her dress, God, he wanted to devour them, he wanted . . .

'Excuse me.'

He heard Eve interrupt his fantasy, as she turned into the bathroom. Panting, he grabbed her hand. She recoiled with a gasp. 'Oh, Eve. I just wanted to say how lovely it is to see you again.' He sighed, leaning in dangerously close to her lips. '*Eve.*'

But before he could kiss her, Eve had darted into the bathroom with a little cry and slammed the door in his face.

Longstaff leant on the other side, trying to catch his breath and calm the torrent of his lust, hoping that none of the staff was lurking nearby. Walking swiftly down the corridor, he swung into a store-room nobody ever used and had a little fiddle into his son's old cricket jumper, just to clear his head, he told himself. Wouldn't be able to concentrate all night, otherwise. Then he adjusted his tie, cleared his throat and headed back to the drawing room to finish drinks and talk politics with that bastard Latner.

Eve was inconsolable on the way home. 'That man is disgusting!' she exclaimed. '*Disgusting*. He makes my skin crawl. You should have seen the way he put his sweaty pink hands on me when he showed me upstairs and tried to stick his tongue down my throat. I swear to you I am never in my life going anywhere near that – that pervert ever again.'

'Eve!' Oliver reprimanded her, a nod towards the driver's head. 'For God's sake, have some discretion.'

'Discretion?' she hissed. 'Discretion? What is that supposed to mean? Don't you even care that some pervert would have tried to kiss your wife? Is that what you call *discretion*, Oliver?'

'Eve, listen to me. Enough. We'll talk about it when we're home.'

'Oh, will we, now?' she said hotly. '*Will* we, now? That's good, Oliver, that's really great. Thanks for your support.' She stared at him then, a look of pure shock etching itself across her delicate features. 'My God,' she gasped, slumping back against the seat, 'you don't believe me?'

Her husband was silent.

'Tell me,' she urged, 'do you even believe what I am telling you? Or are you going to take that revolting . . . *rapist*'s side?'

Oliver gripped her hand then. 'Enough,' he warned her. 'That is quite enough. How dare you speak about a colleague of mine like that?'

She slammed the car door when they arrived, leaving Oliver fuming in the driveway. How much more of this could he take? He was sure that Eve was exaggerating – Rupert Longstaff was head of station here; he was hardly about to risk his reputation by touching up another fellow's wife, was he? And for some reason – who knew why? who could predict such things? – she'd been in a dark, volatile mood all evening, even before they'd left their house; the worst she had been for a while.

Upstairs in the bedroom, Eve refused to talk to him, hunching her girlish body into a corner of the bed as she lay there, sobbing quietly at first, then falling ominously silent. For hours, both lay tense and awake with their backs to each other, until eventually, as a watery blue light started to drift in through the shutters, he heard her breathing slow. When he was sure that his wife was asleep, Oliver hoisted himself up on one elbow and watched Eve at rest in a pool of dawn light, her features now relaxed. She looked like a little girl, and his heart faltered. Would she make up a story like that? Why didn't he believe her? Why was he never quite able to believe her?

'I'm sorry,' he mouthed to her silently. 'I am so sorry.'

But Eve slept on, oblivious.

FOUR

The trouble that had started between Amal and the Palestinians, down at the Rashidiyye camp in Tyre, soon spread up through Sidona and into Beirut. On hearing the news that lethal clashes had broken out in the city once again, Eve decided to take action.

'I'm going back to Paris,' she announced to Oliver one morning.

He looked up, surprised, from his newspaper and grapefruit.

'I just need to get out of here for a time. I feel so sick, I don't know what to do with myself. Something's not right. I'm sorry, Oliver. I just need to go.'

The past few weeks had not been easy. Since that night at the Longstaffs, actually, Eve had slunk back into her scratchiest, gloomiest mode: sullen and weepy sometimes; violently excitable at others; then deathly silent, when she would do nothing except read or write in her diary for hours, even refusing Lara's company. Some nights, as if swept with remorse, she'd clutch at Oliver like a child and sob that she was sorry; she'd sob into Lara's hair and the little girl would become upset too, which would make Oliver furious. Eve had also started to complain of sickness: she was turning down food, saying the Middle Eastern spices made her want to vomit, and was in fact throwing up often; he was worried by how much weight his already slender wife was losing. She was also refusing to accompany him to functions again, after a particularly disastrous reception, soon after the Longstaffs' dinner, at which she had got blisteringly drunk, had some sort of hysterical fit in another room, much to his mortification, and locked herself into a bathroom for the duration of the evening. Poisonously silent on the way home, she had declined to tell him what had gone on at the party to make her so distraught, muttering bitterly that he would not believe her anyway because he didn't care. What with the downturn in the political situation and the increased workload this had brought, Oliver was feeling quite exhausted.

And so he nodded at his wife from across the breakfast table. 'Okay. That's probably not a bad idea.'

'Just for a week or two. I'll take Lara to see my parents. It's been so long. We'll spend a little bit of time in Paris and I'll feel so much different. I'll come back refreshed and renourished and I'll be a better wife for you.'

Oliver sighed and put down his newspaper, reaching out to take her hand. 'Eve. You're a very good wife. Stop that, please.'

She shrugged. 'You know what I mean. I can't sleep, I'm exhausted, I feel so emotional, I keep throwing up, I can't eat, I can't do anything. And I'm so scared about what's going to happen now that I feel completely choked by it. I'm scared, Oliver, and I need to get away from here.'

'So we'll arrange it today.'

'Good. I'll miss you, though.'

'And I'll miss you both too.'

Oliver went back to his breakfast with an odd flash of relief.

Touching down with Lara at Charles de Gaulle airport a few days later, Eve was amazed by how instantly better she felt just to be out of Beirut, out of the long shadow of civil war with its all-pervading smells of cordite and petrol, and its daily death toll. Her parents, Colette and Bernard, met them at the airport – where a crowd had gathered to catch a glimpse of the actress they still thought of as their star, some taking photographs, some thrusting pieces of paper into her hands, all of which she signed. Outside in the bright morning the four of them clambered into Bernard's old blue Citroën and bumped through the streets of Paris back to the apartment on avenue Bosquet that her parents had lived in since the early fifties. Eve wound down the rickety window and leant her head out into the sky, letting the fresh autumnal wind rush through her hair. It felt so good not to be in a leather-upholstered, spiritless armoured car, so good to be chattering in real French and watching the colours of September erupt across her city. Her home. The trees lining the Seine were red and yellow, orange and green, and her heart danced at the first glimpse of the river, quite golden today in the tilting light. She was so proud of her daughter, who was gabbling away in French to her grandparents and then, just as quickly, switching into English when she turned her head to ask something.

'Mummy . . .'

'Chérie, nous pouvons parler français tout le temps maintenant que nous sommes à Paris!'

'Paris!' Lara repeated excitedly. 'Nous sommes à Paris!'

Colette turned around to the back seat and smiled at Eve. 'Qu'elle est adorable!' she exclaimed, with such warmth that Eve wanted to burst. Looking out of the window again as monuments and street names and parks long-beloved flashed past her, she wondered how on earth she had ever been persuaded to leave this city in the first place. It's the centre of life, she thought to herself. *N'est-ce-pas?*

The next few days were a delicious blur of family and love, and Eve folded herself fully back into the embrace of her parents and her Paris, sitting up for hours drinking wine, listening to his records and putting the world to rights with her father; accompanying her mother on her daily errands; meeting her old girlfriends Aurélie and Sophie for a raucous lunch at La Palette; going to mass in Saint-Germain; dropping into the *ateliers* of her favourite couturiers, who even now pressed beautiful dresses into her hands; calling on her old professor Sebastien at the Conservatoire and walking into its hallowed theatre, holding Lara's hand as they stood there in silence, two solitary figures on an empty stage. Most of all, Eve relished being able to walk through her city with her daughter as the season took hold and the sky crisped and the temperature dropped. For the first time in ages, she felt uncomplicatedly happy. There was no war here. No salacious diplomats with fat fingers and brandied breath. No mind-numbing conversations with oily-faced wives. Just Paris.

Nevertheless, after a week, when Eve's mind and her soul felt refreshed and her body stronger thanks to the nourishing wonders of Colette's cooking, the lurking feeling of sickness inside her hadn't subsided. She was alarmed to still be throwing up most days, until finally it dawned on her one morning, counting back the weeks and doing the maths in her head, that she must be pregnant again. Shrieking with glee, she cursed herself for being so *stupid*. Of course!

Secretly, she had wanted and wanted and wanted another baby, longed for it as she'd longed for nothing in her life, but every time she had mentioned it to Oliver, he'd said he didn't think it was the time – and she'd had to admit that perhaps he was right. What with civil war raging around them, and her own emotional flux, did she really want to bring a defenceless, innocent being into all that misery and chaos? But something must have gone wrong with their precautions, because now it was so obvious! The hormonal rages, the tears and tantrums, the nausea. She'd put it down to being stuck out there in that terrifying place, with those awful people, and the war, and not acting, and Oliver so busy, and her with nothing to *do*. But it wasn't that at all! She was pregnant again! It was the most wonderful news she could imagine!

Skipping down the stairs in her parents' apartment, Eve immediately snatched up the white Bakelite telephone in the hallway and dialled the number of the embassy in Beirut.

'I'm sorry, Madame, Monsieur Latner is in a meeting,' she heard his secretary explain.

'Well, tell him to call me as soon as he can, Roula, please!' Eve trilled. 'I have such good news!'

Giggling to herself as she replaced the receiver, she couldn't escape the feeling that she had somehow been saved. Redeemed. If she was pregnant, nothing really mattered except the baby. That she had been feeling so wretched again lately didn't matter. That she had no career any more didn't matter. That there existed in the world creeps like Rupert Longstaff didn't matter. Even being in Beirut didn't really matter. She and Oliver would have another child, she'd stick out the rest of his 'tour', as they called it, and then she would ask him to take up another desk job at the FCO in London, where perhaps she would act again, or perhaps she wouldn't, but even that didn't matter. And how could he refuse her when they had a new baby to love and look after? Maybe he might even decide he'd had enough of this endless upheaval and leave the Foreign Office altogether; assuage his love of the Middle East with sun-soaked holidays to the Levant instead. She was fantasising now, she knew: her husband's sense of vocation meant he would never give up the diplomatic service, he had already made that so clear, but still – still, the news about the baby was like a miracle, and she clapped her hands in joy again as she bounded into the kitchen to tell Colette and Lara, who were busy making animals with pastry.

'Qu'est-ce-qu'il se passe?' Colette cried, as Eve tripped in, grabbed Lara, and twirled her around and around in a circle until the little girl was screaming with laughter. Eve came to a breathless standstill.

'Maman has some very good news,' she cried joyfully, catching Colette's eye. 'I'm going to have another baby!' She ruffled Lara's hair and knelt down so she was at the same level. 'My darling, do you understand? You're going to have a little sister or a little brother!'

'Oh!' Lara exclaimed.

'*Oh!*' Colette gasped, dropping her rolling pin. '*Evie!* Are you sure?'

Eve stood up again and nodded happily. 'I don't see any other reason for my sickness and terrible mood swings. And it makes sense, time-wise.'

'Oh, what wonderful news! What wonderful, wonderful news!' As Colette bent to plant a kiss on Eve's still-taut belly, Lara hopped excitedly on one leg.

'Look, *chérie!*' Colette said, to her granddaughter. 'Another

149

baby growing in here!' Lara's eyes opened wide as she followed her grandmother's example, gently rubbing Eve's stomach.

Eve smiled at her mother. 'Another baby,' she said, in wonder, taking Colette's hand. After Eve, Colette and Bernard had never been able to have another child; and Eve, who was married to another only child (although Oliver's parents had declined to have another for altogether different reasons), had always worried that Lara might be destined for the same peculiar loneliness that came of having no siblings. But clearly not! She let out a musical laugh and cried, 'Where is Papa? Let's ring him and tell him to meet us at the Flore. I want to celebrate!'

Café de Flore was packed, as usual, this lunchtime, but when the manager, Jacques Catroux, spotted Eve Lacloche – as he would always think of her – emerging from the crowds on the boulevard Saint-Germain in a red beret and sunglasses, then pulling open the wrought-iron, glass-fronted door to his restaurant, he snapped his fingers at a nearby waiter and had a word *sotto voce* to ensure that a premium table for four became vacant *immédiatement*. Ah, Eve looked fabulous, Jacques thought – all those years away and in she was gliding, *trop Parisienne*, in a chic little jersey dress, Saint-Laurent no doubt, as if she had never left. His staff, not to mention his regular clientele, would be beside themselves to see her again. He moved swiftly towards the door.

'Jacques!' Eve cried, when she saw him, and rushed over to throw her arms around him. 'Oh, Jacques! Comment vas tu, mon ami?'

'Je suis en pleine forme, ma belle Eve. Ça me fait plaisir de te voir. To what do we owe the pleasure?'

'I came home, Jacques!' Eve told him, eyes shining. 'I just

came home. And we have such good news to celebrate today! Jacques, you know my family?'

'Mais bien sûr,' Jacques assured her. He shook Bernard's hand and kissed Colette's cheek. 'How very nice to see you again, Monsieur et Madame Lacloche.' Reaching down, he gave Lara a little chuck on her nose. 'And this is the little one, eh? My, my, Lara, *ma petite*, how you have grown! And just look at those eyes! I think you must need a hot chocolate, *non?*'

Lara nodded shyly, taking her mother's hand as Jacques showed them to what had once been Eve's favourite table in the corner by the window. Eve took a seat in this wonderfully familiar parlour, site of so many happy days in her twenties, when she would rendezvous here with Paris's most brilliant young filmmakers and poets, fashion designers and musicians, and leant back contentedly. For so long, this had been her natural habitat. How many times had she sat here, at this very table? In how many different manifestations of herself had she luxuriated in the glow from these chandeliered lights? The lights that now blinked again reassuringly, in the huge, brass-framed mirrors of the café, like an impressionist painting, hazy with the steam from the coffee machine and the smoke from a hundred cigarettes and all the reflected glitter and gloss of Rive Gauche Paris. Here she had been as a teenaged student in 1968, after descending with her fellow students on the Bou' Saint-Mich, drinking endless cups of black coffee while deep in impassioned discussion about politics; here she had been as a young actress just graduated from the Conservatoire, flush with her first professional successes and being toasted with champagne by all of Paris; here she had been as a twenty-four-year-old girl, on a cold, bright September afternoon just like this one – falling more in love by the minute with a handsome

English civil servant named Oliver Latner, as they shared a steak on their very first day together, the day after that fated *Phèdre* . . . And now, here she was again today, as Oliver's wife, and a mother!

Eve placed her hands on her promise-filled belly in wonderment, and looked across at her daughter, who had been provided with colouring pencils by Jacques and was now busy drawing on the tablecloth, just as Eve's old poets and politicos had once scribbled love verses to her and manifestos to the state. Imagine – another Lara! Eve had managed to get through to Oliver in his office just before they left the apartment, and he had sounded delighted. 'Oh, that's wonderful, darling,' he'd said, after a moment's stunned pause. 'Gosh, what a surprise! But how wonderful. Well, take care of yourself over there, won't you? Don't gallivant around too much or you'll tire yourself out.'

She had laughed happily. 'I'll be fine, my love! We'll all be just fine. And I'll see you very soon.'

Eve leant over the table and planted a spontaneous kiss on Lara's soft forehead. 'I love you,' she said to her daughter, touching noses. 'I love you so much I could die.'

When their lunch finally arrived, Eve carefully cut up Lara's poulet frites before tucking into her own food, chatting to her parents and occasionally looking up to wave at old friends, familiar faces; all the people who were rushing over in excitement to kiss her cheek and welcome her back and admire the little girl and ask her how she was and whether they could expect the family back in Paris soon and this and that and this and that and then suddenly, a face was sharpening into focus in front of her, and there he was, and *there he was*, and her heart skipped a beat and she dropped her fork onto the plate in shock. 'Dominique!' she gasped.

She had not seen him in so many years.

The director gave a little bow to the table. 'Madame Lacloche,' he greeted Colette, who had stopped eating and whose face had gone a little pale, 'Monsieur Lacloche, how very good to see you again. What a wonderful surprise.'

Bernard managed a gruff '*Bonjour*,' in response, and then Dominique St Clair turned and bowed towards Lara. 'And you must be Lara.'

Lara nodded happily at this stranger dressed all in black. 'Yes!' she assured him, in her sweet, earnest French. 'I'm Lara. Who are you?'

'Me?' he asked. 'That is a good question.' He turned to Eve, for the first time. She was barely breathing. 'Who am I?'

'Lara, *ma chérie*, this is Dominique,' Eve managed, her voice steady, but her hands shaking as she pulled her cutlery together and pushed her plate away. She folded her arms tightly across her chest, protectively across her belly. 'He is somebody Maman used to work with.' She glared at Dominique. 'A very, very long time ago.'

He smirked. 'Not so very long.' His eyes bored into hers and then he looked up. 'It's good to see you all again. *Alors*, I'm afraid I must get back to my rehearsals. *Bonne journée*, everybody. *Au revoir*, Lara.'

'*Au revoir, Monsieur!*' she chirruped. '*Au revoir!*'

And he was gone.

FIVE

They met at a small, unassuming café behind the Bouffes du Nord, where he was in rehearsals; she, five minutes late, with her hair tucked into a sailor's cap, her eyes hidden behind sunglasses, in a mannish jacket from Yves' new collection and a red scarf draped over her shoulders against the wind; he, five minutes early, in his customary uniform of black velvet jacket, polo-neck and trousers. He thought, when he saw her again after that fleeting moment in the Flore, that his whole life had perhaps been leading up to that second when she walked into Bistro Jules and removed her sunglasses, scanning the room until her eyes – *those eyes* – came to rest on him. It was as if all meaning, all point and purpose, everything he had ever done or said or been, all converged headily into that moment, and then time stopped, and it was just him, Dominique St Clair, and her, Eve Lacloche, in a smoke-filled café whose windows were steaming up in the cold September air. Just the two of them, held in this moment, for ever. She broke the spell, however, by storming over to the table, a blur of red shawl and black hair and green eyes still full of the old fury. He leapt up, but she did not take the seat he offered, choosing to remain standing, with her hands planted questioningly on her hips.

'Eve,' he said. 'Eve, my dear. It's so good to see you.' He leant over to kiss her cheek – how could he help himself? it was only polite – and in the split second before she pulled away, he was overwhelmed by a familiar rush, an aching sensation as the scent of this woman filled his nose and he was hurtled back in time, hurtled back into love. Yes, love. Dominique loved Eve as he had never loved another human soul. And here she was. Real and human, no longer the figment of his dreams or a flickering image on a cinema screen. Flesh and blood. With such fire in her eyes.

'I am so glad you agreed to come,' he said quickly. 'I could not let you leave Paris without seeing you again. Eve, please, sit.' He himself sat down, motioning to the chair opposite his.

'What do you want from me, Dominique?' Eve asked stonily, without moving.

He lit a cigarette. 'Sit down and I will tell you.'

She hesitated a second, but eventually scraped the chair back and sat down. 'I'll give you fifteen minutes. I need to get back to look after Lara.'

'You already know the answer to the question, Eve. Of course you do.'

She shook her head. '*Non.* I refuse to accept that you are not working simply because I am not in Paris. I never heard anything so crazy in my life. Especially after what you did.' She leaned forward and looked him directly in the eye. 'Dominique, you nearly ruined *everything* for me.'

'I *am* working,' Dominique demurred, ignoring her last statement. 'Actually, as a matter of fact I am doing a rather extraordinary *Hamlet* right now. I just don't make films any more. For film, I need you.'

Eve looked down. 'We've been through this,' she muttered, as the waiter appeared at the table.

'Can I at least get you a coffee?'

She sighed. 'Fine. One coffee.' She looked up graciously at the waiter, and Dominique felt his heart skitter as Eve's glorious spirit filled the room like music, so that *everybody* in that café was suddenly turning to stare at her do nothing more remarkable than order an espresso and smile. *Merci.*

'You know you have to stop this, don't you?' Eve said, when the waiter had disappeared. 'You are the best filmmaker in France. I can't stop you working.'

'Then come back to me,' Dominique urged. 'Come back to me.'

She met his gaze coolly. 'I can't come back to you, Dominique. You know why.'

'Why?'

'Why? Because I have a whole life, a husband, in another country.' She reflected on this. She had a husband in another country, that was true, but a whole life?

'So why did you agree to meet me today?' he was goading her. 'Why?'

'I—' Oh, Eve had dreaded the question. Why, indeed? Why had she agreed? Because for that brief time after she had seen him, in the Flore, a little giddy on champagne and sunlight and being on the streets of the Left Bank again, she had dared to dream that one day she might be able to come back to all this. The truth was, when Jacques had held her back as she and her family were leaving the restaurant, long after Dominique had gone, and pressed the little note into her hand, and she had seen the words 'Please, just one coffee. Tomorrow, midday. Bistro Jules – D', she had been too weak to resist. The truth was that Dominique St Clair would always have power over her. It was nothing to do with Dominique himself – Eve had long grown out of that girlish dalliance – no, it was what Dominique *created*, the stories he told; the way he in turn enabled her to tell them without either of them quite knowing how or why. Something happened, some inexplicable magic, when Dominique and Eve made films together, and everybody knew it. It happened when they made films together in French – *Le Retour*, when she was just twenty-one, a month out of the Conservatoire; *Quand J'embrasse le Ciel*, which had made them both famous, and of course, *La Belle Hélène*. It happened when they made films together in English – *Blue Gardenia*, *Once More in Eden*, *Remembering the Rain*. It would probably have happened, Eve reflected ruefully, if they had made a film together in gobbledegook. Theirs was simply one of the great filmmaking collaborations, beyond language, beyond even subject matter, and the truth was – oh, God, oh, God, the truth! – that she missed working with him. Missed telling those stories, creating those worlds.

And yet to talk of creation . . . ! Her hands flying instinctively to the almost imperceptible bump of her stomach, Eve gnawed at her lip and reminded herself why she must not allow herself to be sucked back in by Dominique and his promises. She thought of the baby growing inside her – her and Oliver's baby, *their* creation – and remembered the jeopardy that this man, *this very man*, had thrown her into the last time she'd been having a child. How could any film, even the most beautiful film in the world, compare to that? Eve took a sip of coffee and told her heart to be still. Her love for Oliver was everything, her *raison d'être*. She had known it the first night she had seen him, at the *Phèdre* gala dinner. She had known it the day he'd threatened to leave her in Paris, no thanks to Dominique St Clair, and she had suddenly been faced with the prospect of a future without him. And still she knew it today, more so than ever before, even though she was now sitting opposite a man who represented so many of her hopes and dreams – a man who represented an alternative past, and therefore a possible future?

'I came,' Eve answered, her voice steady, 'to tell you, face to face, that you must leave me alone. You must not write to me any more. You must not send me scripts. You must just let me be. Let us all be. I am pregnant again, Dominique.'

Dominique felt his chest tighten. 'Again?' he asked feebly.

'Yes, I am having another child. You nearly destroyed my life the last time I was pregnant, so I am asking you now to respect me, and respect my family.'

Eve crossed her hands in front of her and Dominique caught sight of her hand in close-up, remembering with a wrench of regret its long, elegant fingers, its lovely almond-shaped nails. He had shot that hand so many times on film, let his camera linger over it, caress it in a way he wished his lips could. Eve had an uncanny knack of apparently being completely still on camera, yet able to convey with a mere eyelash or fingernail precisely the emotion she was feeling, or wanted the audience to believe she was feeling. This great stillness, this extraordinary capacity to emote so silently and subtly, was just one of the things that made her a supreme actress. Dominique thought of the shot in *Hélène*, when Eve is left alone towards the end of the film, and how he had decided on a whim to focus on her hand, rather than her face, as she touched the balcony, and how everybody on set had thought he was mad, could not understand what he was doing, why he would waste a shot on a hand when he could have *that* face; but in that one shot, Eve had managed to transmit the whole weight and tragedy of what had just occurred. In the end, that was the moment that made the film, and he was hailed as a genius. But it was all Eve. With the touch of a trembling finger, she had made his name.

Contemplating this, Dominique no longer felt merely sad, or lovesick – he felt quite furious. 'It is a crime, you know,' he could not stop himself from blurting.

'A crime?' Eve echoed in disbelief. 'A crime to have another child?' She frowned. 'Sometimes I think you are sick, Dominique, and you know what? I'm not even angry with you any more. I am just so, so sad for you.'

'A crime that you are not working,' Dominique corrected, lighting another cigarette. 'You know what I mean, Eve.'

She looked at him, her eyes at first angry – and then, instants later, blurring. 'Don't,' she whispered. 'Please, don't do this. You know why I cannot . . . I just cannot.'

'No, Eve. I have no idea why. It seems to me to be a tragic waste of your talent, and of what you and I both know you need.' Dominique placed his hand under Eve's lowered chin and raised her face gently so he could look into her eyes. 'I know you, Evie Cécile, remember. I understand you, better than anyone.'

Eve held his gaze, transfixed for a second, then wrenched her head away. 'No!' she growled. '*Not* better than anyone . . . Not better than Oliver.'

159

The irony that this might not be so struck Eve bitterly, and she felt a great leadenness drag at her heart. She stood up in a rush and swept her new jacket around her shoulders, fishing in her purse for a franc note.

Dominique grabbed her arm. 'Eve, please, sit down. I'm sorry. Please. I say this to you not because I want any of that any more.' He made a dismissive gesture. 'You made your choice, Eve, so very publicly, and I have my dignity, I have my pride. I will not beg you to be with me.' He folded his arms and gave the slightest of sniffs. 'And I am sorry for any pain I caused you in the past. I swear I am. I did stupid, foolish things as a young, proud man, and I am sorry.' He leant forward. 'But you are a great artist, Eve, a truly great artist, and I will *not* allow myself to stand back and watch you waste your life like this. I have to say this to you, as someone who recognises what you are. *Who you are*. I look into your eyes, Eve, and I see that a little piece of you has died. And I am *grieving* for that little piece.' He leant back and paused theatrically. 'I know how to find it again, but you have to come back to me.'

Eve felt the blood humming in her ears, heard the low murmur of chatter from the tables around them, the clink of spoon against coffee cup, faint music coming from somewhere behind the bar. The café smelt of stale smoke and fresh bread. She forced herself to breathe. Dominique was looking at her with such tenacity in his eyes that she felt quite weak in his gaze.

'You have to trust me,' he said, taking her hand again. This time, she did not pull it away but let it lie there, limp, in his. 'I know what you need.'

'How dare you—' she tried to admonish him, then hung her head in mute desperation. What good was admonishment when they both knew he was right?

160

There was a charged silence, and then, very softly, Dominique started to speak again. 'I have a project,' he said, 'a beautiful, beautiful story I was given a couple of years ago. I have been holding on to it because I swore I would never make another film without you, and because this is the film that we need to make together. Knowing how you would feel about it, Evie, I have kept it, I have told the producers I am still considering it, because I don't want anybody else to direct it and I don't want anybody else to star in it. It's for you and me, Eve, this film, I swear to you. It's called *Si Ça C'est Un Jour*. You'll read it and you'll understand what I'm saying, and we'll make it, we'll do it here, in Paris, quickly, this winter, before you have your baby. We'll do it and it will be something so precious, and it will give you back the little piece of you that died, it will give you back your light, and then, I don't care, go back to your Englishman, follow him around the world, do whatever you want. But make this film with me soon. Come back to me, if only this once. One more time, Evie. *Eve.*'

She put a hand to her mouth and he saw a tear gleam in the corner of her eye as she slowly shook her head.

'Don't you understand?' she pleaded, her voice a broken husk. 'I am not *that Eve* any more. I cannot be *that Eve* any more. So please. Don't ever ask me this again. Soon I will leave Paris and go back to my husband, and I will live in Beirut and I will have my child and I will live that life, the life that I *chose . . .*'

The tear escaped down her cheek and Dominique watched her brush it frantically away, aware, now, that he could be a character in one of his own films. He imagined how gorgeous this scene would look: he'd pull away from the two lovers at the table, a crane shot, revealing a sparkling Paris beyond the heartbreak . . .

Eve had stood up and pulled on her little hat, and the fact that she was really leaving him made Dominique snap out of his reverie. He went to grab her arm again but this time Eve yanked it away. 'No!' she cried. 'You have to help me. If you really care about me, as you say you do, you have to *help* me, Dominique. I can't *do* this any more.' She took a deep, racked breath and moved to the door. 'Goodbye, Dominique,' she whispered. 'Goodbye.'

The following morning, Eve let out an anguished shriek as Colette placed the newspaper in front of her daughter. Bernard had taken Lara down the road to the Champ de Mars to look for conkers, and Eve had slept late, rising with a renewed sense of purpose as she banished the conversation with Dominique from her mind and allowed the knowledge that she was pregnant to sink in all over again. The contentment it created spread warmly through her body and made her want to sing.

But now, just half an hour later, singing was the last thing she wanted to do. On the front cover of *Le Monde* there was a shot of Eve and Dominique from yesterday, taken on a long lens through the café window. They were clutching each other's hands and looking into each other's eyes; even she could see why it looked like some kind of tryst. *Damn* those photographers, Eve cursed. Damn them! They were so *clever*. They must literally have have had their lenses trained on her and Dominique throughout their entire meeting and caught them, SNAP!, just at her moment of weakness when she had allowed Dominique to hold onto her hand before she left. It had not occurred to Eve before, but that was certainly a benefit of being a diplomat's wife in a faraway country: no paparazzi stalking you from across the street. She sighed. Underneath the grainy photo, she read the caption.

Le Retour? Eve Lacloche was back in Paris yesterday, alone, for a clandestine meeting with Dominique St Clair. What can this mean? Are the great actress and director planning another film together? Or perhaps a different kind of relationship? Ms Lacloche's husband, a British diplomat, was nowhere to be seen. Turn to p. 3.

She flung down the paper in rage as Colette poured a mug of coffee and rubbed her daughter's shoulders.

'I'm sorry, Evie, *ma chérie*,' Colette said. 'But I thought you should see it.'

Eve stared at the photograph again, then pushed the paper away. 'I don't want to know what they wrote inside,' she croaked, then looked up at her mother pathetically. 'Is it really bad?'

Colette made a clucking noise. 'It's just the usual nonsense,' she soothed. 'Don't worry. Everybody will have forgotten about it by tomorrow.'

'The crazy thing is, I was there turning Dominique down again!' Eve cried. 'He offered me a film, he talked about it, said he would even be able to get it moving quickly enough so I could do it over the next few months before I start to show, but I turned him down!' A hideous thought crossed her mind and her heart began to pound. 'And now *Oliver* will see this, and he's going to think the only reason I came back to Paris . . . oh, *God*, and I'm . . .'

'Ssh, my darling,' Colette urged again, pushing a plate of *pâtisserie* towards her daughter. 'You mustn't panic. Oliver is not going to think anything. For a start, he trusts you, but more to the point, he's not even going to *see* it. Who's going to be reading *Le Monde* all the way over there, eh? Now, calm down and eat, please.'

'I'm not hungry,' Eve said, sullenly.

'*Bof!*' exclaimed Colette. 'I won't have such nonsense talked in my house. Remember, you are eating for two again, now. And you're far too skinny as usual. Eat!'

Eve knew better than to fight with her mother about food, and so, like a grudging teenager, she picked up a croissant and ate.

SIX

Oliver was surprised when Roula called through to his office and told him she had Jeremy Weldon, the deputy head of mission, on the line. 'What on earth does he want?' he asked.

'I don't know, Monsieur, but it sounds pretty urgent.'

'We'd better not keep him waiting, then. Put him through, please.'

'Latner?' he heard after a second.

'DHM. How goes it?'

'Not bad. Listen, old chap, sorry to have to call you up about this but it seems we have a bit of a problem.'

'A problem?'

'Mmm. Bit of a sensitive matter, I'm afraid. Any chance you could pop in later and we'll have a little chat?'

'A little . . . ? Um, sure. What time would you like me?'

'Four okay?'

Oliver scanned the diary on his desk. 'Four's fine,' he said. 'I'll see you there.'

'Capital.'

Replacing the receiver, Oliver scratched his head and tried to work out why Jeremy Weldon would possibly be calling him into his office. It couldn't be about the promotion already, could it? He felt a rush of adrenalin at the prospect, then told himself to stop being so foolish: the bidding process wasn't even due to kick off until November. Unless Weldon was leaving early. He'd said it was a sensitive matter . . .

For the rest of the afternoon he racked his brains over what it could be about, but was none the wiser when the time came to knock on the door of the deputy's rather grander office.

'Drink?'

'Just water, thanks.'

Oliver watched as Jeremy Weldon poured one glass of water and one generous Scotch, and found himself wondering again how anyone in the senior echelons of the Office ever got any work done on post, the amount of alcohol they consumed in the afternoons. 'Thanks,' he said, as Weldon passed him his glass and walked over to the window.

'Terrible what's going on, isn't it?' the deputy head began.

'You mean at the camps? I know. Shocking business.'

'You wonder how it's all going to end, don't you? Seems so bloody irreconcilable. Even I find myself losing track.'

Oliver allowed himself a polite chuckle. 'Indeed,' he said. 'It's hard to keep up sometimes, everyone shifting allegiances and betraying each other all the time. I have trouble trying to explain it to my wife.'

Weldon turned away from the window then and leant his ample frame against the wall. 'Ah, your wife. The lovely Eve.'

Oliver took a sip of water.

'Funnily enough, dear boy,' Weldon continued, 'that's the reason I've got you in here.'

Oliver took a second to register what he had just heard, trying to make sense of it. 'Oh – the reason . . . You mean, all the sectarian stuff?'

Weldon shook his head. ''Fraid not. Your wife, actually.'

Oliver placed his water glass carefully on the coaster beside him. 'My wife?' he said, in a measured voice. 'Eve? What's she . . . ?'

'Mmm. Seems there's been a bit of business.'

'What do you mean, business?'

Weldon crossed the study and settled himself into the chair behind the desk, reasserting his authority over the younger diplomat. 'I hear she's abroad at the moment.'

'That's right. She, er, she took our daughter to Paris to see her grandparents. They'll be coming back next week.'

Weldon nodded thoughtfully. 'Listen, dear boy, there's no easy way to say this. I'm afraid somebody has filed an official complaint about your wife. And unfortunately, as your line manager, it falls upon me to break the news to you.'

Oliver was stunned, wondering if he'd heard correctly. If they'd got the wrong wife. '*Eve?*' he managed, eventually.

Weldon nodded again. 'Eve,' he confirmed.

'What kind of complaint?' Oliver asked, ears hot, cheeks burning. 'And who, may I ask, made it?'

'Mary Longstaff.'

'*Mary Longstaff?*'

'Yes. Mary Longstaff. Well, Rupert made the complaint, really, but on behalf of Mary. I'm afraid it's rather delicate.' Weldon took a sip of his Scotch and regretted that he had to do this. He liked

Latner, they all did, and as for that wife of his – well, she was a beauty. But it had to be done. The complaint had been registered through official channels, and after the latest news that had come through from Paris today via the FCO press office, he now had no choice. 'It seems Mrs Longstaff believes your wife has tried, on a number of occasions, to proposition her husband.'

Oliver laughed out loud then, relieved beyond belief. Clearly it was all a gross mistake. 'Proposition *Rupert*?' he exclaimed, the tension evaporating from his face. 'Mary Longstaff thinks Eve's been trying it on with her husband? Well, honestly, Jeremy, I've never heard anything so ridiculous in my life. Really. Surely this is a joke?'

But Weldon was not smiling. 'I'm afraid not, old boy. Mary's accused Eve of . . . Let's see.' He fished around on his desk for the relevant document. 'Of being rude to her, of, um, apparently *pulling faces* behind her back in public?' He looked up quizzically. 'And of propositioning her husband. She says Rupert has had to "deal with Mrs Latner constantly pestering" him to meet her.' He looked back down again. 'And she claims that on three separate occasions Eve has tried to, er, actually seduce her husband. Sorry.'

Oliver stood up, blood rushing to his head. '*I'm* sorry, sir. I just . . . Well I'm not sure what to say. I happen to know that this is complete tosh. What does Mary Longstaff's official complaint mean? Presumably they have to produce some sort of evidence. And presumably Eve gets a chance to defend herself, does she? I mean, what happens now?'

Weldon stood up and walked around the desk to face Oliver. 'For the moment, it's just a caution, Latner. The board won't need to take it any further so long as there are no more complaints from the Longstaffs. But we had another piece of news that came through on the wire today. Apparently there were a few reports about Eve in a French newspaper yesterday, all gossipy things, probably nothing, but, you see, the thing is they actually mentioned you and the embassy by *name*, which is why the press office picked up on it, of course. Not ideal timing.' Oliver's face paled and Weldon patted his arm. 'All I'm saying, old chap, is I'd be *very* careful, if I were you. You're well liked in the Office, Latner, and you could go far. I know your wife is not exactly one of us, different breed of people those actresses, and we'd all hate to see her ruin things for you. Do you understand what I'm saying?' He held out his hand for Oliver to shake and the younger man stared at it for a second. His mouth felt completely dry, his heart was beating fast, and he still had an urge to laugh, because surely the whole thing was completely absurd. *Eve and Rupert?* Eve was pregnant again, for God's sake – she'd rung to tell him a few days ago!

But what was it that had come out of Paris today? *Probably nothing*, Weldon had said. Probably nothing?

He stood up and shook his senior's hand. 'Thank you, DHM. I understand completely.'

Eve had been rejecting Dominique's telephone calls and had tucked away – unopened, in a box that already contained reams of his past correspondence – every one of the letters that had arrived in his spidery script since the day after the Bistro Jules rendezvous. Furious with herself that she could not simply destroy them, throw them into the fireplace or rip them up and flutter the pieces to the wind over the Seine, she nevertheless could not bring herself to see what he'd written. Had he tipped off the press that day, in a bid to stoke up all the old chaos? Who knew? It did not even matter now, anyway. She had made up her mind that she would never have anything to do with him again. Ever.

Fearful of the paparazzi who lurked outside, and the journalists who had also been calling, day in day out, since the 'story' had broken in *Le Monde*, Eve rarely left the apartment over the next few days, allowing Colette and Bernard to take Lara to the park or shopping for groceries or a new pair of mittens while she curled up on the sofa in her parents' sitting room, writing in her diary and listening to her father's records as she gazed silently out of the window while the light slowly faded from the city and the air turned grey.

One afternoon Lara came back cold-cheeked and red-nosed from playing in Champ de Mars and hopped onto the sofa next to her, saying, 'Mummy, why are all those men waiting outside our house?'

Eve didn't know how to answer, as she stroked her child's shiny dark hair and let her fingers touch the unimaginably soft skin of her neck. She opened her mouth, but said nothing.

Her mother stepped in to assist. 'One day,' Colette ventured, 'when you're a big girl, you can see Maman on the television screen, because she used to be an actress.' Eve winced at her mother's unthinking use of the past tense as Colette tried patiently to explain to a confused Lara, who was looking between her mother and the small television in the corner of the room, why hordes of rapacious photographers were lining a corner of avenue Bosquet beneath them.

Early the next morning, the day Eve and Lara were due to leave for the airport, Dominique himself turned up outside the apartment. Bernard had just been out to load the luggage into the boot of the Citroën and came back into the kitchen with the news.

'What am I supposed to do now?' Eve cursed. She'd been battling a vicious headache all morning and was feeling sick and unsteady on her feet. 'The press will go fucking crazy.' Colette cleared her throat and raised an eyebrow towards Lara, who was in her coat and sitting at the table crayoning a goodbye drawing for her grandparents, humming to herself and apparently oblivious to her mother's language.

'Sorry,' Eve muttered, scraping her hands through her hair. 'I just can't believe he'd be so . . . so *selfish* as to turn up here now. He knows what they're like.' She crossed her arms. 'But what am I talking about? It's Dominique. Of *course* he would be so selfish.'

'I didn't see any photographers down there this morning, Evie,' Bernard said. 'It's very early. Just St Clair.'

'Well, that's a relief,' said Colette. 'Perhaps they've got bored and have finally gone home. *Chérie*, I think you should stop worrying. We'll all go down now, you can talk to him, see what he wants, and then we'll get in the car and go.'

'I know what he wants.' Eve sighed.

On the way to Charles de Gaulle she sat in the back next to Lara and stared out of the car window, clutching the script that Dominique had thrust into her hands out on avenue Bosquet until her fingers turned white. Its cover was a bare page with the words *Si Ça C'est Un Jour* typewritten on it. *If this is a day*. Colette and Lara were singing French nursery rhymes so loudly and merrily that Eve had to bite her lip to stop herself screaming, '*Shut up! Shut up!*' She felt so wrong, so sick. She wondered how she would get through the journey back to the Middle East. The weather had turned, and she watched as sheets of sleety rain fell from a leaden sky onto her city. Her city, but the city she was leaving. She tried to think about Oliver waiting at the other end, how just the sight of him would restore her to herself again, but he had been so brusque with her on the telephone for the past few days, curtailing their conversations with a snap and telling her he was very busy (as if she needed reminding of *that*). Why couldn't he sound happier about the baby? He'd been so delighted when she'd first told him. Why couldn't he be kinder to her, gentler to her, nicer to her? When she heard him address her in that tone of voice, that snippy, short, oh-so-*decorous* voice, as if she were merely an errant member of his staff, she wanted to give up.

Eve blinked, and still the rain fell, turning the river a liquid slate and the pavements glossy. She felt her eyelids prickle. *Il pleure dans mon coeur/Comme il pleut sur la ville*, she thought to herself, the lines of Verlaine once learnt as a schoolgirl arriving in her consciousness like a mournful ghost. *Quelle est cette langueur/Qui pénètre mon coeur?* And the thought, then, that she would never know, never understand what it was – her own 'langueur', a desolation that always lurked in some corner of her soul, threatening to blacken it completely, turning the world dark for apparently no reason and making her want to stop everything, just *stop* – caused Eve's throat to tighten and her heart to pound. In a catastrophic flash she had the sensation that she was about to suffocate.

'*Arrêt!*' she gasped from the back seat. Lara and Colette stopped their chanting immediately, while Bernard's eyes shot up to the rear-view mirror. Eve was tugging madly at the door. 'Papa, stop, please.'

'What is it?' Colette cried, as Bernard pulled over and Eve flung herself out, dropping the script onto the glistening road. She threw up violently on the pavement, and again, and again, before finally gasping for breath and leaning against a lamp-post to steady herself against the spots of blackness that danced vertiginously in front of her eyes. She started to take another gulp of air, holding her face up to the cool rain, but the sickness came again, in a great furious lurch, and the last thing Eve felt, before she collapsed on the rain-darkened ground and the world went black, was the excruciating pain of her stomach in spasm.

SEVEN

After she was released from La Pitié-Salpêtrière, Eve was ordered to remain in Paris until she was stronger and no longer in need of close medical attention. She didn't lose the baby, although she had come very close; the doctors said she'd been extraordinarily lucky. Had Bernard not navigated the car so quickly through the clogged, slippery streets along the Seine to the boulevard de l'Hôpital, the internal haemorrhage that had caused Eve to collapse would have been far worse, and the fragile foetus would not have survived. She had also, they pointed out, been almost miraculously lucky not to hit her head. While Eve and her unborn child recuperated, the media interest in her presence in the city reached fever pitch: reporters turned up at the hospital; photographers hovered on the street outside; flowers, fashion, cards and other gifts were sent to her bedside every day. Oliver made his excuses in Beirut – diabolical timing, but what could he do? – and flew directly to Paris, but this only made the press furore worse: every morning, as he skimmed the French papers trying to keep an eye on what was going on in Lebanon, let alone elsewhere in the world, he was greeted with more gossip about Eve and Dominique; more photographs taken of them holding hands, embracing, during what was so obviously this trip; more snide comments about *le rosbif diplomatique* and speculation about their marriage, even though their concern and support for his wife never wavered. It was as if they *wanted* the marriage to fail, thought Oliver bitterly – as if this vindicated their pro-Dominique stance all those years ago ...

After a fortnight, when Eve's condition had stabilised and he could not stand to be in Paris among the whispers and the mocking any more, Oliver used the worsening situation in Lebanon as an excuse to take his leave, promising to return again as soon as possible. His decision made Eve, who had been instructed by her doctors to remain in France, weep. Although she heard her husband's 'rational' explanation for his departure, his decision – after the blissful comfort of his presence for the past two weeks – felt so heartless, and his absence made her desperate, further slowing her recovery.

For days she lay, at first in her hospital cot and then in her old bed back in her parents' apartment, incapable of doing much but cry – she cried and cried until her eyes were dry, and then she cried some more. She had been forbidden by her doctors to smoke, of course, forbidden to drink, forbidden this and forbidden that, but she had no appetite to do anything anyway. No appetite for anything at all. Each day Colette would come into Eve's room at regular intervals to bring her soup and juice or turn on the radio, and Lara would jump onto her bed with new drawings, or sing new songs she had learnt at the day-nursery Oliver had enrolled her in down the road when Eve had refused to let him take Lara back to Beirut without her. But she could barely even find the energy to smile and kiss her daughter, or mutter a thank-you to her mother.

She felt drained again, like she had done in the worst periods in Beirut, except this was so much worse. She was empty now: empty of everything except this hollow pain; this terrifying black, hollow pain. Allowing Colette to spoon food into her mouth after a stern lecture that she really would lose the baby unless she started to take in some nourishment for both of them, Eve wondered numbly if it might have been better if she had lost the child. Useless as she was, what good would she be in this world to another helpless baby?

For his part, Oliver had still not told Eve about the official complaint filed by the Longstaffs. It seemed unnecessarily cruel to do so now, when she wasn't even in the country, and although he was anxious about his wife's health, and missed her, he thought it was probably fortunate she wasn't in Beirut at the moment. Just as the gossip about him had been malicious in Paris, so it was becoming unbearable about her in Beirut: Mary Longstaff's ridiculous slurs had been inflated by the other wives – who, with nothing better to do than read the French magazines on sale in the international cafés in the Gemmayzeh, were apparently now convinced that *none* of their husbands was safe in the presence of 'that froggy slut'.

Oliver found himself bristling under the stares of his colleagues and their women – some sympathetic, some mocking, some clearly just bloody delighted that Eve Latner in all her dazzling beauty was clearly not to be trusted; delighted that their 'suspicions' had been right all along. To his shame, he occasionally resented *Eve* for having put him in this position, rather than blaming what he knew to be the insular and petty mentality of the expatriate circle. Feeling perversely thankful that the situation on the ground was so bleak – there had even been rumours that the embassy might have to be evacuated, although he chose, on his daily telephone calls to Eve, not to mention this – Oliver simply put his head down and got on with the job.

Nevertheless, the absence of his wife and child from his everyday life was having a profound effect on him, making his days taut with worry and his nights sleepless. Oliver was particularly concerned, once he'd had the assurances from Eve's doctors that she was still making a steady physical improvement (although they did express some concern for her emotional well-being), about his daughter. When he'd left Lara in Paris she had seemed cheerful enough and was being very well looked after, he had to admit, by Colette and Bernard Lacloche; but after he had heard his daughter crying down the telephone on three successive afternoons because she was 'worried about Mummy', he got Colette back on the phone and suggested that perhaps his own parents might come over to Paris to take Lara to their place in Berkshire for a couple of weeks, give her a change in scene, some fresh air and countryside. But Colette, who took no care to disguise the contempt she clearly felt for her son-in-law's decision not to remain by his wife's bedside for the duration of her recovery, rubbished the idea. 'You want to take Lara away from her mother, now?' she exclaimed, in colourful French. 'Ha! You must be joking.'

His parents, Susan and Thomas, did, in fact, fly over to Paris for a few days, chiefly so they could report back to Oliver about the state of Eve and Lara. They stayed in a small hotel near the apartment and came to visit in the afternoons, bringing colouring books and English stories for their granddaughter, and shop-bought *pâtisseries* that Colette put out sniffily alongside her own fabulous creations. Neither Susan nor Thomas was a superb French speaker – they ran to the odd '*bonjour*' but that was about it – and Colette and Bernard had clearly decided to forget every English word they had ever known for the four days of the visit, so the hours spent in the apartment together *en famille* were somewhat awkward, with an unsuspecting Lara being the only thing to defuse the tension as she chatted away in both languages and performed little dances and songs or routines she had made up.

'Goodness, it looks as though the little one has inherited her mother's talents,' said Thomas, one afternoon, evidently keen to make some sort of conversation. He sipped his tea and clapped appreciatively at his granddaughter's dramatic efforts. Eve, slumped on a chair in the corner of the room with a blanket over her knees, raised her eyes and stared at him. 'Perhaps she'll be following you on to the stage one day, my dear,' he added.

To her incredulity, Eve felt a smile tug at the corner of her mouth – it must have been her first in a month. '*Oh!*' she said, looking back at Lara, who was milking the applause. 'I suppose . . . I never . . .'

But Susan was shutting her husband up. 'God forbid,' she hissed. 'Honestly, Thomas. Don't go putting ideas into the girl's head now, please.'

When Eve's doctors advised that she was strong enough to fly back to Lebanon, they instructed her to do as little as possible for the remaining six months of her pregnancy. 'Nothing to worry about there, then,' Eve scoffed, before thanking them for their care and obligingly signing autographs for the staff.

The following morning, the family climbed back into the Citroën, and this time they made it to Charles de Gaulle with no drama. But as Eve crossed the departures hall in the international terminal with Lara, she suddenly found herself doing a double-take. Because there, lounging by the Air France check-in desk, stood Dominique St Clair. He held a huge bouquet of arum lilies and, she could see, another copy of the script she had dropped into a puddle in the rainy road all those weeks ago.

'How did you know I would be here?' she gasped.

'I've been coming here from time to time,' Dominique explained. 'I knew you'd come one day.'

She looked sceptical.

'Okay, so I know a girl who works at your doctor's clinic. I bribed her to tell me when you'd been discharged.'

Eve shook her head, but nevertheless her hands automatically took the script he pushed into them. 'You amaze me,' she said bitterly. 'You know that? You amaze me.'

Dominique shrugged and bent down towards Lara. 'Well, hello again, Mademoiselle Lara!' He grinned and offered her the bouquet.

She beamed. 'Hello,' she replied in French. 'These are pretty flowers.'

'They are for you, little one.'

'Thank you!' Lara took the lilies excitedly, just as Eve grabbed her up into her arms, holding out a warning finger at Dominique.

'Don't you dare try to use her as – as some kind of *pawn*!' she cried. 'Don't you dare!'

Dominique inclined his head. 'Fine, fine. The lilies are for you, Evie. Read it, just read it – please? That's all I ask.'

Eve turned away from him and smiled at the luggage porter, who was hovering nearby with their baggage. He lifted her cases onto the scales, and she pressed a note into his hand. Then, very calmly, very slowly, without meeting Dominique's eyes, she opened her handbag and took out their passports and tickets, placing

179

them on the desk as Lara wriggled out of her grasp to better play with the luscious flowers.

Finally, Eve turned to face Dominique, holding his script at arm's length towards him. 'I don't need to explain myself to you again. I've told you the reasons why I can't do this, and I need you to respect them.' Her voice trembled. 'I need you to respect me. Something is happening to me ... I can't explain ... I am not myself. But, Dominique, please. I need you to help me. Take this back. Please.'

He crossed his arms, refusing the script.

'Fine,' she said, after a moment. Then she turned back brightly to the attendant behind the desk. '*Alors*. We are ready to check in. Would you mind disposing of this for me?'

Eve placed the script, *Si Ça C'est Un Jour*, on the desk and the bored-looking girl chucked it matter-of-factly into the rubbish bin behind her. 'Madame Latner,' the girl started to intone, 'You're seated in row two ...'

As the security questions were duly recited in front of her, Eve turned, for a final time, to look at Dominique. '*Désolée*,' she whispered.

He thrust his hands into his pockets and looked at her, his customary arrogance vanished, his eyes lost. They stared at each other like that for what seemed like for ever, and then he opened his mouth. 'Comme tu veux, Eve,' he muttered. 'Comme tu veux.'

And then he turned, and was gone.

Eve gazed after the black streak of Dominique's receding back for another moment, her head reeling, before she realised that Lara was tugging at her arm. '*Maman*, that lady's still talking to you.'

Eve cleared her throat and apologised to the attendant. 'Excuse me,' she apologised. And then, biting her lip, she said,

'Actually, I'm so sorry, but would you mind giving me back that script?'

The girl stared at Eve as if she were insane, then slowly, deliberately, got up from her chair, walked over to the bin and fished it out. '*Voilà*,' she said, handing it over. 'You're boarding from gate twelve in half an hour. The first-class lounge is that way.'

'*Merci bien.*'

Eve pulled Lara away from the desk and walked purposefully towards the departures gates, but her legs were shaking and her knees felt as though they might give way beneath her.

'*Maman?*' she heard her daughter asking. '*Maman, Maman?* Why are you crying? *Maman!*'

But Eve could not answer.

Lara was still clutching the white lilies as they climbed onto the plane.

Part Three

Part Three

ONE

Date: 5 September

To: alex.craig@gmail.com

From: llama@gmail.com

Re: Phew!

Hey, sexy. So, have survived Day One. Pretty exhausting. Woke up about 4 and couldn't go back to sleep – thanks to helpful combo of being both shit-scared and jet-lagged. We had a big day: meet-and-greet, read-through, costume fittings, makeup & camera tests, etc – and then afterwards, feeling completely shattered and frankly, terrified, I was *desperate* for someone to just go and have a drink with in t'pub but, there being nobody, and actually not even a pub as such, have instead come home to my VAST empty apartment to unpack properly and try to get my head around it all. (Actually not quite true – could have gone and had a drink with Jessica Cole or some of the other cast at their v. swanky hotel, but I just couldn't really face the whole actor-chat thing, 'oh, I worked with so-and-so last year', 'oh, I worked with him on *blah*', 'Oh, really?', 'who's your agent?' blah, blah.) Not sure I'm going to have any kindred spirits on this film, my love, but that's probably no bad thing anyway given HOW MUCH WORK I'VE GOT TO DO AAAAAAARGH.

I'd forgotten how *scary* doing films with Americans is. Everyone is so serious and earnest – as I suppose you would be with that much money at stake. The read-through was at the company offices in TriBeCa – all chrome and glass and sleek black furniture and whatnot. And I swear, it was like a meeting of the UN General Assembly. We each had microphones and posh water and were arranged in order of importance – so there's me, sitting centre stage, in front of about a million Armani-suited exec producers, in practically every frickin' scene, fretting about me accent, me performance, me everything, wondering whether they're going to sack me straight away . . . Apparently they held a cast and crew screening of *La Belle Helene* here last week – thank God I hadn't arrived yet, that would've really done my head in – so I couldn't stop thinking that everyone must be comparing me to Mum already and being like, oh, great, we have to work with *her* instead . . .

Think it went okay, though. Think. Always hard to tell – read-throughs are so weird and anticlimactic, nobody actually does any 'acting' as such so it's hard to get a feel for what people's performances will really be like. The new script's fantastic, though, and Kevin was great – made a nice little speech at the end and was sweetly v. kind to me. The crew seem top-notch – in fact Graham Bell, the DP (that's their way of saying Director of Photography) shot one of your favourite films, *Point of Departure*, so you'll have to chat to him about it when you come out. The writer Martin introduced himself to me afterwards and I half wanted to throw my arms around him and say, 'Thank you so much for writing the best script I've ever read,' and half wanted to punch him and say, 'Why, why, why did you have to write such a perfect script and tempt me into doing this crazy thing?!?!??!?!' Because I still feel so conflicted, Al, about this project. I KNOW you'll tell me I've made the right decision and must now just get on with it, but I can't help this feeling of – well, abject terror really . . .

Tomorrow evening I'm due to meet that woman I told you about, Sabine de Sévigné, who worked as costume designer on the original film and who's acting as a consultant on this one, so that should be interesting – bit nervous – then the next day we start shooting (main studio is in Brooklyn but we're doing lots of stuff out on location too) – very nervous. Guess who's first up on the first day?? Old Muggins here. Thank f*ck it's not *the* most important scene that we're starting with. You always pray that your first day's shooting doesn't contain your first scene, your last scene or your big scene, but on this film I have so many big scenes it's quite remarkable that I'm not kicking the whole thing off with tears and drama!!

Baby, I can't WAIT for you to come out and see this apartment. It's in boring and deeply uncool (but v convenient) midtown, but with the most sensational views, which I suspect I will spend a lot of time staring at. You'll be appalled to learn that I've been assigned my own personal assistant, Madison, as well as a driver, Bobby – poor Madison, she's as nervous as I am! I think her job description is literally 'Do whatever Lara tells you to do and ask no questions.' It's crazy – I think the production were even surprised they had to 'provide' me with one: apparently most actors simply turn up with their own in tow, having had it written into their contract that this PA will fly first class, get all the perks, and generally be the go-to-guy between the star and the plebs. (Of course I told them they didn't have to provide one, before you get all antsy, but by then Madison was already in their employ, and they would not let me refuse her 'vital assistance' . . .) It seems that if you are 'Number One on the Call Sheet' in the US, i.e. the lead in the film, you just *have* to have a personal assistant. Gosh, I don't know how us Brits ever coped without one!

Wish you were awake so we could have a proper chat, but it's the middle of the night for you and I hope you're sleeping tight. I miss you lots and hope all is OK at work, I know you said you had a really heavy couple of weeks coming up on those cases. I should probably go to bed myself now – another early start tomorrow for final costume fittings, etc., and if I sleep as badly as I did last night I'm going to need all the hours I can get. Bleurgh.

Love you, chicken. Say hi to everyone from me, and write soon xxL

Lara pressed send and shut down her laptop, then walked over to the panoramic windows of her living room to lean her nose against the floor-to-ceiling glass. Her apartment was on the seventy-seventh floor of a building halfway down Lexington Avenue and the vertiginous midtown view was like a ludicrous cliché of New York. She could see the outlines of the Empire State and Chrysler Buildings and a hundred other skyscrapers etched against the night, the grand sweep of the avenues clasping the precious green lung of Central Park, bridge lights blinking across the Hudson and East Rivers. If she turned and looked through another window she could see right down to the southernmost tip of the island, to the financial district where Dan and Lucy, her high-flying English friends who'd been headhunted across the Pond, were probably still toiling away, even at this hour, around the ghostly vortex of cranes and construction where the World Trade Center towers had once stood. Lara felt quite peaceful, suspended up here, insulated from the hoot and roar of the chaos below as she gazed out at the galaxy of lights across and beneath her. And how strange it was, she contemplated, that somebody in one of the other skyscrapers over the avenue might at this very moment happen to be glancing at her own glass box, just as she might be glancing at theirs, yet neither of them would ever know. They were that inessential to the life of the city. All of them. Feeling a little rush of freedom, Lara took a last glance at the glittering metropolis spread out beneath her like so many scattered diamonds on velvet, pressed the relevant button on the 'atmosphere' remote control, and marvelled again as the blinds dropped instantly to cocoon her within the room's creamy walls.

Sabine de Sévigné was a small, elegant, grey-haired *Parisienne* who had moved to New York more than twenty years ago after her first marriage had ended in bitter divorce when she fell in love with an American art dealer. In her heyday Sabine had been one of the great costume designers of the era and had worked on a number of classic French films, including, almost thirty years ago, the Dominique St Clair masterpiece *La Belle Hélène*. Kevin Goldberg, a fervent admirer of de Sévigné's work in theatre and film, had tracked her down two years ago to tell her he was soon to be going into production with a remake of *La Belle Hélène* in English, set in modern-day New York. Would she perhaps be prepared to act as a consultant on the film, he had asked her over coffee at the Algonquin – and, better yet, even oversee the costume design?

Sabine had raised an artfully groomed eyebrow and said she would have to think about it: he must know she was working on fewer and fewer films these days? (Secretly Sabine was wondering if this young man, with his greasy hair and tatty leather jacket, really had it in him to treat that wonderful story with the requisite sensitivity.) But she had agreed, graciously, to stay in touch; and as the weeks had gone past and Kevin had eagerly kept her abreast of developments on *This Being Human*, sending her script drafts and storyboards, she had been increasingly compelled by the idea of working on the project. When Goldberg's short film had won the Oscar, she'd been impressed; when his first feature, *Retributive Justice*, had pre-screened at the Lincoln Center, she'd been overwhelmed. And when he'd rung her to tell her that Eve Lacloche's daughter, Lara Latner, had just been attached to play the part of Helen – well, that was when her decision had been made.

Sabine had seen pictures of the girl, of course. Although she had yet to make a name for herself in America, she was enough of a media fascination already to have warranted reviews in the *New York Times* of her performance in a London play – and she knew there was a more than passing resemblance in the girl's face to her mother. But she was not prepared for the shock of seeing Kevin Goldberg walk through the door of the Bull and Bear at the Waldorf Astoria, followed by this Lara. Despite an unmistakably English air of scruffiness and a somewhat taller frame, Lara was absolutely the image of her mother – she was Eve, as Eve had once been, twenty-eight years ago. The presence of this ghost-made-flesh in the room rendered Sabine, usually the very essence of composure, tongue-tied and emotional as she stood up to greet the pair.

'Hi, Sabine,' Kevin was saying, kissing her cheek. 'This is Lara. Lara Latner – Sabine de Sévigné.'

'Why – hello. *Bonjour*,' Sabine managed to utter, as Eve's daughter smiled earnestly at her. 'Lara – yes, of course. *Enchantée*!'

'I'm so pleased to meet you too,' Lara agreed warmly, shaking her hand. 'Kevin's told me you've been such an enormous help putting together the film, and from what I've seen, the costumes look fantastic.'

Sabine had to stop herself staring at the girl's face as she murmured a little something in response and they sat down. But it *was* quite extraordinary. The bone structure was so familiar. Those impossibly high cheekbones, that magnificent mouth, the eyes. Becoming aware that Kevin was talking to her, asking her what she wanted to drink, Sabine eventually drew her eyes away from Lara's haunting face. Yet even as she busied herself with a glance at the wine list, her hand shot out to give the girl's hand a quick squeeze, in a warm and spontaneous gesture that spoke intuitively to Lara of the possibility of confidences to come.

'I'll have white wine,' Sabine announced. 'The Burgundy, please, Kevin.'

'Sure. We'll get a glass of the white Burgundy?' said Kevin to the waiter. 'And I'll get a beer, thanks, a Bud. Lara?'

'Think I'll stick to Coke,' Lara said, with a wry grin. 'First day of shooting tomorrow and all that.'

'But of course!' Sabine exclaimed, in her silvered, whispery voice. 'So tell me, Kevin dear, how are you feeling? How are you both feeling? Excited?'

Kevin lounged back in his chair, the very picture of relaxation. 'I am so psyched,' he said, rubbing his hands together. 'I cannot *wait* to get on that set tomorrow.'

'Well, I'm a *bit* more nervous than he is,' Lara confessed to Sabine. 'A bit . . . terrified, in fact.'

'Oh, but you must not be!' Sabine said.

'Of course she mustn't,' agreed Kevin. 'She's going to melt that screen. Just you wait, Sabine.'

'I have no doubt!'

'We'll see about that,' said Lara, drily, grabbing a handful of peanuts.

'It's funny,' said Sabine. 'Your mother – I remember, she never used to get nervous. Nobody could understand it. Even before the most taxing of scenes, she would not seem even the tiniest bit anxious. She was the most relaxed actress – or actor, for that matter – I ever saw work. You know we did *Quand J'embrasse le Ciel* together too, before *La Belle Hélène*? *When I Kiss the Sky*.' She sighed. 'Ah, she was beautiful in that film . . . beautiful. And, truly, she'd be chatting away to some lowly runner between takes – she was *very* focused, but she would always be so friendly to everybody – and then the cameras would start to roll and the most extraordinary transformation would take place and that would be it! Those performances just seemed to come out of nowhere. And no two takes were ever the same, she did something different every time. It really lifted everybody else's performances, too, because they always had to be on their guard. It was such a privilege to watch, to be present on a set when you knew something magical was happening before your very eyes.'

Now it was Lara's turn to stare at Sabine. This neat, smiling Frenchwoman who smelt of powder and perfume, as familiar as her grandmother, had actually been *on set* to witness her mother's greatest acting moments. She had been there, she'd seen it. The thought made Lara's stomach somersault. 'Well, I'm afraid that's definitely not me.' She laughed. 'I mean, I love filming, but I do get very nervous.'

'Well, you're going to be just fabulous,' Kevin told her decisively. 'Just fabulous.'

'Of course she is!' Sabine agreed, beaming. 'Now, Lara, Kevin said you might have some questions about *La Belle Hélène*? Anything you want to ask me, please, I am always here. I won't be on set every day, of course – I'm a little old for all that now.' She smiled, then tapped her head. 'But this still works quite well. And I have so many memories. So many things to talk about, if you would like to.'

'Yes!' Lara breathed. 'Thank you. Yes – yes, I'd love to.'

'Oh, and photographs, of course,' Sabine added. 'Don't forget, I have so many photographs, many, many albums. All the original costume-department photographs and continuity sketches, and some of my own pictures, too. I always loved to document my work. You are most welcome to come to my house and see them, *chérie*, any time. My husband Frank and I live on the Upper East Side . . .'

Lara's heart jumped at the thought of what Sabine had just said as she vaguely heard the Frenchwoman give an address somewhere up in the Nineties, Carnegie Hill or somewhere. *Photographs.* 'Thank you, Sabine,' she managed in response. 'Thank you. I'd – I'd love to come and see them. It would mean the world to me.'

'*Parfait.* Well, I won't expect you for the next few weeks. I've seen how busy your shooting schedule is!' Sabine elbowed Kevin with a grin. 'But any time you would like, Lara, you can just call. I am always here.'

That night, Lara was as wide awake as the legendarily insomniac metropolis that hummed seventy-seven storeys below her. Tossing and turning in the crisp white linen sheets in her unfamiliar apartment, her body was crying out for rest but her mind was increasingly alert. She was used to pre-shoot jitters, especially the night before filming started, but the rawness and intensity of these particular nerves was new. Every time Lara closed her eyes she saw images of *La Belle Hélène* and felt the fear clutch at her chest again. She wondered how on earth she was going to play this part. Tomorrow. Filming was starting *tomorrow*. Somehow, over the past few weeks, she had talked herself into the idea that by the time it came around to 'turning over' she'd be ready, prepared, calm. She'd know what she was doing. After all, she had played leads before, she'd reminded herself, not quite in Hollywood movies, it was true, but *The Chronicles of Mary* was definitely 'her' show and she was used, as an actress, to carrying big scenes and having a lot of responsibility on set. She'd read and reread her script to the point that she could almost quote the stage directions by heart; she'd thought so hard about her character Helen, so different from herself in her whimsy and lethal ability to deceive and manipulate; she'd watched *La Belle Hélène* more times than was probably helpful, scrutinising her mother's performance and mentally absorbing what Eve had created, apparently effortlessly, in Hélène, gearing herself up to try to do something similar with her own Helen. But now here it was, a few hours away, the start of the shoot – and despite all the preparation, Lara didn't feel ready for what she was about to embark upon at all. Instead, she felt quite petrified.

Rolling onto the other side of the bed, in case the coolness of a fresh pillow and the untouched half of the sheet might help calm her, Lara tried to remind herself sensibly that when she walked into that studio in Brooklyn tomorrow morning, it would be no different from walking into any other studio. Film sets were universal, and she knew the drill as well as anybody. Pick-up. Trailer. Makeup. Blocking rehearsal. Costume. Shoot. Hit your mark, say your lines. Lunch. Shoot. Hit some more marks, say some more lines. Wrap. It wasn't rocket science. She wasn't expected to perform brain surgery, or carry out a rescue mission in Darfur. It was only acting. But what if she *didn't* hit her marks? What if she messed up those lines? What if, when she actually came to speak Helen's words, her mouth dried up and she simply couldn't do it at all? Or what if she did it, but did it badly? It didn't matter that *This Being Human* was recorded film rather than live theatre and they could, if the worst came to the worst, do as many takes as required to get it right: Lara knew that the stakes were so high on this project that anything less than a perfect performance was going to be a compromise, not to mention a very public humiliation. She *had* to get it right, or she'd be letting down so many people. Kevin, Alison, Eric, all the people who'd shown such faith – possibly misguided, she feared – in her ability to play this part. Milton. Alex. Herself. Worst of all, so much worse, she'd be letting down her mother. Lara let out a groan. The other pillow, unsurprisingly, wasn't making any difference at all.

She crunched open her eyes and wondered blearily what the time was now – it had been nearly three a.m. when she'd last checked. Turning back onto the other side of the bed – it always felt strange to be alone in a double bed, no matter how often she went away on location without Alex – she looked towards the clock on her bedside table and saw a neon green 04:08

blinking away unapologetically. Less than three hours until her pick-up, then. Great.

Trying to resist the temptation to call Alex – it was after nine in London, he'd definitely be in his set by now – Lara nevertheless reached for her phone in the darkness and switched it on, illuminating the bedroom in a bluish light. She was being pathetic, she knew, as she pressed Alex's speed-dial number, but he wouldn't mind. He was on voicemail, however, so she left a message. 'Hi, it's me. Can't sleep for nerves. Wanted to talk but you're not there, so will give you a buzz later. Love you lots. Have a good day.' Eventually deferring to her ragged mental state, Lara turned on the light and hauled herself out of bed, then walked to the window in the living room and pressed the remote control to open the blinds.

Manhattan seemed a little less frenetic at this hour in the morning, the action on the muted streets below somehow slowed down, the skyline a little sleepy, less sharp-edged. But it was still pretty much all-go down there. Lights across the city were still blinking madly; yellow taxis still scratched across the grid like toy cars across a board; no doubt half the town was already at work. The realisation that she certainly wasn't the only one awake was a sort of comfort, though, and Lara soon turned away from the mesmerising view and wandered over to the table. She picked up the '*This Being Human* Welcome Pack' they'd all been given at the read-through two days ago. It contained shooting schedules, the latest script draft, cast and crew contact sheets, a New York City and Subway map, a US production cellphone, and also – she knew – an American DVD version of *La Belle Hélène*, to which was attached a note.

MEMO

To: All *This Being Human* Cast & Crew
From:Karina (Production Office)
Re:La Belle Helene

Please find enclosed a DVD copy of *La Belle Helene* for your own
personal reference throughout the shoot as per Kevin's request.
Thanks. K.

For your own personal reference throughout the shoot. In the dawny
half-light, Lara held the DVD box in her hand, as she had once
held a VHS box in her old living room many years ago, and
looked at the image on the front. She glanced up at the wall,
where she had hung the vintage poster her friends had presented
her with on her last night in London, and saw the same image.
Her mother, as Hélène, on a balcony, gazing into the distance,
all of human emotion seemingly contained in her eyes – everyone
who has ever changed you, every thing. And somehow, *tomorrow*,
she was going to have to find within herself the ability to create
something similar.

Lara slumped down on the sofa and wondered bleakly what
quantum leap of faith had ever made her think she might be
up to the task.

TWO

'Quiet on set, please!
  'Turnover!'
  'Rolling!'
  'Sound speed!'
  'Mark it!'
  'Slate one take one. A Camera mark!'
  'B Camera mark!'
  'ACTION!'
Having spent the past six months rehearsing *Night Games* in a dingy Clapham rehearsal room, then taking it to the West End stage, Lara hadn't been on a film set since *Out of the Darkness* last spring. But from the moment she heard Kevin's '*Action!*' and the snap of the clapperboard arm as the loader marked the first slate, she was hurtled back instantaneously into the magic.

As much as she had enjoyed her summer stint at the theatre,

to Lara filming was like nothing else on earth. On her very first acting job, a small part in a BBC production straight after drama school, Lara had fallen instantly for the camaraderie of the set. She loved the bantering, bustling crew; the assistant directors, ADs, rushing around with their radios, barking instructions to the hapless young runners; and always found it reassuring that grips and sparks, the burly, tattooed, shorts-wearing boys who dealt with the camera machinery and the electrics and were never without their big gloves and Leatherman tools, should always look the same, everywhere. She loved the geography of the film studio, with its catering (or, in American parlance, 'Craft Service') tables, and camera trucks, and unit base, where the makeup and costume buses, on-set production office and all the actors' trailers were parked. She loved the back lot itself, with its looming shadows and towering lights, and the meticulous mock-ups of real life that lay on the other side of each fake wall. In short, she loved being in the crucible of make-believe that was a set, and losing herself completely to its other, fantasy world.

Not that it wasn't bloody hard work. By the time they broke for lunch a few hours later and Lara emerged, blinking, out of the darkened sound stage into the hard, bright East Coast daylight, she felt drained. After her sleepless night, she had been more dependent than ever on adrenalin in there; and it had not been the perfect first morning. No disasters, and Kevin had been consistently encouraging, but a couple of times she had fluffed a line or caught herself 'acting'. That was what Lara was trying particularly to avoid. She definitely knew what she was after in this performance, but it wasn't quite happening yet. She wasn't, quite, Helen yet.

Feeling tired and mildly disconsolate, Lara walked back alone from the sound stage towards base, sipping the Diet Coke Madison had handed her as she came off set and warning herself not to worry too much about it. It was only the first morning, and first mornings were always a bit creaky. Every director and crew had a different rhythm, behaviour pattern, style to get acquainted with – and at least this morning's scenes hadn't been the most important. She'd do better to relax this lunch break and focus on the afternoon ahead rather than dwell too much on what had or hadn't happened in the morning.

As Lara turned into unit base, she spotted Jacob Moss sitting on the steps to his trailer, smoking a cigarette. The sight pleased her: she'd been meaning to have a proper chat with him since the read-through, when they hadn't managed to talk at all. There was a biggish scene up after lunch between Helen and his character, Peter, and lunchtime would be a great opportunity to run through it with him.

'Hey, Jacob,' Lara called, smiling.

Jacob looked up lazily, his slate-grey eyes cloudy with some expression she could not read. 'Hey,' he said, after a second's pause. He kept his eyes on her but did not move, and as she stood there, holding her Diet Coke, she felt a flush of awkwardness.

'So – how's it going?' she asked brightly, after another moment, to fill the silence. 'We had a pretty good morning.'

Jacob still didn't say anything, although a mysterious little smile seemed to twitch at his lips.

She ploughed on: 'And we're on schedule, which is great. You're first up with me after lunch, aren't you? Scene forty-six?'

Jacob took a drag of his cigarette. 'Sure,' he said, exhaling a light column of smoke.

Something in his manner further threw Lara, and she suddenly found herself gabbling. 'Well, d'you want to go through lines or anything? Or just talk about the characters and what's going on, even? I'm just along there if you want to . . . I mean, it's not a *huge* scene, I know, but it would be good to try to nail it, don't you think?'

Jacob's eyes flickered, and the hint of a smirk remained on his lips. He took another drag. 'Sure,' he said again, and Lara thought she could detect the faintest trace of irony in his voice. 'Let's try to nail it, Lara.'

'Okay, cool. Great. Well – I'm just along the next row, as I say, so knock on my door whenever.' Lara grinned nervously and gave him a clumsy little wave as she began to move off. 'Okay, then. See you in a bit.'

Lara walked away, flustered by their exchange, wondering why she'd been reduced to such a gibbering idiot around her co-star. She knew Jacob Moss had a reputation for keeping himself to himself – and perhaps, given how his film career had rocketed him into the stratosphere recently, this was not altogether surprising – but she had nevertheless been counting on having a good working relationship with him. Film actors were notoriously lazy, but Lara had been secretly hoping that the other main players in *This Being Human*, particularly Jacob, would share her desire to work really hard on this one. At the very least she was holding out for some line-running between scenes and the odd ice-breaking drink after work. The story between their characters in particular was so intense, it would be a nightmare to have to try to convey all that without getting to know each other a bit off set. As she walked past the other actors' vans towards her own, Lara realised she had no idea how Jacob was even intending to play his part. His performance had been okay at the read-through, but he'd only been reading – it was impossible to tell. Perhaps, Lara fretted now, he wasn't going to get the measure of this part, this story, at all? And where would that leave her? Peter had to be *everything* to Helen.

Reaching her trailer, Lara was temporarily diverted from her anxieties as she marvelled again at its ridiculous size. Much bigger than even the most luxurious 'three-way' Winnebago she'd ever had on a film set in the UK, not only did it boast a sofa, table, double bed, surround-sound entertainment system, fridge, and bathroom stocked with fancy Molton Brown toiletries, but when she'd arrived there this morning, hollow-eyed after her restless night, she'd discovered a 'Welcome To The Production!' gift on the table. It turned out to be the latest video iPod, engraved on the back with her name and '*This Being Human* Cast & Crew, New York'. No wonder Hollywood stars often behaved like spoilt brats, Lara chuckled as she unwrapped the slinky gadget.

Lara was still fiddling with her new toy, and wondering what Alex would have to say about it, when there was a loud knock on her door. She grinned as she went to open it, relieved Jacob had taken her up on her suggestion.

'That was qui—' she started to say. But it wasn't Jacob at all: it was Madison, bearing a lunch tray. Poor Madison, who looked like a Victoria's Secret model, all glossy mane and Barbie-doll figure, and who was desperate, naturally, to break into acting.

'I got your lunch order!' she trilled. 'Want me to lay it out on the table here?'

'Oh,' Lara said, surprised. 'Oh, Madison, that's sweet of you but I really don't mind getting lunch myself in the future.'

'Oh!' Madison blushed. 'Did I get it wrong when you gave me your order? You said you wanted the chicken?'

'I know.' Lara agreed. 'But that's because I thought it

would help the caterers if they knew in advance what we all wanted, not because I wanted you to have to go and get it *for* me!'

Madison looked confused. She held on to the offending item uncomfortably.

'Oh, look, honestly, it's not a problem,' Lara said quickly, taking the tray out of her assistant's hands. 'Of course it's not. Thanks for doing it today. But, as I say, I'll normally be more than happy to go and fetch my own and eat with the crew.'

Madison appeared horrified. 'Eat with the crew?' she echoed.

'Yeah – there must be a crew catering area, isn't there?' Lara asked. 'In fact, I'm sure I saw it on my way through this morning. Just next to the catering truck?'

'Sure, there's crew catering,' Madison confirmed. 'But, like, no *actors* ever eat there. We're supposed to bring you all your lunch at the top of the break, to your personal trailer.'

'Ah.'

'That's kinda how it works, right?'

'Ri-ight. Um, okay. Well, I guess I'll be eating here, then.'

'Okay! You want anything, else with that? I got you the salad and fries too, like you asked. That's so cool that you eat fries, by the way! And here's your soda. If you give me a shout when you're done with this and I'll come by and clear up.'

'Okay. Thanks, Madison. Thanks.'

Lara shut the trailer door after her voluble PA and shook her head, bemused. She put on some music and tucked into her radical fries as she pored over her script sides, waiting expectantly for another knock on the door. It was a bit sad, she thought, eating on her own in her trailer like this – she remembered all the chatter-filled lunches she'd enjoyed with her *Mary* cast-mates on the crew catering bus. That was part of the fun of filming, a little wind-down at lunchtime with everyone. Anyway, where the hell was Jacob? When Lara popped out to indulge in a cigarette on her trailer steps, berating herself for how many she'd already smoked today – it was a habitual, nerve-related temptation of the set, which she had never been able to resist – she kept casting her eyes in the direction of Jacob's trailer. But there was no sign of him. And, once Madison had removed her lunch tray, no further knock on the door either until Greg, the third AD, came by at the end of the break to inform her that Makeup were ready for her checks.

Lara *almost* made a joke about it as one of the runners walked her and Jacob back across unit base to the sound stage after the break – 'You'd bloody well better be word-perfect in that case, Mr Moss.' But something held her back at the last minute: Jacob didn't really seem like someone you could make jokes at, or with. So she smiled instead and was about to say something suitably mindless, like, 'Good lunch?' when Kevin came up behind them to give them a note about the upcoming scene. Lara let her mind drift from what the director was saying as she wondered if Jacob's behaviour might be an attempt at intimidation. She forced herself to shrug off her anxiety, though, reminding herself of a very basic but useful adage from her drama school year. *Take that emotion and use it.* That was what she would do. That was all she could do.

As they blocked the next scene and went into a technical rehearsal for the crew, however, Lara's anxiety around Jacob soon crystallised into frustration: he seemed just as detached and disengaged from her on set as he had done down at base; she felt she wasn't getting anything from his performance at *all*.

Why didn't Kevin say anything? she wondered. Jacob was supposed to be this great actor but, so far, she remained distinctly unimpressed.

When Steve, the first AD, called an end to the crew rehearsal – the cue for the heads of department to move in and light the set, and the actors to step off (to be swiftly replaced by their stand-ins) – Lara followed Jacob outside rather determinedly. 'D'you have another of those?' she asked, as he lit the cigarette that had been tucked behind his ear.

He blew out a stream of smoke, then turned to her. And she wanted to cry in exasperation as, once again, that curious expression twitched at the corner of his mouth. 'Sure, Lara,' he said, digging in the pocket of his costume jacket and pulling out a pack of Lucky Strike. Then, before she even knew what was happening, Jacob had whipped his cigarette out of his mouth and placed it in her own, his fingers grazing the delicate skin around her lips, his eyes catching hers, before, quick as a flash, he turned back to his nonchalant position against the studio wall and lit another cigarette from the pack for himself. It was such an intimate, no, *intrusive* gesture, and over so quickly, that Lara could hardly believe what had just happened.

'Er, thanks,' she gasped, a tingle of something – what? Irritation? Shock? – on her lips where his fingers had just been. Jacob responded with the slightest of grins and continued to lean serenely against the wall.

What a freak, Lara thought as she took a drag of his cigarette and felt herself shiver. The crisp mid-September sky was cloudless, and the air was autumnally chilly. She could easily ask one of the runners for a set 'keep-warm' coat but it didn't seem worth it for the time they'd be out here. Plus, she reminded herself, as she crossed her arms against her chest for warmth, if she was going to say anything to Jacob about the scene, she needed to get on with it. She'd rejected 'Do you think you're really going to play it like that?' as a bit rude, but had settled on something along the lines of 'You know, it would be great for me, really useful, if you could give me more of a *reaction* on the line . . .'

Before she could pluck up the courage to open her mouth, though, Greg was popping his head out of the sound stage. 'Uh, we're ready for you guys,' he said, then intoned into his radio: 'That's Lara and Jacob stepping back in, then. Actors back on set.'

Jacob dropped his cigarette and ground it out with his heel, moving past Lara without another word. She was left staring after him, silently reeling, before stubbing out her own and following Greg in.

And yet, when the cameras started to roll in stage three a few minutes later, something extraordinary happened. As Kevin called 'Action,' Jacob Moss stepped into the light, hit his mark, and promptly disappeared. And suddenly it was Peter, not Jacob, who was standing before Lara, and the reactions she had been seeking during rehearsals were not only there but delivered with a grace and subtlety that made her own Helen snap fully to attention. Lara was astonished when Steve yelled 'Cut' between takes and she found she could breathe again. Something was vibrating in the enchanted space between camera and character that she'd rarely experienced in her life. For those supercharged minutes when they were rolling, Lara had not been Lara, twenty-six-year-old London actress with a barrister boyfriend and a flat in Ladbroke Grove and a deceased French mother. She had been somebody else altogether: Helen, who had her own blessings and her own curses and her own soul. These were the moments you lived for as an actor: the fleeting instants when you lost yourself entirely and weren't acting at all. Lara could count on one hand the times in her career when she'd ever felt that, and it was especially rare on a film, where the very mechanics of the artifice were all around you, often in your eyeline. But now Jacob had come along and made it happen between them in their *very first scene*. She felt her heart beating faster with anticipation as Steve yelled, 'Turn over!' again and they went for another take.

At the end of the day, when Steve called a wrap, Lara burst into relieved laughter. What an afternoon. She was buzzing as she accepted a copy of tomorrow's call sheet from one of the runners and waved goodbye to Kevin and the crew. She turned to say thanks and goodnight to Jacob, who had been there two seconds ago, but he seemed to have vanished. She took a final look for him around the sound stage, where the camera, sound and light boys were busy derigging, but there was definitely no sign of her co-star. Walking back to base, with Madison in tow, she discovered him in the makeup bus, running his head under the tap.

'Hey, there you are!' Lara said shyly, nervous again at the prospect of talking to this person without the protective layer of their being in character. 'I was looking for you. I really wanted to say thanks for a . . . well, for a brilliant afternoon.'

Jacob turned slowly to her and inclined his head. He looked at her curiously for a moment, running his hands through his wet hair. He had such an amazing face, Lara suddenly realised, vulnerable and powerful, ugly and beautiful all at once. 'Honestly, I never imagined that scene could have so much in it,' she carried on. 'Don't you . . . don't you think it went really well?'

'Yeah,' Jacob drawled, his voice betraying a shade of amusement. 'I had fun out there.'

'Me too!' she said eagerly. 'I really enjoyed it. Look, if you ever want to run stuff at lunchtime, or whenever, I'd love that.'

Jacob smiled as he gathered up his things and slung a battered canvas record bag over his shoulder. He pulled out a cigarette and stuck it, unlit, in the corner of his mouth. 'You know what, Lara, I kinda like just to be spontaneous while we're rolling.' He moved past her unapologetically towards the door of the bus. 'Later, everybody.'

Lara turned away, stung, as the makeup girls, who were packing up their kit, chirruped their goodbyes in a collective swoon. Catching sight of her disappointed expression in the mirrors, Lara shot herself a warning glance. It was deflation she was feeling, that was all, and dented pride. That their first scenes together had gone well meant lots to Lara, but there was no reason, she reminded herself, why Jacob Moss should care about this film as much as she did. So he obviously wasn't going to turn into a 'proper' friend in the way Charlie Fox and the gang from *Mary* had done. But so what? Hardly any actors stayed close after jobs. She didn't need Jacob to be a friend to her, just a good actor. If he was offering her some kind of pathetic challenge, with his too-cool-for-school attitude and his condescending smirks and his refusal to rehearse or engage in any kind of off-set conversation, then sod it: she would embrace that challenge, raise her game, prove to Jacob Moss she was more than a match for him. Resolute, Lara sat down at her station, picked up the bottle of cleansing lotion and cotton pad that her makeup artist Ally had just passed to her, and slowly, carefully, wiped the last traces of Helen from her face.

THREE

'Helloooo!' Cassie shrieked, after a single ring.

Grinning, Lara sat up in bed, holding the phone under her chin. Sunlight was falling across the duvet in great bright streaks. 'I've just woken up and it's *such* a glorious day here, Cass, I can't tell you. Just wish you and Liz were around so we could go and have lunch in some chic little eatery downtown, then hit the shops and drink martinis until we pass out.'

'God, that sounds like heaven. It's pissing down here.'

'What you up to?' Lara stretched lazily.

'Just having a drink at the Westbourne with Tash and a wander round Portobello before we meet up with everyone later.'

'Nice. Say hi to Tash. What's the plan?'

'Not sure yet. We'll probably go for some food round here, then out for a bit of a boogie. I have to drive to my parents' for Sunday lunch tomorrow, yawn, so I'm not going to have a late one. How about you?'

Lara smiled to herself. 'I really don't know. It's my first weekend off so got no plans, no nothing, just a whole sunny New York City at my disposal.'

'Mmm. *Delicious.*'

'Isn't it. It's been such a mad fortnight, I really just want to kick back a bit. Might go for a walk around the park, might go to an exhibition or two, *might* just force myself to go shopping. It's a tough life.'

'I don't know how you cope, sister. Hats off. So, how's filming going?'

'Good, I think, just bloody exhausting.'

'How's Jacob? Is he still being a dick?'

'*Total* dick. Still won't speak to me, still won't run lines, still acts as if he's the king of the world, but, whatever, I'm used to it now – and I do have to hand it to him. He's probably the best actor I've ever seen.'

'Shame he has to behave like that, though,' mused Cassie. 'I'd rather set my hopes on him falling in love with you, to no avail of course, and following you back to London where I'd be ready and waiting to ensnare him with my lurve.'

Lara chortled at the ridiculousness of the proposition – on so many levels. 'I'm sure he'd be all over you, C, but trust me, you'd be mighty disappointed.'

Cassie sighed. '*Such* a shame.'

'Anyway, how's everything? You still temping?'

Cassie groaned. 'Yes, I bloody well am. This week I've been discovering the delights of NHS bureaucracy, and next week, joy of joys, I'm headed to some market-research firm.' She let out a chortle. 'Market research? Can you imagine. Only markets I'm remotely interested in researching are the ones selling nice clothes and posh olive oil. Still. Nine quid an hour, and they're letting me off for an audition on Tuesday, so can't complain.'

'That's cool. What's the audition for?'

'Some crappy telly, probably, but anything would be better than market research, right?'

Lara laughed. 'And how's young Ed?'

'Very lovely, thanks for asking.'

Lara feigned a gasp. 'This must be some kind of record for you, Cass, no? How long's it been now? Two whole months?'

'I know. *God.* Really should think about dumping him soon, shouldn't I?' Cassie giggled. 'But, yeah, he's cool. We're quite chilled out – he's off to Leeds to film a new series for ITV any minute now, so that may be that. But we're having lots of fun while it lasts.'

'Good. Well, I won't keep you if you're with Tash, but so lovely to chat a bit and I'm glad all's going well.'

'You too, honeybunch. Great to talk to you, and I'll be in touch again soon.'

'Hey, good luck at your audition. Let me know how it goes.'

'I will. And good luck you with the Moss Monster.'

Lara laughed. 'Cheers, lovely. I'll need it.'

'Byeeee! Oh, and Tash sends her love too.'

'Send mine. Miss you all.'

Lara chuckled again as she put down the phone, then tried to call Alex. He was on voicemail, probably playing cricket – he'd mentioned yesterday that it was the last game of the season. After sending a quick text to her dad to tell him she was fine, had settled in and, yes, had received his email about getting in touch with the Drakes, some friends of his from his UN days, Lara got up, pressing the button to open the blinds in the living room on her way to the bathroom. More

September sunshine streamed in through the windows. What a day. She had told the production office yesterday in no uncertain terms to give both Madison and Bobby the weekend off: she would *not* be needing their assistance, she assured Karina, who nevertheless informed Lara that the pair would be kept on standby *just* in case any 'situation' should arise.

But Lara had been adamant. This would be her day, she decided, as she turned right out of her building and headed down Lexington Avenue in search of breakfast. A day to meander through the streets, a day to indulge herself in this fabulous city, a day to dawdle and gawp, to eat and shop, to do whatever she wanted and not have to talk to anyone if she didn't feel like it – especially not to have to make pointless polite conversation with her driver and PA, sweet though they were. Grabbing a bagel, a *New York Times* and a steaming cup of coffee from a Jewish deli on 53rd Street, Lara marched briskly along Fifth Avenue and over to Central Park, where she found an empty bench by the pond and caught up with the week's news – or tried to, rather: it was hard to concentrate on black-and-white newsprint on a technicolour day like today.

Discarding the paper, she sipped her coffee and gazed at the scene around her: birds dipping in and out of the pond, kids gleefully feeding the ducks, elderly Manhattan couples shuffling past hand in hand, manic joggers pounding the pathways, loony tramps muttering to themselves, stylish young mothers and preppy-looking husbands pushing state-of-the-art buggies towards Madison Avenue brunches. She let her mind wind back over the last two weeks on *This Being Human*, and felt a little gulp of excitement. There had been one or two shaky moments, of course, but on the whole it was going better than she could have imagined. Lara had been running on adrenalin (and black coffee and nicotine) all fortnight – having had a decent night's sleep at last, she felt almost drunk on its benefits now – but the nerves that had been so crippling at the beginning were now, she hoped, pretty much under control, and she was having a great time. The American crew were fun, the cast – with the exception of Jacob – were friendly, and Kevin was proving himself to be an intelligent, brave director; Lara could see why he was being tipped for such great things. He was also a rare and wonderful thing to work with from an actor's point of view: sensitive to their concerns, giving them lots of rehearsal time and blithely ignoring the grumbles of first AD Steve if ever they wanted an extra take when a technically satisfactory one was already in the can. She was also, she hoped, really beginning to get to grips with Helen, who was easily her most challenging part to date. So, all in all, it had been a pretty triumphant fortnight; although, as Lara conceded as she sorted the sections of the unfamiliar newspaper into piles to chuck – the bits she never read: sport, money, business – and keep – news, arts, magazine, travel – there were, of course, still many more weeks of the shoot to go. The worst thing she could do now would be to relax and get complacent. It was, as they said out here, *all still to play for*.

Lara stretched out her legs in front of her and wiggled her feet happily. Then she jumped up, loving the brightness of the sky as she ambled along the row of benches, each with its own little plaque, that dotted the southern perimeter of the park. She wondered where she should go next. Part of her reckoned she should probably turn inwards and head towards the East Side and Museum Mile. There was a 'must-see' Rothko retrospective on at the Met, apparently – she'd just glanced at the glowing reviews in the *Times* culture pages – and she'd enjoyed exploring the whorls of the Guggenheim during visits

213

to her father when he'd been working here a few years ago. And yet she was also eager to get down to SoHo or the Village, find cool coffee shops and bars, trawl bookshops and boutiques, simply hang out. In truth, on this sunny day, she would probably rather potter than be stuck inside an art gallery. And yet if she was on the East Side, she would be well placed to drop in on Sabine and see the promised photographs, which, having had no real time off until now, she hadn't yet managed to do . . .

And that settled it. She would phone Sabine and see if she was in; if not, she would go downtown. Pausing at a different bench so she could find the costumier's number, Lara glanced idly at the inscription on the plaque as she dug inside her bag for her crew list. '*In memory of our dear grandfather Joel,*' the Rosenblatt family had dedicated, '*who had the wisdom to know that if you love the questions, you might one day live your way into the answers. We miss you, Gramps. With all our love from Annie, Benjamin and Rachel. March 2006.*' Lara dialled Sabine's number and pondered the Rosenblatts' phrase as she awaited a response. Love the questions, she mused, as the phone started to ring in Sabine's apartment, and you might live your way into the answers? She was wondering, absent-mindedly, what Joel Rosenblatt might have meant when she heard an American man's voice say, 'Hello?'

As it turned out, Lara's first proper New York Saturday held the best of both worlds. Sabine's husband, Frank Mellon, had explained to Lara that his wife was at her Pilates class, to be followed by lunch with her girlfriends, but that he knew she'd be delighted to see Lara later, so why didn't she swing by the apartment for a drink at, say, six thirty? He gave Lara the 93rd Street address and she scribbled it down. Then, with the afternoon hers to play with, she walked out of Central Park and over to the metro station, wrestling with her subway map and her new MetroCard before depositing herself on one of the rattling silver boxes that was headed for downtown Manhattan.

Emerging at street level a short while later, Lara was a tad dismayed, having prided herself on what she hoped was an ability to navigate herself mapless around the world's great cities, to find herself at the wrong end of 14th Street. (It was too confusing that there should be so many different 14th Street stations!) Gratefully spotting a sign for the Village Vanguard, however, she reoriented herself and followed it down Seventh Avenue, feeling a twist of nostalgia as she recalled how her grandfather had once dreamt of playing there. She remembered him in his and Colette's apartment in Paris when she was a little girl, carefully showing her and Lucas those precious record sleeves – the words *A Night at the Village Vanguard* or *Live from the Blue Note* seeming to fill Bernard's eyes with light, shorthand for some sort of unimaginable magic.

Lara stood on tiptoe now and tried to peer through the shuttered Saturday-afternoon windows of the famous old jazz club. The building looked sad and a little weary this lunchtime: a shell of what it would no doubt become in a few hours' time, when filled again with musicians and drink and sweat and syncopation. She peered at the poster that displayed the programme for the upcoming weeks, and saved the bookings number on her phone. How exciting, she reflected, to be back in the jazz capital of the world: she should honour the spirit and memory of her grandfather by coming to a gig here as soon as possible.

Content to play out the clichés this afternoon, Lara hit

Bleecker Street and decided to indulge herself in a vanilla cupcake and cafè latte at the Magnolia Bakery before browsing the rails at Marc Jacobs on the opposite corner. Almost spoiling herself with a cute little dress but resisting at the last minute, she took a ludicrously overpriced and oversized pair of sunglasses instead. Such a purchase felt justifiable, on a day like today – sun in the sky, New York to dress for, no Alex to make jokes about her profligacy. She could do what she liked.

At the Biography Bookstore across the street, Lara was browsing the second-hand boxes when she spotted an account of Yves Saint-Laurent's life. Instinctively, she checked the index – and, yes, there they were: various entries for 'Lacloche, Eve'. She felt a thrill, but Eve's inclusion was hardly surprising – she had been a contemporary of Saint-Laurent and Pierre Bergé in the heady days of 1970s Paris and had a lasting association with his couture.

Lara flicked to the photographs in the middle of the book and felt a familiar tummy-jumping sensation when she saw a photo of her mother, aged about twenty-four, wearing a seventies *Le Smoking* with her hair slicked back and a capricious glint in her eye; and then another, Eve a little older, in a boxy dress alongside one of Yves' other muses, Loulou de la Falaise. Standing in the musty bookshop now, Lara had a memory of her own excitement as a little girl whenever one of those YSL-monogrammed boxes arrived, wherever her family were in the world: a shimmer of Parisian glamour and promise rustling between the layers of crisp tissue paper. A year or so before she had died, Eve had done a shoot for French *Vogue* to publicise *Si Ça C'est Un Jour*, and had brought her daughter along. Eve had thought it would be fun for Lara to try something on, and had picked out a rather beautiful pink confection for her gangly fifteen year old. The designer of this dress, Eve had explained, with an almost mournful reverence in her voice, was a very dear man. Perhaps a genius. She had known him and his partner Pierre very well, once, although they weren't in touch so much these days. 'But, of course, you weren't only a muse to Saint-*Laurent*!' Lara recalled the fashion director or somebody gushing. 'There is St Clair, too!' And Eve had turned away, suddenly, her face a shadow . . .

Lara dug out a ten-dollar bill and went to pay for the book. Then, after wandering through the rest of the Village, popping into shops and galleries and drinking in the buzz on the streets that told her she could not be in any other city in the world, she headed down Greenwich Street and found the place that Chris, the actor playing Michael in the film, had recommended to her, a bar called the Spotted Pig. She ordered a glass of wine and got lost in her thoughts for an hour or so, people-watching and dreaming until, glancing at her watch, she saw it was much later than she'd expected. A hint of dusk was already whispering over the streets of the West Village, and unless she took a cab she'd be late for Sabine and Frank. Lara got the check and dashed onto the street. But this was New York, of course, and as she headed up West 11th, past the junction with Bleecker and up to Seventh, she was greeted by the sight of ribbons of yellow taxis unspooling down the avenue, illuminating themselves in the falling light. Hailing one, Lara jumped in with her packages and leaned back happily against the shabby leather. She wondered when the last time was that she had felt so relaxed, so happy. She loved it here. She loved the city, the taxis, the dusky light that was settling over everything. And best of all, she realised, she couldn't *wait* to go back to work on Monday morning.

FOUR

When *The Chronicles of Mary* had first become a hit in Britain a couple of years ago, the gossip columns and weekly showbiz magazines had soon cottoned on to the fact that the girl playing Mary, with her striking looks and her famous dead mother, might be a bit of a 'story'. When journalists started to probe, however, Lara had been resolute in her approach. She was never rude, but she never gave anything away. Early on there had been a spate of pieces speculating, perhaps inevitably, about whether she might be 'getting a little too close' to her 'gorgeous' male co-star Charlie Fox or, indeed, any of the other lads from the show. But after a distinct lack of evidence, and negative provocation from Lara and Charlie, the UK press machine lost interest. They might write about Lara's quirky sense of style, or photograph her in beautiful dresses at first nights or film premières; they might run reviews of her work in arts sections or bid for long features in the weekend supplements. But Lara agreed to do personal interviews on only very rare occasions, and only if she had a specific project to discuss. She wasn't interested in promoting herself and, as a result, had almost entirely ceased to be UK tabloid or diary-page fodder. She didn't use them so they couldn't use her. She didn't have a famous boyfriend (she didn't even publicly admit to having a boyfriend, actually: she was perennially tight-lipped about her private life in interviews). She didn't go out to clubs in the West End and flash her knickers to the paparazzi. She didn't, as far as they knew, shovel cocaine up her nose or drink to excess (certainly, to the best of their knowledge, she'd never checked into the Priory). Although 'actress Lara Latner' was always worth a pretty photo or two if she did go out to events, to the people spinning these kinds of stories she was actually a bit square, a bit 'boring'. They didn't know how Lara lived her real life, and that was exactly how she – and Alex – liked to keep it.

It came as something of a shock, then, when Lara strolled into the Brooklyn studio one morning, a month or so into the *This Being Human* shoot and got an appreciative whistle from Billy, the notoriously playful Best-Boy grip.

'Nice pic in the *Express*, Lara.' He winked as she walked past Craft Service, where he was making tea. 'Us boys have had a sweepstake going since we started 'bout how long it'd take you two to get it on. I said a month. Reckon I mighta cleaned up today.' He rubbed his hands together and winked at her again.

Lara stopped dead in her tracks. Had she heard him right? 'What are you talking about, Bill?'

'Oh, come on, sweetie. Remember us grips get to watch you on set all day long. We've known since day one.'

219

'Known what?'

Billy rolled his eyes and tutted indulgently, then pulled a rolled-up copy of the newspaper in question out of his back pocket. He turned to page five and handed it to her.

The gossip page in front of Lara's eyes made her do an almost comedic double-take. Accompanying a story entitled '*Moss gets up Close & Personal with* Human *Co-star*' was a picture of her and Jacob kissing. She recognised the kiss immediately: it was part of a scene from the film. They'd shot it out on location in Manhattan last week. But the image had been cropped in such fashion that you could only make out the two figures, rather than much of the background, and, what was more, the picture had been cleverly doctored so that all sorts of details had been subtly changed: the colour of their clothes, for example. In fact, studying it more closely, it looked as if what they were wearing in the picture had actually been superimposed onto their bodies. Lara gasped.

'Is this some kind of joke?' she asked, blushing hotly. 'This is from the *film*. Billy – you were *there* when we shot this scene. You must know it isn't real?'

Billy took the paper back and stared at the image again. 'Nope,' he teased. 'Can't say I recognise it. Never seen you wearing that.'

'But – they've just Photoshopped it or something!' Lara exclaimed. 'Can't you see?'

Billy grinned. 'Don't get your knickers in a twist about it, honey. No need to be embarrassed. Everyone'll be pleased for ya. He's a lucky man! Now, I gotta get back to work and collect my winnings! May I?'

The technician retrieved his precious *New York Express* from Lara's hands and chuckled his way back to the camera truck, leaving her standing stock-still and stunned. Despite what Billy had just said about the sweepstake – because that must be a joke, surely? – it wasn't the possibility of anyone here actually *believing* she was having an affair with Jacob that bothered her. The idea was ridiculous: they'd still barely spoken to each other off-set. No, it was the flagrantly deceitful way in which the story had been created. Cutting and pasting and Photoshopping a shot, which was obviously a paparazzi grab or a leak from the film set, to make it look real. The sneaks! Whenever she'd had stuff written about her in the trashier UK magazines, it had always been carefully couched within the bounds of 'speculation' and 'possibility' and 'unnamed sources'. Now, here they were, writing about Jacob Moss's latest 'affair' – for it was, of course, Jacob's love life they were interested in, not the unknown British girl's – and presenting this picture as evidence of the fact. It was outrageous! Lara felt her cheeks hum with indignation, then embarrassment, and was wildly relieved when she remembered Jacob wasn't working today and that she wouldn't have to face him until tomorrow.

When Madison popped over to say she was needed on set for rehearsal, Lara asked her to tell Greg she just needed five minutes, then ducked behind one of the flats at the back of the sound stage for a bit of privacy. She hated to hold people up like this, she was allergic to any suggestion of being a diva, but she had to try to get through to Alex; she wouldn't be able to concentrate, otherwise. Thankfully he picked up his phone straight away.

'I just thought you should know,' she said, biting her lip, having duly explained to her boyfriend what had happened.

There was the slightest pause before Alex answered, although that might merely have been a transatlantic time delay. 'O-kay,' he said. 'Well. Thanks for telling me.'

'I was worried it might be picked up at home, somehow, and

221

I wanted you to hear it from me. Oh, God, it's all so *stupid*. I can't actually believe it.'

'I can,' Alex replied, and Lara was grateful to hear levity in his voice. 'You know what these guys are like, La. It's not as if it hasn't happened before. Remember all the stuff that came out about you and Charlie?'

'I know, but it's still infuriating.' Lara sighed. 'And especially as this is just *so* bloody ridiculous. At least Charlie and I were mates. I barely even speak to Jacob when we're not working. He's a total weirdo. Anyway, baby, I've really gotta run. I'm holding everyone up. But just wanted to warn you.'

'Well, thanks. But don't worry about it, princess. It doesn't matter. I think my pride can take it. And, thankfully, none of my QCs or clerks is likely to be well acquainted with the *New York Express*. Although I can't necessarily say the same for some of my clients on remand: I hear that kind of thing's all the rage down in the Scrubs.'

She laughed. 'You're amazing. Thanks for understanding. I'll call you when I'm done, if it's not too late.'

'Cool bananas. We're going to Frankie's thing later, anyway, so call any time, I'll probably be up.'

'*Shit!* I forgot to email him to say good luck. Will you apologise for me?'

'Course I will. You've got a pretty good excuse, though.'

Not really, Lara reproached herself, as she dashed to set. Frankie was one of their good mates from university, and had recently, after slaving for four or five years, been signed to a record label. Tonight was his first public gig and she'd meant to get his home address off Liz or Cassie ages ago and send him a proper good-luck card. Instead, she'd forgotten all about it. Not cool. She hated that about filming, how instantly self-absorbing it became; and, worse, how everyone excused it for being such, when really she should be making *more* of an effort with her friends at home right now, not less.

As much as she tried to concentrate on her acting once the cameras were rolling again, Lara was distracted all morning and her mind kept flicking relentlessly to the photo of her and Jacob. Alex had been typically understanding about it, which was a relief, but that still didn't solve the problem of how she was going to deal with the mortification of seeing Jacob tomorrow. Or, moreover, how she was going to get through the rest of today, when the crew were clearly determined to rib her about it – no matter how affectionately. Even the people who could see that the pictures were faked seemed to suspect there could be a perfectly truthful premise behind it.

'Well, well. All I can say is, you lucky thing!' Jessica Cole joked, as she and Lara went outside for a fag and a cuppa while the crew relit for the next set-up and their stand-ins took their places. 'I've got such a crush on that boy I can barely even get my lines out when I'm doing scenes with him. It's *most* unprofessional.'

'You know it's all bollocks, though, right?'

Jessica gave Lara a sly look. 'If you say so.'

'Of course it is!' Lara exclaimed.

An eyebrow shot up. 'Methinks the lady might be protesting too much.'

'Oh, come *on*,' Lara cried. 'I mean, have you ever even seen me and Jacob together when we're not working?'

Jessica let out a bark of laughter. 'I'm not sure that's a viable defence, Lara. I mean, I've watched the two of you on the monitor, and you're pretty shit-hot up there together.'

'So? That's *acting*! That's not real!'

Jessica studied Lara's face. 'Why are you getting so het-up about it, then?'

'Because it's a load of rubbish, that's why. And it really, *really* pisses me off that they think they can write what they like and get away with it. That stuff can wreak havoc in people's lives and they don't even care!'

'Okay, Lara, calm down,' Jessica soothed. 'Sorry, I didn't mean to touch a raw nerve. And I've just remembered, you have a boyfriend back home, don't you? So I can see that must be weird. Aren't you, like, practically married?'

Lara swung back towards her. 'Whatever gave you that idea?' she asked, irrationally flustered. Why should Jessica's assumption irk her so much? she wondered. *Weren't* she and Alex practically married?

'I don't know, I just remember seeing a story about you somewhere. They had pictures of you and him together. From ages ago, uni or whenever. It wasn't at an *event*. You don't really do that sort of thing, do you?'

Lara pursed her lips. 'No . . .' she murmured. She knew which article Jessica was referring to. It had come out in one of the lower-brow Sunday newspapers a year or so ago, at the beginning of the latest series of *Mary*: an unauthorised account (after she'd refused their request for an interview) full of lazy presumptions and silly mistakes. Her irritation had been nothing, though, to Alex's fury at having been named, pictured and investigated. There were old, faded pictures of him playing football in the Varsity match, and a shot of the outside door of his chambers in the Temple (*fascinating* to the general public, no doubt). She'd never seen Alex so pissed off, and although he later calmed down, saying he accepted it was just one of those things he'd have to get used to the more famous Lara got, she'd understood his anger.

It was one thing for the press to follow her around, take pictures and write nonsense about her, but quite another for them to dig around in Alex's private life. They'd also never been able to work out who had sold the photos of them from their college days, and had felt jointly betrayed by it for some time.

'Seriously, though,' Jessica was chuckling, 'no matter *how* loved-up I was back home, I still wouldn't say no.'

Lara stubbed her cigarette, rolled her eyes at her flame-haired vixen of a cast-mate, and walked back on set.

The rest of the morning passed, thankfully, with little more than a few raised eyebrows and knowing chuckles from the sparks and grip departments; and Lara, after speaking to Alex again at lunchtime and hearing him insist again that it didn't matter, managed to wrestle herself back into her performance and salvage something of the day.

When Bobby dropped her home to Manhattan that night and she went to check her email, however, she was dismayed to discover that her fears about the story crossing the Atlantic before it could be properly buried had come true.

Date: 09 October

To: llama@gmail.com

From: cassiecat@mac.com

Re: Bad news

Hello, dear you. Just wanted to write and send love as I'm sure you've heard by now one of the showbiz blogs had a story up this afternoon that seems to have originated in NY about you and Jacob – I tried to call you earlier but you didn't answer your phone. I imagine it must've been ringing off the hook. Bloody paparazzi. And from what you've told me about Jacob, it's about the most unlikely pairing imaginable – although he does look fit as you like in the shot! (Sorry, that's probably in very bad taste right now – forgive me . . .)

Anyway, I know this is the sort of thing that has vexed you in the past, so wanted to check you're feeling cheery and not worrying about it too much. Obviously nobody gives a shit over here what those idiots write, and anyone who knows you and Al will see it's utter rubbish, but I'm afraid it did make the late edition of the London freesheets, with the same photo, so – just thought you should be aware. Ironically, it ended up being a really positive story about you. As in 'our great Hollywood hope Lara Latner' . . . So please don't fret, my love.

I am assuming, by the way, that you (a) know what I'm talking about and (b) have spoken to Alex about it? I'm supposed to be seeing him later at Frankie's gig, so maybe give us both a call when you wrap, we'll no doubt be up late.

Smooches to you, my darling sister, and lots love Cass xxxxxxxxxxx

Lara frowned as she scrolled down her email inbox and saw how many of the subject lines seemed to refer to the story. Even her brother, who probably wouldn't know what a showbiz blog was if it hit him in the face, had been alerted to the article, it seemed:

Date: 09 October
To: llama@gmail.com
From: lrl27@bristol.ac.uk
Re: eh?

Hey, Lals. Don't know if you've seen it but a mate forwarded me this link earlier and I thought you should know about it if you don't already. It's not true, is it? Enjoyed his film *Long Road Home*, but can't believe this can be true!
html://www.blogspot.moviestarsmisbehaving.com/
jacobmoss&laralatner&newyorkcity%435%899

Hope you're cool out there, anyway. I'll write more soon.

Luc

PS By the way, I spoke to dad recently and he wondered how you were. I know you're busy but maybe give him a call sometime?

Despite her annoyance about what was going on, Lara allowed herself an ironic snort at her brother's cheeky postscript. He was a fine one to talk. How many times had she had Oliver on the phone, anxious, because Luc had disappeared off to West Africa or somewhere in his holidays and wilfully dropped off the communication radar? Still, her brother probably had a point. She'd barely been in contact with Oliver since she arrived in New York, apart from the odd text here and there, and according to the snippets of news she heard, things in his neck of the woods were getting worse. At least, Lara reflected hopefully, that probably meant there was no chance he'd seen the stupid story.

She stared again at the web link Lucas had helpfully forwarded, but found she had no desire whatsoever to click on it. She knew that Cassie was probably right: in the grand scheme of things nobody who mattered would care, and even if it remained on the web for ever, the story would soon lose its currency. It would become, like so many, the proverbial 'tomorrow's-fish-and-chip-paper'. Nevertheless, tonight, thinking about poor Alex, who would have had to face all their mates at Frankie's concert, and wondering how on earth she was going to play it with Jacob in the morning, it was still making her feel jumpy and uncomfortable.

Lara shut down her computer with a bang and paced around the apartment. She should do something to expend some of this nervous energy, she knew, take a late-night jog or go the gym downstairs, whose membership had been part of her deal and which she'd barely visited. But she felt too frustrated, and tired, now, to move. So she slumped instead in front of the TV and finished the leftover takeaway in her fridge from last night in front of *The Daily Show*, then crawled, somewhat grumpily, to bed.

FIVE

Date: 19 October

To: llama@gmail.com

From: alex.craig@gmail.com

Re: Re: Re: Re: Phew!

L, thanks for my text earlier. Sorry to hear things have been stressful on set this week. Was gutted to miss you AGAIN last night, and now tonight by the look of things, but hope things are easing up. I'm gonna crash in a minute as have also been working like a maniac – one of Matthew's cases has listed early (rape, always nice) and I've been assigned to it, hence the extra workload. Which is all a bit rubbish given that my chief priority at the mo is to escape and come and visit my favourite girl. But anyway, I'll leave my phone on so please call me when you wrap if you're not too knackered yourself.

The good news is that I had a chat with the clerks today and it's looking like I'll definitely be able to escape for a few days in about a month, so will start checking flights tomorrow. According to the last schedule you sent me this seems to coincide with some days off for you, although annoyingly I see you have the rest of that week off! Wish I could stay longer than the long weekend but prob unlikely given how busy we are here.

Anyway, hope all is okay and you know that I love you endlessly and think of you all day long even when we don't speak. Take care, pretty girl, and don't work too hard.

A xx

PS Saw Cass and Liz briefly last night at Rosa's bday drinks in the Windsor Castle (popped in for 5 whole mins on my way home). The girls were asking after you, as was everyone, and complaining because apparently you've been a bit crap lately at being in contact. I told them not to worry, and that you were so busy even I'd hardly spoken to you recently. But they sent love and said to drop them a line when you get a chance. Everyone misses you lots. And me the most, just in case you hadn't worked that one out. xxxxxxxx

Lara bit her lip, and pushed her laptop onto the bed beside her, reaching over to light a cigarette. She should hit reply, she knew, or better still, pick up the phone as he had requested. *Even when we don't speak.* It was now more than two days since she and Alex had actually talked to each other – a lifetime for them. Despite Alex's words there had never really been a period before now when they didn't speak. When she'd lived in France during her languages degree they'd chatted all the time; and when she'd gone to LA earlier this year to do *Out of the Darkness* they'd managed to call each other every morning or evening, often both.

But at the moment it was difficult. As the days rolled on and autumn took hold in the city, she was becoming increasingly absorbed in *This Being Human*. The past few days had been particularly fraught, due to scheduling complications and a fault on B Camera, which had lost them half a day's shooting. They'd been dropping scenes and going into overtime – an expensive business in the heavily unionised US industry – which always raised tension; and Lara had been fretting about her performance again after misguidedly rewatching *La Belle Hélène* one night and feeling depressed by the knowledge that she'd never be as good as her mother. At the moment she felt so wrapped up in Helen, and Hélène, that she could hardly bring herself to talk to *anybody* outside the film set – even Alex or her friends back home, who were still dutifully texting on a regular basis. It was so hard to explain the intensity of the shoot, the intensity of the experience of recreating Eve's most famous role, that it seemed an easier option not to speak to anybody at all.

Rolling onto her back, Lara gazed around her bedroom, which was now beginning to feel less like a soulless rented room and more like her own space. She'd put a copy of the iconic Eve/Cleopatra image on the wall and stuck up snaps of Alex and her mates to remind herself of home. Her bed was decorated with a throw Lucas had once brought her back from Mali, and her books, magazines, old call sheets, and the coloured script rewrites issued almost weekly by the production office now covered the smooth white surfaces of the room. The other, assorted bits of clutter she'd chosen to accompany her on her packing afternoon also provided a semblance of familiarity and comfort. Until now, these had been a blessing, but tonight, for some reason, the sight of all these Londonish bits and pieces in this most unreal of New York bedrooms made Lara's stomach lurch. She should ring Alex. Sitting up, vaguely disoriented, she checked her watch. Bobby had dropped her back over Brooklyn Bridge half an hour ago: it was nearly nine thirty. Alex would be fast asleep, and from the sound of things he needed all the sleep he could get. So, no, she decided, exhaling. She wouldn't call him now. She'd drop him a quick email instead, and speak to him tomorrow.

Wandering into the kitchen in search of a snack, in the hope of quelling the weird feeling in her stomach, Lara suddenly heard her phone beep noisily on the table. She jumped, flooded with irrational guilt that it might be Alex wondering why she hadn't called him. Depressed in any case by the sorry contents of the fridge, she took another drag on her Marlboro Light and pressed the envelope icon.

Drink?

Received: Oct 19 Time: 21:32 Sender +19172889064

Lara inspected the number, surprised. She didn't recognise it – a New York cellphone, if the area code was anything to go by. She wondered if it might be Dan Peters or Lucy Drew. She'd dropped them an email at the beginning of the shoot to say she was in town, but had done pitifully little to take them up on their subsequent offers of drinks, dinners and parties. She probably had their New York numbers written down somewhere, but couldn't be bothered to search for them now. It certainly wasn't Jessica or Chris: she had their numbers programmed in. It wasn't Kevin either, or Sabine, with whom she had been in regular contact since that lovely evening spent poring over photographs. It wasn't anybody she could think of. **Sorry**, she tapped back in response. **Don't have many numbers in this phone. Who is this? Lara**.

For a few moments she waited for the phone to beep again with an answer, but it was quiet. Must have been a wrong number. Stubbing her cigarette in the ashtray on the table she walked restlessly back into the bedroom, reopened her laptop and wondered how she should reply to Alex's email.

'Morning,' Lara said, as she stepped off the makeup bus the next day, her hair still in curlers in preparation for the blocking rehearsal ahead. Jacob Moss was standing outside, drinking black coffee out of a styrofoam cup and smoking a Lucky Strike with his customary nonchalance. With any other actor, she would have leant over to kiss them hello, but not this one. He was the least tactile, least *actory* actor she had ever encountered.

'Good morning,' Jacob replied. It was well over a week since the splash about them in the *New York Express*, and to Lara's immense relief, the story seemed to have disappeared. The press had obviously lost interest, and Jacob had never even deigned to mention it. 'You sleep well?'

Lara was amazed. Was this a *conversation* Jacob was starting? 'Fine, thanks,' she said, which was a lie. She'd tossed and turned until three, before dropping into a fraught sleep tormented by a dream about car accidents on snowy streets intercut with fragments of images from *This Being Human* and *La Belle Hélène*. She shuddered now to think about it. 'How about you?'

Jacob looked at her, and the expression in his greyish eyes seemed to have a peculiar effect on her stomach this morning, not unlike the one she'd had in her bedroom last night, actually.

Perhaps it was simply that she'd been up for three hours and had not yet had breakfast.

'I slept okay, thanks. I went to a session at the Vanguard – you know what that is? And then I was kinda buzzed, so I was hanging out for a while.'

Lara was about to open her mouth and say something – how extraordinary, yes, she did indeed know what the Vanguard was and, moreover, how remarkable to hear Jacob string more than three words together in conversation! – but Jacob was suddenly grinding his cigarette under his boot and walking up the stairs to the makeup bus. Before she could gather her thoughts he had disappeared.

Lara stared after her co-star for a second, then shook her head and walked over to her trailer, where her dresser, Jennifer, was waiting outside. 'Morning, Jen.'

'Hey, Lara. You heard they want you in costume for the rehearsal, right?'

'I know, Greg told me. Something to do with the lighting in that location. So what have we got today?'

'Oh, it's beautiful,' Jennifer cooed, as she followed Lara into the cavernous trailer. 'Sabine's done such a great job.'

Sabine. The name made the breath snag in the back of Lara's throat as, with a jolt, she recalled that one of the images in her dream last night had not been from *This Being Human* at all, or even from *La Belle Hélène*. No, it had been from Sabine's photographs. One of the pictures she'd pored over that Saturday evening last month.

'She certainly has,' Lara agreed, suppressing the image as she wriggled out of her tracksuit bums and Alex's old football sweatshirt and into Helen's luxuriously tailored garments. 'She's a genius.'

'I know, right? We're so lucky to have her on board. I've learnt so much from her already.'

'Actually, Jen, is Sabine on set today? I'd like to ask her something.'

'I don't think she's in today. Is it something to do with your costume? I can see if Beth-Anne can help, if you want?'

'No. Don't worry about it. I'll talk to Sabine next time she's on set.'

'Fine, if you're sure. Now, is everything okay with this?'

Jennifer took a step back and looked Lara up and down. They were shooting an evening scene this morning, a party, and she'd been dressed in beautifully cut black cigarette pants and a turquoise silk top, with red patent Louboutin heels. 'That blouse could do with taking in a little, perhaps. But we can pin it for you on set.'

'Okay,' said Lara, kicking off the gorgeous, but towering, heels. It always felt bizarre to be dressed-up and made-up before breakfast. 'Can I wear my Uggs down to rehearsal?'

'They might need the shoes for height. But wear your boots over there and we'll bring them to set. Your jewellery's just there.' Jennifer motioned to the transparent box marked '1: LARA LATNER/HELEN' and grinned. 'And *please* don't forget to wear your wedding ring today!' There had been a continuity issue yesterday when Lara had taken off the ring at lunchtime – wearing it made her feel odd, she couldn't explain why, and she was in the habit of removing it absent-mindedly – and had forgotten to put it back on for the first scene after lunch.

'I promise!' Lara giggled guiltily. 'Sorry, again, about that.'

'No worries. You all set, then?'

'Yep. Thanks, Jen. See you over there.'

When Lara got home that night, mercifully early because they'd actually wrapped on schedule, the first thing she made herself do was call Alex. It was one thirty his time but he'd insisted in his reply to her email of last night that she call him tonight, no matter how late.

'Hello?' she heard a sleepy voice pick up, as she wandered into the kitchen to put on the kettle.

'Hey, it's me, sorry to call so late. I hoped you might still be up.'

'Hey, you!' Alex's lovely northern lilt was warmth to her ears and Lara, tired after shooting big party scenes all day, suddenly just wanted to collapse into bed with him. She could imagine his brain and his body scrambling to attention, the floppy dark hair she adored being pushed out of his eyes, his sleep-fuzzy limbs firm and alert now. Lara couldn't believe she'd left it three whole days to speak to her boy: now that he was actually on the line, she just wanted to talk and talk to him, to explain how tough the past week or so had been, to tell him about her horrible dream and the funny feeling she kept having, and that photograph of Sabine's that had flashed into her dream and then haunted her all day. Acknowledging, with a touch of guilt, that she also had scant idea what was really going on in Alex's life at the moment, she also wanted to say sorry for having been so bad at being in touch of late. She wanted to tell him she loved him.

'You know you can call me any time,' he was saying. 'How's it *going*?'

'Good. It's so bloody busy. I'm sorry I haven't called before. I'm so tired, I feel like a zombie.'

'The sexiest zombie in New York, I bet.'

Lara snorted. 'Oh, right, with the big huge bags under my eyes. Yeah. If you could see me now . . .'

'I wish I *could* see you now. I miss you, miss.'

Lara took a gulp of her tea. 'Me too. How is everything?'

'Also crazy, no thanks to Matthew's rape.'

'Is it – really bad?' She wondered what else to say. If she'd been at home, Alex would have flopped on the sofa and told her all about the grim details of the case, but out here she felt so far away from him and his world of pink-ribboned briefs and horsehair wigs that she didn't even know how to broach a conversation about it. She rubbed her eyes, feeling unspeakably tired all of a sudden.

'It's pretty nasty. A stepbrother and -sister.'

'Seriously?'

'Yeah, it's sad, actually. It's split the whole family up.'

'And you're defending who? The guy?'

'Obviously.'

'Right. So, you're defending another rapist.' Lara could never, quite, come to terms with the strangeness of the fact that Alex, one of the most fiercely principled people she knew, did a job in which he had to represent society's ugliest criminals and strive to get their punishments *reduced*.

'An *alleged* rapist, La. That's how the law works, remember? There are definitely mitigating circumstances.'

'I still find it hard to get my head around it.'

'Well, that's what I've been trying to do all evening, monkey,' Alex yawned, 'on top of all my other cases. I only got home a couple of hours ago.'

'Jesus. You're working filming hours, babe. When was the last time you had a proper day off?'

'I can't remember. The day I played cricket with the lads, I think.'

'*Al!* That's rubbish! You need to look after yourself.'

'I bet you can talk. How many hours' sleep are you getting at the moment?'

Lara sank onto the sofa and put her feet up on the table. 'Fair point. But still.'

'Listen, I love it really, the work. And this case is fascinating, so I shouldn't grumble. The only real problem is it means I haven't been able to come out and see you yet.'

Lara felt a slow worm of betrayal snake through her gut as she realised with a shock that she was secretly *relieved* Alex hadn't come out to see her yet. She knew how distracting set visits from outsiders could be, and she had no doubt she would have had a completely different experience on *This Being Human* if her boyfriend had been out here, requiring time and attention. 'Honestly, it's probably a good thing you haven't,' she assured him. 'I've been working every day and it would have been rubbish not to be able to see you properly.' Feeling restless, she jumped up and went to the window to watch unsuspecting Manhattan going about its nightly twinkle down below.

'And, of course, you've been busy having your affair with Jacob Moss,' Alex quipped. 'Didn't want to get in the way of that.'

'Well, exactly,' she deadpanned back. 'How would I ever have managed *that* if you were over here?'

Alex laughed. 'Are you still having fun, though?'

Lara watched the dot of a yellow taxicab crawl along Lexington Avenue beneath her and found herself marvelling again that she was really here, in New York. 'Am I having *fun?*' she echoed. 'I don't know about fun. But it's very exciting. And, you know, even though there's all the usual crap with filming, the hanging around and the on-set politics and all that, it's so surreal to be here, playing Mum's part, that to me it almost feels like something much more important than just making a film.' She turned back into the living room and pressed the blinds button, giving a little chuckle. 'I mean, if that doesn't sound like the most pretentious thing in the world . . .'

'Doesn't at all, baby,' Alex said again, but she could hear how his voice thickened with tiredness. 'Sounds amazing.'

'Anyway. It's clearly not the time to talk about this. You must be zonked.'

'Oi!' he disagreed, his voice sharper. 'Listen, you. I *really* want to hear about it. I've been a bit worried the past few days.'

Lara closed her eyes. 'Please don't worry. And I'm sorry, again, that I haven't been better at calling recently. I'm just—'

'Ssh!' Alex interrupted. 'I understand. And *I'm* sorry I'm being such a vegetable tonight. Can we find a time to talk properly tomorrow?'

'Of course,' Lara breathed. 'I'll give you a ring when I get into work . . .'

There was a fractional, infinitesimal pause then, which would have been undetectable in normal circumstances. But it was as if both, in that instant, knew that something had shifted ever so slightly in the distance between them; in the air and night and water that separated their two bodies and should not have separated their two souls but, somehow, did.

'Hey – I love you,' Alex said.

Lara bit her lip. 'I love you, too,' she whispered.

No sooner had Lara put down the phone than it beeped with a message. She snatched it up. If Alex had sent her a text, she wanted to send him one back, quickly, while he was still awake, to say that she loved him lots and was sorry about the strangeness of the end of the conversation, and that she would definitely call him earlier tomorrow – because she would, she promised herself.

But the message, Lara discovered, as she pressed open the little envelope icon, was not from her boyfriend at all.

So? How about it?
Received: Oct 20 Time: 21:18 Sender +19172889064

Lara barely had time to read the message before another was buzzing in her hands.

I dare you.
Received: Oct 20 Time: 21:19 Sender +19172889064

And then another:

It's Jacob, by the way.
Received: Oct 20 Time: 21:20 Sender +19172889064

Lara let out a cry of astonishment, and promptly dropped the phone.

SIX

It took her a little over a week to say yes. A week, during which she and Jacob filmed almost all day every day together but still barely spoke to one another off-set, so that the simmering intensity – and, yes, she supposed, *chemistry*, people were still raving about their 'chemistry', even though they had tired of joking about their supposed affair – built up to a pressure that yielded spectacular results on-screen.

After that tricky week of dropped scenes and camera problems and expensive overtime, the production had found its mojo again. Kevin was back on track, the actors were flying, and the sense among the crew that they might be working on something quite special was tangible on set. Lara felt particularly excited by the way all these vital scenes between Helen and Peter were going, and there were moments when she wondered if Jacob had even plotted it this way – like, humour the sweet English chick with all her earnest requests that they run lines and discuss motivation because she wants to make sure their relationship on screen is *viable*, oh, sure, smile at her and ruffle her feathers a little by doing things out of the blue, like the cigarette trick, and then WHAM! Hit her with this!

Such a strategy did not seem entirely unlikely. The more Lara watched Jacob Moss at work, the more she detected within him a scarily intuitive intelligence. One morning, while they were sitting in the artists' green room waiting to go back on set, Jacob had left his script lying around as he went out to take a phone call. Lara, heart thumping, had snatched it up, hoping to discover a clue to Jacob's thought processes; a clue to his uncanny ability to so judge the emotional pitch of a scene that he could turn whatever was on the page into something unexpectedly moving, often jaw-droppingly powerful. With one look, Jacob's performances could force you to ask questions, reveal to you the answers, then force you to ask them all over again; and there seemed to be so much behind his eyes when the cameras were rolling that she expected to see his script covered with ideas and observations – as, indeed, hers was. Instead, Lara found only page after page of complete blankness – until, curiously, at one point he had scrawled, in a touchingly childlike hand, 'pick up boots'. She had stared at the phrase, agape, and then, collecting herself, shoved the script back into its former position as her co-star ambled back in. No, it was not academic intelligence that Jacob had, Lara thought, as she felt, physically *felt*, Jacob's Peter break her Helen's heart on screen half an hour or so later: it was something much more primitive and instinctive. No matter what a treacherous shit Peter was, no matter how he behaved, the way Jacob played him it was impossible not to care about him. Poor old Chris: his Michael should have been far more sympathetic than Peter, yet he was being acted off the screen by his counterpart!

Jacob understood people, Lara was learning, he *got* them. Like Peter, he knew how to control, how to manipulate, and could suck people in before his unwitting victims even realised what was happening.

But she *did* realise what was happening, she told herself, and she would not be so beguiled. Despite an overwhelming impulse to text back 'Yes!' to his drink proposition, she had therefore forced herself to hold back. Jacob was playing a game: she must play one too. Their scenes the morning after his 'I dare you' taunt had been particularly charged, and Lara had spent her lunch break pacing around her trailer, trying to work out what to do. When another text message had arrived on her phone that night, she had been about to write something flippant like **Dare to ask me face to face tomorrow, Mr M, and you might just get an answer** ... but had held back, once again. And then, the next day, there had been more silence, more pretence that none of this was happening – only to be accompanied by another exhilarating morning under the spotlights.

It was *almost* fun, this, seeing how long it would take either of them to crack; but perhaps inevitably it was Lara who finally caved in, the following Friday morning. For the first time that week there had been no text from Jacob the night before, and she had sat in her apartment, trying to go over her lines but unable to focus as she waited expectantly for it, feeling oddly bereft, and then shamefully foolish, as it had never arrived and she'd gone restlessly to bed. It would have been his intention, no doubt, to derail her like that, but despite the alarm bells that rang noisily in her ears, she'd had enough.

They were standing near the Craft Service table outside the sound stage, being fitted with radio-mics in readiness for the following scene. As Lara had her pack fitted to the back of her skirt, she clocked Jacob studiously avoiding her, making a coffee and peeling a banana, whistling to himself. As Tony, the sound assistant, went over to fit Jacob's mic, she caught a flash of her co-star's taut, tattooed belly as he lifted up his shirt to thread the wire up – and had to turn away quickly, her heart banging in her chest. How was it possible that Jacob Moss could still make her feel like this, so flustered and silly and . . . *English*? Once Tony had gone, Lara cleared her throat and said, as coolly as possible, 'So, I thought I might go to the Vanguard tomorrow night. If you want to ever, you know, have that drink, we could meet somewhere down there beforehand. I found this great place – the Spotted Pig?'

Jacob raised an eyebrow and grinned. Then he shrugged. 'Sure. I like the Spotted Pig. And I like the Benny Jones orchestra.'

Lara was taken aback. She hadn't asked him to go to the gig with her! And how come he even knew what was playing there tomorrow night? 'You do?'

'Doesn't everybody?'

That was so typically Jacob, to undermine her even as he was slowly reeling her in. 'I doubt it,' she said, trying to wrest back a little dignity. 'A little too tame for most people's taste, aren't they?'

'For the jazz aficionados, perhaps, sure, but not for regular people.'

Are you a regular person? she wanted to ask. *You?* But she didn't have the guts – and, in any case, they were being called back by Greg onto the set.

That evening Lara was in her apartment, running a bath. It had been a long day, at the end of a long week, and she had declined offers from Chris to go to a dinner and Dan Peters to go to some party, fancying instead an evening in with her feet up and an early night. Dipping her toe into the water to test the temperature, she was wondering idly what Jacob had made of their exchange earlier, and whether his laconic 'sure' would actually materialise into a meeting tomorrow, when her phone beeped in the living room. The sound sent a smile hurtling so quickly to her lips that she was shocked – and then suitably chastened, in any case, when it turned out that the text wasn't from Jacob after all. It was from Sabine, wondering if Lara would like to come to the apartment for lunch tomorrow: she had dug out some more photo albums from Paris in the 1970s and 1980s, she said, and would be delighted to show them to her if she was interested. Lara swallowed her irrational disappointment and texted back to say that, of course, she would love to, she would be there at one. She resolved to get up early, go for a jog around Central Park, and catch the Rothko show she'd been meaning to go to at the Met *en route* to Sabine and Frank's. Then she headed back to the bathroom and climbed into the steaming tub.

When her phone went off again, minutes later, Lara assumed it was Sabine replying, so ignored it. Once out of the bath and in her pyjamas, she switched on CNN – the new president was in Iraq, which the anchor was assuming heralded the beginning of a policy of troop withdrawal – and half watched the footage while she tried to decide what to do with her night off. It was too late to call Alex, but she could watch a movie, or catch up on emails from her friends and family. She could start ploughing through the scripts Milton had been sending her, some of which were direct offers (she could certainly get used to this, never having to audition for a film again!). Or read a book – there was a stash of mostly untouched novels and the Saint-Laurent biography sitting in her bedroom. Not to mention a tub of Häagen-Dazs in the freezer . . .

When Lara did finally pick up her phone on her way to get the ice cream, then, she got a shock.

Tonight?
Received: Oct 28 Time: 21:08 Sender +19172889064

Lara stared at the word, her heart in her mouth. She looked down at her pyjamas, her slippered feet, cast a glance towards her invitingly squashy sofa. The clock on her phone told her it was already nearly nine forty-five. Of course she should not go out for a drink with Jacob *now* . . . She should wait until tomorrow night, as they had planned – or, at least, half planned . . .

What's wrong with tomorrow?

Lara's fingers quivered as she pressed the green 'send' button. It was the first time she had ever replied knowingly to one of Jacob's messages and her heart was beating pathetically fast.

Now, there's a question.
Received: Oct 28 Time: 21:44 Sender +19172889064

Lara let out a squeal of frustration and waited for the next message. Surely, there would be a next message. She stormed into the kitchen and opened the freezer. She would not succumb. She wouldn't! Screw Jacob and his infuriating games: going out now would be a crazy thing to do, crazy. She was so knackered that if she closed her eyes now she would probably fall asleep.

And, yet, it was Friday night . . . She was in New York . . . There was the whole city out there . . . And Jacob, somewhere . . .

He had texted her the address of a bar in a street somewhere off Eleventh Avenue, in the Meatpacking District. Lara was surprised: she knew that was a cool area – she'd had a drink in Soho House nearby a couple of weeks ago, and it hadn't seemed Jacob's style – all hipster media types and expensive martinis. Not, she reflected, that she had any idea what Jacob's 'style' might be. He remained a complete enigma. And *that* was the reason she was going for a drink with him, she reminded herself. She'd spent the last month filming these intimate, emotionally charged scenes with a person who in reality she knew nothing about (although, in extremely uncharacteristic fashion, she had recently been pulling up items about Jacob from Google and Wikipedia, and discovering eye-popping tales about his poverty-stricken, drug-addled past). Now was simply a chance to find out a little bit more, and that was why she'd finally caved in and sent the **Fine, tonight. Where? When?** text.

Despite the temptation to throw back on a pair of jeans and trainers, Lara had learnt that it was better in New York to look the part for wherever you happened to be in the city, so she dressed now in what she hoped might be suitably MePa fashion, in an amazing blue Stella McCartney tunic and some funky little ankle boots from Miu Miu, both gifts from New York fashion PRs that had arrived – to many shrieks of excitement and glee – in Lara's trailer last week. As she brushed her hair and put on some makeup, she recalled how nice it had felt to wipe everything off a few hours ago and get into her jim-jams, and now here she was with a mascara wand in her hand, feeling as nervous and excited as if she were about to go on a first date. Which, obviously, she wasn't. But, oh, God. What *was* she doing? And why was she going out with him now, tonight, when she'd been all but ready for bed half an hour ago? Was she insane? Lara grabbed her lipgloss, her keys, phone and Prada clutch, and fled the apartment before she could change her mind.

When she told the cab driver the address Jacob had sent through, the old man raised his eyebrows. 'You sure, lady?'

'Er, yes. I think so? Why?'

He shrugged. 'Just don't look like the kind of girl who belong down there.'

'Really?' Lara felt a dart of concern, before telling herself not to be so foolish. She'd looked on the map: the street wasn't far from the bright lights and extravagant cocktail lists of Soho House and Hotel Gansevoort. And if she was over-dressed, then sod it: she felt pretty fabulous. If it was weird with Jacob tonight, she'd call Dan and go and join him and Lucy. Everything would be cool. Looking out of the window, though, Lara could see what the driver had been getting at: as they turned off the glossily gentrified main lines of the district, the streets took on an entirely different aspect and atmosphere. They stopped on the intended one, which seemed dark, empty and somewhat forbidding.

'So here we are, lady. Thirteen eighty.'

Lara frowned as she took out her purse. 'This is definitely the right place?'

The driver shrugged. 'What you told me.'

'Okay,' she said, pulling out a twenty-dollar bill. 'Would you do me a favour? I'm supposed to be meeting a friend here, but I can't see him, and I can't for the life of me imagine this can be the right street. Will you wait for me for two minutes while I go and check? Oh, and keep the change.'

'Okay, pretty lady. I wait for you come back here, then.'

Lara got out of the cab and tottered a little further down the street, shivering in the late October wind. There was no sign of any life here, unless you counted the slumped figures in the occasional doorway. Amazing. Everywhere in New York was noise and bustle, energy and movement, and here she was, the only moving life form on the only quiet street in the city. She supposed this was how the Meatpacking District had once been all over: a conglomeration of dark, unlovely streets, cowering in the shadow of industry, before the glitterati entrepreneurs had moved in and transformed some of the grander avenues into shining temples of trend and commerce. No doubt this would have been *fascinating* to see, she thought bitterly, had she been walking around here in daytime. But it was strangely less interesting right now, in this weather, in this outfit. What was Jacob playing at? Cursing her co-star, and herself for having replied to his infuriating text message in the first place, Lara turned swiftly around and walked back down the eerily silent street towards her cab, silly impractical boots clicking on the pavement as she went.

And then, suddenly, there was a burst of light and noise as one of the basement doors along the street was thrown open and she heard loud music, laughter. And now, now there was the familiar sight and shape of him, a tall, sinewy blur of colour and muscle emerging up the wrought-iron stairs, laughing. Lara realised she'd never heard Jacob laugh – not out of character, anyway. It was a good sound: rich and full. He was lighting the cigarette in his mouth and talking to his companion, a giraffe-skinny Japanese girl with long black hair, bright red lips and lots of black eyeliner. He still had not seen her. Lara cleared her throat, nervously, and approached them.

'Hello.'

Jacob spun around to face her, and Lara's heart faltered for a millisecond as she saw the gleam in his eyes. That was *Peter's* gleam; the sort of eye-light she was often dazzled by when she was acting opposite him, as Helen, but which she had never once seen in Jacob himself – for whom the phrase 'turning it on for the camera' had practically been invented. As himself, Jacob usually wore an expression of mildly bored amusement, his eyes cloudy and unreadable.

'Well, hello there,' he said, and then, to her further astonishment, pulled his cigarette out of his mouth and leant over to kiss her cheek. Was that the first physical contact they had ever had as Jacob and Lara rather than as Peter and Helen? She felt her skin blaze where his lips had just been. 'This is Coco.'

'Hi, Lara,' said Coco, grinning. 'It's great to meet you. I *love* your dress, it's so neat.'

'Thanks,' Lara managed, her eyes still fixed on Jacob's face. 'I thought I was totally in the wrong place.'

'Really?' Jacob said, smiling. 'Why would you think that?'

Lara let out a nervous laugh. 'It just wasn't exactly what I was expecting,' she admitted. She remembered her cab, still sitting there, and felt about ten years old, the lamest kid in school, as if her mum and dad had dropped her off at a party and were now hanging around to check up on her. She tried to motion subtly to the cab driver that she was fine now, she had obviously met her 'friends', he needn't wait any longer. But still he sat there, engine humming, waiting for her to come back – just as he had promised to do.

'Hey – uh, I'm just going to get rid of my cab,' Lara said sheepishly. 'I'll see you down there.'

As Jacob brushed past her on his way back down the stairs,

he murmured in her ear, 'I'll always give you what you're not expecting, Lara, remember that.'

She felt a shiver of something pass through her – trepidation? Fear? Excitement? Or, perhaps, merely the autumnal night wind. No matter what it was, a few moments later she was following Jacob down the stairs into the club.

SEVEN

Lara was being ripped out of her sleep-funk by the phone ringing insistently in her apartment. She inched an eye open. It felt crusty, blinded by the light that streamed into her bedroom through the blinds. Her head was pounding. The clock by her bedside table said 11:53. Jesus, it was nearly midday! She was supposed to be at Sabine's for lunch! She threw a hand over to the bedside table and scrabbled around for the offending telephone. 'Hello?' she said groggily.

'Hello, my beautiful.'

'*Al*. Hey. How are you?'

'Did I wake you up?'

'No, no, not at all. I was . . . Yeah, you did, actually. Fucking hell, I can't believe I've slept this late.' Lara eased herself up in bed and rubbed her eyes, her brain grumbling wildly as its contents slid messily back into place.

'Were you working late?'

'No-o, not really. I actually went out. And I must've really needed to blow off some steam or something, because it turned out to be a bit of a large one.'

It had been after seven, according to her trusty bedside clock, when she had collapsed into this bed. Not that long ago, come to think of it. No wonder she felt so monstrous.

'Probably good for you, miss.'

She grunted in response.

'So, who'd you go out with? Film people?'

Lara swallowed, repulsed by her sorry state. Her mouth felt like it was full of brick dust and she could smell the toxicity coming off her breath. 'Mmm. Jacob, actually, took – took some people to this little club, in a basement in the Meatpacking. You'd never even know it was there if you weren't looking. It's a real dive, kind of Prohibition-chic, all unnamed liquor bottles and achingly cool girls in lots of eyeliner. But the best music. Seriously, I've never heard such amazing music.' It was true: she'd danced all night in appreciation.

'Sounds fun.'

'Yeah,' Lara replied. 'It was kind of fun.' Jacob – who, Lara had noticed, didn't seem to drink alcohol himself – had thrown two shots of some indescribable combination down her throat as she'd joined him and Coco at the bar, and it had been five a.m. before she'd even known it. 'A bit of a New York night, I suppose, everyone a little wacky and crazy, but really interesting.'

'Well, you deserve to let your hair down. And what are you up to for the rest of the day?'

'I'm due at Sabine's in about an hour, so I should get a move on. And then, I don't know what. I was thinking about going to a gig at the Village Vanguard tonight, but I'm not sure I can face it now . . .' Memories of drunkenly making Jacob promise

253

to meet her there as originally planned swam in her head. She felt nauseous. 'What about you, babe? What are your plans? Did you play footie today?'

'Nah. Had to go on a prison visit this morning with one of the silks so I missed the game. I'm meeting up with the boys in a bit, though. Think I'll just go for a few beers and head back for an early one.' He adopted a silly voice: 'Cuz I is cream-crackered, like.'

Lara chuckled, despite herself. 'Poor you. You're working too hard.'

'*You*'re working too hard by the sound of things. But, hey, guess what?'

'What?' she asked.

'I've booked my flights for the nineteenth. And I'll be there for five whole nights.'

Lara gulped. 'Brilliant!' she managed to say. 'That's so exciting.'

'I can't wait to see you, miss.'

'Can't wait to see you too.' She grimaced. 'I'd better get up now.'

'Okay, lazy-bones. Have a nice day.'

'You too. Say hi to the guys.'

Lara put down the phone and felt her eyes sting. She seemed almost impossibly far away from Alex at the moment, and not just because of the hangover. It hurt. As nobly as they were both trying, it was always difficult to conduct a relationship telephonically or by email. She'd known so many actors break up with their partners while they were away on location (or soon afterwards) and it was easy to see why. *This*, this life, was not conducive to maintaining a grip on reality, and relationships back home invariably suffered as much as the other neglected elements of real life; the difference being that those other things –

friendships, parking fines, overdue library books – were more easily rectified. It was much harder to mend broken connections with loved ones. Being away filming seemed to widen the distance between people in a much more than physical sense. It allowed cracks – the normal cracks that were part and parcel of any relationship between two individuals and could easily be filled by proximity and shared conversation and the touch of the other during sleep – to open, to grow.

Alex had once joked to Lara that her work was like a kind of paid summer camp for grown-ups, and he was right. You went to a place you didn't know, you met the random people you would be working with for a finite period, and immediately those people would become your friends, your colleagues, your brothers, your sisters, your lovers. You would all work with the utmost focus and intensity to one shared end; you'd spend seventeen, eighteen hours a day in a small closed box with them, a box full of lights and costumes and make-believe; and then, more often than not, you'd go home with some of them – go home for a drink, a wind-down chat or, sometimes, more. And then, at the end of the fixed period, it would be over: you'd be released back into real time and real life, often never to see any of those people again. The only thing that would endure of your lives together was the film, your shared offspring, always there to remind you of a character you once played, a life you once lived, a world you once inhabited fully and wholly, but only for a moment. And by then, of course, you'd already be off on another adventure – a new story, a new family, new brothers, sisters, friends, colleagues, lovers . . . And what of the people left behind each time?

What of the people left behind? Lara folded her arms across her chest and gazed around her luxurious rented bedroom. She *knew* what really mattered in her life, and it certainly was not this. Any of this. But she and Al had always been okay while she was away: their relationship had never floundered in the five years she'd been acting. Partly because Alex was secure in his love and unfazed by the vicissitudes of his girlfriend's industry – as demonstrated most recently in his reaction to the New York tabloid gossip. But also because the unspoken love contract between the two of them had always implied, It's you, and I know what is important in life. *You*. So long as they both kept their side of the bargain, they would always be okay.

But now, this morning, her head still ringing with the alcohol that Jacob Moss had poured down her throat last night, before walking her home for two hours through the streets of Manhattan as the sun began to rise, Lara began to see that she had grown worryingly complacent about her relationship with Alex. Talking to him just then, he had felt so like a stranger: his world somehow less immediate, less real than the one she was inhabiting now. It would be easy enough to blame that on the long-distance telephony, but it had never happened before while she'd been away. Ever. Faced, for the first time in six years, with the nagging possibility that she might be capable of *not* honouring her own part in that contract, Lara felt a cold anxiety creep through her that was almost instantly overcome by another bolt of hangover nausea. Dragging herself out of bed, she clutched her aching head and went in urgent search of a painkiller.

Frank and Sabine Mellon's apartment was the archetypal Upper East Side pad: large, tasteful, elegant, with plush cream carpets and huge, famous-looking canvases on the wall – probably originals, given Frank's line of work. Everything was spotless, just so. Although she had dressed carefully for the occasion, Lara felt horribly out of place this lunchtime, as she followed Frank through the hallway into the drawing room, as if no amount of sharp tailoring could hide the fact that she was hungover as a beast and might keel over at any minute.

She'd taken the hottest, most scalding shower she could bear, standing under the jet and willing her head to settle, her mind to clear. She'd made a cafetière of eye-wateringly strong coffee and glugged the remains of a carton of orange juice that was in the fridge. There wasn't much to eat in her kitchen, and she didn't have time anyway, so she'd done as tourists do and bought a disappointing pretzel for a dollar from the street vendor at her corner of Lexington. She'd chewed off a salty corner in the cab – she would not feel guilty about taking cabs here, she'd already decided: she was on a hundred dollars *per diem* for expenses and hardly spending any of it, and besides, they were so cheap compared to London – then tossed the remains of the doughy knot in the trash can outside the Mellons' portered block. In the mirror in the elevator on the way up to the eighteenth floor, Lara had run her hands through her hair, still damp from her recent shower, and yanked it into a ponytail, then pulled a lipgloss out of her bag and applied a quick slick. Baby steps, she told herself. Hair. Lipgloss. Smile. You can get through this.

Frank Mellon, a dapper man in his late sixties, opened the door and ushered Lara into the drawing room, offering her a drink. Champagne? White wine? A Bloody Mary? Lara opted gratefully for the latter, her stomach doing flips, and asked if she might also have a glass of water.

When Sabine came through she gave Lara a kiss on the cheek. 'Bonjour, chèrie!' she greeted her. 'Tu vas bien?'

Lara managed a smile as she kissed Sabine back, hoping the blessed Tabasco and tomato juice might already be hiding the poison she could still taste lingering on her breath from last night. 'Je vais bien, merci, Sabine, et toi?'

It was always a pleasure to speak French with Sabine and her husband, but today Lara could have done without the extra mental pressure as she tried to construct sentences over lunch – perfect, restorative Dover sole, *boulanger* potatoes and *haricots verts*, made by the live-in French cook – in her second language. It would have been difficult enough to accomplish that today in her first. After general chit-chat about how she was getting on, what she had been doing in New York – had she seen the Rothko at the Met? Frank wondered helpfully – they mostly asked her about the film, to which she tried to respond as neutrally as possible. Sabine was saying that Kevin had shown her some rushes already – dailies, she called them, of course, having lived in America for two decades – and that Lara looked 'fantastic' up there on screen. 'Just like your mother . . .'

Lara smiled bravely and arranged her knife and fork together. She felt so far from fantastic right now, inside and out, that it seemed an outrageous slight against Eve to even mention mother and daughter in the same breath. 'You're too kind, Sabine,' she said, taking a sip of water.

'Not at all, just saying the truth. Have you seen any of the film yourself yet?'

'Some of the others have been bugging Kevin to let them watch the rushes, but I can't quite bring myself to do it. I feel nervous even thinking about it.'

'Are you modelling your own performance on your mother's?' Frank asked.

It was a reasonable enough enquiry, but made Lara's fragile head pound even harder. This was a question so complex she dreaded thinking about it at the best of times, let alone in her current, frayed state of mind. 'Ye-es, I suppose I am. It was hard to know what to do – whether, you know, to not watch the original and just play the part that was on the page in front of me, or whether to really study Mum's interpretation and try to capture something similar, which I think is what Kevin is after.' She let out a self-deprecating chuckle. 'Obviously I realise that's a pretty tall order, to recreate what she did, but I'm trying.'

'You know, I was actually a little surprised when I looked at the dailies,' said Sabine. 'You *look* so like Eve, but I think in life you are quite different.' This made Lara sit up sharply, as Sabine continued, 'You have a wonderful – *comment est-ce qu'on dit?* – a *realness* to you, that your mother, who was one of life's dreamers, never seemed to have. And so I was expecting your Hélène to be so different from hers. But on the screen it is all there again in you: all her fragility, all her lightness.' Sabine smiled kindly. 'Not that you haven't also created your own interesting dynamic for this character, of course. I think you are working well with Jacob, *non?*'

Lara loved how Sabine said his name. *Jacob*, as in rue Jacob, as in where her mother and father had once lived, before they were married, before she was born. The smooth swish of the '*ja*', as she spoke it in her heavy French accent, reminded Lara of how Eve used to say the word, and she wondered, disconnectedly, what on earth her mother would have made of her enigmatic co-star, source of such bewilderment over the past few weeks and now, unbelievably, the reason for this deathly hangover.

'Mmm.' She nodded. 'It took a while, but we're getting on quite well now.' She closed her mouth, respectful of the instinct warning her inside that if she started talking about Jacob to Sabine she might never stop.

Sabine laughed fondly. 'Yes, I imagine it would. He is not the most forthcoming of creatures, that one, but I have to say I find him fascinating.'

Lara smiled valiantly, and murmured another 'Mmm' in response. Then she turned to Frank and promptly changed the subject. 'May I have some more potatoes, please?'

After dessert, they retired with coffee to the drawing room, at which point Sabine brought over the albums she'd mentioned on the phone. The first time Lara had come here, Sabine had shown her the original costume designs for *La Belle Hélène*, as well as sketches and continuity pictures taken from the Paris set, all of which were arranged in special albums showcasing the whole of the de Sévigné *oeuvre*. There were pictures, too, of Eve in the film *Quand J'embrasse le Ciel*, also directed by Dominique St Clair. These images had been remarkable to Lara, things of unthinkable magnificence, but today's offerings were somehow much more poignant. Sabine had dug out her personal collection of photographs from that time, and now here they were, sitting in front of her. History and memory and beauty interleaved across three large books.

After a while Frank and Sabine left Lara alone to turn wordlessly the pages of the old blue albums. Here – in both black and white and brash 1970s technicolour – was Eve chatting on set, smoking, or laughing, or clutching at her co-star Gabriel Dufy's arm in a fit of mirth, her head thrown back in the giant roar that Lara remembered well. Here was Eve in costume during what must have been a rehearsal or a take on *Hélène* – she immediately recognised the film set in the background of the picture. Here was Eve off-duty, still in costume, her arms flung around Dominique St Clair. And here, again, another: the director's arm around the actress's shoulders, her head leaning on it, eyes closed in a state of apparently blissful contentment. Here was one, a twenty-something Eve giggling playfully at the centre of a group of camera crew, that made Lara smile. It could have been herself on set last week – or, indeed, any pretty young actress – indulging the grips and sparks with a photo.

In the decade since her mother's accident, Lara had, of course, gone back to pore over the family snaps they had at home. She had also asked Colette to dig out as many old photos of her daughter as she could find, from when she was a little girl, a teenager, a student . . . And there were many. She had seen many. The world was not short of pictures of Eve Lacloche. In her time, Eve had been one of France's most photographed women. As well as all the film or theatre stills, such as Cleopatra, and the more artistic portraits that graced the pages of Christie's and Sotheby's catalogues and occasionally turned up in auction houses around the world, there were fashion magazines, film magazines, books on French style, books chronicling the wild era of post-1968 Paris and its cast of characters, which Eve Lacloche had, in her own way, helped to define. But these – these were different, somehow. Taken over a relatively short period – the dates seemed to suggest 1975 to 1982 – they captured Eve as she had once been at a very specific moment in her life. Grief itched at Lara's throat now as she discovered image after image of her mother at a time when she had clearly taken such uncomplicated pleasure in the world. Eve's face was so lovely and open in these shots, it seemed to call out to Lara across the decades, 'Look! Look at me! Look how happy I am!' In the pictures from *La Belle Hélène*, Lara liked to imagine that an element of her mother's radiance might have come not only from the fact that she was in love with Oliver but from the fact she was newly pregnant. Lara scrutinised the photos to try to spot the small bump that was herself on her mother's slender frame, which you could see at certain angles in the film, and in some precious frames, you definitely could: in one, a beaming Eve even had her hands clasped protectively over her belly!

Life for Eve would soon turn, Lara knew, as she started on the second album; things would change when her mother and father left for London soon after this. Eve would not always find life so joyful and free from struggle, and later there would be all those days when she could or would not get out of bed, the times when Lara and Lucas would telephone her from school and her once smoky, teasing voice would instead be dull and exhausted. But this was before all that, and it was touchingly life-affirming to see her mother as she had once been, the very essence of girlish energy and joy. Lara remembered her father at lunch that day in the summer, telling her how Eve, when he met her, had been 'like sunlight'. *She'd arrive somewhere*, Lara could hear Oliver's voice recounting, *and everyone would light up*. Lara could practically see that process happening in these photographs. She held up the album to study more closely the stills from the set, and there – yes, there it was. All eyes on Eve, everybody turning their faces towards hers, sharing in her infectious laughter. Sabine had evidently loved to take pictures during rehearsals: there were numerous shots of Eve, deep in concentration with Dominique, or Gabriel, or André Labeque, or Edouard Valence, her leading man in *Quand J'embrasse*, and in every one it was the same. Lara wasn't sure whether it was a trick of the light, or her fancy, but in each photo, it seemed, Eve somehow appeared to be in sharper, more dazzling focus than anybody else.

The last album was one not of photographs but of press clippings, which Sabine had meticulously archived if they related to her or her work. Among the many features about actresses and models Sabine had dressed or styled that had been snipped from the pages of fashion and society magazines – here was Emmanuelle Riva, Brigitte Bardot, Simone Signoret, Cathérine Deneuve, Claudia Cardinale – there were a number of articles about Eve, who had once been the starriest girl of them all. There were plenty of images from premières and parties, including one, Lara was enthralled to discover, of her mother *and* her father, in black tie, both looking heartbreakingly young and beautiful at what seemed to be a state function. Sabine had apparently been the official dresser on this occasion and had attached a note to the image: 'Fonction officielle pour les droits des femmes, Château de Versailles – S. Veil, *Christian Dior*. E. Lacloche, *YSL*. M. Pelletier & F. Giroud, *Chanel*. Juillet, 1980.'

After that one, however, there were few pictures of Eve with Oliver. Her father had probably been like Alex was now, Lara supposed, determined to keep as far out of the public eye as he could; so far, in fact, that he didn't even accompany his girlfriend, and later wife, to awards ceremonies. Lara went on to discover pages of cuttings from Cannes, the Venice film festival, even the Oscars, relating to *Quand J'embrasse le Ciel* and *La Belle Hélène* – Sabine herself had been regularly nominated for awards – but there was never a sighting of Oliver. Instead, Eve seemed mostly to be photographed, eyes glittering, on the arm of her director, Dominique St Clair.

Staring at a *Paris Match* feature on the Oscars' ceremony in 1982 – which had taken place just a few months after she'd been born, she knew – Lara felt her cheeks prickle and her breath catch as something unimaginable occurred to her. Frantically, she rushed back to the other albums, including the ones Sabine had shown her last time she was here, when one image in particular had caught her eye. Yes, there it was, a picture of Eve, on set as Hélène, staring at her director, with a particular expression in her eyes. An expression of giddy, drunken – *love*. The expression, in fact, that even just an hour or so ago she had confidently assumed derived from the love affair her mother would have been conducting with her father at the time the photograph was taken. But again and again there were Eve and Dominique, Eve and Dominique, Eve and Dominique . . . Lara closed the photograph album and leant back against the soft cream sofa. Her head was throbbing.

The light was fading from the sky when she emerged from the drawing room. She'd lost track of time and felt guilty for having taken up so much of the Mellons' Saturday afternoon. She opened the kitchen door, shyly, to find Sabine and Frank engaged in the *New York Times* crossword, heads together. They looked up and smiled as she walked in. 'Thank you so much for letting me see them,' Lara said quietly, in English. 'They're wonderful.'

Sabine found herself intensely moved by the image of Eve's very English daughter, standing tall and brave at the doorway of her kitchen. She stood up and went to embrace Lara, who buckled in the face of such kindness and choked out a sob.

'I'm sorry,' Lara whispered, into the peach cashmere of Sabine's cardigan. 'I'm sorry, I just . . . I don't know. It was the picture of my mother with my father that . . .' She looked up apologetically and bit her lip. 'Sorry. I'm just a bit of a mess at the moment. I think it's the film . . .'

'Oh, *chérie*!' Sabine murmured comfortingly, as Frank rose discreetly and disappeared from the kitchen. 'Of course! You must be exhausted, my poor, lovely girl. Come on.' She motioned to the table. 'We will make a little cup of tea, *non*?'

'Oh, Sabine, no, please don't worry. I should just go home. You've been so kind. I have so many questions, so many things to ask you about. I just don't think I can do it now, if you don't mind.'

'Of course, *chérie*, of course. But you are welcome any time, you know that? And if there are any of those pictures you would like, you will tell me and I will get copies made for you, yes?'

Lara smiled appreciatively. 'Thanks, Sabine. There is one, in particular, actually . . . And I'd love to be able to show some of them to my little brother, Lucas. You know, it will be ten years this December since Mum died.'

Ten years. Sabine nodded gravely, and reached across the kitchen to take Lara's hand in her own. 'I know. And it still feels like yesterday. Oh, Lara. I adored your mother. *Everyone* who was lucky enough to work with her adored her. She was a real glory.' Sabine's eyes shone, but she blinked the tears quickly away. It would not be fair on Eve's daughter to weep in front of her. 'You know, Lara, to work with Eve was empowering. It was to be taken to the very edge of what you can do, and to be made better. Oh, *chérie*, please don't cry. Your mother would have been so proud of you.'

Lara tried to force down the lump in her throat. She wondered if that was true; if Eve really would be proud of her. 'Thank you, Sabine. I can't tell you how much I appreciate that. Will you say thanks to Frank, too?'

'Of course.' Sabine cast her eyes heavenward. 'Although I think I've lost him to the baseball for the rest of the afternoon. Now, I will be on set at the end of the week to see how everything's going, but will you promise to call me if you want to talk about anything before that? And you must tell me any photographs you want and I'll take them to Giorgio, my nice Italian printer in Chelsea.'

Lara went to give her a hug. 'I will, I promise.' She kissed Sabine's papery-soft cheek, breathing in the scent of old-Parisian-lady face powder: the most comforting smell in the world, the smell of her grandmother Colette. 'Thanks again.'

'*De rien*,' insisted Sabine.

But as she saw Lara out of her front door and watched the girl move along the carpeted corridor to the elevator, Sabine's pale blue eyes misted over. '*De rien*,' she whispered to herself, with the smallest shake of her head.

EIGHT

It had been a difficult thing to admit – her heart already belonging elsewhere – but Lara had finally faced up to the fact that she had fallen in love. Deeply, helplessly, swooningly in love. She'd always been intoxicated by New York when she'd come to stay with Oliver during his tenure at the UN, but now – more than two months into her time shooting *This Being Human*, and still filled with dizzy wonder each time she woke up and thought, Er, hello, here I am in my apartment in *New York* – it was the real deal. Lara had hurtled headlong, happily, into the starry-eyed state that rejected all the bad press about the city and subscribed breathlessly to the clichés: that New York was energy; New York was possibility; New York was novelty (enshrined in its very name, no less!); that New York, essentially, was life. Yes, she'd lost her heart to the city, and her old flames Paris and London would simply have to deal with it.

As Lara waited with two piping hot cappuccinos at the arrivals gate at JFK – Alex would be grateful for the caffeine, she was sure – she reflected back over the past months in amazement. It was nearing the end of *November*. Hard to believe she'd been out here for so long already: in some ways it still felt like yesterday that she had been arriving in this very airport, her skin brown from the London summer and her heart knocking against her ribs for fear of what she was about to embark on. And yet, in other ways, she felt as if she had been here for ever.

The love affair had started, she reckoned, hopping impatiently as she scanned the arrivals board for information about Alex's delayed flight, after the weekend she had first gone drinking with Jacob and his crazy friends in the grotty bowels of the Meatpacking District. Until then Lara had rather floated along the city's surface, happily conforming to fun stereotypes, getting whiplash from craning her neck to gawp at skyscrapers and feeling very Carrie Bradshaw as she drank twenty-dollar lavender martinis in zinc cocktail bars after splashing all her *per diem* on shoes at Macy's. With Jacob, however, she had been shown a different side of the city. Fooling the paparazzi – who, in any case, had gone off the Jacob-Lara scent weeks ago – with hats and goofy sunglasses, her elusive co-star (still not making much conversation with her on set) had turned out to be the best tour guide imaginable, whisking Lara off on unexpected adventures that invariably ended up in dark basements, where cheap red wine flowed into chipped glass beakers until sunrise and the smoking ban was flouted with zesty dedication. With Jacob, she'd discovered art galleries you couldn't just turn up at, clubs you could never find, karaoke bars you had to have a special password to get into, restaurants you could never read about, theatres you couldn't buy tickets for – and always secretly, after they'd wrapped and each had been dropped at their respective apartments from the studio. (Sometimes Lara would wave goodbye to Bobby on the street, wait for his Lexus to disappear out of view as she pretended to search for her keys, then hail a cab to meet Jacob straight away, with a little thrill in her heart.)

Lara glanced up at the display screen and noticed that Alex's flight had landed, although it would still be a while before he came through, what with the endless extra immigration checks, these days. His coffee was getting cold. Lara took another slug of hers. She was knackered. They'd gone to one of Coco's friends' art openings in a gallery downtown last night, and Jacob, his eyes unfairly persuasive, had been insistent everyone went dancing afterwards. The club had been in Alphabet City somewhere, a typical Jacob hangout: impossible to find, you'd never know it was there from the street, but once inside, a veritable trove of great music and eccentric people. She'd got over her sensation of feeling desperately uncool and boring and English around Jacob and his gang, and now found them funny, bright and different. Certainly they made Lara's previous social options in New York – the other actors from *This Being Human* or her expat university friends and their circle – feel boring by comparison. She did still occasionally go out with Jessica and Chris and everyone, but found her cast-mates were still swapping anecdotes about previous jobs and gossip about fellow actors, their horizons as narrow as their waists; while Dan and Lucy, she had discovered, were hanging out with investment bankers who seemed mostly interested in credit crunches and Fed cuts – things Lara neither understood ('Sorry, can you please explain what a derivative is again?') nor was *remotely* interested in.

Mind you, she thought, rubbing her eyes and emitting a little yawn, she could have done with Jacob and Co. being a little less funny and bright last night. Sitting down cross-legged on the floor, Lara checked her phone to see if Alex had texted her from the other side and found instead a message from Jacob:

Can't believe you split so early man, you missed a sunrise breakfast on Clarence's roof plus impromptu live session from that band we took home with us. Gotta love this city!
Received: Nov 20 Time: 08:04 Sender +19172889064

Lara, having fallen into bed at around five, let out a snort. The boy was crazy. As she'd got to know Jacob better over the past few weeks (and heard from the horse's mouth which of the Wikipedia stories were true: yes, he had run away from a Midwest trailer park aged fourteen when his mom was arrested for dealing heroin; yes, he was picked up off the street in the Lower East Side by a casting scout for Miramax; no, he'd never slept in the doorways of the Bowery where he now owned a million-dollar loft; no, he hadn't fucked two of last year's Best Supporting Actress Oscar nominees simultaneously in an elevator at the Kodak Theater in LA) she was finding it increasingly fantastic that they could have come from *such* unrecognisable worlds and ended up as friends. Their frames of reference on life were totally polarised, him having dropped out of school as a teenaged crack addict and never travelled outside the US; Lara, globetrotting diplomat's daughter, having been affectionately nicknamed 'Lame-arse Latner' among her cooler friends due to her reluctance to indulge in any drug harder than the odd joint. And yet, even on that first night out in the Meatpacking, when he had insisted on walking her all the way home to show her the city as the stars faded and dawn began to nudge over the streets, Lara had felt a surge of connection with Jacob. She'd felt something similar on set before, but only between Peter and Helen, never between Jacob and Lara. And now here it was, fizzing between them, definitely between *them*, under a lightening Manhattan sky. She'd had to keep checking, as she followed him through the skein of streets that had not quite made it into the grid until, finally, Ninth Avenue appeared and they were at right-angles again: was this really *Jacob*, her aloof and disengaged co-star, who was now chatting away so easily? *Jacob*, who had spent the past month apparently ignoring her, patronising her, challenging her, making her feel as uncomfortable as possible? But, yes, the grey eyes were definitely his, the twitching jawline, the fuzzy brown hair, the tattoo-streaked, sinewy forearms still bearing the faded track scars of an unimaginable past. Yep, it was definitely him.

They had not been in communication again that first weekend. Lara had come home from Sabine's and spent the evening trying to make sense of the emotions that had been generated by staring at pictures of her dead mother all afternoon; and on Monday morning at work it was as if their Friday-night escapade hadn't happened. Jacob didn't mention it and had been as detached as ever, which had driven Lara mad until she realised that she'd just given what was probably the performance of her life in a particularly devastating scene between Helen and Peter. And then, that night, Jacob had sent her a message, and she'd sent one back, and before she knew it, they were having a conversation. The next day it was the same story – cool civility on set, betraying nothing – while later that evening he had turned up out of the blue on Lexington and called her to say she needed to come downstairs: he had somewhere to take her (some random blues bar in Hell's Kitchen, as it turned out). Every night that week and, indeed, in the weeks that followed, they'd ended up either having long conversations on the phone or meeting each other in some place or other of Jacob's choosing; the following days on set, though, they would barely acknowledge one another. It was weirdly fun. And while she often wished she could make reference at work to whatever they'd been discussing the night before – sometimes profound, mostly rubbish – Lara had soon got used to the thrilling duplicity of their friendship. To her, it was a secret narrative that was unspooling innocently and unpredictably between them, after hours, while their characters Peter and Helen played out a different drama daily on set.

Jacob had done a thousand different things that had surprised her since they'd been hanging out. Like the time when, out of nowhere, he'd said; 'So, do you think about her every day?' He'd just stuck an early *Kind of Blue* session on the gramophone, and Lara had been sitting on his couch, drinking a beer, listening to the melting wail of Coltrane's sax and thinking again of how her brother would go nuts about this place with its stacks and stacks of vintage vinyl.

'Do I think about who?' she'd replied. 'Helen?'

'Eve.'

Lara had taken in a little scoop of air then, which promptly got stuck in her lungs. That, she had not been expecting. If people talked about Eve in front of her, it was usually to say, kindly but somewhat blandly, what a great actress she was, what a beauty, all the usual, obvious things. They never asked, though some must have been curious, what losing her had felt like, whether it got better, whether the fact of it ever left her alone or whether it was with her all day long, every day. If they had asked her, she could have told them. It's there in every piece of music, every tube stop, every shift in the light, every cup of coffee, every ray of sunshine, every drop of rain, every kiss, every tear. It's there in every other human being who has dared to survive in this world after Mum was gone.

'Every day,' she had said, her voice very steady.

And Jacob had turned to look at her and nodded thoughtfully. 'Life and death, it's an equation, right? A love equation. I bet your relationship to your mother continues to change, doesn't it, even though she's dead?'

Lara had faltered. 'Maybe . . .' she stuttered. 'Maybe, yes, the relationship does change. I don't really know.'

'That's cos you love her, and love changes every day.'

Love changes every day, Lara had wondered. *Who is this person?*

'Can you picture what happened to her the day she died? Does it haunt you?'

Lara frowned. 'We'll never know what actually happened. I mean, I can picture what she *looked* like, unconscious, in the hospital, in the hours before she . . . but . . .' Lara had tailed off helplessly. 'Of course it haunts me. I have an imagination, don't I?'

'Yes, you certainly do.' He grinned. 'So, what did she look like?'

'What are you, Moss, some kind of sicko?'

'Not at all. I've seen dying people, I've seen dead people, but they were junkies, man. Their spirits were already way spent. Their souls were dead long before their bodies were. I always imagined that the still-alive dying would have a different look. I always wondered if you could see all that unspent love on their faces.'

Lara had closed her eyes as an old grief tore up through her throat, her nostrils, her skull. 'Blue in Green' was crackling its way around the gramophone and the combination of the jazz and the beer and Jacob's strange grey eyes seemed to be unravelling her emotions until suddenly they were all over the place. Was she really going to open up to Jacob Moss about this, the most personal thing in her life? She'd never talked to *anybody* about the hours she and Lucas and Colette had spent in that room in the hospital in Paris, her father still on an aeroplane in the sky somewhere as the three of them sat there silently, on orange plastic chairs, paralysed, powerless, watching Eve's life gradually ebb away: the whisper of a cough, the slight shudder of her chest, the flicker of an eyelash and then that total, terrible stillness.

'No,' she said quietly. In that hospital bed Eve had not seemed to hold a lifetime's wasted love on her bruised but largely undamaged face. Rather, her mother's unconscious visage, eerily stilled when in life it had always been so animated, had looked aghast, regretful. Lara had always imagined her mother inside, screaming to be let out, to be released back into life and to all the multitudinous things she still had to do. 'No,' she repeated. 'It was more that she looked sorry, somehow. As if she had done something appalling in getting hit by that car and would we, could we, ever forgive her for dying before her time?'

'Would you, could you?'

'Forgive her?'

'Yeah.'

'Of course. What is there to forgive? It was an accident.'

Jacob had held Lara's gaze then, questioningly, almost chillingly, for a split second, before jumping up to put another record on.

Alex's flight now had a baggage-carousel number attached to it, which was a good sign. Lara took another sip of her coffee and wondered how she was really feeling about his visit. They hadn't spoken much over the past few weeks, and she knew, with a guilty lurch, that she'd been working so hard and having so much fun in New York she'd hardly worried about it. She and Al would be fine, at the end of the day, because they always were, but still, it was a shock to think she could be so out of touch with Alex's day-to-day life. Was his rape case done and dusted? Had he scored at football last weekend? Who was it he'd said he'd gone to dinner with last week? She either couldn't remember or had never asked. Horrified at the prospect that Al might have picked up on her disengagement, Lara was resolving to make a huge effort with him while he was there, when she spotted a familiar figure ambling through the arrivals channel. And at that moment, when she saw him, everything – everyone – else faded into the background. Alex was here. *Alex*. As he caught sight of her too, he broke into a gigantic grin, then pulled a silly face and dodged nimbly around the passengers in front of him until he was there, free of the barrier, dropping his bag at Lara's feet. He swept her up into his arms and she wrapped her legs around him and they kissed each other, not so much passionately as with a great swell of relief: for here they were, Alex and Lara, lovers of old, two halves, best mates, reunited with each other after her too-long absence. And it felt good, Lara had to admit. Good to be back in Alex's arms, the place where she still, after all these years, felt safest and most adored.

'Hello, miss,' Alex said, eventually letting her down but keeping his arms wrapped tightly around her waist. He was still grinning.

'Hello, you,' she replied, smiling back at him and handing over the other coffee. 'Here, I thought you might need this, although you took so long to come through it's probably gone cold.'

'You little star,' he said, taking the paper cup and having a swig. 'It's perfect.'

'You're perfect,' she said reflexively, taking his hand and feeling genuinely happy at the prospect of him being here for five whole days (and why shouldn't she be happy? She allowed a flutter of the question, then stifled it immediately). He swung his arm around her shoulder and put his nose in her hair as she led him outside.

'The production office were insistent I should get Bobby to take us back into the city,' Lara was explaining. 'Bobby, that's my driver. Lovely guy. But I thought, I'm not filming today, so he's got a day off, and why should he have to waste it coming all the way to JFK? Besides, I wanted you to myself and he would have wanted to talk your ear off on the way home.'

'Much better plan, then,' said Alex. Having deposited his bag in the boot of the cab and chucked away their cups, he grabbed Lara before she could slide into the back seat, and put his arms around her neck. 'Fuck me, it's good to see you,' he said.

'Charmed, I'm sure!' She laughed, wriggling out of his grip and into the cab. 'But maybe when we get back, if you're lucky . . .'

As far as he was concerned, Alex would have been perfectly happy to spend his entire five days in New York holed up in Lara's very swish apartment, talking to his girlfriend, having sex, talking to his girlfriend, having sex, talking to his girlfriend, having sex. Maybe sometimes at the same time. Maybe sometimes with some food thrown in. But basically not moving, not seeing anyone else, not having to make polite conversation with people he didn't know and would never meet again – just talking to his girlfriend, and having sex.

Lara, however, clearly had different ideas, and seemed to have scheduled a manic few days of activity. His face must have betrayed him when she started outlining her plans to him as they left the apartment (after having sex, thank God) to pick up some lunch, because hers fell.

'What?' she said. 'Do you not like the sound of that? I just want you to get a sense of what I've been doing out here, who I've been spending time with . . .' (Not strictly true, she admitted, she probably wouldn't be introducing him to Jacob's crowd: Alex just wouldn't *get* those kinds of people, with their wacky flea-market clothes and not a regular job between them.) 'I just want you to see what my life is like here.' She tried not to sound whingey: she knew she should be glad that her boyfriend wanted her to himself. That was, after all, a pretty normal expectation, when they hadn't seen each other for so long. But the prospect of spending the next five days with Alex alone was giving her a mild sensation of vertigo. 'I mean, I want to introduce you to Sabine and Frank, I want you to meet Chris and Jess and,' she swallowed, 'Jacob. Everyone's so looking forward to meeting you. Then Dan and Lucy and I have been emailing to work out a time for us all to go to dinner. My friend Johnny from the crew said he might be able to get us Yankees tickets. There's this concert that looked really cool down at Lincoln Center, a couple of films I thought we could see. I want to take you up to the Cloisters because they're so *beautiful* on a day like today, and I really just want to walk around a lot, show you this place—'

Alex stopped in his tracks and pulled Lara into him. Cold white November sunlight was pouring between the cracks in the skyline and illuminating the top of her dark hair like a halo. 'Lara, ssh!' He laughed. 'Listen, you crazy girl, I'm happy to do whatever you want to do. I just want to see you. So, I'm in your hands. Take me wherever you want to go.'

Lara smiled again. 'Right answer, Craig,' she said, with a wink, taking his hand and pulling him down the avenue. 'We are going to have so much fun. You have no idea.'

And for the first couple of days of Alex's visit, they did indeed have fun. Lara was so proud to be showing him around the famous, thrilling streets of her adopted city – which had deigned to be on its best behaviour this weekend, waking them up with sunshine and dazzlingly crisp skies – that she barely let herself think about anything else. She missed the buzz of being on set, of course, and the camaraderie, and the work, but also knew it was no bad thing to step out of the filming bubble for a bit.

She and Alex had soon slipped back into years-old habits of conversation and touch, and it was nice to just sit around and catch up with each other's lives. He had clearly been reluctant to plague Lara with his work anxieties when she was on the other side of the Atlantic and had her own pressures to contend with, but as he explained more fully what had been going on in chambers, how many cases he was juggling and why he had been so busy of late, she understood how stressed he must have been. She felt guilty, again, for not having been a better absent girlfriend and for allowing *This Being Human* and New York to become the centre of her world. Because 'life' in New York was not, she reminded herself, really 'life', it was a very beguiling, very easy and very artificial approximation of it; and she knew that if she were to fall into the age-old actor's trap of thinking that location existence was actually real, she was in serious trouble.

'Anyway, I want to know about you,' Alex said, as Lara swung around on the sofa and put her socked feet on his legs one afternoon. 'Tell me more about the film. How's it been?'

Lara leant over to stroke his cheek. Bless him, he was so

clueless about her world yet always so interested. 'Incredible,' she said. 'Although I've never worked so hard in my life.'

'Aah. My poor little princess,' Alex teased, stroking her feet. 'Never done a hard day's work in her life.'

'Shut up, you bastard!'

'Only joking. And how is it, playing your mum's part?'

She contemplated. 'Weird. Powerful. Quite spooky, actually. Sometimes I'll be playing a scene and I'll have a sense that she's *with* me somehow . . . as if I can almost feel her watching me. It's very bizarre, but also amazing. And I do feel closer to her, in some sort of way.'

Alex grinned, his brown eyes full of love. 'See? I told you you had nothing to worry about, you brilliant thing. So, what's been the best bit so far, then?'

Lara inclined her head and hesitated. 'You coming to see me,' she said a touch disingenuously. 'That's been the best bit. Shall we go for a walk?'

Alex glanced towards the bedroom door and gave her feet a little squeeze.

'I've got a much better idea,' he said.

The problem wasn't that she *didn't* want to talk about the so-called 'best bit', Lara reflected, a short while later as she lay staring at the ceiling in the twisted bed-linen, Alex snoozing gently on her chest. It was how much she *did*. Her excitement about doing *This Being Human*, her new love affair with New York, her unfolding friendship with Jacob, Sabine's evocative photographs, the profound, inexplicable connections she felt with her mother, being here, playing this part; all of this was almost overwhelming – and for reasons she had not even articulated to herself yet. If she started to talk about it now, with Alex, she might never stop. And that, she admitted, as she stroked Alex's hair while he slept, might be very dangerous indeed. With an ominous shiver, Lara manoeuvred him off her body and rolled out of bed.

NINE

The second half of Alex's visit, for reasons neither of them really wanted to face, was less fun. After the initial comforting blur of arrival and touchingly fumbly catch-up sex and hand-holding and general sense of 'hello, you!', the couple were left facing a hollower truth: that since Lara had left for New York, something, slight and imperceptible to the naked eye but *something*, had changed between them. Lara knew this something was her doing, but she neither wanted it to be true nor wanted to change anything about her life in New York, so she tried, brightly and breezily, to ignore it.

And Alex, it seemed, was now endeavouring to do something similar. Despite his earlier protestations, he had since come round to Lara's idea of packing their schedule with as many diversions as possible – he too could sense it, in the apartment, sitting there just the two of them, some microscopic shift in their relationship. It made the blood hum in his brain and, whatever it was, he didn't want to deal with it now either.

The city, needless to say, was more than happy to oblige them with distractions, and they donned brave faces along with woolly hats (for the mercury was dropping by the day) as they zipped up and down the grid, shopping, eating, visiting museums – finally, Lara got to her Rothko – and generally hanging out. Sitting in the Spotted Pig as they munched twenty-dollar hamburgers with Dan and Lucy, everyone chatting easily about mutual friends, shared experiences, London, old jokes, Lara had the distinct impression that this scene could have been copied and pasted from some location in Kentish Town or Westbourne Grove or Shoreditch to here, half a world away. In some sense, this was a comfort: she could relax, be off her guard. Yet it also disconcerted her, this shifting between worlds, between roles, and she felt, suddenly, profoundly alienated by it. These people – not Alex himself, but Alex in this *context* – felt so uncolourful, these days. Part of what excited her so much about Jacob and his eclectic friends was how *unusual* they felt. And yet, surely, she couldn't say that Jacob's crew were her people. They would no more translate back to London and her real life than Dan Peters and Lucy Drew would make sense in a shitty dive down in Alphabet City. With a burgeoning sense of oncoming doom, Lara was beginning to wonder, deep down, how easily she herself would be translating back to London and her real life when all this was over.

But they tried hard. She took Alex to brunch at Café des Artistes with Sabine and Frank, and was reminded of just how wonderful he could be. He knew nothing about either costume design or fine-art collecting – and probably couldn't have given a monkey's about them, either, Lara knew – yet from the way he engaged with the couple you would have thought he'd had a lifelong passion for both. Sabine clearly adored him. She kept throwing Lara girlish winks, and as she pressed a package into Lara's hands at the end of the meal, the copies of the photographs of Eve that Lara had requested, she whispered, 'Now, he is a precious one, *ma chérie*. Look after him, won't you?' Lara had smiled bravely, but had been relieved once she and Alex had seen Sabine and Frank into their cab outside on West 67th and they could drop the charade that everything between them was normal.

'You okay?' Alex had asked, as they wandered in silence back down Central Park West towards Columbus Circle.

She motioned to the pack of pictures, wrapped in their protective paper. 'Yup,' she'd responded, her voice unnaturally bright. 'Just these. They make me feel a bit funny.'

'Of course they do. Hey, maybe you can show them to me when we get back. I'd love to see them.'

Lara hadn't shown them to him, though, fearful that if she did, she'd have to air her suspicions about Eve's own conduct on *La Belle Hélène*. Which would beg all sorts of other questions, all sorts of other complications . . . No, Lara had decided, now was not the time to bring those dark thoughts to light.

On his penultimate evening in New York, Lara and Alex joined some of her *This Being Human* crowd at the Waverly Inn. When they walked through the door, Lara nearly fainted with shock to see Jacob Moss sitting at the table with Jessica, who'd organised the dinner, Chris, Amelia, Robert and Kevin. This must be the first time, literally *the first time* in more than two months, that Jacob had ever deigned to go out with the *TBH* cast. Introducing Alex to everyone, Lara had downed the best part of a glass of wine as he, shaking hands across the table with Jacob, had cheerfully made a joke. 'Aha! My love rival. Good to meet you,

283

buddy.' Everybody had laughed; nobody had seemed to notice Lara going white in the corner.

Amazingly, the actors were on mercifully less solipsistic form tonight, and Alex soon settled into a colourful discussion with Kevin, Robert and Jacob about the new US administration, and what this latest Iraq policy might mean for the rest of the world. Lara joined in occasionally, with the odd nervy laugh and disconnected sentence. When her food came, though, her stomach was churning so much she could barely pick at it, and she soon slunk into coiled, frantic silence as she watched Alex and Jacob chatting amiably to each other. Extraordinarily, she found she couldn't meet Jacob's eyes.

Guzzling yet another glass of wine and trying to stay focused on the conversation she was half having with Amelia and Jessica, Lara beckoned the waiter over and ordered another bottle. When her phone vibrated in her pocket, she was relieved. Thank God, a distraction, and hopefully Lucy or Dan telling them where they were so she and Al could get out of here asap: they'd vaguely arranged to meet up with the uni gang for a drink after dinner. Lara picked up the phone and pressed the envelope icon.

You're ignoring me and I'm ignoring you so why does it feel like we're the only two people in this room?
Received: Nov 24 Time: 21:04 Sender +19172889064

Lara's heart stopped. She read the message again, quickly, her face burning and her hands shaking. 'Excuse me,' she said, in what she hoped was a normal voice, scraping her chair away from Alex's and clutching the phone. 'Just going to call Luce.' She had to get away from the table. Resting her forehead against the cool tiles of a toilet cubicle a few seconds later, Lara held her hand against her chest and felt her heart thumping manically inside. *She was in her film*, she realised, in a crushing wave of comprehension. *Her film. She could have been playing out a scene from her film.* One girl, two boys, an epic love story with a tragic ending. *Fuck.* How could this be happening? She stared at her phone again, and Jacob's words seared into her eyes with their terrible implication.

Crashing out of the cubicle, Lara caught sight of herself in the demonic neon light of the bathroom and searched there for some clue, some truth, some – perhaps? – guilt. And, yes, there it was: a room full of people, a table full of cast-mates, a boyfriend by her side, and the person she had been so achingly conscious of in there had been – Jacob. How could this have *happened*? Lara stared again at herself in the mirror. Could it not perhaps be merely her wine-soaked brain and the recent weirdness with Alex playing tricks with her head? Not to mention the inherent strangeness of introducing your boyfriend to the person you've been pretending to be in love with on screen for the past ten weeks? But that was the point: *pretending*. After all, she had been getting paid to appear as if she was falling in love with people on stage and screen for the past half-decade. It was no big deal; as much a part of filming as smoking too much and sitting around in your trailer doing nothing for hours. She and her actor friends had discussed it a thousand times, how you just switch that bit of yourself off. Sure, you're lying in bed half naked with a heart-throb, but you never *go* there. You cauterise all normal responses, all possibilities. Anyway, she'd filmed with guys far more beautiful than stubbly old tattoo-freak Jacob Moss in the past and never fallen in love with them.

Fallen in *love*?

Are you in love with Jacob Moss? Is that what this is all, really, about? No. *No*. It couldn't be. Lara dropped her head, stuck it under the tap and took a long slug from the stream of cold water, hoping the lady applying lipstick at the other end of the mirror didn't think she was crazy. Whatever this meant, and might mean, she could not deal with it now. She had to get herself together. Splashing water on her face, Lara ran her hands through her hair, dried them on her jeans and picked up her phone.

You're ignoring me and I'm ignoring you so why does it feel like we're the only two people in this room?

Steadily, Lara pressed the 'delete' button. And then she told herself to get back into her role. Smile. Breathe. It's not real. Whatever this means, it is not going to be addressed here, tonight. Everything's going to be okay. Jacob's just messing with your head, because that's what he does. You know that's what he does. You thought you were above it, but you're not. So just calm the fuck down, Lara, and play the part.

Taking a deep breath, and giving the lipstick lady an apologetic smile, Lara walked bravely back towards the Waverly dining room and rejoined the conversation. And when Alex stretched out his hand to be held under the table a couple of minutes later, she took it and squeezed it tightly.

Hers, he noticed, was as cold as ice.

Lara was up with the larks the next day. Even in the warmth of the apartment she could tell the temperature outside had dropped again, and it was raining for the first time in weeks. The sky was the colour of gunmetal. Lara made coffee and switched on CNN, grinding her fists into her eyes and trying to ignore the sinking feeling in her stomach. She had lain rigid and awake for hours last night. Alex, she knew, had also not slept much, although he had kept his eyes closed and his back turned away from her in a touching attempt to hide it. But she knew: she had spent enough wakeful nights in his company, while he slept blissfully on, to know what he sounded like, felt like, lay like when he was truly asleep. His shoulders were never tense like that; his breathing never so jagged. She wondered why Alex couldn't sleep, whether it was just the combination of job stress and jet-lag, or whether there was something else on his mind; and she wished, more than anything, that she could ask him. But she had denied herself that luxury, she reproached herself now, plunging the cafetière, the moment she had started to shut him out of her life here and allowed herself to get carried away by something – or, rather, someone – tantalising and different and dangerous. In a streak of panic, Lara wondered what Alex might know. But then, she reminded herself stupidly, there was nothing *to* 'know'. Nothing had actually happened.

They'd made a few plans for the day, but Lara, who was technically on stand-by, ended up being called into work to shoot a weather cover scene due to the rain. (Thankfully, a scene that was just Helen on her own, no dialogue, no fellow actors, no Peter.) 'Sorry about this, babe,' Lara said, leaning over the kitchen counter to kiss Alex goodbye after Bobby had beeped to let her know he was downstairs. 'It's just a small scene, shouldn't take too long. You're more than welcome to come to set with me if you want, but it'll be terribly boring.'

'It's cool. I'll probably stay here and get through a few emails,' he told her. 'BlackBerry's been going a bit mad. Then I'll go shopping. I want to get something for Mum and Dad, and I thought I might start looking for a wedding present for Nick and Kate.'

'Good plan,' Lara said. 'Well, keep your phone on. I'll call you as soon as I'm done.'

Alex smiled at her – a touch wanly, she thought. 'Hey, come here, you,' he said. 'Give us a proper hug.'

She duly did, and the embrace was warm, and true, and an unexpectedly tender comfort to both. Lara bit her lip as she broke away. The idea of leaving Alex in there, alone, in that alien place with its fancy furniture and its billion-dollar view that had nothing whatsoever to do with their shared life, was too sad for words.

'Gotta go,' she apologised. 'I'll see you later.'

When Lara returned from her filming in the late afternoon she discovered a huge bunch of flowers on the dining-table. Alex had also tidied the flat and done their washing-up, which had been piling up over the last few days.

'What's all this in aid of, eh?' she called, dumping her bag and wandering into the apartment to look for him.

He emerged from the bedroom, grinning. 'Nothing much. Just cos I love you lots.'

'Well, thanks, chicken. I love you too.'

'How was filming?'

'Fine – bit of a non-event, really. It was just second unit weather cover, fairly unexciting. Sorry I had to miss your last afternoon. Did you have fun?'

'I did,' he said, pulling Lara over to the big chair and sitting her down on his lap. 'I went down to SoHo and bought Dad a mini-iPod from the Apple store, a *nanissimo* or whatever it's called. Nick tells me he's got very into his podcasts, apparently

– loves all the academic stuff and the news. Then I went to Bloomingdales and bought Mum a scarf.'

'Very impressive,' Lara said, punching him lightly in the chest. 'Never had you down as a Bloomingdales kinda guy, Craig.'

'Well, I'm not,' admitted Alex. 'I got lost almost as soon as I walked through the door, and it took me half the bloody afternoon to find the scarf department. But Mum'll like it, I hope, so it'll be worth the trauma.'

'Did you find anything for Nick and Kate?'

'Not really. Few ideas.'

'We can always look for something together when I'm back in London.'

In London. The words hung weightily between them. In London. Would all be okay in London? Would normality be restored in London?

'Yeah,' said Alex. 'We can always do that.'

He tightened his arms around her, and Lara leant her head on his shoulder, watching the sky change colour outside the window. It had stopped raining, and the Sunday dusk now seemed curiously to be lightening, rather than darkening, the sky as the evening dripped past.

She had done a lot of thinking this afternoon, on set; or, rather, given herself a good talking-to. Last night had given her a shock. Alex was too precious for her to keep indulging in the delusion that her underground friendship with Jacob was somehow legitimate because it was part of the process of making *This Being Human* and being in New York. Their connection, Lara knew, had gone instantly, dangerously, much deeper than that – and how would she feel if her boyfriend was cultivating something similar with some unknown girl at home? Lara had been flooded with shame as she'd had to admit she'd barely given a thought to how Alex might feel if he knew what she and Jacob got up to into the early hours each morning – all those conversations shared over a rare record and a cigarette and a box of noodles from the Korean grocer down on the Bowery, or the falling asleep on his sofa until it was time to scoot home before her pick-up, or the dawn walks at the end of raucous nights out. It was no good excusing her behaviour as if it were somehow being committed by somebody else – a New York Lara who temporarily inhabited her being and was not really her. It *was* her, the London Lara who in real life held fidelity dear; and she knew, deep down, that it was irrelevant that she and Jacob – as opposed to Helen and Peter – had never even kissed. Your soul has its touchstone, she knew. You are what you do.

And so Lara had decided that she would do better. It was not too late, and tonight was a good place to start. She had managed to get them a table at Cibo, the coolest new restaurant in New York – she'd had to pull a lot of favours, even on a Sunday night, but it was supposed to be amazing – and she wanted to surprise him. She was going to get dressed up, she'd decided, and tell him to put on a shirt and jacket, and they were going to make an effort together, and she was going to treat him to a fabulous meal with expensive wine in the greatest city in the world, then bring him back here and fuck his brains out. After a flurry of activity at the beginning of his visit, they hadn't had sex for the past two nights; and perhaps, she hoped, it would help things if she actually did a little work in that department.

'So, I also did some food shopping', Alex was saying conversationally, breaking her reverie. 'I thought we could stay in tonight and cook dinner. I got a nice bottle of wine and everything.'

Lara took a short, sharp breath. She shifted position on

Alex's lap so that she could face him. 'Oh,' she said, unable to keep the edge out of her voice. 'Oh, right.'

'Is that okay?'

'Sure – if that's what you want to do.'

'Well, yeah, I just thought it would be fun. Cosy. Don't you?'

'Cosy,' she repeated, her voice draining. 'The thing is, Al, I'd actually booked us a table somewhere, at this place Cibo that's just opened. It's supposed to be really great food and it's, like, *impossible* to get into . . . I thought it'd be a treat for your last night.'

Alex rearranged his face diplomatically, but the hairline crack in his voice betrayed him nonetheless. 'Okay, miss. Whatever you want. We can go out, that's cool. Good plan.'

Lara scrambled up, her cheeks prickling. 'No, it's fine, I'll cancel the booking.'

'Don't do that. We'll take it.'

'But are you sure?'

'Lara, this is the most retarded conversation we've ever had. I couldn't care less where we eat tonight, so long as we're together.'

Before she could help it, a yelp of indignation had escaped Lara's lips: 'Well, if you don't care, there's not much point in us going out, is there?'

'Oh, come on, baby, you know I didn't mean it like that!'

'No, I don't know! All I *know* is, I thought it would be nice to make a night of it, seeing as you're leaving tomorrow.' She looked down in disgust at her film-set attire of old tracksuit bottoms and Ugg boots. 'I was going to put a dress on and everything. But it's fine. Honestly. It's fine, it really doesn't matter.'

'Hang on, hang on,' Alex countered, his voice a shade less mollifying now. 'I didn't *say* I didn't want to make a night of it, Lara. I'm not suggesting a trip to the movies and a Maccy D's.

I thought it would be fun to stay in and cook, get drunk together, and just talk without the distractions of anyone else around us. That's all.'

Lara hesitated, because she knew she was behaving irrationally, like a manipulative, spoilt child, and frankly she was scared of what might come out of her mouth next.

'Why are we fighting about this, baby?' Alex asked, after a moment. 'It really doesn't matter.'

'Alex, it's our last night together, it *does* matter!' Lara heard herself cry. Too late: she'd snapped. Alex stood up and tried to put his arms around her, but she pulled back. She couldn't handle the feeling of him, of his arms anywhere near her, right now. 'It *does* matter somehow. I know it does. I just don't know *why* . . .'

'Okay.' He shrugged, nobly resisting the urge to throw up his hands in exasperation. 'Okay.'

Alex walked over to the window and Lara dropped down on the sofa, pulling her knees up tight under her chin. He remained looking out at the city for a minute, then turned around. 'La, I don't really know how to say this. But . . . I don't know . . .' He turned back to the window, and said quietly, to the glass, 'I don't understand what's happening to us. Why are we fighting like this? Is there anything you want to talk about?'

Lara bit her lip. The words sounded so awkward coming out of his mouth. Somebody else's words. *Anything you want to talk about?* That wasn't Alex at all. That wasn't *them*. Should she talk about it? Forget what she'd decided this afternoon and instead just tell him everything? 'I'm sorry I've been such a rubbish girlfriend for the last two months, and I'm sorry I can't tell you what's wrong with me, and I'm sorry, I *might* be going mad, but I'm beginning to think my mother may have had an affair while she did *La Belle Hélène*, and that maybe she might even have got pregnant with me by somebody else, which would explain why I look nothing like my father and why the two of them always behaved so oddly whenever that film came up in conversation. And I'm particularly sorry to have to tell you this, but the *reason* I'm beginning to think Mum might have had an affair, apart from what looks like quite telling photographic evidence, is because something very strange has also been happening in my *own* head and heart out here, playing this part, this supreme adulteress, and, well, I'm sorry, but I think I may be in love with Jacob Moss. Oh, and I'm *sorry* I'm doing this to you on your last night.'

'No,' she whispered. 'There's nothing.'

Alex studied Lara's face for a moment, then walked back to the sofa. Perching himself on the edge, he reached out his hand gently and, to his great relief, she took it. But as she did, a single tear trickled down her cheek, and she put her head in her hands. 'I'm sorry,' she gulped.

Alex dropped down onto the sofa and put his arms around her. 'Hey. You've got nothing to say sorry about. Please. Don't be sad. I love you so much.' He tucked a finger under her chin, tipped her head back and kissed her tear-wet eyelids so tenderly it made her want to cry again.

'No, you're wrong. I've got lots to be sorry about,' Lara sobbed. 'I've been so selfish. You've had so much going on and I've been so self-absorbed out here, so caught up in my own stupid world I didn't even know how bad things had been at work for you. I've been shit with *everyone*.' She raked her hands down her face. 'Cassie sent me an email nearly two *weeks* ago, saying she'd got that part in the Austen thing, and I haven't even rung her yet to congratulate her. How rubbish is that?'

'Baby, it's fine. Cass knows how busy you've been, I know

how busy you've been. And I know things have felt a bit weird between us recently, but it's only because we're both exhausted, and it's no fun being apart. That's all. Hey, come here, you.'

As he held her close, he said, 'I'm sorry I even brought up the staying-in plan. It was lame. It's a much better idea to go out.' He tweaked her nose. 'Thank God one of us knows how to have a good time.'

Lara looked at him, managing a bleak smile. 'Are you sure?' she said. 'Because I *honestly* don't mind cancelling the—'

'Shut up, you prawn. We're going out.'

'Okay', she said, wiping her eyes with a sleeve. 'Thank you for my flowers.'

'Thank you for my Lara.'

Lara wanted to fall back on her usual 'Thank you for the sunshine in my head,' but found, with a clench, that she couldn't quite get back there yet. 'I love you,' she said. 'I hope you know that.'

'Of course I do.' Alex patted her bum and pushed her gently off the sofa. 'I love you too. Now, go and put on that sexy little dress you promised, and let's get out there and paint that town red.'

TEN

The apartment was deathly quiet as Lara let herself in after dropping Alex at JFK. She removed her coat and hung it up on one of the pegs behind the front door to dry. It was bucketing down again outside. The post that had arrived that morning was curled wet at the edges and the ink had run on the top letter, a thick envelope bearing her agency logo. Another script, presumably. Unimaginably. Lara couldn't contemplate doing a job after this. She couldn't imagine what life might hold after this. Putting the damp pile of unopened letters down on the table, she stood still, trying to collect herself.

Alex was gone. And her resolve of yesterday afternoon had seemed to fade with every minute that her cab had brought her closer back to Manhattan. As it crossed the Queensboro Bridge, Lara had seen with a breaking heart that the coquettish island was still the colour of wet flint, the sky pregnant with rainclouds that loomed ominously over the jagged spikes of the skyline.

New York's truculent weather felt appropriate, somehow. Londonish. As if to say: Serves you bloody well right. You weren't so foolish as to think I was in love with you too, were you? After all, Lara thought bitterly, what was one more breaking heart to this city of so many? This city where people got lost like tears in rain and love disappeared and everybody was too busy going somewhere or making money or being seduced by the forbidden themselves even to care.

Lara gazed around the silent apartment. It felt dangerously empty now, without Alex's trainers by the front door and his jumper on the sofa, and his boxers lying on the floor in the bedroom. Last week's *Economist*, the one he'd read coming over on the plane and that had been sitting on the coffee-table ever since, was still there, open at the article he'd wanted to show her. She picked up the magazine and flicked listlessly through it. New American president on the cover, some typically witty headline, and the column that had made Alex laugh so much displaying a cartoon of their own beleaguered prime minister. Hard to believe it was less than a *week* ago that he had first come here with this, dropping his bag in the hallway as they had wrestled each other's clothes off in an automatic reclamation of long-beloved flesh and staggered into the bedroom. So much seemed already lost, somehow.

And yet nothing *had* actually been lost, Lara tried to remind herself numbly, dropping the magazine and scooping up their empty coffee cups discarded in the morning's rush to the airport. Nothing had actually *happened*. She only had twenty-two more days to get through on the film – she knew, she'd counted them – and then Jacob would simply become like all her other co-stars: some guy she once worked with . . . Some guy. Past tense. Twenty-two days. Lara shoved the cups into the dishwasher and walked over to the sink to get herself a glass of water. You are still in control of this, she told herself, as she gulped it madly down. Think. What do you know to be the *truth*? The truth is that your mother loved your father. The truth is that you love Alex. The truth is that no amount of late-night music sessions and downtown adventures and starlit metropolitan walks can add up to what you and Al have created over the past six years. She poured another glass of water. The truth, Lara, is that you cannot trust your emotions at the moment anyway. It's not real. New York is not your life. You are not your mother. You are not, repeat *not*, Helen . . .

But in that instant, a cold, cancerous certainty tore up through her gut and Lara was suddenly bent over the sink, throwing up. Alex was gone, but it was Jacob she missed. Alex had been here, in her arms, but she had wanted Jacob. She *still* wanted Jacob. And there it was. Lara shook as her body expelled the contents of her guts, then staggered to her feet, gasping. She ran the tap again and forced her head under it, breathing deeply. Oh, God, Jacob.

Jacob.

He wasn't filming today, she knew. She'd already consulted the schedule this morning while Alex packed, under some feeble pretence of wanting to check when she was next in herself. (Not until Sunday, as she knew very well; she had almost a whole bloody week to get through, with no possible distraction of work.) So Jacob was in the city. Somewhere. In this city. Walking, perhaps? He so liked to walk. Drinking coffee downtown with Clarence and Coco, maybe? Sitting in his apartment, smoking and listening to Bill Evans? What was it he'd said to her, one night, after they'd picked up some rare treasure at one of his beloved record shops? 'You and me,' he'd murmured, 'we're the two lonely people.' And when she'd looked at him, quizzically, a funny feeling in her tummy, he'd laughed at her and said, 'It's the title of the track, dumb-ass,' then pointed it out to her: 'The Two Lonely People . . .'. Of course. The track.

She should go out and do something, she knew, but what? Every damned street down there reminded her of the very person whose presence she was trying to forget. Every art gallery. Every street café. He could be anywhere . . . And it was *New York*: wherever he was in the city, she could be there too, in a matter of moments. Lara stalked back into the living room and grabbed her phone; and then, in the nick of time, dropped it again. Do not do this, a voice inside her warned. Call Sabine, call Jessica, call Chris, call Lucy, call Dan; hell, call your gym instructor, your dry-cleaner. Call anyone but him. Her hands were shaking. If only she were filming today. If only she had something to *do*, to divert her mind from him . . .

Lara went on into her bedroom and scrabbled around the dressing-table for a pack of cigarettes – Lucky Strike. Jacob's brand. Pathetic, how everything reminded her. She sucked in a great jag of nicotine and felt giddy with fear. She must do something. She could ring her father: she badly owed him a call. Or Cassie! Yes, Cass. Lara had not only been too preoccupied with her own dramas of late to call her best mate: she had been scared that, if she did, she might inadvertently give something away about her compromised state of mind. It had been so long since they'd had a proper chat, Cassie was bound to ask loads of questions about how filming was going, some of which would almost certainly involve Jacob. Lara was not certain she was a good enough actress to answer those questions now without a clotted throat, a giveaway crack in her voice . . . So, no. Not Cassie, after all. Lara fingered the phone, that most everyday of objects that looked so innocent but contained within it such a treacherous possibility. *Call him*, the phone seemed to say. *That's what I'm here for. Call him.* If she screwed up her eyes she could still see the image of his text message burnt mockingly onto her retina.

You're ignoring me and I'm ignoring you so why does it feel like we're the only two people in this room?

Lara flung the phone until it skittered to a stop against the window, marched to the front door and stormed back outside into the sodden city.

ELEVEN

When they were children, Lara and Lucas Latner had been taught by their mother that missing someone, like dreaming about someone, is a way of secretly spending time with that someone. Clutching her children's hands and kissing their hair before she saw them tearfully off on a flight or a train journey, Eve used to remind them that, although they were about to be separated by vast oceans and different skies and crackly telephone lines, they all knew where they could go and spend time with each other if they missed each other. *I'll see you on the other side of the stars*, she would whisper in their ears as she hugged them tightly goodbye. *N'oubliez pas! L'autre côté des étoiles . . .*

As tempting as it was to 'spend time' with Jacob by sitting in her flat all day missing him, then, in the torturously empty days after Alex had left and she wasn't filming, Lara forced herself to find means of distraction. First, she armed herself with a store of excuses for when Jacob next got in touch. She was running out of time here: there were so many things she'd been meaning to do in New York since she'd arrived and had never got round to. She had to meet her father's old UN acquaintances, Catherine and Mark Drake, for supper. She should spend more time with Sabine. With Dan and Lucy. She needed to see the New York casting directors and producers with whom Milton had long been trying to set up meetings while she was 'in town'.

And it was true: she did have stuff to do. On Tuesday she hired a bike and cycled around Prospect Park in the bracing cold and drizzle, her cheeks raw, then spent the afternoon, charmed, at the Frick Collection. On Wednesday morning she took a subway down to Cortlandt Street and felt the usual eerie sensation as she paused for a few minutes to watch the construction workers at Ground Zero plough that emotionally freighted ground with their cranes and JCBs, before sheepishly entering Century 21, the massive discount department store opposite that everyone always raved about. On Thursday the weather was so bad she stayed in and spent an hour on the phone to Alex. Both were valiantly playing along with the idea that normality between them had been restored, that the fracture in New York had merely been a feature of distance and time, a not entirely unexpected consequence of her going off filming for three months. So they made jokey conversation about superficial things. What she'd seen at the Frick. Man City's midweek triumph. The ongoing crappy weather in New York. Emma and Tom's engagement. Her plans for Christmas in Paris. His suggestion that he'd join her there for New Year's Eve. And yet, although they rang off with the usual ironic nicknames and promises to speak again soon, both remained aware of a new shard of uncertainty that splintered their every exchange.

Lara got off the phone from Alex feeling wretched, and promptly opened her computer. She must not allow these feelings airspace, for they would lead automatically to thoughts of somebody else – somebody forbidden. She started to type.

> Date: 29 November
> To: oliver.latner@fco.gov.uk, colettelacloche@wanadoo.fr
> CC: lrl27@bristol.ac.uk
> From: llama@gmail.com
> Re: Christmas?

Dearest Pa, Mamie, Luc – sorry been so out of touch the last few weeks, things a bit crazy here as film nears completion, but all generally well and I hope with you too. I was wondering what our plan was over Xmas? I wrap here on 14 Dec, leave on 15th or 16th and will probably head back to London for a couple of days to sort my life out. So if it suits you, Mamie, how about Luc and I get a Eurostar on about the 20th? (Luc, how are you fixed? I know you said you had loads of DJing gigs over the Xmas period, but would be fun to travel to Paris together, no? Let me know and I'll book asap.)

Anyway – am in middle of a rare few days off filming and PROMISE to be better at emailing/phone calls from now on in, let me know thoughts.

Je vous embrasse,

Lals x

The Other Side of the Stars

Remarkably enough, it was Lucas who responded first.

Date: 29 November
To: llama@gmail.com
From: lrl27@bristol.ac.uk
Re: Re: Christmas?

Hey, 20th works for me but have a gig on 19th in Brighton so
not too early please ☺ What are your plans for New Year? I
spoke to dad and apparently he doesn't want us to make a big
deal of it . . . So will you pls book my ticket to come back to
London on 28th? Been booked to play at what should be a
pretty cool party in east london if you and Alex and Cass or
anyone want to come down – can get you on the guest list. Let
me know.

Luc

To be swiftly followed by their grandmother.

Date: 29 November
To: llama@gmail.com, lrl27@bristol.ac.uk
From: colettelacloche@wanadoo.fr
Re: Re: Christmas?

Delighted to have you both whenever you can get here!!

Mamie C x

Thank goodness for that, Lara thought, rerouting straight to the Eurostar website.

> Date: 29 November
> To: lrl27@bristol.ac.uk
> CC: colettelacloche@wanadoo.fr, oliver.latner@fco.gov.uk
> From: llama@gmail.com
> Fwd: Booking Reference

Dear Eurostar customer,

Please find below your booking reference for the following journey:

EXCVYJ

Passengers: 2/Miss Lara Eloise Latner, Mr Lucas Raphael Latner
Route: London St Pancras – Paris Gare du Nord
Depart: 20 December 1310 arr. 1645
Seats: 43b, 43c standard class

She must have caught her brother at an uncharacteristically sedentary moment, for his response was again almost instant.

> Date: 29 November
> From: llama@gmail.com
> To: lrl27@bristol.ac.uk
> Re: Fwd: Booking Reference

Cool, cheers. Looking forward to it. I'll bring some new tunes. Enjoy your last few days. L

The next day, Lara spent the morning doing her laundry and then, on a whim, went to a yoga class Amelia had recommended. She had never really got the yoga thing in the past, but she was willing to try anything right now if it promised to take her out of her own head space and deliver some sense of inner peace.

After staggering out into Union Square with sore limbs and too-many stifled giggles, however, Lara was so desperate to speak to Cassie – who would also have been in hysterics in there – that she called her. They laughed for half an hour and talked about everything and nothing, and when the inevitable Jacob question came up, Lara found she was able to breeze over it. 'Yeah, fine. Had most of the last week and a half off actually, so haven't seen anyone in ages.' Cassie was too excited about her BBC drama and her burgeoning relationship with Ed Fletcher to suspect anything anyway – why would she? – and Lara saw how idiotic she'd been not to call Cassie ages ago. As she caught up with the developments in her friends' lives and realised how many things she'd missed over the past few months – engagements, birthdays, new jobs, new relationships – she was surprised to find herself genuinely looking forward to seeing everyone in a couple of weeks' time, even though that would mean she was back in London: away from here, away from him.

Hopping onto the subway back to her apartment she allowed herself the tiniest murmur of self-congratulation. She'd got through the five days since Alex had left without succumbing to her craving to see or speak to Jacob once! Now there was only *one more day* until she could go back to work and throw herself into the end of *This Being Human*. And in two weeks she could go home.

It was Saturday that broke her.

Lara woke up that day with sweat pouring down her brow and her heart racing. She had been dreaming about one of the earliest scenes she'd shot in *This Being Human* – a love scene between Helen and Peter, now morphed graphically into her and Jacob. As the memory of Jacob's mouth, his body, faded slowly into the grey light of day and she thought guiltily of poor Alex, Lara totally crumbled. She switched on her phone, and the fact that an entire week – but could it really be only a week? – had passed since Jacob's Waverly bombshell smacked her in the face. She stared at the phone, conscious of the bitter irony that despite all her watertight excuses as to why she wouldn't have been able to see him this week, she'd had no need to employ them. Because, just as if they were back at the beginning of the shoot, as if none of the intervening weeks had happened, Jacob had reassumed total radio silence. For the past seven days there had been no more messages, no more invitations to unlikely nocturnal Manhattan escapades, no nothing. Lara thought back to the first few weeks of their 'friendship', when his texts would come in thick and fast. She wondered how could she have taken them for granted like that. What would she give for one tiny, innocent little **Drink?** now?

Before she even knew what she was doing Lara was suddenly up and dressed and out of her front door. Without being able to stop them, her legs simply kept going, walking, walking, until now she was down on the Bowery and pausing helplessly outside the door to Jacob's apartment. For a long time she stared dumbly up at his windows, morning drizzle matting her eyelashes. And then, slowly, deliberately, Lara tapped out the word **Hello** on a text message, letting her thumb hover over the green 'send' button for a perilous second.

She nearly jumped out of her skin an instant later, when the phone screen suddenly vibrated in her hand. But it was only Sabine, bless her: Sabine, calling like an unwitting angel of fate, to intervene before Lara could commit such folly. 'Sabine, hi!' she gasped, relieved. The sound of the Frenchwoman's voice asking her if she'd like to come over for supper, though, brought last night's illicit dream flooding back, as she contemplated that 93rd Street living room and recalled the disturbing suspicions she'd had there about her mother and Dominique St Clair . . . What was going on? Had Eve fallen in love with Dominique? Had Lara fallen in love with Jacob? Was she somehow destined to step into her dead mother's shoes in more ways than one? 'I'm so sorry, Sabine,' she lied, hurrying away from the Bowery and getting swallowed up in the crowds on East Houston Street, 'but I've already made plans.'

That afternoon, Lara was sitting on her bench in Central Park, the script of *This Being Human* in her lap. She was nervous about being back on set tomorrow after so much time off and was now trying to concentrate on becoming Helen again. She was going through her lines in her head, her eyes closed, when she heard someone call her name.

She thought she must be hallucinating as her eyes opened around the shape that had materialised in front of her. 'Hey,' the shape was saying, as it dropped down onto the green bench beside her. 'I thought it was you. How you doing?'

Lara was struggling to get air in or out of her lungs. Was this real? Or was she dreaming? No. Here she was. At her bench. Hers and the Rosenblatts', of course, but nobody else's. *Love the questions and maybe you'll live your way into the answers.* Yes, here she was. On her bench, in the rain. But why was Jacob Moss sitting next to her on her bench? She looked at the script on her lap. Maybe she was confused, and this was actually a scene from her film. Yes . . . the film . . . But hadn't she and Jacob already shot this sequence, weeks back, very early on, a clever mock-up of a Manhattan Street in a Brooklyn studio? The moment when, having forbidden herself to see Peter, the man she really loves, after all that trauma and heartache, Helen simply bumps into him on the street one day. *Peter*. Yes. And how blissful and brutal it is that life can do that to you. Here you go, plonk. Here he is. You may think you can hide from him, but you can't. You're in the city. He's in the city. He exists, he is real and, oh! what a surprise, you're still in love with him. Oops.

'How − how did you get here?' she heard a voice asking thickly; it was hers, she was sure, but it sounded distant and weird to her ears, as if she were speaking under water.

The shape was chuckling at her. 'Well, hey, I did this really outlandish thing,' it was saying. Was she mad, talking to this figure as if it really was Jacob Moss, and he really was sitting on a bench next to her, in Central Park, on a miserable, wintry afternoon, his body so close she could actually reach out and touch it? She'd seen enough tramps sitting on park benches in this city conducting animated one-way conversations with themselves. Had she simply, in all her confusion of the last few weeks, become one of them? 'I decided to go for a walk. That's how I got here. Pretty crazy, huh?'

'You *walked* here?'

'Yeah. I love this city in the rain. You know that. And I have the day off. You probably know that too. So I was just walking. Through the park. And then, whaddayaknow, I spy this little person sitting on my favourite bench in a little blue hat and I think, Hey, I know that little person sitting on my favourite bench in her little blue hat.'

Lara's hand flew instinctively to the stupid beanie on her head. It was Alex's: he'd had it since he was a kid. It was pale blue and bobbled with age. Manchester City colours, apparently, horrible synthetic material but she had always had a fond affection for it. Lara glanced towards Jacob, and knew, then, in a catastrophic instant, that the person on the bench next to her really was real, that this moment was actually happening.

'This is your favourite bench?' she asked, incredulous.

It really was him.

He'd found her.

A whole city at their disposal and they'd ended up at the same moment in the same park on the same bench in the same rain.

'It's got the best message on it,' he explained. 'It's Rilke, right?'

Lara stared at him. Rilke? Her mother's favourite poet? How had she not spotted it?

She paused. 'I didn't know you ever came here.'

'Yeah, radical. I mean, who ever comes to Central Park?'

He grinned, but Lara did not smile back.

'Hey,' said Jacob, after a second. 'Hey, you.'

Lara swallowed tightly, willing her eyes to stay focused on the park scene in front of her. Normal people. Day-to-day lives. Rain. Trees. Think, Lara. Think.

'How you doing?' he asked again. 'You okay?'

She held her head back to the storm-darkened sky and felt the rain cool on her face. Was she okay? She had just been sitting here, and Jacob had found her, practically the only place in the city they had never been together, the only place in the city she felt was truly, privately hers, and now here he was. Here they were. She had forced herself not to see him or speak to him for a week and was *so* close to getting through it, and now he had just walked up to her. As if he had been there, watching her, all along. Just waiting for his moment. Like an actor with perfect timing delivering a killer line.

'Not really,' she said, bringing her face back down.

Jacob was silent. Lara could feel his eyes watching her, and she wondered for a terrible second if he was going to touch her. She felt her resolve start to dissolve like the edges of the park around her. Tears in rain. Rain on the sea.

Helpless.

'I know,' said Jacob. He had not moved.

Lara screwed her eyes shut and told her heart to stop pounding. Then she opened her mouth to ask, although she already knew, just *what* it was that he knew. But in that second the great expanse of Manhattan sky above them cracked open in a thunderous roar, and the storm broke on their heads, drenching them in a torrent of rain so ferocious it made them gasp. There were shrieks all around as everyone else unlucky enough to be caught in the open space of a park in a Saturday-afternoon thunderstorm started to rush towards shelter – moms with prams and lone tramps and a few tourists with sodden maps and expensive photography equipment now being swaddled desperately in wet jackets, *no time to open cases or bags just run*!

'Come on!' Jacob laughed, grabbing Lara's arm as if to do the same. But Lara remained frozen on her bench. She threw her head back to the sky once again and let the raindrops slip faster and more furiously over her face. *I love you*, she confessed to the rain. The sky split open again and a streak of lightning illuminated the sky, violent and beautiful and terrifying. Jacob's hand was clasped tightly around her arm. *I've been trying not to. I really, really have been trying. I love Alex too. But I love you and I love you and I love you.*

And now Jacob's face was in focus, in front of hers, his eyes glittering like black onyx, irises the same colour as the lightning-rent sky above them. Rain was runnelling off his nose, his hair was plastered over his face.

I love you.

'It's okay,' Jacob was saying, his hand still firm around her arm, and she could feel the faint electricity his grip generated inside her, even under the layers of coat and jumper. 'Lara. It's okay.'

The rain kept falling, and now neither of them moved.

Love the questions.

'What, Jacob?' Lara asked eventually, rain in her eyes and tears in her mouth. 'What is okay?'

Live your way into the answers.

'I'm in love with you too.'

Part Four

ONE

The funeral of Eve Lacloche was to be held at l'Église Saint-Germain-des-Prés on a bitter, brilliant January morning, twelve days after the accident in a freak snowstorm that had claimed the actress's life at the age of forty-five. Despite the pleas from the Latner family for privacy at this difficult time, by early morning on the day hordes of weeping mourners and well-wishers had already started to descend on the square outside the church, clutching photographs of the deceased (and cameras in the hope of snapping one of the glamorous personages they imagined would later be shuffling in to pay their respects). A small police detail had been dedicated to the event to control the expected crowds, and a phone call now to Monsieur Latner, who was still waiting for the hearse with his son and daughter at the apartment that had been lent to him by the British Embassy, confirmed that the strategy had been necessary. Eve's most distraught fans had been congregating from as early as six a.m., the police *préfet* was telling Oliver, and they were expecting larger crowds to gather as the day went on. 'I think you can take solace in the fact that your wife was much loved in this city, Monsieur,' the *préfet* concluded.

'Yes, indeed.' Oliver thanked him, and put down the phone. He sighed. He would have preferred to bury his wife somewhere much more private, precisely to prevent this sort of thing, but Colette had been determined and impassioned. Saint-Germain was the very heart of Eve's city, the grief-hobbled mother had croaked. This was her favourite church, the very oldest in Paris. And, yes, Oliver did realise, thank you, Colette, it was also mere steps away from where Eve and he had lived, down on rue Jacob, when they were first twenty-something lovers all those years ago. Old Jacques Catroux, still holding the fort at Café de Flore across the road from the church, had offered to close the restaurant to the public on the day of the funeral in honour of Eve's memory, and had insisted they hold some sort of wake there after the burial, which was to take place at Père-Lachaise.

Oliver, reluctant at first – it felt so inappropriate to throw a 'party' for Eve in a place that represented such frivolity and pleasure in her life – had soon accepted Jacques' offer gratefully. Colette was certainly in no fit state to host anything at hers – it was the first time Oliver had ever seen his mother-in-law incapable of eating, let alone spending entire days in the kitchen. Colette seemed barely to have moved from the spot in the drawing room where Oliver had found her when he'd finally arrived back in Paris, grey and broken off that plane, one precious hour too late; Eve already dead. In any case, the apartment was too small to hold everyone, and the prospect of having someone else organise anything in these days of paralysis and shock was, in fact, a blessed relief.

316

Oliver stood by the telephone for a moment, gathering himself, then turned around. Lara was dropping slowly down the stairs of the borrowed embassy apartment, clutching a magazine. At the sight of his daughter Oliver's heart faltered again. Lara, coltish teenage almost-beauty, was dressed in a black lace and silk dress, a touch too sophisticated for her girlish figure, perhaps, but exquisite nonetheless. Her haunted Eve-eyes were rimmed red with crying, and she still wore the expression of absolute disbelief that united them all in these impossible days.

Oliver heard his daughter's breath catch in her throat, and he reached out a hand to take her skinny arm as she reached the bottom of the stairs. 'What is it, darling?'

Lara's lower lip trembled miserably. She held up the magazine. It was the latest edition of *Paris Match*. 'I was just reading this, and . . . Oh, *Dad*.'

'I know, sweetheart. I know,' Oliver soothed, taking the offending magazine out of her hands. 'You shouldn't read that now. Not today.' There was a feature in there about a taxi driver named Rémy Briand, 53, from Noilly-sur-Seine, who was claiming to be the last person to have seen Eve alive. (The driver of the car that had actually hit her had explained, traumatised, that in the flurry of chaos as his vehicle ploughed into something solid that had seemingly stepped into his path out of nowhere, he had never even *seen* her, not until she was lying unconscious and bleeding on the street, red blood seeping into white snow.) This Briand fellow had given a rather lachrymose, not to mention self-important, account of picking Eve up at Charles de Gaulle airport. He'd mentioned proudly that the world-famous actress had had no money on her, and he'd given her the ride for free.

Needless to say the French media had covered column inches galore with Eve's death; the Briand '*exclusif!*' was just one of a number of pages inside this magazine alone dedicated to the accident. Other 'witnesses' from Charles de Gaulle Terminal One talked about seeing Eve there too: one man, Pierre somebody, had come forward to say he approached the actress with a pen and paper outside, in the hope of getting an autograph, but she had turned away from him. This 'detail' bothered Oliver intensely, for it was most unlike Eve, who had been famously gracious to her fans and always made certain to sign every paper pushed in her direction. Anyway. Whether they were true or false, the magazine stories were causing extra, and as far as he was concerned completely unnecessary, upset in this house of already uncontrollable sorrow.

'It just seems so *unfair*,' Lara was sobbing now, 'how this random *taxi* driver got to share Mum's last few alive moments with her, and we couldn't. We didn't even know she was in Paris, we thought she'd gone back to Lebanon with you. I still just can't believe it.'

Oliver extended his arms to give her a hug. He rubbed her back, and something in the touch of her dress snagged on his memory. 'I know, sweetheart, I know. It certainly isn't fair.'

'I don't understand, Dad. Why did she decide to stay in Paris?'

Oliver released Lara in her dress and wondered how he could answer that question when he didn't really know himself. 'Lara,' he said gently. 'You know how impetuous Mum could be.' It was still a struggle to have to force his mouth around the necessary past tense. 'We were transitting here, as you know, and she simply decided she wanted to come back for a few days and spend some time with Grandma, having not seen her over Christmas. And I said I thought it was probably not a bad idea if she did . . .'

Oliver had been over and over that final airport exchange in his mind. They had spent a lovely Christmas at his parents' house; the first happy time for ages, actually. To his surprise and relief, after a very difficult year, Eve had been back at her sparkling best. The kids had refrained from their normal bickering and been delightful; his parents had been more relaxed than expected; and even the toxic tension that usually charged any room containing his wife and mother had been surprisingly absent. One morning after Christmas, in fact, lying in his arms after they'd just made love, Eve had looked up at him, her eyes shining, and said, 'Oh, Oliver, I'm so happy I could *die*.' Oliver, remembering this now, shuddered to think of life's cruel irony.

On the last day of the year the whole family had driven to Heathrow. He was due back in Beirut for urgent meetings the day after tomorrow, so he and Eve were flying that day, via Paris. The plan was that Susan and Thomas would take Lara and Luc back to Berkshire with them and keep them there until school started in a week's time. Eve had been crying as they took off from London, but no more so than she always did when she said goodbye to the kids, and then, as they had touched down in Paris to change planes, she had become preternaturally calm. She said she'd had a 'perfect idea', that she was going to stay on in Paris, to see Colette, and that she would join him in Lebanon in a day or two.

Oliver had at first been surprised, but had seen the sense in the plan; even felt some relief at the prospect of Eve not coming straight back with him if she was going to be maudlin and moping while he was caught up in busy meetings for the next few days. 'I can't believe we didn't think of that before!' he had even remarked, as he wondered if she had enough of her things in Paris to see her through. Eve had looked momentarily confused

– things? What need had she for things? But that was so like Eve: in her world of romance and daydream, there was no place for unpoetic practicalities like knickers and toothbrushes. When Oliver had explained what he meant, she had recovered immediately. 'Oh, of course!' she had said. '*Oui*, I have all that at Maman's.'

As Oliver had kissed his wife goodbye, Eve had clung to him so fiercely that he'd actually pulled away and murmured, 'Darling?' And what Oliver had wanted to say was: I will cancel my meetings for you, if you want me to, I will stay in Paris with you if you need me here. But those were not the words that had come out of his mouth, and in any case Eve had already been saying goodbye. '*Au revoir, mon amour*,' she had whispered as she kissed him. '*Je t'adore.*' Then she had fled, as if to wait an instant longer in that terminal would be enough to change her mind. It was only after Eve had long disappeared through the doors that Oliver had realised she had left her handbag in his hand-luggage case. He had dashed out of the terminal building after her, to be greeted, to his surprise, by the sight of snow falling, but it had been too late. She had already disappeared. So, heeding the 'urgent call for Passenger Latner to make his way to Gate 17B', he had hurried back into the airport building in order that his plane could take off before the quickening snow outside prevented it departing at all.

'So that was why she decided to stay in Paris,' Oliver told Lara, clearing his throat. 'Just to see Gran and spend a couple of days here.'

She looked grave; the irony clearly not lost on her either. They stood in silence for a moment, a broken father and a shell of a daughter. Then, Lara said simply, thoughtfully, 'And she was so happy over Christmas.'

'She was, yes . . .' Oliver agreed, surprised. It was possibly the first time Lara had ever implied an awareness that her mother was sometimes *not* happy. Usually Eve was so elated to see the children that her blues melted away as soon as the school holidays arrived. She used to make such an effort around them that it was heartbreaking, in fact, to witness, knowing what she was like when the kids weren't there. 'Yes,' he said again, softly. 'She had been in good sorts.'

'I suppose that's the only comfort, then,' Lara sighed, 'that she died happy, in the city she loved most in the world.'

Oliver smiled at the youthful wisdom and gave her arm another squeeze. 'You're absolutely right, sweetheart,' he said. 'We must try to focus on that.'

'I just don't understand why they can't leave her alone, now she's . . .' Lara glanced again at the *Paris Match*, which Oliver had dropped unceremoniously onto the hallway table next to the telephone.

'I know. It's rotten. And unfortunately they can write what they like, because none of us will ever really know what happened that day.' He patted her back. Again, the touch of that dress – what was it? 'It's not fair. But I need you to be strong, today, for Mummy. And for Grandma, and for Luc, and for me. Okay?'

Lara frowned. 'Dad, I'm really worried about Lucas. He hasn't spoken a word since we left the hospital.'

Oliver sighed. 'I know. But he'll be all right. He'll come through. It's just his way of dealing with it.'

Lara felt a deep judder of woe in her chest. The thought of her little brother upstairs, motherless at eleven, was almost harder to bear than her own loss.

'I'll go up and have a word with him now, shall I?' Oliver said. 'Is he dressed, do you know?'

'Yeah. He's just sitting up there, on the bed, not speaking. I keep trying to comfort him but it's not working.'

'It will, though, Lara. You're a wonderful sister and Luc is going to need you to be really brave over the next few days and weeks and months. Okay?'

Lara nodded morosely. 'Okay.'

'Good girl.'

Was it *Eve's*, the dress? Was that why it was triggering such a feeling inside him, some deeply buried nostalgia, a memory almost too lovely to bear? But surely he would not remember this particular garment, even if it were. His wife had been the Queen of the Little Black Dress, after all: he must have seen her wearing hundreds of different versions throughout their life together. 'Where did your dress come from, by the way?' he asked lightly. 'Was it one of Mum's?'

Lara touched the silk of the skirt almost reverently. 'Yes. Gran found it for me yesterday. She said that Mum had cherished it but that she hadn't worn it in years.' She looked up at her father anxiously. 'Do you mind me wearing it? I just – I can't explain it . . . It just makes me feel better.'

Oliver gave a slight cough. 'Not at all, darling. If it makes you feel better, you must definitely wear it. And you look lovely. Now, will you stay down here and listen out for the car while I go and see how Luc's doing?'

'Yes,' she said hesitantly. Then, 'Dad?'

'Mmm?'

'You're okay, aren't you?'

The diplomatically trained muscles in Oliver's face somehow found a way to arrange themselves into a half-smile. 'Me?' he said. 'Of course I'm okay, Lara. We'll all be okay. I promise.'

At the top of the stairs, though, as soon as he was out of

view, Oliver slumped, weak with grief. Oh, God. *That dress*. The single act of impetuosity Oliver Latner had ever committed in his *life*; that dress. Lives changed for ever in a single moment, a single spin of the world on its axis. *Où allez-vous, Monsieur Olivier?* she had asked. *C'est parfait!* How would his life have turned out had he not dared to help her on with her jacket over *that dress*? Well, it was inconceivable now, of course. And Eve wouldn't have let him consider any other possibility anyway: she later confessed she had 'just known', then and there, that she was going to marry the man who was helping her on with her jacket so 'Englishly'. And that was one of life's great mysteries, she always used to say, how your whole world can change in a heartbeat, for ever . . . Oliver forced himself to stagger upright again. He must resist this, the inevitable slide into self-pity and grief. He must find his wounded, newly silent son; he must check that Lara had her poem ready for the service; he must go and see about the car. His children needed him: those lovely children, Eve's darlings; the children she had been forced to spend so many years apart from because of his job. Today of all days Lara and Lucas needed him to be strong. They were about to bury their mother. Their *mother*.

Eve was dead.

Lara was right: it was unthinkable, unbearable. But he must not cry. He must do as he had just instructed his daughter to do. He must get through this, somehow, for them.

The sense of stunned grief among the mourners was tangible, and the French had seen little need to hide their emotions. There had been loud weeping from almost all corners of the church, especially among the many theatrical professionals (the only notable absence from the congregation, to Oliver's great relief,

323

being Dominique St Clair). Oliver, Lara and Lucas had sat in silent shock as they watched Eve's coffin being borne the length of the church and come to rest in front of the altar. The rosewood coffin held a photograph of her, laughing, circled by arum lilies, her favourite flower.

The priest, who had known Eve personally, opened proceedings. Sebastien Delacroix, Eve's mentor and professor from the Conservatoire, delivered a eulogy that touched on her great talent as an actress, while her oldest friend Sophie talked movingly about her very special spirit as a human being. A choir made up of Eve's friends from the Paris Opéra sang a Duruflé mass so beautiful it seemed to split the very air inside the church. Lara, very bravely, stood up to read one of Eve's most cherished poems, an elegy of Rilke translated from the German into French, and drew heart-wrenching gasps from the assembled company with her instinctive timing and delivery of the line 'Aber weil Hierssein viel ist': *because to be here is much*. Eve's fellow actors read other pieces; her favourite hymns were sung; the coffin was lifted away; and then out they all staggered into the disbelieving, fractured light of a Paris that had just bid goodbye to one of its most cherished daughters.

At the gathering at Café de Flore, everybody – how could there still be all these people, Oliver wondered, when she had not lived here for so many years? – remarked on how moving the funeral service had been. Through the bewildered blur of well-wishers and their clichéd but heartfelt ministrations of sympathy and remembrance, he was trying to keep an eye on his children, who were sitting in the corner and struggling not to fall apart by the look of things – little Luc had gone slightly green, and Lara was now putting her arm around him – when a vaguely familiar figure sharpened into focus in front of him. *Jesus Christ*. It was Mary Longstaff.

'We are *so* sorry for your loss, Oliver,' Mary was saying, holding out her older but still meaty face to kiss him. What the hell was she doing here? 'We heard the news down in Nice. You know Rupe's consul there at the moment? Thought we'd come up and pay our respects. Must be hell on earth.'

'Ah, Latner,' Rupert joined them. 'So sorry, old chap. She was such a great girl, old Eve. Horrible way to go, too, car crash.'

Oliver stared at the man. Come to think about it, he had been dimly aware that the Longstaffs were in France, somewhere; had seen Rupert's name on an FCO telegram not so long ago. But here? Now? For *Eve*?

'Indeed,' he managed.

'Kids bearing up, are they? Must say we thought the girl read jolly nicely,' Rupert said appreciatively. He'd noticed Lara's uncanny resemblance to her beautiful dead mother immediately in the church, and had been surprised to find that the image stirred up an old feeling inside him and made him rather genuinely sad. 'Jolly brave.'

'Mmm,' said Oliver, casting around desperately for a way to escape. 'In fact, talking about Lara, I really must go and check on my children. Will you excuse me, please? So good of you to come.'

It was the presence of the Longstaffs at Eve's funeral that finally undid Oliver. In the nightmarish fortnight he had somehow just endured, he had not yet buckled. When he had received that frantic phone call from Colette as he landed back in Lebanon, saying that Eve had been hit by a car in Paris – *Paris!* Colette was screaming. What was Eve even doing in *Paris*? – four hours ago and was now in a coma in La Pitié-Salpêtrière, Oliver's emergency diplomatic training had kicked in instantaneously. These are words you know and understand, he reminded himself.

Accident. Loss of blood. Unconscious. Life support. Think. React. Stay calm. In the face of the tumultuous news, then, Oliver had remained composed, trying to pacify his mother-in-law, enquiring about the children – had his own parents been contacted? Were they getting the kids onto a train or plane asap? – while retracing his steps directly back into the airport and walking briskly over to the ticket desk. He had booked himself on the next flight to Paris, which was leaving in six hours, French weather conditions permitting, and had preferred to wait in the airport as the precious minutes ticked by just in case anything should change, putting through the requisite calls to his office to explain the emergency and making all the necessary arrangements.

He had spoken to Colette just moments before boarding – she was still alive, Colette was weeping, the doctors were saying she would probably survive the night but it was critical – and had even managed to sleep on the flight, knowing he would need all the energy he could possibly conserve for whatever the next few days might have in store for him. And then, on eventually touching down at Charles de Gaulle, delayed thanks to the continuing snow, Oliver had even managed to take on the chin the news that he had been too late, that Eve had died a little over an hour ago. 'Right,' he had said. 'Okay. Well. Tell the kids I'm on my way. I'll be there soon.'

And through all these grief-soaked, wifeless days in Paris, he had managed to be strong, to take care of Colette, and Lara, and Lucas; to arrange the funeral; to deal with the press and media, the police, the lawyers, the estate, the florists; to field the endless stream of sympathetic phone calls from his and Eve's colleagues and friends. He had survived all this, the funeral, the platitudes, the finger food and the tear-streaked faces in the Flore. But now this! The *Longstaffs* – who with their ridiculous and, as it was proved, unfounded allegations about Eve, had been the source of all that malice and angst in Beirut all those years ago – having the gall to turn up at Eve's funeral. It was too much for Oliver to bear.

Remembering the existence of a back door Eve had often used in the old days, when she'd wanted to slip out of this establishment unnoticed by the paparazzi who would sometimes collect on the main boulevard, Oliver found it again and emerged into a small courtyard where some of the restaurant staff were lounging around, smoking. Mustering every last drop of strength he had inside him not to crumble in front of them, Oliver rushed through the courtyard and out onto the grey street, and finally, after thirteen days of sheer hell, collapsed to the ground in despair.

TWO

Another week or so went by, and the Latners were still in shock, sleep-walking through the endless days, wide awake though the lonely nights, trying to look after each other as best they could but learning the hard way that they were never going to be quite enough to each other to escape the horror of what had happened. No amount of hugs from their father could erase for Lara and Lucas the harrowing truth that they would never again be touched by their mother. No amount of their mother in his children's faces, in Lara's green eyes or Lucas's fine nose, could soothe for Oliver the agony that he would never again see those features in his wife. So they sat, and they tried to get through the days. Clocks ticked. Hearts beat. Sometimes hours passed without anybody even moving or speaking. Lucas had still not opened his mouth at all. Sooner or later, someone would get up and do something – go to the toilet, fetch a glass of water, look out of the window. And then they would sit down again. Oliver occasionally picked up the phone, sometimes typed out a letter. He was in the process of trying to 'sort everything out': will and testament, estate, Eve's papers, the children's schools – *would* they be needing bereavement counselling? He had no idea, had never been a great believer in all that, but keep an eye on them, yes, please, and do whatever you think is best – not to mention his own situation. The Foreign Office pastoral-care bureaucracy was putting pressure on him to take 'gardening leave' with immediate effect, but Oliver was resisting. The grief might be debilitating at the moment, but he knew that in time he would need to focus all his energy on something bigger than himself, bigger even than his children, bigger than all their unimaginable sorrow put together. He would need to go back to work.

It was a relief, Oliver had to admit, to be staying somewhere in Paris where Eve had never been. Colette's old apartment, currently still populated by other family members who had stayed on after the funeral, had been desiccatingly painful in the days immediately after Eve's death: they had all kept expecting her to bound back into the kitchen with some story or other, hear her singing in the shower, or see her joining them at the table for dinner. At least here, in this unfamiliar, generically furnished place, there were no memories of Eve in its actual walls, in its glasses and stairs and furniture and doorknobs. Here, she was in their heads and their hearts only. Here, they could almost pretend that she was not with them simply because she was somewhere else.

Almost. Because it only took a lethal split second of focus for the truth to come crashing back in: that Eve was not here because she was dead. She wasn't away on a film set, or rehearsing in a theatre, or doing a photo-shoot, or visiting friends. She was dead. And when this hit home, it seemed to the Latners that there was nothing holding them together any more, no centre. They were just a collection of strangers in a strange room, not knowing what to say to each other, entirely beyond consolation. Sometimes, in a sort of reflex, they would stop to give each other a hug, or squeeze a hand, or offer a sympathetic smile that tried to say: I understand, I'm going through this too. But all that those pitiful gestures could do was remind them of what they were supposed to be taking comfort from. And, of course, there was no comfort to be taken from that at all. None at all.

It was another few days, but one morning Lucas simply decided to speak again. He had come downstairs and sat at the table and eaten his cereal and looked out of the window and said, seemingly out of nowhere, 'Are we going back to England soon?' There had been a clatter of spoons and muffled gasps as his sister and father had stared at each other and wondered what to say in response.

'Where did you go?' Lara asked her little brother now, intensely curious.

They were sitting next to each other on the Eurostar that was hurtling them back to London again, where normal life awaited: streets, trees, friends, boys, and, preposterously, school. Last week, there had been some question as to whether Lucas would be going back to school at all this term. Lara had heard her dad on the telephone in the embassy flat a few days ago, talking to his headmaster in hushed tones and trying to explain that his son had not uttered a syllable since his mother's death nearly three weeks ago. 'Not sure of the best course of action,' she had heard him mutter. 'Sounds eminently sensible. Yup. We'll wait and see.'

But then, the very next day, Lucas had started talking again, and when Oliver had sat them both down and asked them gently what they would like to do now – would they like to go back to school? Or stay with Granny and Grandpa Latner for a little while in England? Or go back to Beirut with him? – both brother and sister had said, in unison, 'School, please.' That had surprised, momentarily, all three of them; and then Oliver had smiled, thanked God for the fact that his children had developed his own sense of getting-on-with-it, and given them both a quick hug. He would be needing to go back to England and see them much more often now, he knew, but that Lara and Luc had the courage to start facing their newly motherless lives at all was encouraging to him: a load off his mind. 'Right, then,' he had said. 'I'll get on to your head teachers this afternoon, and we'll see about taking you back there in the next couple of days. We'll all go to England, I'll settle you in, and then I'll come back here to finish sorting through Mummy's things.'

'Lucas?' Lara asked again on the train. 'Where did you go while you weren't speaking? You seemed so far away.'

'Just somewhere,' Lucas told his sister, calmly but defensively. He glanced at their father, who was reading *Le Monde* in the window seat opposite Lara's.

'And why did you decide to come back?' Lara prodded him.

'Because I found out what I was checking up on.'

'Checking up on? Luc, what are you talking about?'

Lucas flicked his blue eyes shyly towards Oliver, but his father was still apparently immersed in the newspaper and showed no sign of listening to their conversation. Lucas leant his hand on his sister's shoulder and put his face close to Lara's ear. 'I just went to the other side of the stars,' he explained, in a very earnest whisper. 'To see if what Mum said was true. And it was. It's all right, Lals. She's there, waiting for us. I spoke to her. She said she loves us very much and she'll always be there when we miss her. It's like before. All we have to do is go and see her, and she'll always be there.'

Lucas sat back on his seat, and smiled beatifically.

Lara felt a tear roll slowly down her cheek.

THREE

'Thanks, William.' Oliver stood up and reached over to shake his Head of Department's hand. 'Thanks. You've been a real brick.'

'Not at all. Always thought it was ludicrous that we had a set policy for this kind of thing. Perfectly obvious that people might have different ways of dealing with things, and strikes me you've made absolutely the right decision.' William Davenport released Oliver's hand from his own firm grip. 'Nevertheless, you know where to find me. Keep in touch out there and give me a ring if you change your mind.'

'I will. But I don't expect that to happen.'

'I'll see you at the Peace Process conference in Cairo in a couple of months, anyway. Let's catch up then.'

'Grand.'

'Safe flight.'

Oliver closed the door of Davenport's office and walked briskly down the corridor, past the Goetze murals, down the opulent double staircase of the Ambassadors' Entrance and out through the security gate. Then he turned right down King Charles Street, dropped two at a time down the steps under the statue of Clive, and entered St James's Park.

Davenport's no-nonsense response to his request to go back to post within a week or so, once everything was tied up in Paris, had been such a relief. Crunching through the winter-hard ground past rows of shivering snowdrops and the odd early crocus, Oliver felt the tension in his stomach ease in the knowledge that, with his children now safely delivered back to respective head teachers, he would no longer have to stew in quiet rooms with his questions and his memories, and could rather head back over the Mediterranean to his responsibilities in the Middle East. Taking in a cold lungful of the late January air, he felt refreshed and revivified for the first time in weeks: it was good just to be outside, walking, rather than sitting in that stifling embassy apartment, listening to the radiators gurgle and the clocks tick and his poor children trying to choke back their tears.

Quickening his pace, Oliver checked his watch and calculated that he had time for a further diversion around Green Park: it would only take fifteen minutes or so to get back to Tachbrook Street, where he needed to pick up his things before catching a train back to Paris. Enjoying the sensation of his feet pounding the Mall beneath him as he instinctively broke into a run, not out of any time pressure but from the sheer need to expend some physical energy after the long weeks of mental grief, Oliver revelled in the rush of endorphins that now coursed through his body. The satisfying snap of twigs under the soles of his shoes as he entered the second park, the whip of the cold wind past his ears, the burr of traffic from Piccadilly on his right and Constitution Hill on his left; the feel of his sluggish blood waking up and moving through his body again, all of this told him he was alive, that he was going to be all right, that he had it in him to get through this.

Life had been a struggle for Eve in the months before she died, there was no question about it, and as Oliver jogged past Lancaster House now, his muscles responding instantly to the signal from his brain that he needed to release something, to run, to be free, he realised how ground down he, too, had been by his wife's oscillating unhappiness. It was the not being able to predict her state of mind or help her that had been so debilitating. She would be fine one day, happy, getting on with things, exploring books and languages or volunteering in the refugee camps, and then, seemingly without warning, everything would stop, the mood would darken over the residence, and that would be that for days, sometimes weeks. Over the past two years the bad patches had been exacerbated by certain events, and had far outnumbered the good. She had been inconsolable, for example, after the miscarriage, coming as it did so soon after Bernard's heart attack; although her doctors had assured her that early natural miscarriages such as this were very common, she had blown it out of all proportion and started to insist that it was her fault her baby had died.

'It is my punishment,' she would mutter in distress, her eyes dull. 'I am such a bad mother. I do not deserve another child.' She would clutch at her empty belly and weep, and tear at her hair, and sometimes let out the most gut-wrenching cries; and then she would collapse, again, in bed, refusing everything – food, comfort, love, explanation.

'Darling?' Oliver would keep asking, regardless, stroking his wife's matted fringe away from her forehead as she curled up like a weary child. Her unwashed hair now hung lankly around her grey face, and she had lost so much weight since the miscarriage he couldn't help but stare uncomfortably when faced with his wife's naked form. 'Can I do anything? Can I help? Can you tell me what's the matter?' But she would turn away from him, sometimes angrily, sometimes miserably, each time her eyes terrifyingly empty. As Eve continued to shut Oliver out from whatever internal torment she was battling, and the distance between them seemed to calcify into something harder each night when he arrived home from the office, Oliver had begun to despair. When these occasional episodes had started, what?, ten, fifteen years ago, when they had first gone to Beirut, Oliver had taken to seeing his wife's behaviour as a rather theatrical form of sulking, as if to punish him for the fact that they had left the bright lights of Paris and her acting world. But he had felt suitably justified at that stage in getting on with things: Eve had made a choice, in Paris, to be with him, and Oliver would *not* be made to feel guilty for doing his job.

Later, though, the dynamics of their relationship had so shifted, and Eve's periods of unhappiness so intensified, that Oliver, despite his long-buried insecurities from the past, had made a suggestion that surprised them both.

'I've been thinking,' he'd ventured one evening, bringing a glass of water to their bed where Eve was propped up on pillows. He'd arrived back at the residence that night to discover his wife sobbing wildly over the children's most recent letters from school. He had calmed her down, although her tears had so smudged the blue Parker pen ink of Lara and Lucas's neat childish hands, explaining what they'd had for breakfast and where they were going on their next field trip, that she'd soon been set off again. 'Maybe you should go back to Paris and start working again, do another film. Or a play. Would that make you feel better?'

He held the water glass gently to her lips and she took a small sip and stared up at him, her eyes foggy and confused.

'What – what would I do?'

'Well, darling, you'd know that better than I. But there must still be projects out there for you.' It was true that in recent years the phone calls from her agent had gradually decreased, the scripts had stopped arriving so regularly, but she was Eve Lacloche, for God's sake. Somebody must still want to employ her.

Eve had shrugged. 'I just don't know any more.' Then he had seen the light shift in her eyes, as she swallowed another sip of water and looked tentatively up at him. 'Although, there is something . . .'

She tailed off, and Oliver waited a moment before asking, 'Well? What is it?'

Eve frowned, then shook her head. 'I can't.'

'Eve, what is it?'

She did not answer him, merely fiddled agitatedly with the edge of the bedsheet.

'Eve?'

'It's – Dominique's film.'

Oliver had clenched his fists, then. Just to hear that man's name still made his skin flash in fury. But there were bigger things at stake than his old pride. Much more important things. 'Well, if that's what it has to be, that's what it has to be,' he reasoned. 'If that's what you most want to do, you should do it.'

Eve had stared at him and started to cry helplessly. 'But are you sure you wouldn't mind?'

Oliver had forced himself to smile as the old cogs of jealousy in his mind began to whirr and he wondered how it was that Eve even *knew* Dominique had another film for her in the pipeline. Had she been in contact with him again recently? Had they been communicating behind his back?

'Darling,' he soothed, taking his wife's cold hand in his, 'if it's going to help you feel better, I don't mind what you do. Whatever you think best.' His voice had faltered slightly, though, as he asked, 'What's it called, then, this one?'

'*Si Ça C'est Un Jour*,' she had whispered, her eyes now clear. And then, for the first time in what must have been weeks, she had flung her bony arms around him, kissing his face and grasping at his shirt buttons. 'I need you to make love to me', she had breathed. 'Please . . .'

Eve's doing that film had ultimately been a disaster, though, Oliver reflected again now, as he came to a pause by a bench and got his breath back. His impetuous dash through two of London's great parks in his work shoes and suit had rubbed a blister into his heel and he cursed himself for his boyish stupidity. When Colette had telephoned him a few weeks into the *Si Ça* shoot, saying Eve seemed to be having some kind of panic-attack, he had feared the worst. Was this going to be it, then? Was this going to be the moment he had been secretly dreading all these years, the moment when she finally told him what he was most terrified of hearing? Arriving in Paris to collect her, as requested by Colette, though, Oliver had been faced only with a hollow-eyed, distraught shadow of his wife, who kept repeating that she had failed herself, failed everybody. It turned out filming hadn't gone well: she'd been understandably rusty after all those years out of practice and, from what he could gather, had had trouble learning her lines and concentrating on set. Oliver remembered again how relieved he had been to discover that this was the only problem, and how essentially dismissive he had been of Eve's sense of personal trauma. 'You'll be wonderful, darling,' he had told her patiently, like a parent intoning automatic assurances to a nervous child while concentrating on something apparently much more important. 'You'll be wonderful. Now, please stop worrying and let's go home, eh?'

When Oliver recalled now how Eve had turned on him after that, the muddy disappointment in her eyes, which seemed to say, *You really don't care, do you?* the great energy rush that he had felt upon leaving the Foreign Office half an hour ago seemed to drain instantly from his body.

Grimacing through the pain of his blister, Oliver limped slowly, grimly back to the empty house on Tachbrook Street that he and his dead wife had once made home together, and began to pack his suitcase.

FOUR

Colette Lacloche was spooning coffee very carefully into the pot when she heard her son-in-law walking down the stairs and depositing his bag in the hallway. These were the little things she had to focus on, now, in these empty, silent, confusing days. Don't spill the coffee grounds on the floor. Don't splash the milk on the kitchen surface. Having taken the children back to their schools in England, Oliver had been back in Paris for a little over a week, wrapping up the loose ends of Eve's affairs. He seemed to be content that everything was 'in place' with her daughter's estate and all the legalities, and was heading back to Lebanon that afternoon. Colette had been grateful that Oliver was willing and able to deal with the official processes required after the accident: she herself could not bear the cold formality of it at all. Even *seeing* the words 'Concernant la femme décédée: Mme Eve Cécile Latner, neé Lacloche' and Eve's dates of birth and death at the top of one of the letters that had arrived last week had cut her adrift and sent her spiralling back into paroxysms of grief. It was enough, for Colette, to have to deal with the more personal aspect of what Eve had left behind – the letters, the notes, the thousands of pages of diaries, the fan mail, the photographs, the original scripts of all her films and her old dog-eared playtexts, empty of markings inside but for the very occasional, very simple direction to herself: *Je touche la table*, perhaps, or, *je tourne à gauche*.

When Colette, sorting through these seemingly endless archives of her daughter's life, had last week come upon a letter addressed inexplicably and shockingly to herself and Oliver, she had stopped still in her tracks. Oliver, though back in Paris, had not been in the house: he had gone that morning to a meeting at Eve's lawyers. He would be back within an hour or two, but she could not wait. With trembling hands and sinking heart, Colette had eased open the envelope and read the words that lay, innocent and unknowing of their devastating content, on the page in front of her. She had sat down, suddenly, on Eve's old bed, blood hurtling to her head. And then she had read the letter again, very carefully, slowly, as if not quite able to trust that her brain was not deceiving her in its maddened grief. But no. Her daughter's words at least were clear, if their implication was more ambiguous. She had risen to her feet, gone downstairs and waited for her son-in-law to come home.

And now, after those few strangest of days, Oliver was once again knocking gently on the kitchen door and coming to say goodbye. Colette wished that he did not have to leave so soon.

'Right. I'm off, I think,' he announced. 'Unless there's anything else you need me to do?'

Colette turned, coffee spoon in hand. 'You're sure you have

to go back today?' she asked. 'You know you are welcome to stay here for as long as you like.'

'I know, Colette, and thanks. But – well. I need to go back to work. It's time.'

He was wearing a navy cashmere jumper that brought out the blue in his eyes, and had shaved, and combed the chestnut hair which was now greying, slightly, at the temples. With that morning's *Le Monde* tucked under his arm, Oliver looked quite the diplomat again, and Colette felt a sudden wrenching sorrow for Eve's poor husband. In the past she and he had never quite seen eye to eye on many things: to Colette, Oliver had often seemed a little remote – all stiff-upper-lip and terribly *English* in the way he conducted himself; and, of course, they had all been horrified when Eve had announced, aged twenty-seven, that she was going to marry this man and leave Paris. But Eve had loved Oliver Latner with her entire soul and being, had insisted that beneath the cool diplomatic exterior he had poetry in his soul; and now, Colette had to admit, she was beginning to understand it, to understand at least how much Oliver had loved Eve too. He had shown a more sensitive side of himself in these horrific weeks, and this new-found vulnerability, not to mention the way he adored and worried about those children, had touched her deeply.

On the day of the funeral, Colette had slipped out of Café de Flore for some air, and, turning the corner to get away from the crowds on busy boulevard Saint-Germain, had spotted her son-in-law on the street, weeping and crumpled. Her instinct had been to rush over, to hold Eve's husband in her arms, to share his tears and let him know that he was not alone in this world, that she, of all people, understood. But Colette had also had the foresight to know that such actions would mortify Oliver, clearly somebody who needed to do his grieving in private.

So she had turned away and left him alone. But the image of that most upright and composed of men quite disintegrating in sorrow had lodged in her consciousness ever since, and awoken in her a deep fondness for him.

'You know, Oliver, we have a lot more in common than you think,' Colette interjected now, as her son-in-law leant over to kiss her goodbye. She smiled. 'You and I. I know it doesn't often feel like it, but we do.'

Oliver smiled back, puzzled. As far as he was concerned there was little to link him and his mother-in-law, apart from their mutual love for Eve, Lara and Lucas – and now, of course, what had been revealed in that letter last week.

'Really?'

'Eve was very like her father in some ways. So I know what it is like to be married to somebody who has something inside them, a talent so big it can exhaust them even as it elevates them, and which you yourself can never be part of, no matter how much you care about them. I adored Bernard's music, I loved what he could do, but trying to navigate the highs and lows before and after his performances was one of the hardest things about my marriage. And it must have been difficult for you, too, with Eve being what she was.'

Oliver stared at his wise old mother-in-law, then recovered himself. 'Yes,' he admitted, surprised. 'It was, rather.' And now the desire to talk about this, to confess to somebody who might understand just *how* difficult it had been, flooded Oliver in most uncharacteristic fashion. When Colette motioned again at her coffee pot, he nodded helplessly.

'Talk to me?' she asked gently.

And the temptation to finally open up was so great that Oliver, sighing, found he could not resist.

'You know, when Eve and I first met we may as well have come from different planets,' he mused, dropping into one of the chairs around the kitchen table. 'I had so little idea about her world, she was like an alien to me. I remember one evening not many months after we met, going to see her in another play, a Molière she was doing. I went alone. She didn't know I was in the audience. It was the first time I had ever gone to the theatre of my own volition in my entire life, and I could not believe what I was seeing, or the effect it was having on me.' He crossed his arms over his chest in a gesture that spoke to Colette of still-latent insecurity or defensiveness about this. 'I didn't understand it,' he was continuing. 'I didn't understand what Eve could do. Maybe I was even a little scared of it. It was so unpredictable.' Oliver allowed himself a wry chuckle. 'And, when all is said and done, I suppose I'm a person who likes things to be predictable.'

Oliver tried bravely to grin at his mother-in-law as she set his coffee in front of him, but Colette could see the pain and confusion that marked the blue of his eyes. He hung his head. 'I've been thinking, over these past few days, since . . . My God, Colette, I loved her so much, but I don't know if I ever really . . . *understood* her, and . . . Well. Perhaps I didn't always deal with that lack of understanding very brilliantly.'

Colette reached over to touch his arm as she sat down. 'Oliver. Please. You must not blame yourself for that. Nobody truly understood Eve, least of all Eve.'

'Do you really believe that?'

'Yes – that was part of the problem, her sense that when she was acting she was a sort of vessel for something outside her, beyond her, over which she had no control. I know she didn't understand that. She used to feel very undermined and scared by it.'

Colette stirred her coffee thoughtfully, a memory shadow passing over her grief-worn face. 'I remember, when Eve was just a little girl doing a school nativity play, she was only about five, Bernard and I were driving her home afterwards and she was in the back, just shaking. And we said, "Evie, *chérie*, whatever is the matter?" And she looked so terrified as she stared up at me and said, "Maman, I don't know where I went." And Bernard and I looked at each other and thought, What on earth does she mean? Does she mean she doesn't know where she went *wrong*?' Colette smiled. 'She'd been playing a donkey, and very well too, as it happened. We doting parents certainly hadn't noticed any slip-ups. We let it go, but the image of that little face, so puzzled and frightened, never left me. And, you know, later, when Evie was about eighteen and at the Conservatoire, she said something similar. She'd been given quite a small role in the first production of her year, but she had really thrown herself into it, of course, and after the performance we took her out to dinner as a little celebration. She looked utterly shell-shocked, drained, even though there was this *light* in her eyes . . . And I was reminded of that moment in the car, more than a decade previously, as she tried to explain to me what it felt like, that process of exiting her own self and becoming somebody else. "I don't really know where I go," she confessed. "It's terrifying." I, of course, couldn't imagine *what* she was talking about, I knew only that for some inexplicable reason I had given birth to a child who had this great talent. That night, Bernard tried to explain to me what he thought Eve was getting at: it wasn't a million miles away from the transition that used to happen when he was playing, he told me. You know him, he was hardly a man of many words, God rest his soul, so it still didn't make much sense to me. But I had been aware of the

345

emotional ups and downs he was prone to, of course I had, and I started to see more and more of them in Eve as time went by. I lived through them – here, actually, in this very room – the breathless happinesses and the plunging miseries, all the dancing and the tears and the tantrums. And Evie did once admit to me, later on, that although to act was a *compulsion* for her, she knew she had to do it, it never ceased to scare her. She said that after each performance she never knew if she, the real Eve, was going to come back afterwards, and after a while who, indeed, the real Eve was.'

Colette smiled wanly at Oliver, who was dumbly staring at his coffee cup as he grasped too late how skewed his own impressions of his wife's acting talent had been. What had worried Oliver over the years was the *ease* with which Eve had just seemed to slip in and out of character; that ease had always nagged at him in their private life. Was she acting with him? How would he ever know if she was? It had never crossed his mind that she might actually have found acting difficult, intrusive, that each performance might chip away at her own soul until she did not know what was left of it.

'I have to say I hadn't ever looked at it like that,' he said quietly.

'Well, of course, that was why it was almost a relief for her when she married you,' Colette explained. 'To be taken away from a world in which the temptation to act was always in front of her. Demanding of her. But being away was also difficult, of course, because there was a part of her that did *need* to do it.'

'Yes,' Oliver agreed, too late.

'I think perhaps . . .' Colette began, searching for the words, '. . . that perhaps Eve's battle was between her need to create and her need simply to – *be*. Maybe those two impulses are not always reconcilable, maybe they created in her a little madness that . . .' She tailed off, and glanced warily at him. 'Well, maybe that's the reason.'

Oliver cleared his throat. 'Yes,' he repeated. 'I expect you're right.'

He fingered his coffee cup and thought, Tread carefully, now. But he had to ask. It was the one thing they had not touched upon in the past, even more perplexing, few days. 'Do you think they need to know about the letter?'

'The children?' Colette paused, and uttered her words equally deliberately: 'No. I do not think they need to know.'

Oliver swallowed, relieved. 'I agree,' he said. 'I don't think we need to make this any harder for them than it already is.' He stood up, a touch shakily. 'So, we'll keep it between ourselves, then?'

'And Eve, of course.'

'And Eve, of course.'

'It can remain her secret.'

'Yes. Her secret.'

'Well, then.' Colette smiled at her son-in-law, and stood up beside him. 'You should probably be going.'

Oliver checked his watch. 'So I should.'

They embraced briefly, but warmly, and Oliver found himself feeling genuinely moved as he bade goodbye to his mother-in-law, who was going to help him maintain the memory of the Eve they had all known and loved. 'Thanks again for everything, Colette,' he said, picking up his suitcase, 'and please take care of yourself. I'll be in touch at the other end.'

Colette smiled bravely. 'Good luck, Oliver my dear,' she murmured, as he made his way out of the front door and down the steps. '*Bonne chance.*'

Part Five

ONE

Lara was waiting on the corner of rue de Seine and rue du Buci, distractedly biting a fingernail as the nerves gnawed at her stomach. She could hear Christmas carols being piped out of shopfronts all around her, and the streets at this historic intersection had been decorated in typically Left Bank chic, with tasteful Christmas trees and silver stars. No corny electric Santas and Rudolphs for the well-heeled denizens of Saint-Germain, then, she reflected wryly. She checked her watch. He was late. She wondered if she would recognise him from his photographs, and turned again to peer into the bustling interior of Bar du Marché, just in case she had missed him the first few times she'd looked. No, he definitely wasn't there yet. Just 'Jingle Bells' playing on a loop and a faint smell of mulled wine.

Lara dug her hands into her pockets, her right hand closing over her phone. It was switched off – she was having to be militant about not checking it constantly for messages from New

York – but she wondered if there might be some problem with the arranged rendezvous? Then she remembered that he didn't have her mobile number anyway, so if he wasn't going to show up, she'd have to find that out the hard way – by waiting. She wondered what she was going to say to him anyway. How did one broach this sort of thing when it came down to it? *'Hi, did you by any chance sleep with my mother, say, about twenty-seven years ago? Is there any possibility you might actually be my father?'* Er, no. Maybe she should forget the whole idea, continue to live in blissful ignorance, skedaddle, now, before he even arrived, while she still had the chance.

It had all been such a blur. She'd landed at Heathrow Terminal Five from New York yesterday morning, but instead of getting into the car that had been sent by the film company to pick her up and take her home to St Charles Square, Lara had, in a fit of impulsive desperation, collected her small suitcase (the rest of her luggage having been freighted from Manhattan last week, such was the Hollywood treatment) and walked directly back to the departures area. She had enquired as to when the next flight to Paris Charles de Gaulle might be, then bought a seat on the plane, cancelled the car, called Alex to explain apologetically that she was going to Paris earlier than planned in a bid to discover the truth about her mother's relationship with Dominique St Clair – not strictly true, but true enough that he wouldn't suspect her real reasons for being unable to face going home yet – and had promptly boarded said flight. When she had arrived at Colette's apartment, her grandmother had taken one look at her standing sheepishly on the doorstep, muttered a knowing 'Oh, *chérie*,' then promptly bundled her into the warmth of the kitchen.

Meeting him had seemed such a good idea when she'd made

the phone call last night, carefully dialling the number Sabine had found for her on Colette's trusty old Bakelite telephone in the hallway. Nervous anticipation had fizzed in her heart, but she had been convinced she was doing the right thing. Now, though, in the actual moment, in the cold blue light of this December afternoon, Lara was regretting her impetuosity. Jesus, she was nervous. She shifted her weight from one leg to the other and wished she had a cigarette. Did she even want to know the truth? She had a *right* to know, obviously, but did she really *want* to?

Lara's back was turned to the street when she felt somebody tap her shoulder. She spun around. 'Oh!' she exclaimed – because it was him, of course. She recognised him instantly. His hair was grey and thinning, his body a bit doughy, but it was definitely him. The great visionary director, the *auteur*, a touch depleted-looking, these days, but with an intriguing gleam in his eye nonetheless. 'Dominique?'

'Ah, *oui*, *bien sûr*, Mademoiselle Lara. I recognised you even from the back. You could not be anybody but your mother's child.'

Lara managed a smile, wondering if he was being deliberately cryptic or if his English was just a bit ropey. 'That's very observant of you, Dominique,' she replied in French. 'Shall we go in and sit down?'

'*Oui-oui*,' he said, following her through. 'I am so sorry I am so late. My rehearsal went on. You know how they do. I am doing Verdi's *Otello* at the Opéra. First time I ever directed an opera. That was your mother's favourite play, you know. I could never direct it again, after . . . But the opera, it's okay. It's a good enough substitute.' He gave a little wink.

'Of course,' Lara murmured, as they sat down at a quieter table in the corner next to a huge Christmas tree decorated with

353

red and gold baubles. Her heart was thudding in her chest just to hear this stranger talk about her mother in such familiar terms. She forced herself to smile. 'I imagine it is. Dominique, thanks for coming to meet me today, especially at such short notice and especially when you're in the middle of rehearsals. I really appreciate it.'

'Not at all, Lara, not at all. It's so wonderful to see you again.'

Lara's heart faltered as she wondered if she had heard correctly. *Je suis content de te revoir*, he had said. *Revoir.*

Revoir?

'*See me again?*' she echoed.

Dominique caught her eye, apparently surprised by her question. She opened her mouth to repeat it, but he was now looking up at the waitress who had appeared alongside their table.

'Avez-vous choisi?'

'I will take a double espresso and a glass of water,' he announced. 'And a *croque* with *frites*, please.' He looked up at Lara apologetically. 'Forgive me, Mademoiselle Lara, I have not eaten this lunch break. And what would you like?'

'Uh, just a *café crème*, please,' Lara said. She watched the girl disappear into the smoky steam of the bar before she turned back to Dominique. 'Again?' she said, tentatively. 'What do you mean, again?'

Dominique pulled a pack of skinny white cigarettes out of his black corduroy jacket pocket and offered one to Lara. He placed one in his mouth and lit it, somewhat theatrically. Then he studied her face and looked directly into her eyes.

'Why, *bien sûr*, dear Lara. This is not the *first* time we have met. You do realise that?'

*   *   *

Oliver slowly replaced the receiver of the phone in his office. And so it was. All summer, all autumn, ever since he'd learnt of Lara's damned film in fact, he had known that this possibility loomed large on the horizon. And now it seemed inevitable. That had been Colette on the phone. Lara had turned up on her doorstep the day before, apparently, straight off a plane from New York even though they were all due there anyway in three days. She was nervy and exhausted, Colette told him, but more to the point, full of questions. She had just left Colette a note to say she was going to meet Dominique St Clair for coffee, so it was, presumably, only a matter of time . . .

Oliver glanced at the clock and stood up, pressing the intercom to go through to Julia in the outer office. 'Cancel my four o'clock with the second sec for me, will you, Julia? I need to pop out for a bit.'

'Of course, sir,' came back the response. 'Everything all right?'

'Yup. Everything's fine,' Oliver said, clearing his throat. 'Put any urgent calls through to my mobile, please, otherwise take messages.'

'No problem. Any idea when you might be back?'

Oliver sighed. He badly needed to get out of this room, clear his head, take in some fresh air. If possible, he would like to get down to the coast. 'Chance I may not make it back this afternoon, actually, but call me if there's anything that looks serious.'

'I will do, sir.'

Oliver grabbed his phone, keys and diplomatic ID from his desk, and retrieved his jacket from behind the door. 'Thanks, Julia,' he said, and was gone.

Oliver left Tel Aviv via the simplest checkpoint, moving relatively quickly through the diplomatic channel, thanks to his blessed dip plates and paperwork. He pointed the car north up the freeway towards Haifa, although he wouldn't go that far – just to Natanya, perhaps. Thirty kilometres or so. He only wanted to get out of the city. The sky over this benighted land today was as blue as it would be in a child's picture book, the Mediterranean sparkling cheerfully in the wintry afternoon light. Oh, what you must have seen, Oliver thought, as he let the image of the waves crashing on the deserted beaches to his left calm his brain. What you must have seen, and still you keep on, back and forth, in and out, heroic perpetual motion. How he loved the sea. 'Somebody told me,' he remembered Eve saying to him once, in almost child-like wonder as they strolled along a beach somewhere, salt wind in their hair, a sea filtering through their toes, 'that Beethoven wrote all his music without ever having seen the sea. Can you imagine?' No, Oliver had agreed, laughing, he couldn't. How could anyone do anything without the sea?

That had to be one of the best things about this job, he contemplated, as he rolled along the coastal road. Apart from the intellectual challenge, of course – the seas, the skies, the space, the chance to escape. He had always been a wanderer: *itchy feet*, his mother, Susan, used to tut, not altogether approvingly, the implication being that it was somehow better to stay in the Home Counties and play bridge all one's life. Oliver remembered the first time he'd been told about the Foreign Service at school. That there was a Very Respectable Profession that would send him all over the world and teach him languages *and* pay him to live by the sea had seemed too good to be true. He had done Sandhurst and Northern Ireland out of a quiet sense of duty after Oxford, but had taken the civil-service exams in secret and quit the army in jubilation when his results came in. And he would never forget his first day in King Charles Street: sniffing the air in those hallowed old corridors – that scent of secrets, and dust, and wood polish, its particular promise of different skies and different tongues and unimaginable freedom.

It was freedom for which he had always yearned, Oliver reflected now, as he parked in one of the small seaside towns up the coast, between Herzlia and Natanya. Checking that his phone was in his pocket in case Julia rang with an emergency, he pulled off his shoes and socks and rolled up his trouser legs. Then he locked the car and walked down to the shore. It was warm today, must be about 22° centigrade, but the place was quiet and deserted, exuding the muted poignancy of any off-season seaside town. Cafés shuttered. Colourful wooden beach huts padlocked together. A lone blue plastic chair sitting on the promenade, discarded and forgotten. The emptiness was hardly surprising: it was a Wednesday afternoon in mid-December. Oliver was glad to have the beachfront to himself, his feet thudding along the sand, which still contained the sun's late warmth compacted in its grains. The water that foamed over his toes was cold but bracing, and helpful. He needed to clear his head, and walk, and think, because if what Colette had said was true, it looked likely that any day now he was going to be required to have the hardest conversation imaginable with his daughter. And he needed to work out what, in his defence, he was going to say.

Colette had seen the note, in Lara's charmingly mistake-laden written French, as soon as she had walked into the kitchen after running her errands. It was stuck to the fridge with a blue magnet.

Chère Mamie Colette,
Sorry I slept so late and didn't see you this morning – I seem to be
completely knackered from the film and just couldn't wake up!
Hope your doctor's appointment went OK.

Just so you know: I've gone to meet Dominique St Clair for coffee. I got his number from Sabine, the costume designer I was telling you about . . . I've been feeling for a long time that I need to talk to him. I hope you understand. I wanted to get in touch with him before I shot This Being Human, *but now, as I'm here anyway, it seems like the right thing to do – just an instinct I have about something . . . Sorry to be cryptic: I actually hope we'll be able to talk properly about all this when you get back, as I'll probably have a few questions for you, too.*

Je t'embrasse,

Lals x

Colette had dropped her grocery bags on the table. So Lara had gone to see Dominique. *And so,* she had thought, *it is time . . .*

First of all, she had telephoned Oliver, via the Foreign Office switchboard in London, to warn him that Lara was here, unexpectedly early, and that she had gone off to see St Clair. His daughter, if and when she found out what had really happened, was going to need a lot of questions answered and he would do well to prepare himself for that eventuality before he came over for Christmas. She would do the same. Oliver had sounded grimly resolute, and thanked her for the advice. Then Colette had gone upstairs to the drawer by her bedside table and scrabbled around in it until she found what she was looking for: a battered old green ring-box, which had once contained the simple diamond engagement ring with which Bernard had proposed to her, and which she still wore on her gnarled left hand. Nestled on a dark lock of her daughter's baby hair inside the box was the object she was looking for. Colette had picked it up, and held it up to the light. *And so it is time.*

She had then walked slowly, boldly, down the stairs to the living room.

And when Lara burst through the door of her grandmother's flat, an hour or so later, her face flushed and her mind reeling after everything Dominique had told her in the café, she had found her grandmother in the drawing room, seemingly prepared. Colette was sitting in Bernard's old armchair, holding a small, silver key.

TWO

Dominique St Clair and Eve Lacloche had indeed been lovers, once.

But the story Dominique told his former lover's daughter, as they drank coffee and smoked endless cigarettes in the Bar du Marché, was not quite what Lara had expected.

They had met while she was still a student at the Conservatoire. Like many others, Dominique had been besotted with Eve's beauty and her talent, but she in turn had been impressed with the idealistic young director and his big ideas. They had made a film together almost as soon as she graduated, *Le Retour*, which was critically fêted and put them both on the map. Eve and Dominique had a special connection, it seemed, both professionally and personally and, perhaps inevitably, they would sometimes sleep together. 'Hey, we were kids of '68,' Dominique had shrugged. 'We were all sleeping together.' But Eve was not in love with him, Dominique knew: she never had been. She had all sorts of other boyfriends in that period, for a start. 'Eve could take her pick in those days, movie roles, dresses, men. Anything she wanted, the whole world was hers to play with. But she always seemed to be searching for something deeper than that, something beyond all the frippery and fun.' And when a certain English diplomat named Oliver Latner had arrived on the scene one autumn, well, that had apparently been that. Out of the blue Eve had suddenly been off-limits to them all. 'It was as if she had changed, for ever, overnight,' Dominique said, chewing his sandwich a little morosely. 'I remember having lunch with her a day or so after she'd first spent the night with *le rosbif diplomatique* – sorry, that was our nickname for him, which unfortunately got leaked to the gossip pages – and she just had this light in her eyes as she gabbled on, telling me how she had fallen in love for the first time in her life. Being Eve, of course, she had no idea that I was in love with *her*. She wasn't trying to hurt my feelings, she just couldn't have known the effect she had on me – the effect she had on most people. I certainly wasn't the only man in Paris to be in despair that Eve Lacloche had got herself a proper boyfriend!' He had smiled again, stirring a lump of sugar into his second coffee. 'Of course, we were all young and arrogant and we thought we owned Paris. We demanded to know what exactly this English fellow had that was so great he'd popped up in our territory, out of nowhere, and managed to usurp us. I mean, he wasn't a poet, an artist, a musician, an actor, a writer, the things that *we* were, and that Eve had always surrounded herself with. And when we met him, Oliver wasn't what we were expecting at all. I mean, he was beautiful, sure, and he spoke wonderful French, but he was so *academic*, so political – but not even in the way that *we* were political – so very *English*. And let's just say the incomprehension was mutual: he didn't seem to like us much, either. But Eve was clearly crazy about him, and you could see he was crazy about her, too. There was a glow about them when they were together, and for the rest of us miserable fools watching, it was obvious they were painfully in love.'

'So how was it filming with her once she'd started going out with my – with Oliver?' Lara had asked, nervously lighting another cigarette.

'Oh, no, nothing really changed in our professional relationship,' Dominique explained. 'That remained very much the same.'

'Can you tell me what it was like working with my mother?'

'Of course. Eve was . . . Well, she was the hardest-working actress I ever saw, which was strange given that she was also a complete natural. She had such curiosity about the parts she played: what has happened in this person's world to make them behave like this, say this, think this? She always wanted to look the world in the eye, whatever it had to hold back up at her, and to bring that new understanding to bear for her character.' Dominique had smiled sadly as he seemed to rifle through the many memories in his mind. 'And woe betide you if you did not apply the same rigour to your own work! Eve was always very exacting, you know, she did not let up. She pushed you to the limits of what you thought you were capable of – as a director or an actor or a person – and, *bof*, with a twinkle of her eye, before you even knew it, she had forced you over the edge, and suddenly you were doing something different, scary, but, my God, you were doing it.'

Dominique had chuckled, as Lara had closed her eyes, thinking of how apt a description that would be for another actor: Jacob Moss.

'Eve was particularly hard on me,' he continued. 'You know, Lara, these days I'm a teddy bear, but, *oh, la la*, back then I was tough. I was young and celebrated and arrogant and passionate. I was mean to people, so they feared me, but they also respected me because of the work I was doing – and they wanted to keep working with me. So they lay down. They were afraid of who they thought I was, and they let me walk all over them. But Eve – pah! She knew who I was, and she showed me up in front of everybody for what I was: a bright young kid with some ideas and a bit of *chutzpah* and a hell of a lot of luck. She did not lie down, she was fearless, and as a result I learnt so much from her.' He looked wistful. 'My God, we learnt a lot from each other.'

Lara had prepared herself, suspecting this wistfulness might perhaps be a cue for something else. And, indeed, the next thing Dominique had said was, 'Now, what you need to know is, what I need to confess to you is, the stupidest thing I ever did in my life, and the thing I regret the most in my life.'

Lara had nodded, but not without trepidation, wondering again if she was really ready to hear this.

'One night at the end of *La Belle Hélène*, the night we wrapped on the movie actually, we all went out to La Coupole or somewhere for dinner. Eve, I remember, was so shattered. She had worked so hard on that film and she had not been sleeping well because she was pregnant –' Dominique smiled at Lara '– with you, of course, and having terrible sicknesses in the mornings. But that night she was back on her enchanted form again, an angel of grace and wit and spice. She was high, I guess you might say, high from the film, and the glory of being adored, high from Paris and, who knows, perhaps the pregnancy hormones. She kept talking incessantly about her new fiancé

363

Oliver and telling us that he had been away on a trip for the past week and how she could not wait to see him tomorrow. We were jeering – "Eh, tomorrow is another day, stay out with us tonight!" – and because she was in such a good mood, she did, she stayed out with us. And it was the first time in such a long while that we had seen her, as Eve, off set, not working so hard as Hélène, it was too delightful. Too delightful for us to have her back, out on the streets of Paris, celebrating, without an Englishman in sight. I remember we were buzzing around her like naughty bees that night, shameful creatures that we were. Myself, Gabriel Dufy, Édouard Valence, all the crew. Tell me, Lara, do you know what I mean, if I say *faire des bêtises*?'

Lara remembered the phrase from her childhood, her and Luc being scolded by their mother for some naughtiness or other. 'You mean, like, mischief-making?'

'*Exactement*. It was too much, to have her back in our midst again without *le rosbif*, forgive me, sneering down his nose at us. So we made some mischief. We ate dinner and we all drank too much champagne and we went dancing somewhere, and Eve, who was a little drunk, too, I am afraid to say – this was the early eighties, nobody worried too much about drinking during their pregnancies – was telling me very earnestly, as we walked arm in arm along the street to the nightclub, how she would always love me, in a way, because of what happened when we made films together, because of our very special connection. And I was wilfully misinterpreting this, of course, in my mind. She loves me! The fool. Anyway. We stayed out until the sun rose in Paris and she was very tired and drunk by this stage, and I promised her I would take her home. But when she was saying this in the club, "Take me home, Dominique, take me home" – and she was almost collapsing she was so exhausted

– as I say, I was deliberately misinterpreting her words. I did indeed take her home: it just happened to be my home. My apartment on rue de Fleurus. And she passed out immediately on the sofa – it was mostly exhaustion, my dear Lara, I promise you, she was not *so* very drunk. So I picked her up and I put her in my bed and then I climbed in next to her, and the two of us, like stupid teenagers, promptly passed out.'

'What happened?' Lara had asked, anxiously but without judgement: didn't she, of all people, know how high emotions ran when wrapping on a film?

'Well, silly Eve had convinced herself she was just going to come out for one glass of champagne because she was so tired. And she was supposed to be meeting her Englishman at the airport, back from his trip, in the morning. When she didn't turn up at Charles de Gaulle as planned and he couldn't get through to her at the flat on rue Jacob, or at her mother and father's, Oliver was very surprised. Now we forget, in those days, no mobiles, how frustrating not to be able to get in touch with people. Eve had not left him a message at the airport, or at the British Embassy, or anywhere. He came back into the city and went home, assuming that Eve had just been a little scatty and he would probably find her still in bed, fast asleep. But Eve, of course, was not there and had left no message to say she was doing anything else, and when he went upstairs, the bed was made, everything was in order, she had obviously gone somewhere. He was starting to get worried – she had sounded so tired, what with the pregnancy, and the film, when he had spoken to her this week from abroad. Where could she be? She should be resting. He told himself to stop fretting: perhaps she was just out shopping for some lunch. So. He waited a while longer, and then he started to phone some other people, her friends Sophie and Aurélie, other acquaintances, a bit more frantically now. He called Colette again, who told him to ring some of the people from the film, perhaps. And then, upon hearing this, and remembering that Eve had mentioned she might go out for a wrap drink with the cast and crew last night, Oliver, being a clever man, but also a jealous man – for he had always mistrusted me – made a lethal connection in his head. He looked up my address and he took a taxi to rue de Fleurus where, meanwhile, Eve and I were, of course, still passed out in my bed. He waited for the next two hours, outside the apartment, pinned down by this instinct that his pregnant fiancée might be inside. Eventually, Eve woke up because she had to be sick – and she was aghast, mortified, *furious* to find herself in my bed, with me snoring away next to her. She had a hangover from the champagne and the too-much sleep and was very sick. My God, Lara, she was *incandescent* with rage – hitting me, pummelling me, how could I have done such a thing? Taken advantage of her in this way? She knew, of course, that nothing had *happened*, I hadn't so much as kissed her, but she was going crazy, when she saw the time and remembered she was supposed to have met Oliver at the airport four hours ago. She flew down the stairs and out onto the street where, of course, your father was standing. Just standing there, watching the front door, waiting.'

Lara had been horrified for her poor mother and father, and the creeping realisation that she might herself have got something terribly wrong about her mother had begun to hum in her brain like a demented insect. 'And I suppose he didn't believe her that it was innocent?' she'd asked gingerly.

'Well, it certainly didn't help that she was hungover and it was nearly four in the afternoon and she was wearing last night's dress.'

Lara's heart had broken, then, for her dad. 'Did he come upstairs and threaten to kill you?'

'No. He behaved like the perfect English gentleman he is. He walked away, quite calmly, quietly, down the street. But he also told Eve that he was moving out of her flat in rue Jacob immediately and leaving her. He was due to return to London quite soon after that anyway.'

'So what did Mum do?'

'She went completely out of her mind and begged him not to leave her. Then she asked me to help, seeing as it was all my fault anyway. And this was when I did what I regret most in the world.'

'What did you do?'

'Eve wanted me to tell Oliver the truth, that we had been lovers once – as he probably knew – but not for years. And that on the night in question it had been, as you say, all innocent.'

'But?'

'But instead of doing that, as I should have done, and because I was proud and lovesick and foolish and arrogant, and I knew it was Eve's word against mine, I not only let Oliver believe that we had slept together that night, I let him believe that we had been sleeping together on other occasions throughout their relationship. Worst of all, I let him believe that the child Eve was carrying in her belly might be mine. I let him think that you might be mine.'

Lara had dropped her head, sickened by the thought that she might ever have contemplated this possibility herself; might ever have doubted her mother in such a fashion; might have let her own baseless suspicions about Eve's conduct colour her own behaviour in New York. And when she looked up, she saw how her own bitter self-reproach was mirrored dramatically in Dominique's eyes.

'I have never forgiven myself, Lara,' he said, his voice cut with remorse. 'I loved Eve so much, and I did her such a grievous wrong. How could I have done that? It was all so pointless, anyway: their love was strong enough to withstand even my attempts to jeopardise it. Eve swore to Oliver on her unborn baby's life that the child was his, and that she could not live without him, and that if he would only believe her and marry her and bring this child up with her, she would do *anything* for him. She would even leave Paris, quit acting, go with him *anywhere in the world*. I don't know whether Oliver fully believed her then, or when he may have started to, but I think at that point he interpreted her begging as evidence of guilt. But, you know, he loved this girl. He wanted to be with her, even if he could no longer trust her. He just needed to get her out of Paris, away from her naughty world with all its debauched filmmakers and actors, away from me. So Oliver, on Eve's promise that she would leave Paris and make a life with him in international diplomacy, capitulated. And they were married. They left Paris. It seems that when you were born – helpfully looking *nothing* like your father, by all accounts – Oliver assured Eve that he did believe her, did trust that she had never been unfaithful to him with me. But who knows if he ever could, quite, believe it? We men are very proud, you know, and our pride disables us. Makes us stupid. I know that Eve certainly worried about that – about her husband's lack of *absolute* faith in her – for the rest of her life.' His shoulders visibly slumped. 'It nearly destroyed her . . . and it was all thanks to me and my stupid ego.'

Dominique's eyes had widened in apparent horror as he contemplated again what he had done, and Lara, though stunned by what she was hearing, had felt almost sorry for him at this point.

'But how do you know all this, Dominique?' Lara asked gently.

He looked up at her. 'I know from what Eve told me at the time, and what she told me later on, and because I filled in the blanks. In those first few days after our little sleepover disaster, even though she was furious with me, she needed me to help her win back Oliver – she could hardly have known what wickedness I was capable of. So, she told me what was happening, with him threatening to break off the engagement and leave Paris without her and all the rest. She would ring me up to scream at me. "*Do you know what you've done, Dominique? How could you do this to me?*" After they got married and left France, for a long time she refused to talk to me. Even when we were photographed together at the Oscars and on all those occasions, she would be polite and civil in front of the cameras, but would not actually speak to me unless absolutely required to.'

Lara felt sick as she remembered studying those pictures of the two of them in Sabine's living room, letting her own twisted convictions run away with her.

'And then many years later,' Dominique carried on, 'we bumped into each other in Paris at the Café de Flore. That was where I met you for the first time, Lara, as a little girl colouring in the tablecloth with old Jacques Catroux's crayons. When she miraculously agreed to meet me the next day I begged her to come back and make another film with me. She, of course, refused point-blank, and it killed me. Sorry. It devastated me. I had missed her terribly over the years, for despite everything, Eve and I did have a very great friendship, a special understanding. It had simply been muddied by my other feelings for her. As I began to comprehend how badly I had behaved, I started sending her letters, apologising more profusely for my unforgivable actions of all those years ago. I told her to forget about the script I had given her, *Si Ça C'est Un Jour*, to forget about working with me ever again. I only begged for her forgiveness on a human level. And, because your mother was one of the most generous souls alive, eventually she did forgive me. Then we started to write to each other quite often – you know how lonely she was while Oliver was away working and you and your brother were at school – and, to my amazement, many years later, she out of the blue telephoned me to say she had changed her mind: she wanted to come to Paris and make *Si Ça* with me. And that, of course, was a shock, but nothing like the shock I had when she actually arrived and we started to work. Doing that film with her was when I saw just how bad things had got, when I really started to worry . . .'

He had tailed off, and Lara had frowned. 'What do you mean, "just how bad things had got"?'

Dominique had wrung his hands, then, and pulled yet another cigarette from the packet on the table. This one he did not light but instead rolled back and forth between his hands. His features were knotted in an anguished grimace. 'Lara, it is not my place to tell you this, but I do believe you need to know. Or, perhaps, you know already, in which case I hope you'll forgive me my impudence. But that is not the impression I got from your grandmother.'

Lara was shocked. She had no idea Colette and Dominique St Clair had ever had anything to do with each other, apart from in the most peripheral of ways.

'Know . . . what?'

Dominique leant his head back and groaned. 'Oh, *mon dieu*, how can I put this? Lara, Eve suffered from serious depression. She was tragically good at hiding it, of course, what with all that acting ability, and in those days people did not think about depression in the same way they do now. Nowadays they would probably diagnose her as a manic, a bipolar, or at least as someone with acute clinical depression and prone to psychotic interludes. She would be prescribed drugs, and she would be okay. But in those days there were no such trendy labels, not widespread, anyway, and I am sure your father would not have been someone to encourage that in any case. He strikes me as quite a "keep buggering on!" sort of an Englishman, no?'

Lara nodded mutely. She couldn't deny that, although the cultural stereotyping irked her. Dominique's observation seemed to be tinged with criticism of Oliver, which in turn made her want to defend her dad ferociously: Lara herself had always been a bit sceptical of the actors she knew who claimed to be 'depressed', many of them on Prozac and wearing it like some kind of badge of honour, some specious designer label. But Eve? Depressed? Lara didn't want to believe Dominique's words were true, but they were resonating with something very deeply embedded in her subconscious.

'Eve's depression was serious, though, and by the time I recognised it when we did *Si Ça* and I was so appalled to discover how bad she had become, it was too late. I tried to tell her that what was happening to her was an illness because, you know, she was so *scared* of it, those feelings of such intense despair and pointlessness. I tried to explain that she was sick, that she could get help, that there were pills she could take to equalise her mind, that she could be happy again if only she admitted to a doctor how she felt. But she had already worked herself up into such a state of conviction that it was all her fault, that she was somehow being punished by her misery for some wrong she must have done – to Oliver, to you and your brother, to the dead baby, to me, to all of us.'

371

Lara remained silent, dumbstruck, as she listened to the terrible irony of these words.

'And then, of course, the film came out and expectations were so high – Eve Lacloche and Dominique St Clair working together again after all these years! It was critically trashed, as you know, and rightly so. It wasn't just that we hadn't met their unreasonable expectations, it truly was not a good movie – well, you have probably seen it?'

Lara cleared her throat. 'Yes – I have. It's . . .'

'Well, that film required Eve to be *Eve* when she came to her character of Isabelle, and I'm sorry to say that, when we made it, she simply was no longer Eve. It was like she had gone blank inside. It was the most tragic thing I ever saw: Eve on camera, *Eve*, and her eyes totally dead. Not an ounce of energy coming out of her. Eve! But the criticism, of course, for her was just the cruellest thing. All these years stuck abroad with Oliver, having to attend cocktail parties and state functions, she had been holding up acting, and that particular film – with which I had tempted her many years ago – as a sort of salvation, a sort of "If only I could go and do that again, live that life again, I would be happy again." But, tragically, by the time she got there, more than a decade on, it was already hopeless . . .' He had shaken his head. 'My God, when I went to see your grandmother a month after the funeral – which I simply could not face, by the way – and she told me what she had discovered . . . Well, I just wish we could have got to her sooner, before it was too late.'

Lara had felt a disturbing cadence of time, then, the minutes and seconds all out of place as she struggled to come to terms with what Dominique St Clair was really saying. Everything was slowing down, her brain seemed to be whirring strangely in her head. 'What do you mean, too late?' she had whispered.

Dominique had blinked, his eyes laced with sorrow and regret. 'Lara, I am sorry to be the one to tell you this, but I believe it is time you and your brother knew the truth.'

She could feel the world spinning ever more slowly on its axis and her heart gently decelerating until, finally, it was completely still.

'More than a year before she died, your mother wrote a letter explaining that on various occasions she had contemplated suicide, and warning Colette and your father that she might do so again. She had convinced herself that it would be better for everyone if she was gone, that there was nothing left to live for. She hid the letter, which Colette discovered after her death. Perhaps the car hitting her that day really was an accident. But your mother was in the grip of an illness that she refused to face, and I, for one, have no doubt that she fully intended to kill herself.'

THREE

14 sept
Paris.
Chère Maman, et Oliver, mon amour,

*If you are reading this, it is because I will finally have done
something which I often think about doing, which I almost
did again today but which I was prevented from doing by a
series of fateful coincidences, and which I know I may well
have to do one day in the future. If this is indeed what has
happened, I do not want you to spend the rest of your lives
wondering why, so I hope this letter will perhaps answer
some of your questions, and that you will forgive me if there
are some that remained unanswered.*

*My darling mother, and the most cherished love of my
life, Oliver, as you know I have been wrestling with the
blackness inside me for so many years now, and the periods*

of light have become increasingly fleeting, and rare. The only thing that has given me joy is you both and Papa and my Lara and Lucas, but I see, Maman, how you cope without Papa and I know how well you will cope without me. I see, Oliver, how busy you are and how your worries about me get in the way of your very important work; I see how without me you will be able to work so much harder and do so much more good for the world. And I see, now, how Lucas and Lara do not need me any more, how they do not feel the same way about their mother as they used to. And so if I have finally decided to do what I fear I must do, this painful and inescapable truth will have been part of my decision.

It has been a particularly bad time recently, after Papa and the miscarriage and the film and the raking up of all the old feelings in Beirut, a place I associate with the darkest thoughts because that is where they first started to plague me for long periods without relief. I want you to know that I am not blaming anybody except myself, but for so many years I have found each day a struggle and have had to act my way through life just to endure each day. Well, I am sorry, but I cannot act any more. I am exhausted.

For many years I convinced myself that my feelings of despair and pointlessness were being caused by my not being an actress, as in not physically working on the stage or screen. Well, you might say, 'But an actress is still an actress even if she is not actually "acting"!' But I started to understand that this is not true: that I could not think of myself as an actress if I was not working. And then I thought, Well, what am I here for, what is the point? I somehow convinced myself that if I were to go back to the

375

theatre or the film set everything would be restored again – I often looked back to what the press refer to as my 'glory days' here in Paris when I was in my twenties and thirties, and I suppose I bought into the cruel lie: I told myself that if only I were to relive that time, I would also be able to rediscover a former self. A former Eve. An Eve who was happy and who loved life. It was a tantalising excuse, and underpinned the reason why I eventually decided to do Si Ça C'est Un Jour *(on dear Oliver's most generous and considerate suggestion).*

This, as we all know, was a terrible decision but in fact I am almost grateful for what my experience on that film revealed. Dominique told me that the reason he could not get the performances out of me that he used to get was because there was something wrong with me. 'Yes!' I said. 'Me. I am all wrong!' He ignored this and told me I was 'depressed', that my lethargy and my inability to learn my lines or do what he asked of me was not my fault. He tried to tell me that I was very sick, and must get myself to a doctor immediately. But, as usual, Dominique was talking rubbish. I am not going to blame my own failures on a supposed 'disease' one cannot even see. I am not going to evade my own responsibilities. The truth is, I am a failure. The thing I have held up all these years as some kind of pathetic proof that I am actually worth something in this world has been exposed as a lie. And in the process, I and everything I have told myself I believed in have been exposed as the same.

For what is Eve Lacloche if she is not an actress, you might ask?

I have asked myself this so many times, and at my more deluded moments I have sometimes entertained the consolation of 'Well, Eve Lacloche is also Eve Latner, and Eve Latner is a wife and mother, is she not?' Because, Oliver, I love you as I have never loved another human soul, and the passion I feel for Lara and Lucas is also so overwhelming as to be beyond my understanding. But I have been a bad mother, haven't I? That is why I lost my baby – I did not deserve another child. I have been so selfish, I have abandoned my own darling children in faraway countries and left them in the hands of strangers. I remembered recently that once, when I was very miserable in our second year in Kinshasa, facing life without Lara and Luc at home, one of the other diplomatic wives told me, 'We can make a choice in this position, Eve. We can either stay with our husbands and look after our marriages, or we can go with our children and look after them. But remember, ultimately, if your marriage is okay, your children will be okay.' And she was right, in a way, this woman, but she was also wrong. For yes, the children are 'okay', but they have grown up not needing me any more, not loving me any more. So it is no surprise to me that my baby died: why should I have been allowed another child, simply to abandon it again in this way? When I read their letters I see how independent Lara and Luc are now, how they do not have any further use for their mother, how they will not only survive well after I am gone but will in fact be better off without me.

Just as you all will be better off without me.

The revelation of Si Ça C'est Un Jour *that I literally cannot act any more (as Eve Lacloche) has made me desperately scared I will soon lose my ability to act the part of wife and mother (Eve Latner) too. If I cannot keep acting for the children, hiding from them the way I truly feel about life, as I have been doing for so many years now, they will start to hate me even more. And that I truly cannot bear.*

So, I hope you will see in time why this is the best way, and feel no grief for me. You must know I have loved you both, and Papa, and Lara, and dear little Lucas, with all my soul, and always will.

Je suis desolée et je vous embrasse toujours.

Your loving

Eve

PS It would be better I think if the children never knew of the existence of this letter – I do not want them to be tormented, or to blame themselves in any way. They, like you, are of course perfectly blameless: the fault lies entirely with me, as I am sure they in time will also come to understand. I am trusting you both therefore to destroy it, and forget about it, and I know, of course, that you will not betray me on this most important of matters. Thank you – E

FOUR

'Do you think he meant it when he said he was sorry?'

Lara and Lucas were lying, as they had once liked to do as illicitly smoking teenagers, among the water towers and insulation units on the roof of their grandparents' seventh *arrondissement* apartment. Christmas night in Paris was freezing and starry this year, and they had pulled various old blankets up the ladder with them, along with Lucas's drum and his guitar, to keep themselves warm as they munched Colette's famous Christmas biscuits and smoked Lucas's weed.

'What are you talking about?' asked Lucas. 'Of course he meant it.'

Lara paused. 'I just cannot believe they could have kept it a secret for so long.'

'She asked them to,' Lucas pointed out. 'You read the letter.'

'Yeah, but she was sick! She was ill!'

'So, what? They should have disregarded her dying wish and abused that trust?'

'Isn't it an abuse of our trust that they lied to us like that?'

Lucas dwelt on this for a moment. 'No. Because they didn't lie to us. They told us Mum got hit by a car, which was true. Maybe she didn't actually commit suicide that day, maybe it was really an accident. Her letter was written more than a year before she died. Who knows? So they didn't exactly lie to us, they just kept the extent of her depression, and her declared intentions, a secret.'

'So why did Dad look so contrite and regretful and sorry?'

'Because he is contrite and regretful and sorry.'

'Ha! Why, if he's been doing the right thing all this time?'

Lucas hauled himself up onto his elbows and passed his sister the joint. 'You know, Lals, for someone who's supposed to be quite bright, you *can* be a bit stupid sometimes.'

Lara gasped indignantly and chucked her half-eaten biscuit at him. 'What the hell is that supposed to mean?'

'Well, you must know by now that there's no such thing in life as right or wrong?' Luc chuckled fondly at his sister. 'What did Dad say? He said, "Lara. Lucas. I know it seems indefensible now, but at the time, I genuinely, honestly believed that in my silence I was protecting the three people I loved best in the world. Eve, and the two of you. I am bitterly sorry."'

Lara laughed despite herself at her brother's pitch-perfect impression of their father.

'So, if he had told us ten years ago, he would equally have been doing the wrong thing for Mum,' Lucas continued reasonably. 'Anyway. Maybe Dad was right and we *were* better off not knowing.'

'You really believe that? You think it's right we didn't know the truth until now?'

Lucas shrugged. 'I don't know, man.' He sighed. 'I just miss her, that's all.'

Lara wrapped her blanket tighter around her and took a deep drag of the spliff. Me too, she thought. Me too.

'Luc?' she said, after a moment.

'Yes, La?'

'You didn't really seem surprised.'

Lucas was silent.

'Were you?'

'Maybe I sort of knew,' he said.

'You *what*?'

Lucas gave another shrug. 'I spent a lot of time kind of talking to her after she was gone. Do you remember, when we were little, on the nights before we went back to school or whatever, she would take us outside and hold our hands and we'd look up at the sky and she'd explain that we could all spend time together even when we were apart? Up there on the other side? *L'autre côté des étoiles*, as she used to call it. I know now, of course, that she wasn't *really* there, but I must've worked something out . . .'

'Yeah, I remember those evenings,' murmured Lara. 'Of course I do. But I had no idea . . .'

'It's okay, Lals. Don't beat yourself up. Remember, I was a bit of a weird kid. I preferred talking to her than making conversation with the outside world. Still do, in a way.'

Brother and sister were silent for a while, lying head to head, looking up at the stars hovering over the city as the chemicals in the marijuana gradually kicked in and slowed down their racing brains. How strange it was, Lara thought, that in the wake of Eve's death, once they'd gone back to school, she could hardly bear to see Luc, so painful was it to be reminded of what her family had once been. And yet now, in the wake of learning the *truth* about that death, it had turned out that Lucas was the only person in the world she wanted to see. It had been such a relief to meet him off the train at the Gare du Nord the other day, the train she herself was supposed to be on, to see him ambling along the platform with his record bag and a football. She'd given him a hug and driven him back to Colette's in the old Citroën, making small-talk along the way – she'd sworn to Oliver and Colette she wouldn't tell him about Eve until they got home.

But then, after parking on avenue Bosquet outside Colette's building, Lara had suddenly broken down. As she leant over the steering-wheel and sobbed, Lucas had sat there silently, letting her cry, asking no questions, only reaching over at one point to put a hand on her shoulder. Then, without a word of explanation, Lara had wiped her eyes, twisted the key in the ignition again, put the car into gear, and driven him out to Père-Lachaise. And there, over Eve's flower-bedecked grave, in defiance of the wishes of her father and grandmother, she had told her brother what she now understood to be the truth about their mother's death. And he had taken the news in typical Lucas fashion: calmly, quietly, stooping to touch the latest messages that her fans, conscious of the anniversary, had recently left; and then standing for a while, just standing, speechless, motionless, a distant look in his blue eyes. For someone whose life was all about rhythm and making people get up and move, Lara reflected, that boy had such a capacity for stillness in him it was remarkable. They hadn't said much on the way back to Colette's, but Lara had felt crystallise in the air between them an understanding that said, I'm with you. We'll look after each other. Everything'll be okay. And she had felt – for the first time since she'd grasped Dominique's tumultuous news and confronted her father and grandmother and read her mother's pre-emptive suicide note – as if it just might.

Lara took another deep pull on the joint and felt further calmed by the sound of her brother breathing next to her. She wondered if she'd ever felt so close to Lucas as she had these past few days, and found, with a trace of surprise, that she wanted to open up to him about everything – Alex, Jacob, everything. It seemed trivial to talk about her relationship troubles in the wake of their recent news, but she wanted to know what he would say if she told him the truth. Would he pass judgement, worshipping Alex as he did? Would he tell her she'd made the biggest mistake of her life? Would he tell her she was going to regret it for ever?

'I've really fucked up, Luc,' she said, after a few minutes, still lying on her back staring at the velvety black sky.

He didn't respond for a while. 'Why?' he asked eventually.

'I fell in love with someone while I was in New York.'

'Oh.'

'But not *so* in love that I don't love Alex any more. It sounds impossible, I know, but it's true. I never thought you could actually love two people at the same time, but it turns out you can.'

'Who's the other guy?'

Lara hesitated. The joint was burning down to her fingers. 'Jacob Moss.'

Lucas sat up. 'Oh, right. Of course.' He scratched his head.

'No, you don't understand. When those tabloid and blog stories came out it was all rubbish. Nothing had happened. It was only much later . . . I can't really explain it . . .' She sat up too. 'Oh, God, I'm such a bitch.'

'Yeah, stop hogging the doobie, bitch.'

Lara scrambled to her feet, suddenly restless as she

contemplated anew the chaos of her love life. 'It's done, man. Roll another one.'

'So, what happened?' Lucas said, a few minutes later. He'd picked up his guitar and was strumming a few random chords, very gently.

Lara was leaning against one of the air-conditioner units. She closed her eyes for a moment. How she loved to hear her brother play the guitar. 'I don't know, really,' she admitted. 'I got so confused. The film was messing with my head, New York was messing with my head, and Jacob just seemed to unleash something inside me. I don't know . . . He made me hungry for the world, alive to each second. Every day with him was an adventure, and it was addictive.' Lara walked to the edge of the roof and looked out across Eve's city; at the Eiffel Tower, prettily illuminated for the season, so close to them here in the Seventh it looked unreal, like a movie set mock-up. 'I think that even before I left I'd been subconsciously worrying about my relationship with Alex. Don't get me wrong, I adore him, and I love living with him and everything, but it was like, we bought the flat and then everyone was just expecting us to settle down and get married.'

Lucas strummed. 'You still in love with him?'

Lara sighed, and walked back to sit cross-legged next to him. She stuck his freshly rolled joint in her mouth and lit it. 'I know I still *love* him but . . .' She exhaled.

'Oh. Yeah, that.'

Lara allowed herself a giggle. It wasn't funny, in fact it was kind of tragic, but the dope rush was going to her head.

'Am I a really bad person, Luc?'

He grinned, and put the guitar down. 'Don't flatter yourself, Lals. You're just a person.'

Lara let out another little shriek. 'What do you mean, flatter myself?'

'I mean, you're just a person. It's not like you can control who you fall in love with. It's not like you intended to hurt Alex. This shit just happens.'

'Does it?'

'No, Lara, you're the only person in the world, in the whole of history, who's ever fallen for someone else while you're still in a relationship.' Lucas rolled his eyes at her.

'You are so annoying.' She stuck out her tongue at him. 'You *know* what I meant.'

'Okay. But yes, this shit happens, of course it does. It's like Mamie and Dad not telling us about Mum.'

'Excuse me? How is it like *that*?'

'Because, like I just said, it's hard to do right in life without also doing some sort of wrong. With you and Jacob, it probably felt right, didn't it, to be together? And yet, obviously, it was also all wrong.'

Lara stared at him. 'You know what? You're amazing.'

'Ah, shut up, man. Gimme back the spliff.'

She handed it to him and they faded back into silence again.

'I just can't believe she didn't *trust* us,' Lara murmured, after a moment. 'I can't believe she thought we didn't love her any more, that she couldn't tell us the truth about how she was really feeling.' She felt a new ache pressing down on her chest. 'I can't tell you how sad that makes me, Luc.'

'She didn't trust herself, remember. She didn't want to deal with the truth about what was going on inside her until it was too late.' Lucas leant over to take Lara's hand in a gesture of fraternal affection that nearly broke her. 'But La, it's okay. Mum loved us a lot. I mean, if she was alive now she'd probably be up here with us, getting stoned on Christmas night and looking at the stars while Mamie and Dad did the washing-up. In fact, maybe she can see us.' He gave a little wave heavenwards. 'Hi, Mum.' He turned back to his sister. 'And, you know, she certainly wasn't perfect.'

Lara gulped. 'No.'

'She was just a person, too.'

'Yes.'

'But she would have been really proud of you.'

Lara bit her lip. 'Do you really think so? What would she have to say about me falling in love with Jacob Moss?'

'She wouldn't say anything, much. She'd just expect you to learn the hard way, like she did, that love's not easy, that not all love's good love, but that when you do fall in love you've got no choice but to live your way through it. "Follow your heart," she'd say, though probably a bit more poetically than that.' Lucas blew out a perfect smoke ring and turned to his sister. 'And that's what you should do. That's all you can do.'

'Why, thank you, O Wise One. What makes you such an expert on these matters, anyway?'

'Aha. That'd be telling.'

'Are you in love, Luc?'

'We'll talk about me tomorrow.' He grinned. 'So, anyway, La, I've been thinking.'

'Jesus, Luc. Not *thinking*? Are you okay?'

'Shut up, man. Why don't you take a break from acting? I don't think it's very good for your soul.'

'What little soul I still have left, you mean?' She laughed.

'I'm serious. Get out there and do something that isn't all about you.'

Lara stopped laughing. 'Ouch.'

'Well, it's true, isn't it? You're in the most self-obsessed, self-absorbed profession in the world. Go and do something else for a bit. I'm not talking about for ever, just for a year or so.'

'I'm sorry, am I really hearing this? I can't believe I'm taking career advice from my stoner little brother.'

'Fine, fuck you.' Lucas chuckled. 'But I know you'd be happier if you listened to me.'

Lara watched him for a while, as he leant back with his hands stretched behind his head, and she saw what she knew was contentment spread across his lovely features. Where does that come from, Lucas Latner? she wanted to ask him. That easy peace? That reconciliation with the world? But perhaps he had already told her.

'Fine,' she said. 'I'll think about it. Now, will you please just shut up and play something properly?'

'I can't, man.' He groaned. 'My fingers are frozen.'

'Don't be so pathetic. Play!'

Lucas sighed, then smiled, and picked up his guitar.

FIVE

Lara was taking the Hammersmith & City line across London from St Pancras. Standing in the packed rush-hour carriage, squashed tight between a fat man reading the *Evening Standard* and a pretty Indian girl wearing too much makeup, she glanced around the familiar tube carriage and was struck with mute amazement. Yep, here she was. Definitely in London. Home, in other words. But what did 'home' mean any more? Home was the flat, she reminded herself; and home was Portobello and home was Westminster Abbey and Hampstead Heath and Borough Market and Hyde Park, and home was the South Bank and the National Theatre and the Royal Court and the Tate, and home was the Windsor Castle and the Electric and breakfast at the Wolseley. And home was Alex . . . Or, rather, home had been Alex.

Lara watched with a sense of numb inevitability as the tube chugged its way westwards across the city and crowds flowed off and on through Euston and Baker Street and Edgware Road and Paddington, and all the other junctures where she too could have got off and got lost and gone somewhere else but didn't, until eventually she was at Ladbroke Grove station, and that really did signify: home. She had to come here now, to the flat she had not seen since the earliest days of September, nearly a third of a year ago, because she needed to remind herself that this was all real: that she had a life, a house, a mortgage here. With Alex.

Lara beeped her Oyster card on the machine and the attendant let her through the luggage gate with her small suitcase. Then she dodged past the usual drunks and drug dealers who hung around outside the station, and walked briskly up Ladbroke Grove to her street. *London.* Usually, this city could be counted on as an ally whenever she returned from being away for any period of time. *Here you are, my child. Welcome. Come into my arms, my soulful dusk, my ancient streets. Come home.* But today, on this late, grey afternoon, St Charles Square looked neither welcoming nor soulful, merely cold and dirty and, to be frank, entirely indifferent to the return of this its most troubled of denizens. Lara screwed up her eyes to try to work out if anything had changed, on the outside at least. Not really. New scaffolding had gone up on one of the flats opposite. She spotted a few more for-sale signs here and there. But the magic had gone, somehow, wiped out for ever by her own treacherous relationship with another city, New York. Lara opened the front door to their house and let herself in. Then she trudged up the stairs to the top floor and turned the key to their flat.

Alex had put up a little Christmas tree in the corner of the living room and decorated it with gold and silver stars. There were still presents underneath it, a small pile with her name on;

the sight of which filled her with self-loathing. Their first Christmas in their own flat, and she hadn't even been here. Alex's breakfast things were still on the table: a half-empty coffee cup, plate full of toast crumbs pushed hurriedly into the sink, the newspaper lying open on the table. To see this place now, full of the material totems that make up a life that two people build together over the years but empty of those same people, Lara felt physically sick. She remembered how she had stalked around the flat on the morning she left for New York, a few months but another life ago now, full of excitement and a little trepidation, but with no comprehension of the double calamity that was about to befall her. Her centre, as it turned out, had not held; things had fallen apart. And now here she was again. Home.

Lara forced herself to go into the bedroom, where again, as downstairs, a sense of loss clung resolutely to everything. Even the wands of ashy light that fell through the slats in the bedroom shutters seemed tinged with melancholy. She sat down at Eve's old dressing-table and looked in the mirror, expecting a new tidal wave of misery to wash over her as she searched restlessly for her mother in the glass, as always. And yet, staring at her own face, her own features, Lara was overcome with an unexpected sense of peace. Eve was gone. She had accompanied her daughter as far on this emotional journey as she could, and now she was gone. Now it was Lara who had to take responsibility for her own self, her own life. Lara felt a sudden rush, as if she had just been released, and, remembering how she had instinctively planted a kiss on the mirror the morning she'd left for New York, felt compelled to do the same again now.

'Thank you,' she whispered, breathing in the scent of the old wood, resting her nose there for a moment and closing her eyes. 'Thank you for setting me free.'

Lara opened her eyes. And at that moment, although it may of course have been a mere trick of the light, it seemed for an instant as if the green eyes that smiled back at her really were her mother's.

'Goodbye,' she breathed, and stood up.

She went to the window. Opening the shutters, she gazed down at the empty deck, where a few wind-strewn bits of London debris had settled. If she half closed her eyes, she could picture the night of the flatwarming party below, friends laughing, sun setting, boyfriend hosting, brother playing. Happiness. But she'd had a feeling here, right here, hadn't she? A feeling that her life was teetering on the edge of something, some great unknown. And the very next day the offer to do *This Being Human* had come in . . . And yet, Lara wondered, gazing out across London, if she could rewind to that first night of July, knowing what she knew now, after this strange and sad voyage of discovery, would she do things any differently? Would she listen to her father and grandmother and turn down *This Being Human*? Even if she did the film, would she behave differently in New York, forsake all contact with Jacob Moss, spend more time nurturing her relationship with Alex at home? And therefore have no reason to suspect her mother of what she herself was guilty of – in turn meaning no truth-seeking mission to Paris to track down Dominique St Clair?

Lara brought her head back into her bedroom and locked the shutters. Perhaps the most perplexing thing of all, the answer was: 'No.' As regretful as she was for what she was about to tell Alex, for the hurt she was about to cause him, she could not, she had to admit, contemplate changing a thing.

SIX

When she'd called him from Heathrow on the day she was due back, saying she was going straight to Paris and not coming home as planned, the lurking fear he had nurtured since New York had gripped his body like a fever. You're supposed to be leaving for Paris in two days' time anyway! he'd felt like pointing out, desperately. Why can't you just come home for a bit first? What difference would it make? But Lara kept saying she had found out something about Eve and Dominique St Clair and had to go to Paris discover the 'truth' before Oliver and Lucas arrived at the weekend. So, what choice did he have but to let her go, and graciously, without grumbling, without complaining that he really needed to see her? 'Okay, he'd said. 'If you gotta go you gotta go. I'll miss you, though.' He'd then gone up to his parents', and when Lara had rung him a day or so later, in a state, to explain that contrary to what she'd thought she was going to find out about Eve and Dominique St Clair, she had actually discovered something much worse: that her mother had been secretly battling depression for the last fifteen years of her life and had probably killed herself, Alex had felt flooded with guilt. How could he be moping around his boyhood room feeling hard done by because his girlfriend had decided not to come and see him before she went to be with her family for Christmas when she now had to deal with *that*? He'd been full of remorse, and shock, and apology, and sympathy, offering to leave Manchester immediately and catch a train to Paris to be with her. His parents would understand. But she had said no: no, no. This was her family crisis, her family time. She needed to be there with Luc, and her father, and her grandmother, as they all came to terms with it. And he, of course had understood. 'Okay, well, I'll see you on the twenty-eighth,' he'd said. 'I love you.'

'Yes,' she had agreed, her voice a little shaky. 'See you on the twenty-eighth.'

But when she'd rung him from Paris yesterday to tell him *not* to come out for New Year's Eve as planned, he had feared the worst. She was coming home to see him, she said, in a funny voice, and suddenly he was hearing words down the phone line whose implication he understood but which he had not believed could ever apply to their relationship. 'A break,' she was saying. 'Get my head around things.' He'd been silent. 'Maybe it's best if we . . .'

He'd been on the way back from Manchester and his stomach had lurched faster than the Pendolino train he was sitting on. The past few months had certainly been difficult for them. He had known something was different in New York. But he had told himself that, whatever it was, it would be surmountable: this was him and Lara, for Christ's sake, of course they'd be okay. But now the cold hard fact of it announced itself as real.

Here I am. The day you thought would never happen is about to happen. Lara, the girl you always thought, nay, 'knew' you were going to spend the rest of your life with, is saying the words: 'a break'. And everyone knows what that means.

It would be 'best', they had agreed, to go somewhere neutral in the city, somewhere memory- and significance-free. She'd suggested an All Bar One or a Pitcher & Piano or some other such generic establishment, and he'd said fine. Leicester Square, then. Technically he had the day off, was not supposed to be working until the new year, but he had gone into the Temple after breakfast that day anyway, just to keep his head occupied and stop himself charging around their empty flat like a madman. Alex still could not believe this was real. Mid-morning, he had looked at his watch, numb with the irony that if all had gone to plan he would be boarding his Eurostar to Paris about now, yet instead Lara was on one heading back to London. *We need to talk.* The train tickets were on his desk, and he had ripped them up in a fury, sweeping the pieces onto the floor. Then he had slumped again in disbelief, before sitting upright in shock, when he remembered Lara's discovery about Eve's suicide and how that must be affecting her. He felt guilty again, for feeling so angry with her, until he recalled what it had been like those last couple of days in New York. That had brought the anger flooding back. And, yes, anger, he had found, thumping his computer keyboard as he bashed out emails and stomped around his empty chambers, with its poxy Christmas decorations, to go and make coffee, anger was the best way of preparing himself for whatever it was his girl was going to say.

The anger evaporated, of course, as soon as Alex spotted Lara dashing up to the glass front door of the bar that evening. The sheer relief of seeing her, after all these weeks apart, was so welcome that it temporarily obliterated any other emotions in his head and told him a simple thing: you love this girl. And you will fight to keep her.

Christ, she was beautiful.

'Hello, you,' he said bravely, as she pulled off her coat and unwound her scarf and moved anxiously towards him.

'Hi,' she said. They went awkwardly to kiss each other, neither knowing quite where – cheek? lips? – and ended up missing everything.

'Well, that wasn't weird at all, was it?' he quipped, but she barely cracked a smile. 'Drink?'

'I'll just have a Coke, thanks.'

'Oh, Lara, come on. Whatever you want to tell me that's so bad we have to do it in the middle of Leicester Square, at least do me the honour of telling me over a proper drink.'

Lara seemed to detect the rare flint in Alex's voice, and a look passed between them.

'Okay,' she said. 'Let's get a bottle of wine, then, shall we?'

'Good idea. Red or white.'

'I honestly don't mind. You choose.'

'Red okay, then?'

'Red's fine. Thanks.'

Alex came back from the bar with the bottle and glasses a few minutes later and paused behind Lara's back. He cherished this person more than he could explain, understand, bear; and while she was here, still officially his, still able to be kissed and held, he was desperate simply to kiss her and hold her, to assure her that, whatever it was, it was going to be all right. But he must restrain himself, he knew; shore up his defences. He sat down opposite her.

'So,' he said.

'So.'

'What do you want to talk about?'

Lara bit her lip. 'How were your parents? How was Christmas?'

'That's what you want to talk about?'

She hung her head. 'No.'

Alex went to pour them both a glass of wine, and neither said anything for a moment. He wondered what people must think, seeing the two of them sitting there so awkwardly like this. Who were this poor couple? Work colleagues? Internet daters on a first rendezvous? Hapless victims of a disastrous blind date? Not partners of the past six years, surely. Not best friends, soul-mates, joint signatories on a Halifax mortgage. No way.

'No,' she whispered. 'It isn't that. Obviously. It's . . . I don't think . . . Oh, God, I'm so sorry, Al. I don't know what's happened, I'm sorry . . . I just don't think I can do this any more . . .'

Alex was motionless, looking at her. He did not so much as blink. Then he put down the wine bottle, his hand shaking almost imperceptibly.

'I don't know how to say this,' Lara was managing to say. 'Partly because I don't know *what* I'm trying to say. You're going to want answers that I won't be able to give you. You're going to make assumptions that are completely understandable, given the circumstances, but also wrong. You're going to wonder how it's possible that I –'

Don't second-guess me, Lara Latner, Alex thought, watching her stutter helplessly. You have no idea what I might do. You have no idea of the reserves of love for you that I have inside me, of what you might be about to tell me that I might be able to forgive.

'– I think I might be in love with Jacob Moss.'

Alex closed his eyes.

'It's not what you think, I didn't have – an *affair* with him, nothing happened, really it's not . . .'

Or maybe not. Just like that, with those ten measly words, Lara had crossed the line of the possibly-forgivable. And that was that.

'So it was true all along?' he said, trying to keep his voice steady as the stunned fury churned in his gut. 'The stories you *swore* to me were made up, and which I went around telling everyone were bullshit, were actually true?'

'No, they weren't, I promise! Alex, I swear on my life, nothing had *ever* happened with Jacob—'

'Had? What about while I was there? Had you slept with him then? Oh, *God*, and I sat there through that fucking dinner, talking to him, and you'd—'

'Alex, no, *listen* to me. I swear—'

'As soon as I was gone, then? What happened? You waited until I was safely back on a plane home, back to our flat, and jumped straight into his bed?'

'*No!*' Lara cried. 'Listen to me. I never slept with Jacob, I promise. You have to believe me.'

Alex crashed back in his chair. He looked at Lara, looked deep into her complicated green eyes, and shook his head. He had been mentally preparing himself for this meeting all day. He'd been expecting *something*, an 'I think I'm not ready to settle down yet', or an 'I need some time and space while I get my head around the truth about Mum.' Or something. But this? This was too much. This was a quantum leap from love to loss. Nought to sixty in ten words. *I think I might be in love with Jacob Moss.*

'But you wanted to,' he croaked. 'That's what you're saying. You *wanted* to sleep with him, so much so that you're sitting here telling me you might be *in love* with him, which is –' it occurred to him '– actually much worse than if you'd just fucked him, isn't it?'

Alex felt his heart shatter as the betrayal hit him fully, somewhere in the solar plexus. It had been one of their oldest bedtime contracts, lying naked and earnest and talking into each other's eyes. Infidelity of the mind is just as bad as infidelity of the body, agreed? Agreed. Sometimes it's worse. Yes, sometimes it's worse. Promise me you'll tell me if it happens? Promise. But it'll never happen. You? Promise. But it'll never happen. Good. Good. Love you. Love you.

And now here it was. And Lara was crying. 'I've just been so confused,' she choked. 'I really have been trying to do the right thing. I'm trying to be honest with you, Al, because I love you so much and I can't bear to hurt you, and nothing really happened with Jacob, and I don't know what's *going* to happen but . . .'

'So why are you telling me all this?' he muttered. 'I don't understand.'

'I don't understand it either. That's my point. Something happened to my head while I was away, it was all so weird and so bound up in my character, and New York, and the film, and Mum, and—'

'Lara. Do me a favour. Don't bring your poor mother into this. Please. This has got fuck-all to do with Eve.'

'I know that *now* . . . but at the time . . .'

'At the time, what? You fancied your co-star so you convinced yourself your *mother* must also have had an affair with someone on her set, just so you could justify your own fucked-up head?'

Lara gasped. 'No!' she cried, then dropped her face into her hands. 'Maybe,' she muttered. 'Maybe you're right. Maybe I do have a fucked-up head.'

Alex sighed. Despite everything, despite this rage and this shock and this *unbelievable* pain, he felt horrible for her. 'I didn't mean that,' he said quietly.

'I did,' she said.

'You don't have a fucked-up head, Lara, you've got a lovely head. And that's all part of the problem.'

'What do you mean?'

'Well, I love you, and your lovely head. And I can't—'

Alex couldn't finish his sentence. He wanted to say, 'I can't believe it.' Or 'I can't live without you.' But something had just changed in him for ever. Alex Craig was an uncomplicated soul. He had his family, his job, his football team, his mates, and he had his girlfriend. His main sense of trust and security in life was predicated on the knowledge – not hope, not expectation, but *knowledge* – that he and Lara were going to be together always. So how could he believe it, what she was telling him here this evening? And yet, as he stared at her, something deep inside him knew that he could and did; and, worse, that maybe he could and would live without her. Irony of ironies, it was something that Lara had once said that lodged itself like a piece of grit in Alex's bruised memory now. It had been a few years ago, and she'd been talking about her mother. *Initially, the tragedy is that it's happened at all,* she had told him. *But then the tragedy is that you can bear it. You start to get on with your life. And that's somehow the most unbearable thing of all.* The possibility that he might both accept what Lara was telling him *and bear it* was worse, almost, than the very fact of her infidelity. The idea that somewhere along the line he, Alex Craig, had become somebody who, faced with the words *I think I might be in love with Jacob Moss*, could and did believe them was suddenly the saddest thing in the world.

'You can't believe it, I know,' Lara offered.

Alex swallowed painfully, feeling his heart thudding dully in his chest. He had to ask – he couldn't bear to know the answer, but he had to ask. 'So what's going on with you and Jacob now?'

'Nothing. I haven't even spoken to him since I came back from New York.'

'Does he – does he *feel the same way*?' Alex heard himself rehearsing the lines from a cheesy soap opera or an agony-aunt column and wanted to punch something. He clenched his fists.

'I think we both knew there was a – connection,' Lara ventured, eyeing him warily. 'Although, it was hard to know what it meant. Where our characters ended and the real people began. I still don't know what it means.' She looked at him pleadingly, and he saw that her eyes were liquid, desperate. 'That's why I didn't act on it.'

'Well, well done, you,' Alex said, and instantly regretted it.

Lara looked down again.

'So. Did you talk to each other about how you felt?'

Lara hesitated. 'Yes.'

'So you *told* him you were in love with him?'

'Sort of.'

'Sort of. And he told you he was in love with you?'

'Yes.'

'And did he kiss you?'

Silence.

'Lara. Did he kiss you?'

'Yes.'

'And you kissed him back.'

'Yes.'

'A proper kiss?'

'Does it matter?'

'Er, yes. But I think you've answered that one anyway, thanks.'

She looked up again, found his eyes. 'I am so sorry,' she whispered. 'I know you don't believe me, and I understand why. But I am.'

Alex stared at her, then reached down to pick up his coat and his wallet, his newspaper, his glasses, all the pointless detritus of his life.

'Where are you going to go?' she was asking. He did not respond, just stood still for a moment, staring out of the window. 'Al, what are you going to do?'

Eventually he turned back to face her. 'I don't know. And I think you need to be asking yourself that question too, miss.'

The old term of affection seemed to undo her; Lara gasped, and put her head in her hands again. But he did know what he was going to do: he was going to walk out of here and get on his bike and go to Euston and buy a ticket for the first train back to Manchester. He didn't know what he would do after *that*, but he knew absolutely that he could not bear to be in London, knowing that she was here in this city too. God, it was so ironic. While Lara was away, the memory of her presence on every street corner, in pubs they liked, down on Portobello, in Sainsbury's, in the parks – that had been a sort of sustaining force. Feeling Lara's presence here had been a way of imagining her back, and missing her less. But to know now that she *was* here, that they were in the same city, just streets away from each other, a handful of stops on a tube line, a walk, a bus journey, but *apart*, and maybe for ever apart – no, that was unbearable.

401

'Al,' she said quietly. 'I won't go back to the flat tonight – obviously. I'll stay at Dad's place. You must stay there.'

'I don't think so,' he said.

'One of us might as well be there.'

'Well, you take it, if you want.'

'No, I couldn't. I don't – want to be there.'

'Well, that's funny. Neither do I, particularly.'

'Alex,' Lara pleaded, her voice cracking on the last syllable. 'I am so, so sorry. Please, you have to believe me . . .'

Alex took a long last look at Lara, sitting there, his hunched-up, hollow-eyed, beautiful girl, and cursed himself bitterly for how much he loved her. Then he pushed open the swinging glass door of All Bar One, and was soon just another lost soul in the crowd of many pushing through Leicester Square.

SEVEN

Cassie pressed a pink-painted fingernail on the top buzzer of number twenty-nine and looked around the square in mild disbelief. It seemed like only five minutes since she'd been ringing this very doorbell to go up to Alex and Lara's flatwarming party back in July. But that had been half a whole year ago, and life, unimaginably, had changed beyond recognition for them all. She still couldn't believe what Lara had garbled to her over the phone, between breath-snatching, body-racking sobs. Lara and Alex? Broken up? It just wasn't possible!

'Hey, lady,' she said, when a shockingly skinny and grey-faced Lara let her silently in upstairs. 'Oh. My God. Come here.' Enveloping her best friend in a huge hug, Cassie held onto Lara tightly as she shook, sobbing, her body heaving. Bloody hell, she thought, life was weird. How many times over the years had Lara been the one looking after Cassie as she wept miserably over some boy or other? And now how the tables had turned.

'Come on, love,' she soothed, rubbing Lara's back. 'There, there. Get it all out.'

'Thanks, Cass.' Lara sighed, lifting up her head and wiping her red-rimmed eyes on her sleeve. She was wearing a ratty old college netball sweatshirt and tracky bums and looked – to Cassie, who was dressed in a fabulous sparkly number in preparation for the New Year's Eve party she *had* been going to before Lara had rung in a fit of hysterics half an hour ago – as if she were about twelve years old. Her unwashed hair was scraped back in a ponytail, her eyes were puffy and dull as dishwater, and her usually glowing skin was blotchy and pale. Cassie had to admit it: Lara looked rough. 'Thanks so much. I'm so glad you're here.'

'Be a pretty rubbish friend if I wasn't, wouldn't I? Now, go and wash your face, darlin', and I'll crack open these. Liz is on her way.' Cassie pulled out the two bottles of chilled champers she'd been taking to the pre-New-Year's-Eve-party dinner from her bag and kicked off her silver heels.

Lara took one look at her friend in all her black-dressed, glittery-eyeshadowed glory, and managed a laugh. 'God, I've missed you two,' she said.

A few hours later, the three of them were lying around the living room in Lara and Alex's flat, surrounded by wads of tear-sodden tissues, empty champagne bottles and half-melted tubs of ice cream. Lara's face was still streaked from crying, but she had managed to laugh as well as weep as – on the tenth anniversary of the day her mother had probably committed suicide – she'd gradually choked out the whole story of the past few months from beginning to end. New York, *This Being Human*, Sabine,

Jacob, Dominique, Paris, Colette, the truth about her mum – and now Alex. Somehow, telling Cassie and Liz the truth, and receiving no moral judgement, just empathetic tears and sympathetic ears and a few sound pearls of wisdom, had brought into sharper focus how much she needed their friendship, and how crazy she'd been to neglect it in New York.

'So that's, basically, what's been going on,' Lara concluded. She downed the rest of her champagne miserably.

There was a pause.

'Well, I don't know what you're moaning about, really,' quipped Cassie, with another quick dab to her eyes. She and Liz had spent most of the past couple of hours weeping too, especially when they'd learnt about Eve's depression and the possibility she might have killed herself. They'd all cried buckets over that one, and Cassie still couldn't really believe it. *Suicide.* It seemed too distressing to bear: no wonder Lara looked like a shell-shocked ghost. But, still, she had to keep the mood up, had to keep her best friend buoyant, which was why she was trying to inject a little levity now. 'Hasn't been much of an eventful few months at *all*, then.'

'Exactly,' added Liz, clearly exercising a similar impulse. 'God, La, I can't believe you made me leave my dinner party for *such* an insignificant reason.'

'Ha bloody ha,' Lara slurred. 'I'm a dreadful friend. I dragged you away from your boys and ruined your night.'

'Wait a minute.' Cassie grinned, pointing at the three of them. 'I'm drunk as a skunk on New Year's Eve with my two best mates in the world. I'm happy as Larry, me.'

'Me too,' said Liz, holding her glass in the air. 'As Larry! Cheers!'

'Cheers!'

'But what am I going to do?' Lara said after a moment, her voice wobbling dangerously. 'I mean, seriously, what the *hell* am I going to do? What am I going to do about Alex? And Jacob?' Cassie instantly shoved a tissue in Lara's hand and splashed some more champagne into her glass.

'What you are going to do is, you are *not* going to worry about anything right now, except how bad your hangover is going to be tomorrow. Okay? You and Al will work things out, if that's the right thing to do. And if it's not, well, who knows? Maybe you and Jacob will. These things happen, La, life has to run its course. You never know, maybe you'll decide you don't want either of them and you'll grow up to be a spinster. Or a lesbian.' Cassie leant back with a saucy wink and took another swig of champers. 'Oh, shit, fuck, bollocks, what's the time? Have we missed it?'

All three scrambled to their feet and Lara switched on the TV. According to Big Ben, it was three minutes to midnight. Just then they heard the faint splutter and pop of fireworks outside.

'Quick, let's go out on the deck!'

Lara unlocked the french windows as Cassie and Liz grabbed scarves and coats and phones to call their respective loved ones. Watching her friends busy composing text messages to the boyfriends they had abandoned to come and look after her, Lara allowed herself to wonder wistfully about Alex: where he was, who he was with, what he was doing, how he was feeling. And she wondered about Jacob, too: early evening in New York City, what would he be getting up to tonight? Some mad party in the Meatpacking with his gang? A rooftop extravaganza on the Lower East Side? She thought about her brother, wise old soul at twenty-one, DJing somewhere east of here; and her father, who'd stayed on in Paris with Colette. Lara marvelled again to think of those two, formerly the unlikeliest of allies, now taking solace in each other on this most painful of anniversaries. Gosh, how life changed. And love changed. What was it Jacob had once said to her? *Love changes every day.* A firework exploded prettily over her head and cascaded in a shower of red and blue down towards the square, then another, and another until the sky was illuminated. *Love changes every day.* Big Ben's bongs started to boom out from inside the telly, as more fireworks snapped and crackled in the air above them and a scatter of whoops and laughter came from a party down the street. Looking out across London, twisted city, starless city, but *her* city, for the first time in weeks, Lara thought: I am going to be fine.

And then suddenly the clock had struck midnight and the year had turned. 'Happy new year, girls!' she said, with a bittersweet smile. Cassie and Liz threw their arms around her, and the three of them raised their glasses heavenwards. 'Happy new year!'

EIGHT

Awaking in the tiny spare bedroom in Oliver's flat two weeks later, Lara was reminded again, just by dint of opening her eyes and seeing a whole new morning settling onto the bedsheets around her, of the strange truth that whatever life chucked at you things just carried on. Calamity changed you but it did not really change you. You felt as if you'd never do anything normal again, but sooner or later you just did. You discovered your mother had probably killed herself, but you went to bed and you got up, regardless of whether you'd slept or not. You left your boyfriend, whom you still loved, but you bought groceries and fixed dinner. You emailed. You texted. You did your laundry. You took out the rubbish. You helped your best friend learn her lines. You recharged your Oyster card. You paid mortgage bills and somehow tried to file your tax return before the deadline. You renewed your gym membership, even though you rarely went. You washed and brushed and clipped and recycled. You rang your dad and your grandmother to say you loved them and had forgiven them. You made plans to go to lunch with your agent. You read emails from your boyfriend that broke your heart, then reread them only to discover that they still broke your heart.

Date: 14 January
To: llama@gmail.com
From: alex.craig@gmail.com
Re: flat

Lara. As I'm sure you're aware, we urgently need to do something about St Charles Square. I had a meeting with a financial adviser yesterday who suggested that we put it on the market asap rather than rent it out for any period of time. It looks like the credit crunch is about to get much worse, and property prices are likely to drop another 20–30% next year, even in central London. Needless to say I can't afford to keep paying the mortgage on it while I'm not living there, and I am reluctant to go into negative equity – as, I'm sure, are you. He seems to think if we get it on the market sooner rather than later we'll still get a decent enough price for it, given location, standard of furnishings, etc., so that would be preferable to anything else. Even within the next six months it may have dropped considerably in value, and it might be 5–10 years before property prices hit what they were when we bought it. Please therefore let me know if you agree with this, and I will instruct lawyers, estate agents, etc. Happy to deal with admin from my end but will obviously be needing your signature on certain documents. Can get these put in the post to you as and when if you remind me of the Pimlico flat address.

Alex

Jesus, Al, Lara thought, after reading it a third time. What did you do, get the financial adviser to *write* the damned thing too? Walking down Moreton Place towards Pimlico tube, on her way to meet Milton for lunch, she mulled over what Alex had said. The prospect of selling their flat made her feel wretched for a number of obvious reasons, and yet look at her, cramped in Oliver's spare bedroom because she hadn't been able to face being in St Charles Square since New Year's Eve. She couldn't stay there for ever. And she knew that Alex was right: it was pointless, not to mention financially crippling, to leave empty a two-bed flat on a massive mortgage. Liz and Joe were talking about getting a place together, so maybe Cassie could move in with her, Lara pondered, when Liz moved out; she could probably buy Alex out and manage for a while if Cassie paid her a decentish rent? But that felt all wrong, too, being there with anybody who wasn't Alex. In fact, being anywhere with anybody who wasn't Alex was beginning to feel all wrong.

Not for the first time, as Lara touched in her Oyster and descended into the bowels of the tube station, did she question what the hell she was doing . . .

Nevertheless, the sight of Milton's smiling face as she was ushered into the clinking warm interior of the Ivy – he was taking her for a post-film 'treat', as he often did when she finished jobs – was cheering. He gave her a roar of a hello, and an enormous hug, but then, after a moment, pulled a face in apparent disgust. 'What on earth has happened to you?' he asked. 'You've shrunk!'

'And a happy new year to you too!' Lara sighed wearily as she gave her agent a kiss and sat down on the banquette opposite him. 'Let's just say I haven't had much of an appetite recently.'

'Well, then, we'd better get some food down you, hadn't we?'

'You sound like my grandmother,' she chuckled, obligingly opening the menu.

'So,' Milton said, breaking off a chunk of baguette and slathering it with butter, 'was it gruesome, the film? Last time I spoke to you in New York I thought it sounded as though you were having a rather wonderful time.'

'I was having a wonderful time, sort of. It was pretty life-changing. But it's also . . .' Lara wondered how to put this '. . . wreaked havoc.'

'Ah, one of *those* jobs. Life-changing and havoc-wreaking. So what happened? Fall in love with your co-star, did you? Ha! Only joking.'

Lara looked down quickly to the menu again. 'You shouldn't joke about these things, you know,' she said.

'I'm not really, darling. But blow me down, if I took extra commission from every job where a client's ended up running off with someone on the set, I'd be eating in here every day!' Milton cackled, then reached over to squeeze her hand.

'You practically do that anyway,' she pointed out drily.

He let out another roar. 'Oh, look, darling, I'm only joshing because I know how dotty you are about that nice clever boyfriend of yours, and I can't exactly imagine you throwing it all away to bonk some idiot with coke up his nose and socks for brains. Anyway. What are you having?'

Lara bit her lip, then looked up and smiled at the waiter who had appeared at their table. 'I'll have the duck and watercress salad to start,' she said, 'and the salmon, please.'

'Very good, Miss Latner. And for you, sir?'

'That doesn't sound like a lunch to fatten you up. Bring her some chips, too, will you? I'll have the sautéed *foie gras* and the

411

poulet des Landes. And we'll take a bottle of the Pouilly-Fuissé, thanks. My usual.'

'Of course, sir. And would you care for a glass of champagne to start with?'

Milton looked over to Lara, who rolled her eyes.

'Why not?' Milton smiled. 'Excellent idea.'

They were half-way through their starters when Lara started to explain what had happened. 'So,' she began, taking a deep breath, 'while I was filming I somehow managed to convince myself that Mum had had an affair while she did *La Belle Hélène*, and maybe even got pregnant with me by someone who wasn't my father. By Dominique St Clair, in fact.'

Milton raised an eyebrow and stopped his *foie-gras*-laden fork halfway to his mouth. 'My God!' he said. 'And there I was making silly jokes – goodness, Lara, I'm sorry.'

'It's fine,' Lara said, gearing up for her now-familiar recital. 'Because that isn't actually what happened. But I was so sure of it that I went on a kind of truth-mission, to find out. I went back to Paris to challenge St Clair himself and discovered something much worse.'

'Worse?' Milton frowned.

'Yes. I won't go into the whole story now, but it turns out my mother had been suffering for years with depression. Like, proper depression. Lucas and I had no idea how bad it was because her moods swung up and down all the time, and we didn't ever see the worst of it. Anyway, there was a period of time when things got really bad – Dad ended up being called back to Beirut, my grandfather died, Mum had a miscarriage, Luc and I were unaware of how miserable she was and were writing her really inane things from school, like what we had for tea, which she thought proved we didn't love her any more, didn't need her. And she decided that the only thing she could do to make herself feel better again, prove she had some sort of purpose in life, was to act. So she rang up Dominique, they made *Si Ça C'est Un Jour*, she fell apart, it came out and got panned, and then she sank into something much more intractable. She'd been suffering from what I've since learnt are called "psychotic interludes". Which was why she left my father at Charles de Gaulle on New Year's Eve and decided to stay in Paris. She had every intention of killing herself. She'd apparently been contemplating doing it for a year or so. And, after a particularly lovely Christmas with us all, which was basically too much happiness for her to bear, that seems to be what she did. She walked into the path of an oncoming car, in a snowstorm, and she killed herself.'

Milton's fork clattered to his plate. Lara reached over to touch his arm. 'I'm sorry, Mil. I know it's a shock. I've just about learnt how to say it now. I've learnt a script, almost – how to tell people. But it still doesn't seem real.'

'I'll say,' said Milton, his face ashen. 'Oh, Lara, you poor thing. Have you—'

But Milton didn't get to finish his sentence, because a voice behind them was exclaiming, 'Well, *hello* there! Fancy seeing you two!' Lara and Milton looked up in dismay at having been interrupted at this critical moment. It was Miles Badenoch, one of the UK's top film producers. Milton just about recovered, and accepted Miles's hand, before Miles turned to give Lara a kiss on her cheek.

'Hello, Miles,' she said. 'Great to see you.'

'And you, Lara!' As Miles stepped back, he revealed his pretty lunch date.

'Oh, my gosh, *Jess*!' Lara cried.

'*Lara!*'

'Ah, of course!' Miles exclaimed. 'You must know each other from *This Being Human*. How did you find it, Lara? Alison Kennedy's an old friend of mine. She seems to think it's going to be something pretty special?'

Lara smiled. 'Hopefully,' she said.

'It will be,' Jessica announced confidently. 'You know I was back in New York last week? We had a couple of reshoots. I saw some of the rushes and it looks *inc-red-ib-le*. You are *amazing* in it.' She turned to Milton. 'Hi, I'm Jessica Cole, by the way. It's *so* good to meet you. I've heard so much about you.'

Lara was struggling to breathe as Jessica fluttered her eyelashes at Lara's famously powerful agent. No, she did not know anything about reshoots! She hadn't heard from Kevin for a while, and was on a total, self-imposed communication embargo with Jacob. My God. Jessica had been back there last week? Had she seen him?

'How – how was it?' Suddenly Lara found her mind drained of everything except the sheer relief of seeing Jess, a link to the film, to him. The desire to say his name out loud engulfed her. 'New York, I mean. How was—'

'Yeah, it was fun.' Jessica smiled, a touch slyly. 'But look, what are you doing after lunch? Why don't we grab a coffee and catch up properly?'

Lara knew she must not say yes. Even talking about New York, about *This Being Human*, was tantamount to inviting Jacob back into her life, and she was not ready to go there yet. It had barely been two weeks since she had broken up with Alex, and she was trying to test what Jacob really meant to her by seeing how long she could go without speaking to him, without contacting him at all. She had to know if he really was worth jettisoning her relationship for. So, no, she must not say yes.

'Yes,' Lara breathed.

'How about the Monmouth Coffee Co. at three?'

'Perfect.'

'Bye, Mr Hewison, it was so good to meet you.'

'Nice to see you both,' Miles said. 'Lara, it was a pleasure, as always. And you, old boy – we must catch up soon. Lunch next week?'

'Er, yup. Sounds marvellous,' managed poor Milton, still pale after Lara's revelation. 'Give me a buzz, Miles, won't you? Haven't got the old diary on me right now . . .'

Once Miles and Jessica had sat down in another corner of the restaurant, Lara and Milton turned back to each other. Milton's reflexive flippancy seemed to have quite evaporated in the face of Lara's news. 'I am so sorry,' he told her. 'I don't know what to say. How utterly, utterly ghastly for you. *Suicide.* My God. Unbelievable.'

Jessica Cole was squealing as she clutched Lara's hand.

'Oh. My. God. Have I got news for you!' she giggled, as they stood in line at the Monmouth a short while later.

'What's that, then?' Lara asked, curious. She was desperate to hear the latest from the film but was trying to work out how she could ask lots of questions about Jacob without it seeming really obvious.

'Just some *serious* gossip, that's all,' Jessica replied, 'but you have to promise not to tell another human *soul*.'

'I – won't. Hey, I've got these,' said Lara, handing over a fiver to the barista. 'Of course I won't. Tell me!'

'Okay, then . . .' They were standing at the end of the bar now, waiting for their coffee to arrive, and Lara had just picked hers up when Jessica leant over and murmured in her ear: '*I slept with Jacob!*'

She couldn't help it. The shock was so immediate, her hands so powerless in its wake, her normal defences so instantaneously annihilated by those four little words, that suddenly the scalding coffee was everywhere, all down Lara's cream jumper and jeans and boots, all over her hands, burning, and the gasp she emitted in the moment of dropping the cup was assumed by those in the café who heard it to be a direct consequence of the dropping itself; and nothing to do with the phrase that had triggered it. There was a suspended second of inaction, and then people were moving, dashing over to give the vaguely familiar-looking dark-haired girl wodges of paper napkins and cups of cold water to splash on her hands.

'*Jesus!*' Jessica was yelling at the entirely innocent girl who'd just handed Lara her cappuccino, as she tried to mop down Lara's jumper. 'Are you completely *retarded*? Why didn't you put the lid on that cup properly? My friend here could have *seriously* burnt herself.'

The poor girl behind the counter looked mortified. 'I so sorry,' she kept saying, in a heavy Eastern European accent. 'Really, so sorry. I was certain I had put. But so sorry.' Now her boss was ticking her off too. 'You *know* you're supposed to make sure the lids are on carefully, Milla,' he was hissing. 'How many times do you have to be told that?'

'Please, it's okay,' Lara looked up, her voice a strange husk of disbelief. 'It was my fault, I'm sure. Honestly, please don't be angry with her. It was my fault for picking it up like that.'

'Well, we are *so* very sorry,' the boss barista was saying, a touch obsequiously. 'Would you like another coffee? Anything at all we can do for you?'

416

Lara struggled to focus on the question in front of her, to remind herself how it was that one answered these things. *Play the role.* Would she like another coffee? 'Um, actually, I think I'm okay.' She grimaced. 'Maybe I've had enough for today.' She went to turn around.

'No problem,' the guy called after her. 'Can I just say, though, that *The Chronicles of Mary* is one of my all-time *favourite* programmes? Would you – uh, I know this is a bit awkward, given what's just happened, but would you mind signing an autograph for me?'

Lara stopped in her tracks. Oh, the irony. And she could sense Jessica buzzing impatiently next to her, desperate to get back to their gossip session. *I slept with Jacob.* Jess had no idea about her secret relationship with Jacob, and even if she had, she owed Lara no loyalty: the betrayal lay fair and square with him. But, still, the sight of the other actress hovering there, beaming, smirking, was truly sickening. Lara felt dizzy with shock and was tempted simply to rush out of the door and down the street, putting as much distance between her and Jessica as possible. But the barista was still grinning inanely at her, holding up a pen and paper expectantly.

'Of course,' Lara said, reaching out graciously to take the pen. 'Who shall I make it out to?'

NINE

She ran all the way from Covent Garden to Pimlico, the adrenalin coursing through her body as she pounded London's unforgiving grey pavements until reaching her father's flat. Gasping for breath, Lara let herself in and dropped her coat and bag in the hallway. She walked into Oliver's study and sat down at the desk, her chest heaving. Snatching up the cordless telephone, she waited for a minute for her breathing to slow down. She knew his number off by heart, of course. And now, having restrained herself from doing so for a month, she pressed those fateful numbers.

It was lunchtime in New York City, but Jacob sounded a touch foggy when he picked up, as if she had just woken him.

'You *slept* with Jessica Cole?' Lara cried. 'You slept with *Jessica Cole*?'

There was a shocked silence. 'Whoa. Lara. Calm down.'

'You told me you were in love with me and then two minutes later you go and sleep with her?'

'It wasn't two minutes, Lara,' Jacob said. He sounded a little more alert now.

'Fine, two weeks, then.'

'It wasn't two weeks, Lara, it was a month. A whole month. Tell me, what have you been doing in that month, eh? How's your boyfriend?'

Lara let out a gasp of indignation and began to pace the length of the study. 'How *dare* you? I've had about the worst month of my life, actually, and as it happens I don't *know* how Alex is, Jacob, other than probably pretty heartbroken, because we're separated, aren't we, Jacob, thanks to *you*?'

'Thanks to me?' Jacob chortled. 'Lara, honey, don't kid yourself. None of this has got anything to do with me.'

'What do you mean it hasn't got anything to do with you? It's got *everything* to do with you.'

'Oh, come on, Lara. Get over yourself. This is all about you.'

'What do you mean?' she cried. 'How can this not be about you? I was in *love* with you! That's why I left Alex.'

'And I'm still in love with you!'

Lara choked in a gulp of air. It was wildly, ludicrously, *crazily* irrational, not to mention dangerous and stupid, she knew, to let Jacob's words affect her, but she couldn't help it. Just to hear him say, 'I'm still in love with you' and she felt instantly less desperate. The sound of his voice was slowly disabling her, but she must not let it. He had *slept* with Jessica Cole! And what else? Walked Jessica through the streets of New York too, filling her head with *faux*-philosophical nonsense? Had her round to his apartment to woo her with cold beers and vintage jazz? Taken her dancing underneath tenement blocks in Harlem or the Lower East Side? She felt sick with his betrayal, enraged by it.

419

And yet he had said he was *still in love with her* . . .

Dropping into Oliver's leather armchair Lara found she could not speak.

'You haven't really left Alex, though, right?' she heard Jacob ask into the transatlantic void, a moment or so later. 'Otherwise you'd be out here, like you said. Wouldn't you?'

'I was coming!' she cried miserably. 'I booked a plane ticket for the end of the month. I just—'

'You just what, Lara? You told me you loved me but, hey, you wouldn't sleep with me' – Lara caught her breath at the memory of those nights after the Central Park storm. A desire more powerful than anything she had ever known had coursed through her, making her skin tingle and her insides dissolve, and it had only been Alex's face, hovering somewhere in her compromised conscience, that had enabled her to restrain herself. Thinking of Jacob's body now, though, that beautiful flesh so surprisingly smooth to the touch despite the shallow ridges of his tattoos and the faded track marks that scored the inside of his forearms, Lara felt her legs turn to jelly again as Jacob carried on talking – 'And then you got on a plane. And I ain't heard *jack* from you since. Tell me, what am I supposed to do? Sit around New York and wait for you to decide whether you want to turn up again on my doorstep, however many months later?'

YES! Lara wanted to scream. That's exactly what you were supposed to do! You were supposed to have more *soul*! With a dismal jolt of clarity, she realised that the idealised version of Jacob Moss she'd cultivated in her head all these weeks – romantic night-poet and charismatic pedlar of syncopation and adventure – was a crass delusion. At the end of the day, Jacob was just another guy; and a guy, as it happened, who'd sleep with the first hot redhead who came his way.

'And what if you don't turn up?' he continued.

'And what if Jess Cole turns up instead?' Lara asked bitterly. 'Tell me, Jacob, did you fancy her all the way through the shoot? Why didn't you just fuck her then instead?'

She heard him click his teeth in exasperation, and light a cigarette. That was a good idea, *cigarette*! She didn't like to smoke inside her dad's place but, Christ, she needed one right now. Lara stormed to her feet again and went to rifle inside her bag for the pack of honestly-I'm-giving-up Silk Cut that she knew was in there. 'No, tell me,' she continued. 'I really want to know. Why didn't you shag her then, while I was out there?' She threw her hands up in despair. 'Or maybe you did! What the hell would I know?'

'Lara, will you please shut up and listen to yourself? When was I supposed to sleep with Jess while you were there, eh? You spent practically every night in my apartment, for Christ's sake.'

Lara gasped. 'I thought that's what you *wanted*!' she cried. 'I thought you liked having me over!'

'Of course I did, you idiot. Will you just calm down, please, Lara. This really doesn't have to be such a big deal.'

Lara took a furious, futile drag and collapsed back onto the chair. Then she leant over, opened the window by the desk and chucked the rest of the cigarette out in frustration. 'I can't believe you're not even taking responsibility for this!' she exclaimed. 'You told me you were in *love* with me, and then you go and sleep with someone else. How could you do that? I mean how could you, actually, at the end of the day, *do* that?'

'Lara, how many times do I have to say this to you? I am so in love with you it's insane. I'm here, waiting, whenever you make up your mind what you want. Me, Alex. Whatever you decide. But you clearly got a lot of other shit to sort out first, and 'til you make up your mind, I kinda have to get on with my life.'

Lara's head slumped into her hands. She felt a tear run down her cheek and splash woefully onto her dad's old-fashioned blotter. 'But Jacob, you could have any girl in New York,' she wept. 'Any girl in the world, probably. Why did you have to *get on with your life* by sleeping with *Jessica Cole*? The only other London actress on that shoot! Who I bumped into today, and am going to have to constantly bump into for the rest of my life in this city!'

'Ah, listen. Jess Cole didn't mean anything to me – we'd been working twenty hours in the studio that day, it was all crazy, I was drunk and I fucked her.'

Lara's heart skipped a beat. Jacob had always told her he'd been teetotal since he came off crack and heroin as a teenager. 'You what?' she said. 'You were what?' She'd never even seen a drop of booze pass his lips.

'Yeah, I was drunk. And I fucked her.'

'Drunk?'

'Yeah. I kind of had a relapse after you'd gone.'

Lara gasped. 'Jacob, no!'

'Yeah. Sorry to say. But it's okay. It was only vodka and a few lines of coke. Nothing too major. I knew what was happening and I took myself back to rehab the next day. Which is where I'm headed now, in fact. Oh, joy of joys.' He let out a long sigh, and Lara could imagine him stretched out on his sofa, flexing his feet. 'But yes, I did sleep with Jess, once, while under the influence, and hey, I am sorry for that. I truly never meant to hurt you.'

Lara rocked back and forth on the chair. That Jacob had relapsed again scared her so much: his drug-addled past was one of the things about him she was least capable of understanding, and most terrified of. The thought that somehow *she* might have caused it made her mind blur. She had no idea how to react to this news.

'Listen,' Jacob said after a moment, his voice a little broken, 'I really miss you, Lara. Will you just please come over here and see me? I wanna be with you so much right now it hurts.'

Lara took a deep breath, trying to ignore how his words tugged at her heart. 'Jacob. When I got back from New York, I went to Paris and discovered that my mother probably killed herself—'

'Whoa! What? *Lara!*'

'It's good of you to sound surprised, Jacob, you're a good actor,' Lara continued, her voice steely. 'But I have a funny feeling you knew all along. You once asked me if I'd ever forgive her for what she'd done, and I didn't understand, at the time, but I caught the expression in your eyes and I think you knew. But anyway. Let's just park that for a moment, shall we? So, I found out my mother committed suicide and my father and grandmother had been lying to me and my brother for the past decade. Then I came back here and told my boyfriend of six years that not *only* had my manic-depressive mother killed herself – she was also a pretty good actress by the way, cos we certainly never knew – but, you know that guy all the tabloids said I was having an affair with? Well, surprise! I *might* just possibly be in love with him. So suddenly we're breaking up and going through divorce motions and it's hideous, and although he's behaving very well I'm sure he must really hate me because I've ruined his life. So that's all a picnic. And then what happens? *Then* I bump into one Jessica Cole, and guess what she tells me? She tells me, hey, she's just *slept* with the guy I'm possibly in love with. And after all that, just to put the cherry on top of the cake, the guy I'm possibly, probably, in love with, the former junkie, let's not forget, tells me he's recently relapsed and is back in rehab but, hey, is definitely *still in love* with me.' She exhaled. 'So, weirdly enough, Jacob, no. No. I don't think I'm coming back to New York in the *very* near future.'

There was a pause. Lara listened to Jacob smoke his cigarette and discovered that, if she strained her ears, she could just hear the undulations of a jazz piano melody in the background of his apartment. The music sounded achingly familiar. Was it Bill Evans? She couldn't even speak.

'Okay,' Jacob said, finally. 'Okay. I get it. I'm so sorry to hear about your mom. I did wonder . . . But you know, you gotta know, Lara, this is your call. I'm always here. I ain't never felt like this in my life about anyone. There's something between us, and whatever it is, there always will be.'

He paused, and she heard the faint twists of the piano riff in the background – yes, it was Evans and she knew exactly which track it was too – she could imagine the little smile, the expression she had once found so irritating, then so maddeningly attractive, curling along one side of Jacob's lips. '*You and me,*' he'd said, '*we're the two lonely people.*' Tears sprang to Lara's eyes. I can't do this, she thought. I simply cannot do this. *I love you and I love you and I love you.*

But, like the obliging actress she was, she forced herself to say lines she knew she must say. 'I need to go now, Jacob,' she said. 'I have to say goodbye.'

424

The sun moved in the sky, then, and at that moment a lone shard of watery, late-afternoon light clambered through the window and came to rest on Oliver's desk in front of her, creating a little pool of hope in the middle of the dark mahogany table. And Lara, staring dumbly at it as she replaced the phone in its cradle, was suddenly reminded of something. What was it Lucas had said to her, up on that rooftop in Paris on Christmas night? *You're in the most self-obsessed, self-absorbed profession in the world . . . Get out there and do something that isn't all about you.*

Her mind now whirring, alert, Lara grabbed the phone again before she could change her mind. When the bleep of the answerphone filled her ears she nearly bottled it, but forced herself to speak, just in time. 'Dad? Hey, it's me, Lals. Listen, you can say no to this, but I've been thinking . . . How would you feel about me coming to stay over there for a bit? I mean for a couple of months, or maybe even longer? Please call me back when you can. You'll probably think I'm crazy, but I've had this idea . . .'

Then Lara switched on Oliver's computer and brought up her gmail account. *Love the questions,* she reminded herself, *and maybe you'll live your way into the answers.* She began to type.

Date: 15 January
  To: alex.craig@gmail.com
From: llama@gmail.com
  Re: Re: flat

Dear Alex

Thanks for your message, and for looking into the best options for St Charles Square. I'm sure you and your financial adviser are right and that, if we are going to sell it, we should get it on the market asap. But my instinct is we should hang on to it. I may come to regret this decision, I know, but I suspect this is going to be a period in my life when I look back and regret many of the decisions I made, so I am prepared to take that risk. I can cover the mortgage on my own for a bit, so I am hoping that you will bear with me, for at least a few months. Let's rent it out, then I can pay the mortgage and we can split the rental income, so that if you need extra money to live elsewhere, you've got it. I hope you'll agree with this plan, but let me know if there's a problem and we can revert to yours immediately.

I've just decided – on Lucas's suggestion, bizarrely – that I'm going to leave London and do something completely different with my life for a while, nothing to do with acting, nothing to do with me. I hope this will provide me with a degree of headspace and clarity. I feel I've been so caught up in myself over the past few months I can't bear to look at myself in the mirror. I know it sounds corny and silly but I need to go and remind myself what really matters in the world. Because it isn't acting, that's for sure.

Alex I know you don't need to hear this again, but I need to say it anyway. You're the most precious person in the world to me, and I'm so sorry for the pain and hurt I've caused you over the past few months. I have let you down, grievously, and I have betrayed you, and I don't expect your forgiveness. But I hope with all my heart that we will see each other again, whenever you are ready, because I miss you every day and I can't bear to lose you.

You have behaved with utter grace and dignity when I have barely deserved it, and for that I am so grateful. You've somehow made this easier for me, when you could have made it so much harder, because that is your way, and I love you all the more for it.

You know how to get hold of me. Please keep in touch.
I'm sorry.

Take care of yourself, beautiful boy,

Your monkey Lara x

And then, crossing her fingers, Lara took a deep breath and pressed 'send'.

EPILOGUE

As she steps out of the limousine, the flashbulbs that immediately begin popping in her face are quite blinding. She places a Jimmy Chooed foot on the red carpet, first one, then the other, as she has been earnestly taught to do by the style people over the past couple of days, and she eases herself as gracefully as possible out of the sleek black vehicle. She can hear people shouting her name, and everything all around her is instantaneously a dizzying blur of colour and flashes and tuxedos and microphones and red carpet and glossy hair and diamonds. Flash, flash. Somebody has grabbed her arm and is now guiding her along this red carpet, thank goodness, or she would probably still be sitting in the car like a lemon; and the people are shouting her name again, and now she seems to be surrounded by a braying bank of monsters with long black plastic snouts that dazzle her as they pop, flash-flash-flash in her eyes.

'Lara!' the monsters are screaming. 'Lara!' 'Over here, Lara!'

'This way, Lara!' 'How does it feel to be nominated for your mother's most famous role, Lara?' 'Lara, who designed your gown tonight? Can I ask who your jewels are by, Lara?' 'Lara, give us a smile, Lara, that's right, this way, just a second, Lara, lovely, thanks, Lara!'

The person clutching her arm indicates that she should stop, here, and the flashbulbs go berserk once again. Someone is pointing a microphone in her face, and asking her questions, but she's okay, she can answer these, she thinks.

'It's Yves Saint-Laurent,' she answers, to the enquiry.

'Vintage?'

'Yes. He made it for my mother for the 1982 ceremony, and it hasn't been worn since.'

This information seems to unleash the photographers' might again, flash-flash-flash-flash, and draws oohs and aahs from the very shiny American lady who is interviewing her and who has turned to relay this fascinating information to her camera team and her viewers back home. Lara is asked another question, about how she feels to have been nominated in the Best Actress category tonight, and again, she thinks she can do it.

'I'm thrilled to have been nominated. It's such an honour to have been included among a list of such illustrious actresses. So yes, I'm very happy to be here, thanks.'

'Does it feel particularly significant,' a man with another logo-ed microphone is now asking, 'given that *This Being Human* is essentially a remake of your mother's greatest film? Because, ladies and gentlemen at home, let's not forget that Lara's mother was the great French actress Eve Lacloche, and she was nominated for an Oscar for *La Belle Hélène*, isn't that right, Lara?'

'I'm just happy to be here, and happy that the recognition

Kevin's film is getting may bring more people back to the original.'

'Well, Lara, best of luck! Ladies and gentlemen, the British actress Lara Latner, nominated tonight in the Best Actress category for her role in *This Being Human*, which is up for seven awards in total, including Best Film, Best Director and Best Actor. Hey, Nicole! Over here, Nicole!'

Lara is steered a little further up the red carpet, where there is more of the same 'How does it feel to be . . .' and 'Who designed . . .' interrogation. But then there is a further eruption of mayhem at the other end of the carpet as another star arrives. Like everybody else Lara turns automatically to see who it is. And there, in the maelstrom of flashing lights and slinky gowns and beefy security guards, is suddenly Jacob Moss. He is clean-shaven and has put on a tux for the occasion, but still, it is Jacob. Lara has not seen this person in the flesh for well over a year, fifteen months, but she is ambushed by time: it is as if all the intervening days and weeks have melted away, and life has converged in this instant. Her heart falters for a beat as Jacob spots her and catches her eye. He smiles, and the whole world, Lara thinks, is contained in that smile. She wobbles, ever so slightly, on her pretty six-inch stilettos and reminds herself to keep breathing. It will not do to faint here, on the red carpet at the Kodak Theater in Hollywood, in front of Jacob Moss and the world's television screens. No, that will not do, at all.

She steadies herself. The hunters are calling his name now. 'Jacob! Jacob!' they yell, and as they do so, she allows herself to formulate the same word on her own lips. She says it to herself, 'Jacob,' and, as Jacob has not yet taken his eyes off her, he notices this. She sees him shape her own name back at her.

'Lara,' he mouths. 'Hi.'

'Hey! Lara!' somebody is screaming. 'We get a shot of you and Jacob together?'

And the photographer who has made this suggestion is surrounded by his fellow beasts, who join in the chorus: 'Yeah! Jacob! Lara! Jacob! Lara!'

The girl with the clipboard who has been directing Lara's proceedings on the red carpet also seems to think this is a wonderful idea. She beckons Jacob over, and, before she even has time to take on board what is happening, Lara can sense Jacob Moss in the space next to her, she can smell his very intoxicating smell, can feel his muscular arm around her waist. And in that instant she is convinced that the whole universe, let alone the millions of people watching the Oscars tonight, must be able to hear her heart pounding deafeningly in her chest as Jacob leans over and says in her ear, very simply, 'Hello.'

Lara manages to keep looking straight ahead, at the cameras, and smile.

'Hello,' she says, and the flashbulbs promptly explode in their faces.

When, a few hours later, Lara's name is called out by the handsome movie star with the envelope on the stage, she cannot believe her ears, and for a long moment she does not move. But suddenly lots of people are leaping to their feet around her, cheering, kissing, clutching, crying, and she is being dragged upwards. Kevin is there, and Alison Kennedy, and Eric Liebermann. Beneath the gaggle of the movie people around her, though, Lara looks down at her father. Oliver is still sitting in his seat. He is reaching over to take Colette's hand, and he has a tear in his eye, something Lara has never seen in her life. She has never seen her father cry, she realises. And now she is aware of Jacob

Moss again, very close to her face, and he is murmuring, 'I got you a bench, Lara. Number 495, opposite the pond.' She stares at him, and he grins. 'You and me, remember. We're the two lonely people.'

Lara absorbs this message with as much equanimity as she can muster, then walks as elegantly as possible to the stage. She will not think about Jacob and his bench now. One day, maybe, but not now. She climbs the stairs carefully, in her borrowed Jimmy Choos, and she can hear the wild applause still reverberating around the Kodak Theater as she walks towards the podium and accepts, first, a kiss from the handsome movie star, and then the familiar gold statuette with her name engraved at the bottom. It is heavier than she expects it to be and she almost drops it. Whoops! Lara takes a deep breath and opens her mouth, and the applause in the huge auditorium gradually dies down.

'Wow,' she says automatically, although she has always wished that actors wouldn't say 'wow' when they accept awards. 'Thank you so, so much. I'm sure I don't need to tell you how much this means to me, for reasons both obvious and not obvious. I always hoped that doing *This Being Human* would bring me closer to my mother and it has – although not necessarily in the way I expected. So. Thank you.' Lara pauses, and collects herself. Concentrate. Don't forget anyone. 'Um. For having the vision to get this project off the ground and directing it so beautifully, and for insisting that an unknown little Brit played the role when there are so many wonderful actresses out here in Hollywood, I have to thank Kevin Goldberg. He's an old hand at this Oscar thing so would probably be doing a much better job than I am up here.' (Laughter from the auditorium.) 'Kevin, thank you, beyond words, for the opportunity you gave me. I'm also grateful to the producers, Alison Kennedy and Eric Liebermann, all the production team, my wonderful co-stars Christopher, Robert, Amelia, Jessica and, of course . . .' somehow her voice manages to stay steady '. . . Jacob, without whom my performance would have been meaningless. Also a particular thanks to Sabine de Sévigné, who worked on the original film *La Belle Hélène* with my mother and was such an amazing support to me in New York. I thank my agent, Milton Hewison, for his dogged persistence, my friends for putting up with me, especially during what was quite a rollercoaster ride emotionally, and the most profound gratitude to my father, grandmother and brother – for everything, but most of all for understanding why I had to do this film in a year that was difficult for all of us.'

Lara swallows and, for a split second, takes in the scene in front of her: thousands of rapt faces, hanging on her every word. She had better make each one count. 'I also want to say one last thing,' she continues, and her voice betrays an almost imperceptible waver of emotion. 'I discovered something pretty devastating about my mother, Eve, just after finishing this film, and it has made me think long and hard about what it is that we do in this world. Eve had great creativity as an actress, and that has brought so much joy to so many people. But ultimately, the thing one makes must be worth what it takes, and I'm not sure, in Eve's case, that it was. So. While I dedicate this Oscar to the memory of my mother, I have decided to take a break from acting for a while –' (here, there is a slight but audible gasp from the auditorium, as if to say, *collecting your Best Actress Oscar is not the moment that you announce your retirement from the profession, Lara!*) '– and I am in the process of setting up the Eve Lacloche Memorial Foundation for Music and Drama, which will operate in the Middle East and Africa, offering free arts education and support to kids in

433

the refugee camps there. Mum cared a lot about the children in those places when she lived there, and I hope you will continue to support her – and my – work by visiting the website and giving generously. Thanks again. Oh! And I have to thank one more person out there. You know who you are.' She gives a tiny, rueful smile. 'Thank you for the sunshine in my head.'

There are more cheers then, as a moving montage of scenes from *La Belle Hélène* and *This Being Human* plays on the screen behind Lara's head. Lara is guided off the stage, her Oscar clutched tightly in her trembling hands, and as she makes her way backstage for the winners' photocall the adrenalin that has been pumping so furiously inside her all night eases, and her hands stop shaking, and she is able to compose herself. Afterwards, sitting back in the plush auditorium between Oliver, who looks as though he might burst with pride, and dear old Colette, who cannot stop smiling, Lara takes her phone out of her jewelled clutch bag. Cassie and Liz have been hosting an all-night 'Live Lara Love-In' at Liz and Joe's flat, and euphoric text messages are flooding in from her friends.

There is one that makes Lara catch her breath.

Thanks for that, miss. She would have been so proud of you. And so am I.
Received: March 25 Time: 19:04 Sender: Alex +447803412980

It has been half a year since Lara and Alex last saw each other, although in recent months they've been communicating a little more. Their flat in St Charles Square is still being rented out; the mortgage is still in both their names. Lara wonders if she can bring herself to press 'reply', but she hesitates. Not now. There is too much to say. And there will be plenty of time. Alex.

Jacob. Her story will play itself out, somehow. But for the moment, this golden moment, she is here. Just here. Lara takes her father's hand in one of hers, and her grandmother's in the other. And then she closes her eyes, and smiles.

ACKNOWLEDGMENTS

Heartfelt thanks, first and foremost, to Rowan Lawton at William Morris and Mary-Anne Harrington at Headline Review. A lovelier agent and editor it is not possible to imagine, and I am so grateful for their brilliant ideas and unceasing support in what could have been a very daunting process. Thanks also to Harriet Evans, Leah Woodburn, Alice Shepherd, Georgina Moore, Maura Brickell, Kim Hardie, Diane Griffith, Paul Erdpresser and the Headline sales team, Raffaela de Angelis and the WMA foreign rights team, Caroline Taylor, Melissa Johnson-Peters, and everyone else at Headline and William Morris who helped make that process such fun, and so exciting.

Although the cast and plot of *The Other Side of the Stars* are of course entirely fictional, I would probably never have dreamt up the story had I not spent rather a lot of time hanging around on film and TV sets over the past few years. Thank you therefore to Gilly Sanguinetti and all at Ken McReddie Associates, and to the producers at Company Pictures, who (unwittingly) cast me in the job on which I began to scribble down this book – in my trailer, hair in rollers, between takes . . .

Lara is right when she observes that most actors don't stay friends after the cameras stop rolling and everyone goes home, but I am fortunate to count among my nearest and dearest some very wonderful actors indeed. Profoundest thanks, in particular, to my old mucker Eddie Redmayne, who read the book in draft form and made some hilarious comments (it's true, Hollywood read-throughs really do resemble the UN General Assembly). Also to Sam West, who once taught me that some actors pick up boots while others palliate follies, and whose observations on acting, family, love and life have nourished me alongside many a Joe Allen margarita over the years. Amber Sainsbury and Alicia Witt have proved that despite the bad press, some actresses really can make the best of friends; and Rupert Evans: thanks for all those conversations about the weirdness of being stuck away on location as we blew all our *per diem* on iTunes.

I am ever-grateful to my family – my nieces Elodie and Carys, my brothers Perry and Elliot, my sisters-in-law Lisa and Katey, and Bobby and Stacia. Not to mention my dad, Humphrey, who helpfully made a bet with me he'd finish his book first (sorry). I also owe major thanks to: my parents-in-law Eli and Lawrie Geller, who offered me refuge and excellent roast potatoes when deadlines were getting critical; Hazel Orme for her diligent copy-editing; Coleman Barks, for graciously allowing me to use his Rumi; Emily Speers Mears for her translation of Rilke's 'Ninth Elegy'; AC Farstad for her French; and Matthew D'Ancona and all the other newspaper editors who have enabled me to combine acting with journalism and therefore stopped me going loopy with boredom during long days on film sets.

This book is dedicated to my mother, Gillian – best friend, critic extraordinaire, general inspiration and font of wisdom. I owe her far too much to put into words, but I hope she will know what I mean when I say that I couldn't have done this (or indeed much else) without her.

And lastly, but certainly not least, I would like to thank my husband James. Again, for much more than I could possibly express here, but most importantly, for giving me that which none of my poor characters are fortunate enough to have in their own lives.